"IF YOU ARE STUPID ENOUGH TO MARRY ME, MILORD, I PROMISE I WILL DO MY BEST TO DISGRACE YOU!"

He took her by the shoulders and shook her. "I warn you, that's enough. Persist in this and, by God, you'll drive me to violence."

Her lips trembled and her eyelashes were wet with tears, then she felt the rough sweetness of his kisses. He couldn't help himself. She was so desirable, at once earthy and ethereal, a combination guaranteed to drug him and become habit forming.

"Don't!" She pulled his hand from her breast. "You think you can hurt me one minute and rape my mouth the next. We are mis-matched, unsuited . . . leave me at once!"

"Opposites attract!" he insisted. "For a man and a woman to love each other, they don't have to be cut from the same cloth."

"Love?" She laughed derisively. "I'll never love you!"

He towered over her, his green eyes blazing with unquenched passion at the challenge she threw at him.

"You shall," he vowed. "You shall!"

Also by Virginia Henley:

THE RAVEN AND THE ROSE
THE HAWK AND THE DOVE,
    winner of the 1988 *Romantic Times*
    award for Best Elizabethan
    Historical Romance

THE FALCON
AND
THE FLOWER

Virginia Henley

A DELL BOOK

Published by
Dell Publishing
a division of
Bantam Doubleday Dell Publishing Group, Inc.
666 Fifth Avenue
New York, New York 10103

ISBN: 0-440-20429-1

Printed in the United States of America
Published simultaneously in Canada

September 1989

10 9 8 7 6 5 4 3 2 1

KRI

For my husband Arthur.
When we married thirty-three
years ago, we were the same age;
now, however, I'm *much* younger!

The recipes and magic potions referred to herein are historically accurate, based on the ancient work, *Culpeper's Complete Herbal,* written by the astrologer/physician Nicholas Culpeper. These recipes are included merely to enhance the medieval atmosphere of this novel and are in no way recommended for use by anyone.

Chapter 1

The young virgin lifted her arms high while the old woman adorned her naked form with a silvery robe as finely spun as a spider's web. The filmy material drifted down to her ankles, which were encircled by delicate golden chains studded with amber, chosen for its mystic qualities. The maiden's hair, pale as moonbeams, was unbound in all its glory and fell to her waist in curling tendrils.

The old woman pulled back into the shadows of the high tower room, while the girl went forward gracefully, stepping inside the circle of thirteen green candles. She moved with such fluid grace the flames barely flickered before they rose up straight again, burning yellow, then narrowing and lengthening to blue flame.

She began the ritual by crushing herbs and spices in an alabaster bowl, then setting them to smolder with a long taper. The scent of rosemary, cloves, and myrrh spiraled into an aromatic smoke that filled the senses headily. As she had been taught, she lifted the jeweled chalice and sipped the blood-red wine, then in a beautiful, clear voice she chanted the magic wish:

"I call upon all the Powers of the Universe to send the king and queen to England to set up their royal court. Blessed be."

She then gazed intensely into a crystal orb, which seemed to fill and swirl with gray smoke before slowly clearing. Her eyes were an unusual lavender color that darkened to purple as she stared into the sphere. She willed herself to "see" a royal couple upon thrones with crowns upon their heads. The gray smoke swirled up in the crystal orb, then cleared again to show the king and queen on a ship crossing the sea from the Continent to England.

The old woman watched her granddaughter with pride and possessiveness through shrewd, hooded eyes that had once been as beautiful as the maiden's. "Bastard of a bastard," Estelle whispered as she watched the girl, then her hand reached up to pluck the ugly words from the air before they had a chance to float off into time and space. There were, at the very least, two ways of looking at everything. Jasmine was a love child, and she had drummed into the girl's head since childhood that by blood she was a royal princess!

The late, great King Henry II's illegitimate son, William Longsword, had taken Estelle's lovely daughter for his mistress. The planting of his seed had killed her. She had been too delicate and small to bear a child, yet even though the babe had been a puny and sickly thing, through Estelle's determined efforts it had survived. Jasmine, she mused, fragile and delicate as the flower for which she was named, would soon be eighteen summers. Briefly she wished she could keep her a child forever, then she quickly made a cabalistic sign to erase the selfish wish.

Suddenly Jasmine laughed and ran from the circle of candles. "Estelle, I'm freezing, get my woolen robe." Her grandmother hurried forward and wrapped her warmly, then bent to snuff the candles.

"It was perfect, Jasmine. We will do it exactly so when we have the village women here tomorrow night."

"This time I actually saw the king and queen. Perhaps it would have been stronger magic if I'd invoked their names, Richard and Barengaria?"

"Nay," said Estelle, shaking her head firmly. "Always remember to never be too specific because it narrows the odds of getting your wish. All you want is a royal court set up in England so that you can become a lady to the queen—any queen."

Jasmine laughed and nodded her agreement. "Even Queen Eleanor."

"Never underestimate her jealousy! She never forgave Henry for being unfaithful with Rosamund Clifford, and she never forgave him for begetting your father, William. Ah yes, she accepts and honors him as the great Earl of Salisbury, but you being his love child and so exquisitely beautiful would be a constant thorn to prick jealous memories. She is an old she-wolf who would not hesitate to destroy you."

Jasmine quickly changed the subject. "Do you really think I shall be able to convince the women of the village that I can cast magic spells?"

"It will be child's play, my love. Peasants' lives are ruled by superstition. I've convinced them of my powers for years. And you are pure, a virgin, so your powers are twice as strong as mine. Besides, what spells do they ever need? Cures for the evils visited upon them by men!"

She said this last word with total loathing. Her lectures on the subject of men were as endless as they were lurid. Her own husband had beaten her savagely whenever he had gotten drunk, and she knew full well she would have poisoned him if he hadn't died from an enemy's sword thrust. The only thing she had cherished from that ill-fated marriage had been her beautiful child. But that beauty had turned out to be a curse because it had attracted an earl who lost no time in getting her daughter fatally pregnant. All men were created evil according to Dame Estelle Winwood, whether they be king, peasant, or anything between, and she had dedicated her life to keeping Jasmine safely isolated from them.

"The peasant women start out wanting a love potion to attract a male, progress to a talisman to keep them from conceiving, then end up begging for an abortificant. Do you recall them asking for aught else?"

Jasmine's eyes twinkled. "Only ointments and electuaries to heal their wounds from a beating!"

"Just so," Estelle said with satisfaction. "Mark you well and inwardly digest it!"

"Speaking of electuaries, I wanted to get one more page finished in the herbal book before bed. I've written up hemlock. Would you check it for me before I paint in the illustration?" asked Jasmine.

Estelle walked across to the large oaken desk and ran her fingers down the parchment of the page. "Let's see . . . 'The common great hemlock grows up with a green stalk, four or five feet high, full of red spots. At the joints are very large winged leaves, one set against the other, dented about the edges, of a sad green color. It is full of umbels of white flowers, with whitish flat seeds in July. The whole plant has a strong, heady, and ill-favored scent. Saturn claims dominion over this herb. Hemlock is exceedingly cold, and very dangerous, especially taken inwardly. It may safely be applied to inflammations, tumults, and swellings in any part of the body as well as to St. Anthony's fire, wheals, pushes, and creeping ulcers. The leaves, bruised and laid to the forehead, are good for red and swollen eyes. The root, roasted and applied to the hands, helps the gout. Pure wine is the best antidote if too much of this herb is taken.' " Estelle smiled with satisfaction. "That is excellent, but then you have had the benefit of such a magnificent teacher. Good night, child, don't sit up painting all night. I'll send Meg up with a tray. We must try to put a little meat on your bones."

Jasmine loved to paint. She had an eye for light and shadow that made the flowers appear so real you could smell them or reach out a finger to touch the drop of dew upon a leaf.

The moment she sat down at the desk a sparrow flew

down onto the rim of her wine chalice. "Shoo, Feather, shoo," Jasmine said, gently wafting her hand so the little pet bird flew off to perch in the rafters. With the tip of her tongue between her teeth, Jasmine soon became absorbed in the illustration of the hemlock plant. She didn't notice Feather fly back down to perch upon the edge of the goblet and dip its beak into the blood-red wine, then tilt its throat back to swallow greedily. She was cleaning her brushes when Meg, the young maid, came in with a tray and set it down on the great desk.

"Oooh, my lady, the wee birdie is dead!" she cried with alarm as she saw the little sparrow on its back with its feet sticking straight up.

Jasmine looked around startled, then she laughed. "No, he's not dead, he's just drunk again. You naughty boy, Feather," she scolded as she scooped him up and dropped a kiss upon his head. She finished the wine, wiped out the goblet with a napkin, and popped him into the bowl of the chalice. "You'll be safe there till morning."

Dame Winwood resided in Winwood Keep, a small manor with a high tower deeded to her by the Earl of Salisbury. It was located on the remote edge of the Salisbury Plain, close upon Stonehenge. The people who served the manor were all drawn from the nearby village. Estelle preferred women servants, but in the stables where male strength was a necessity, she took boys only to the age of fourteen. It was a lawless time, because Richard Coeur de Lion chose to be a king *in absentia* and England was ruled by mighty barons who warred with each other for castles, land, and power. Yet the household of women lived without fear for it enjoyed the protection of the mighty Earl of Salisbury, half brother to the king. Though his seat of Salisbury where his main castle was located was a mere twelve miles from

Winwood Keep, Jasmine saw little of her father, for he was a marcher lord, pledged to keep the marches into Wales safe for the crown. He commanded a hundred knights and nearly two hundred men-at-arms, so Estelle saw to it that Jasmine visited only briefly and always kept her strictly within the women's quarters of the castle.

The earl had two legitimate daughters who were the heirs to his vast lands. They had been brought up to be competent chatelaines and were expected to make good marriages. Though William had loved the baby Jasmine dearly, he had found it beyond him to keep the puny little scrap alive and willingly placed her in the hands of her natural grandmother, who had taken her and breathed life into her. Jasmine had had an unconventional upbringing, to say the least. The child, much too small and fragile to train up as future wife and mother, was taught instead the finer arts of music, painting, writing, botany, poetry, and magic. Her life was a blend of fact and fantasy, ideally suited to one so delicate.

Dawn brought one of the loveliest mornings of the year. April's end seemingly brought forth a blossom on every tree bough, and the birds had been singing their throats out since first light. Estelle came into Jasmine's bedchamber as she was dressing. "I'm glad you're up early. We have a busy day ahead if we are to be prepared for tonight's gathering."

Jasmine rolled the spiny ball of a hedgehog from her slipper and smiled at the tiny squeak of protest it made at being disturbed. "Hush, Quill, you kept me awake half the night rustling about, but now that you want to sleep, it is another matter entirely."

"He's nocturnal, Jasmine. A leopard can't change his spots, you know. Why didn't you leave him up in the tower room?" asked Estelle.

Jasmine confessed, "Feather got dead drunk again and I was afraid Quill might forage for him."

"Mmm," said Estelle, pursing her lips. "Typical male behavior."

Winwood Keep's gardens were a riot of color as the two women stepped out into the warm sunshine. Jasmine saw a honeybee drowning and dipped her finger into the stone birdbath to pick it up. It clung on, holding perfectly still for a couple of seconds, then immediately set about wiping its face and antennae with its front legs. Since their first stop was the beehives anyway, to gather the honey, Jasmine let the furry creature stay on her finger until they reached the hives. Everything in this first garden had been planted to attract bees and butterflies. Beneath the hawthorne, cherry, and crabapple trees bloomed borders of phlox, pinks, lemon verbena, primroses, and hyacinths. The lawn was dotted with buttercups, clover, and daisies, all swarming with honeybees.

Estelle wrapped the honeycombs in cheesecloth, put them into her basket, and the women moved through the hedge into the herb garden. There they gathered sage, mint, angelica, poppy, and alkanet, then left the garden for the nearby woods where they gathered hemlock and arrach.

That night they dispensed to the women of the village most of the materials they had gathered. Arrach was given to the few who were barren and wished to be fruitful, poppy was dispensed for toothaches, alkanet for burns, angelica for black-and-blue bruises, but most of the peasant women had come for electuaries to feed their husbands. One was of hemlock to stop a man's lust; the other was mint to provoke a man's lust and stir up venery! The rest had come to the high tower room for magic spells. As she had the previous night, Estelle adorned Jasmine with the finely spun silken robe and the girl glided into the circle of thirteen green candles. Again she began the ritual by crushing the herbs in the alabaster bowl and smoldering them to a heady, spiraling fragrance. Then she sipped the blood-red wine from the jewel-encrusted chalice and chanted each wish, calling upon the Powers of the Universe. She gazed into the crystal orb and told each woman exactly what she wished to hear. Yes, the love of a certain youth would be revealed before the next full moon; yes, the child that was on the way would be male rather than female; yes, the husband would stray no more; yes, the hunting would be bountiful this season.

The women were totally bedazzled by the maiden's sheer physical perfection. Her cloak of silvery gold hair fell about her delicately boned body giving her an ethereal, other-world quality. The candles' glow formed a nimbus around her, and not one soul doubted that she was a fairy princess who could foresee the future and cast magic spells.

It was almost midnight before the last guest left and they were alone. Jasmine spoke worriedly to her grandmother. "Estelle, I didn't have one single vision, I 'saw' nothing!"

"My dearest child, true visions are few and far between, but you acted like an adept and carried on as if you were a high priestess of the Universe."

"But I feel like such a fraud," she explained.

"Never, ever think you have perpetrated a hoax. As I've told you before many times, we are not really dealing in magic and miracles. What we are dealing in is belief, faith. If they believe strongly enough, then it will happen for them. People of every walk of life, not just peasants, but the highborn too, are infinitely better off and happier if they have something they believe in. Well, I'm off to bed; I find there is nothing quite so exhausting as the hoi polloi."

Jasmine watched her grandmother affectionately as she

walked to the tower room door. Though she must be near sixty years old, her back was straight as a poker and her mind as keenly convoluted as it had been at twenty; perhaps even more so.

Jasmine experienced a mild disappointment because of her power, or more to the point her lack of power. She slipped off the silvery robe and reached for a warm velvet bedgown, but suddenly stayed her hand. Something compelled her to try one last time. Perhaps alone she would command more concentration. She bent and carefully relighted the green candles, then stepped naked within the magic circle. Patiently she observed the rules of the ritual and gazed intensely into the crystal orb. Suddenly from inside the globe came a flash of lightning. She was paralyzed; the one thing that had always struck unreasoning fear in her was thunder and lightning. As she stood momentarily transfixed, a dark figurehead appeared in the crystal. It was the face of a man, so darkly forbidding she fell back with a cry. The vision disappeared instantly yet as she hurried from the tower room to the sanctuary of her warm bedchamber, it persisted in her mind. The face had been partially obscured by a helmet with a metal noseguard, but the eyes had burned with a fierce, cruel brilliance, and she shivered from head to toe, convinced that she had glimpsed the Devil.

Chapter 2

William, the marshal of all England, was in residence at his great castle of Chepstow on the border between England and Wales, yet he hadn't enjoyed the comforts of sleeping in his own bed for over a week. A hundred tents

had been set up in one of his meadows along the Severn
River to accommodate the barons who had any holdings
in Wales. Lord Llewelyn, self-styled King of Wales, had
agitated an uprising, and once again the land was aflame
with rebellion.

William Marshal, the Earl of Pembroke, was the greatest landholder in Wales and held the county of Pembroke,
which stretched from Saint Bride's Bay to Carmarthen.
But he was by no means the only one with vast interests
in Wales. William Longsword, the Earl of Salisbury, had
brought his knights and men-at-arms to the war confer-
ence, and his tents were set up next to those of Hubert de
Burgh, Keeper of the Welsh Marches.

One of the scouts they had sent out had just returned,
and the leaders hurried to the large war tent they were
using as headquarters. The scout, disguised as a Welshman with long mustaches, leather tunic, and bare arms
with gold bracelets clasped above his biceps, threw off his
sodden, mud-spattered, scarlet cloak and gratefully
quaffed a tankard of ale that a quick-witted young squire
had poured for him. "My lords," he said, gasping, as he
set the empty vessel down on the large map table, "the
army Llewelyn has amassed is larger than we suspected.
They have several castles under siege in the southwest."
He looked at William Marshal as he said this, for the
southwest was his. "Others dotted throughout the south-
east have already fallen. One at Bridgend and one at
Mountain Ash, and one—"

"By the breath of God, Mountain Ash is mine!" thundered Falcon de Burgh, his fierce eyes burning holes into
the tired messenger. "De Burgh, to me!" he shouted at
the top of his lungs. The family name was used as a
rallying battle cry and his knights responded immediately, running to attend their commander's call for aid.
He quit the tent instantly, waiting to hear no more. He
had earned the nickname Prince of Darkness, for when

seen in the madness of battle this dark young man resembled the devil himself.

At the sudden departure William Longsword raised his brows and William Marshal answered his unasked question. Chuckling, he said, "By the bones of Christ, our enemy picked on the wrong man to steal from this time. De Burgh has only one castle, and if I know aught he will hold what is his."

Hubert de Burgh spoke up. "Horses sink exhausted beneath him; when his men beg leave to rest he leaves them in his dust with a snort of contempt. He is a truly stark Norman lord with fire in his belly."

The Earl of Salisbury, who had only daughters, said to Hubert, "You must be exceeding proud of such a son."

Hubert shook his head regretfully. "I am not his sire, milord, merely his uncle."

The war council dragged on until late into the night. One plan of action after another was examined and discarded because of its flaws. The next day saw some agreement among the barons and a plan of action was decided upon. The third day saw the order to strike camp, but not until day four did the large assembly of soldiers put out their last campfires.

The Earl of Salisbury was just about to mount his great destrier when he saw a young knight he thought he recognized. "Aren't you one of Falcon de Burgh's men?" he asked, puzzled.

Normand Gervase was amazed that the king's half brother had just spoken to him. "Aye, milord earl," he answered guardedly, wondering why he had been singled out.

"Did you not accompany him to Mountain Ash? He rode out of here like the Angel of Death to retake his castle."

"We are back, milord earl," Gervase said simply.

"But what of Mountain Ash?" he probed.

"He retook the castle. Discovered treachery from within. The castellan's head now decorates the portcullis."

"But there was no time for a siege! How did he retake it?"

"He scaled the walls, milord earl," Gervase replied as if it were the most natural thing in the world.

The Earl of Salisbury was stunned. "Ask de Burgh if he would speak with me," he requested.

It was some hours later when Falcon de Burgh, astride his great black destrier, Lightning, rode up beside William Longsword, Earl of Salisbury. The earl's squire dropped behind respectfully to allow the fierce knight access to his lord. William scrutinized de Burgh thoroughly, noting the powerful thighs, the great length of his sword arm, and the ferocity of his dark countenance. Then his eyes narrowed and he came straight to the point without wasting any time on greetings. "Is it true you scaled the walls?"

"They underestimated my anger. They will never make that mistake again," he said quietly.

"How can you be sure it won't happen again?" Salisbury asked reasonably.

Falcon de Burgh's wolf grin flashed and was gone. "I took the new castellan's son as hostage. He knows if he betrays me I will not hesitate to take the lad's life."

William nodded, satisfied. He had taken the measure of the man and liked what he saw. Falcon was a member of the powerful de Burgh family. His great-grandfather had come over with William of Normandy and had conquered Ireland alongside of him. His father had met an untimely death, but his father's brother was Hubert de Burgh, Marcher Lord of Wales and sheriff of Hereford, Dorset, Somerset, and Berkshire. Falcon's other uncle, William de Burgh, was the Lord of Connaught and Lord of the Limerick Region, which covered almost a fifth of Ireland.

Finally Salisbury put his thoughts into words. "Is either of your de Burgh uncles your overlord?"

Falcon shook his head. "Nay, milord. I own only one castle yet, but control of this land is absolute. I owe only fealty to the crown."

"Then I would be honored if you would fight beside me, under my banner."

Falcon de Burgh answered him without hesitation. "The honor is mine, milord. I will fight beside you, but I will fight under my own banner."

The Earl of Salisbury took no offense. Young de Burgh was his own man and made no bones about it! Over the next two days and nights Salisbury was able to observe the young knight at close hand. He always wore full armor; it almost made one tired watching him carry all that steel upon his body. Salisbury never saw him sleep. He knew his men by name, not only his knights but his vassals and castellans also. Whenever they made camp he moved about, stopping to speak to his men, to answer their questions, to look at their horses. He even took time to speak to the common men-at-arms so that he knew how much he could count on each man when it came to fighting. He handled his men with total authority, yet with such seeming ease that Salisbury was greatly impressed.

That night while other leaders drank, gambled, and whored, Salisbury joined de Burgh at his campfire. "I think you'll do a better job than my own captains. If I give you fifty of my knights and a hundred men-at-arms to command, could you handle them as well as your own men?"

"You know I could, milord, or you wouldn't offer," Falcon de Burgh said with amusement glittering in his eyes.

"We reach Bridgend tomorrow. They are yours for this first skirmish."

"I would meet them tonight so I can get to know them and they can learn what to expect from me."

William groaned. "Tonight? God's bones, boy, don't you ever sleep?"

The wolf's grin appeared. "I can sleep when I'm dead!"

The Anglo-Norman army on the march moved slowly through the April rains that dampened every article of clothing the men wore until their woolens chafed and their chain mail rusted. Their supply wagons and siege engines, brought to batter down walls with large stones shot from mangonels or trenchbuts, bogged down at the most inconvenient times, rubbing the men's tempers as raw as their arses.

Falcon de Burgh kept his knights so busy they had no time to whine or complain. He took full advantage of the slow-moving army, knowing he could withdraw his men for a couple of days at a time then rejoin the mass. It was early in the morn, the mists still not cleared, when Falcon de Burgh, intent upon taking a castle before the sun set that day, was taken by surprise. The Welsh band hidden in a small copse loosed their arrows upon the enemy. Retreat and cover were not in de Burgh's vocabulary. His men were under orders to wear their armor and chain mail at all times, so any who disobeyed and were foolish enough to be vulnerable to Welsh bowmen, the best in the world, received no sympathy.

He led the way full gallop into the woods to rout and trample the enemy. The sounds and smells of battle assailed him: arrows whistling through the air then thunking into soft flesh or pinging against metal shields; the hot metallic smell of blood and sweat and vomit and panic. The moans and sobs and screams faded away as the pounding of his own heart in his ears obliterated all else. This early in the day he wielded his sword without effort, for he had been trained to fight from dawn to dusk long after the muscled sword arm was numbed.

He had annihilated a dozen Welshmen, some going beneath his destrier's hooves to make the ground slick with brains and guts. Lightning, his war-horse, had been trained to be fierce and savage and attack strangers. Falcon glimpsed a leather-tunicked youth fall back from the snarling teeth and rolling wild eyes of his destrier. As the youth hit the hard earth, the impact dislodged his helm and long, black, silken tresses came tumbling down. Falcon was stunned to realize it was a female who was almost beneath Lightning's hooves. He was off the horse in a flash. He removed a heavy gauntlet and ran his calloused hand over the girl's strong limbs. She spat into his face. Without hesitation he brought his fist up and rendered her unconscious with the blow. He slung her limp form across his saddle and rejoined the melee.

When the skirmish was over all but half a dozen Welsh were dead or dying, and these they took as hostages along with the girl and a herd of about thirty cattle that had been hidden in the woods.

By the end of the first week Falcon had taken two castles, Skenfrith and Llantilio, and intended to apply to the crown to keep them for himself.

William Marshal's forces were only awaiting supply wagon reinforcements before they moved on to Pembroke, leaving Salisbury and Hubert de Burgh's fighting men to take all between.

At last the supply wagons arrived with food and fodder gathered from the marshal's demesnes of Striguil, Weston, and Badgworth. Supplies were the one big headache for an army on the march, and later that night the atmosphere was almost one of celebration as the leaders relaxed about the warm brazier in Marshal's tent, enjoying the new supply of ale and a large wheel of cheese his thoughtful wife had included.

"You're a lucky man, William," said Salisbury, wiping an appreciative hand across his mouth. "A supportive wife is worth her weight in gold."

Hubert de Burgh slapped his nephew Falcon heartily on the back. "That's what I've been telling the lad here, and now that he has three castles of his own, he's going to be hard-pressed to manage without one."

Falcon grinned. "I'm not sure I want a wife, but I readily admit that I do indeed need one."

Hubert pressed on, for in his opinion it was time Falcon strengthened the great de Burgh family with his sons. "Warwick's widow is available, but she'll be snatched like a ripe plum for the lands she would bring to marriage."

Falcon de Burgh drew his brows together. "I'd rather win my lands in battle or through service to the crown."

"That's to your credit, but don't turn your nose up at a woman because she comes well dowered," cautioned Salisbury. "Since I have no male heirs, my two daughters, Ela and Isobel, will inherit. I would prefer a landless knight for a son-in-law who was strong enough to hold what was my daughter's rather than some titled baron or earl without iron in his gut."

The men refilled their leather tankards and laughed heartily as they advised young Falcon de Burgh on the fine points to look for in a wife. The list was simple but it was to the point. First and foremost she must be a bearer of strong sons. Second she must be trained from birth as a chatelaine to handle the thousand and one duties required to run many households smoothly and efficiently. And last but certainly not least, she should bring much land, castles, towns, and villages with their knight's fees, vassals, and peasants.

The talk of women soon had the men's lust aroused, and one by one they slipped from the tent to ease their loins with the camp followers who were ever present whenever an army was on the march. Hubert de Burgh walked beside Falcon as he sought his own tent. "By God's glove, boy, I think Salisbury has you in mind for son-in-law. Mayhap you were right to turn up your nose at a countess," he said, referring to Warwick's widow.

Falcon shook his head. "I admit to being ambitious, Hubert, but Salisbury is half brother to the king. Don't you think that's raising my sights a little too high?"

"De Burgh blood is as good as Plantagenet any day . . . mayhap better! We're not tainted with the Plantagenet temper that borders on madness."

"Are we not, Hubert? I've been accused of it often enough," Falcon said with his wolf's grin.

"That's just fire in your belly!" Hubert said with pride.

Gervase hovered about the entrance to de Burgh's tent with a worried frown between his brows. He said in a low voice, "My lord, one of the hostages begs audience."

"Tell him no," de Burgh said shortly.

The squire hesitated. "It is the woman, sir."

"Tell her no," Falcon repeated.

Gervase cleared his throat nervously. "She wouldn't take no for an answer, my lord. She awaits you within." He felt he must warn his lord further. "Have a care, sir, the Welsh use their women to lure us to our graves."

Falcon's dark brow slanted up like a raven's wing and he let out a yelp of laughter at his squire's obvious devotion. Then Falcon de Burgh lifted the flap of his pavilion and entered.

Morganna's eyes widened momentarily as his gigantic shadow loomed across the tent. The candles in metal holders had been lighted and sat atop his war chests, illuminating the interior of the red silken pavilion. Without his helmet Falcon de Burgh had a dark, masculine beauty, but he gave off an unmistakable aura of danger. He swept her with one bold, speculative glance that

stripped her of the short leather tunic and golden arm
bracelets. He looked directly into the green eyes that
slanted above sculpted cheekbones and let the silence
stretch out between them until she blurted, "I wished to
speak with you."

"If I'd wished to speak with you," he said with contempt, "I would have had you summoned." He was
amused to see the anger flare in the green eyes. How easy
she was to bait!

"I've seen you watching me for days," she threw at
him.

"And I've seen you watching *me* for days . . . with
lust!" he threw back.

She tossed her head and her black hair swung down
her back like a silken waterfall. Again the silence
stretched out between them. With a shrug of her bared
shoulder she turned her back upon him and strolled over
to his high map table. There she let her fingers trail
across the parchments. "Don't you want to know what
I've come for?" she asked archly.

"I know what you've come for tonight," he said, closing the distance between them in three long strides.
"You've come to be fucked. It is what you want for tomorrow that I'm curious about." He put two strong
hands on her slim hips and lifted her to sit before him on
the high table.

Morganna clenched her fists into small iron balls and
thumped him upon the chest. His hands closed over hers
cruelly and squeezed until she ceased pounding him. She
gasped with pain and his mouth came down to thoroughly devour her. Falcon's strength was like an aphrodisiac to her, and she took his tongue inside her mouth,
sucking with all the sensuality he aroused in her.

Falcon glanced ruefully at the bed across the tent and
knew they would never make it that far. He opened her
legs and pulled her hard against his body as he stepped

between. As he tore off her leather tunic, she freed his engorged member from his chausses, one as eager as the other to mate with such new and exciting physical perfection.

He bent his knees slightly and thrust upward into the girl's body, holding her buttocks firmly in both hands. She writhed upon him in a frenzy. Never before had she been aroused so quickly or so violently. His raw male strength stripped away every inhibition, and as he brought her to shuddering climax she dug her nails into the skin of his shoulders and an eerie wail was torn from her throat.

With her still impaled upon him, he lifted her from the table and strode toward the bed. It was a long time since he had had a woman and he was ready again instantly. He laid her upon the bed and hung over her, taking most of his own weight on his braced forearms. She was small, olive-skinned, and beautifully proportioned. Her hair was as black as his own and her eyes glittered with an animal quality that screamed her sexuality to a male as virile as de Burgh. He took her again swiftly without kisses or love words, and she was amazed that she reached another climax, this one greater than the first.

He rolled off her, but instead of lying beside her, two strong hands lifted her above him to straddle his muscled thighs. She wished she could dissolve in his arms and fall asleep next to him. Her limbs were turned to water, her eyes half-closed in satiety as a great languor stole over her naked body. He watched her through narrowed eyes. A girl this beautiful would never have escaped the notice of Llewelyn. "Do I make a welcome change from Welsh peasants?" he asked.

"The king himself enjoys my favors," she said with pride. Her value as a hostage rose considerably as she unwittingly confirmed her status.

"Llewelyn is lord, not king," he corrected her sharply.

She shrugged her supple brown shoulders, not wishing to argue. Since he would not let her sleep, she decided to explore the magnificent warrior's body beneath her. She ran her palms across the thick slabs of muscle in his chest. The dark mat of hair upon it was crisp to her fingertips. She slid them along the faint outline of his ribs and down across his hard, flat belly. By the time her hands had reached his groin, his shaft was hard again, standing erect, pulsating with blood. She stared in disbelief. Surely he couldn't take her a third time?

Suddenly her blood was on fire. He must find her very exciting if he were this insatiable. She smiled secretly. She would make him her slave. She arched her body up and impaled herself upon him. Inside her he felt like steel sheathed in silk. She bent forward to taste his mouth and moaned with deepest pleasure as he began to thrust savagely into her.

Hours later, when he lay sated and she curled against him in utter exhaustion, he asked, "What is it you want from me?"

She gasped, for she assumed her body had emptied his mind of any coherent thought. "I don't want to be taken to England as a hostage," she said desperately. "I don't want to be humiliated when English women look at me with contempt." She had little chance of appealing to an inner softness for she instinctively knew he had none, and so it was that she trembled uncontrollably with relief as he murmured,

"I'll send you to Mountain Ash, perhaps."

One hour after dawn William Marshal's vast army of nearly two hundred knights and three hundred men-at-arms, along with his supply wagons and siege engines, was ready to depart camp for Pembroke. Before they moved out, however, messengers rode in with such momentous news that it put an instant end to the Welsh campaign.

King Richard had been wounded and might even die. He had ordered his marshal to take ship for Rouen where the state treasury of Normandy was kept. The entire camp was in shock, and little by little as the details came out, the barons were sickened that King Richard's insatiable greed over a few gold coins had ended in disaster. Apparently a golden shield and a trove of ancient coins had been unearthed in a field at Chalus. King Richard took a handful of his knights hotfoot to Chalus to demand the treasure, and an arrow from the castle walls had struck him down. The man who had survived the great crusades and fought the berserk infidel, the man who was reputed to be the greatest warrior-king who had ever lived, was now losing his life's breath over a handful of coins.

William Marshal crossed the River Severn, rode across Wessex, and took his own ship to Normandy and the city of Rouen on the River Seine to stand guard over the treasury.

Falcon de Burgh rode beside Salisbury on the journey back into England. He chose his words with great care for he knew he could quite easily be caught between the kettle and the coals. King Richard was an absentee king who preferred the glory of battle to ruling his kingdoms. He cared so little for England that, in order to finance his crusades, he would have sold London if he had had a buyer. And yet with his faults, he was still preferable to either of the two remaining Plantagenet heirs to the throne. Richard's brother Geoffrey had been killed in a tournament, but Geoffrey's young son Arthur was next in line. The boy was only thirteen years old and had never set foot on English soil. His mother was Constance of Brittany and he shared all her hatreds. One such hatred was for the queen mother, Eleanor of Aquitaine. Philip of

France was such a threat to England that it would be tantamount to suicide to crown young Arthur king.

That left only Richard's youngest brother, Count John of Mortain. John would have virtually ruled England and Ireland in Richard's absence if it hadn't been for the powerful barons. There was not one of them who did not secretly dread the thought that John might become king.

Falcon de Burgh had come to know and like Salisbury well, and he knew that the man's greatest virtue was loyalty. He did not wish to say anything to William that would sound like criticism of his royal half brothers. "It will be a sad day for England, milord, if Richard's wound proves fatal."

"Never!" William cried with conviction. "He's survived a dozen worse woundings than this. Mark my words, we'll be back in Wales before the month is out."

Falcon cleared his throat, wondering if William was deliberately wearing blinders in this situation. After all, they were on their way to England in case the barons were called to Normandy for the king's funeral and the crowning of a new king. "I hope with all my heart that you are right, milord, yet would William Marshal have been ordered to Normandy if the situation was not critical?" he asked carefully.

"William Marshal is the only baron whose honor comes before self-interest. He is the kind of man who comes along only once in a century. If Richard is chained to a sickbed because of his wounds, there is only one man he would trust with his treasury." He winked at de Burgh. "We all know how important money is to our king."

Falcon laughed, relieved that William had been the one to say it. "Aye, the marshal is a man you could trust with your life—or your wife," he joked. The subject of Arthur and John had not been broached between them, so Salisbury decided to let de Burgh know exactly how he felt.

"You know, I always tell myself that I inherited my courage and my fighting skills from my father, King Henry, and yet I lack that ruthless ambition for the throne that drives my brothers. So I also tell myself the driving ambition that crushes everything and everyone in its path was passed down to my brothers through their mother, Queen Eleanor. Mercifully I had another dam. I am not blind to Arthur's shortcomings or John's faults, but they are royal princes and both in line to the throne. Should the day arrive when either is crowned king, I am his man . . . to the death!"

Falcon de Burgh wished he himself saw things in such a simple, straightforward way. If only things were cut and dried, black and white, how simple life would be. But things were not black and white these days, they tended to fall into the vast area of gray with its infinite shadings.

William's voice brought him back to the present. "I extend the hospitality of Salisbury to you and your knights, de Burgh. I would like you to meet my daughters, but of course there is a catch. I have an ulterior motive," he said frankly.

Falcon de Burgh was flattered and honored. Salisbury was making it plain that he viewed him favorably as a suitor.

William continued, "I should like to ride straight home in case there is urgent news, and yet Berkley Castle and Castle Combe have not been visited this year. Would it be too much of an imposition to ask you to inspect them in my stead?"

"You do me great honor, William, to trust me with such a task." The words came from his heart. Falcon was being trusted to collect Salisbury's share of the produce of the two demesnes along with the rents of his tenants. He would have to inspect the men-at-arms and defenses of the keeps, listen to any complaints, go over the accounts and tally sticks. It was not lost on him that William was also showing him two of the holdings that his daughters would inherit.

Falcon wheeled his great destrier about and rode down the line to his own men. Immediately Normand Gervase and Walter de Roche flanked him.

"Sir Walter, I want you to take half the knights and men-at-arms to Mountain Ash. The other half will come with me to England. I am putting you in charge at Mountain Ash. Your word is law so be heedful that if anything goes amiss, I will hold you responsible."

"Rest easy, my lord," said de Roche, grinning with deep pleasure at his newfound authority. He dropped back to select his men as impartially as he could, for de Burgh would need good men to accompany him into England.

Falcon said to his squire, "Gervase, I want you to go to Mountain Ash also, but when your task is completed you will catch up with me as soon as may be. We are invited to Salisbury."

"Then it is true! William Longsword is giving you your choice of his daughters for your wife."

"Softly, man. I think the wind lies in that direction, but there's many a slip twixt cup and lip," he cautioned. He winked at Gervase. "I will need you at Salisbury . . . to help me choose!"

"God's nightshirt, you know I've had little experience with the fairer sex; they scare the shit out of me."

Falcon chuckled. "I'm giving you an opportunity to gain some experience. The female hostage, Morganna . . . see her safely to Mountain Ash."

Gervase paled visibly. "My lord, I command men easily, you've been a good teacher, but a woman is another matter . . . especially this woman. Why, she is as fierce as a young warrior. I-I have doubts that she would heed my authority," he confessed bluntly.

"Come," said Falcon, "I'll give you a short lesson."

They rode down the line to where the hostages rode on their sturdy Welsh ponies. De Burgh signaled to Morganna, who eagerly guided her mount to his side. Rumors were rife that King Richard, Coeur de Lion, was dead, and she planned to get the answers to a dozen questions when he bedded her tonight.

"My squire here, Normand Gervase, will see you safely to Mountain Ash. His word is my command. You will obey him to the letter," he said in a tone that brooked no disobedience.

Her face fell with disappointment, then her eyes glittered with anger. "You do not come with us, Lord de Burgh?" The other rumors must be true, she thought. He is going to England to wed Salisbury's daughter. Her heart twisted with bitterness. She had vowed to own a piece of this magnificent man, but what chance did she have if he was off to court an Englishwoman? "Is it true the king is dead?" she demanded, knowing she would not be sharing de Burgh's bed this night or for many nights to come.

"That is of no concern to you, Morganna. What is of concern is your behavior." Falcon turned his head to Gervase. "If she disobeys you, take away her pony and make her walk."

She threw up her head proudly. "I could walk! To England and back if necessary! I've climbed Welsh mountains all my life."

"You'd be so thin and scrawny, your legs so well muscled, what good would you be in bed? A man could get more pleasure from buggering his page!" Falcon said with contempt.

Gervase was impressed at the way de Burgh's words had silenced the girl and drained away her arrogance, leaving only meekness in its stead. However, he had his doubts she would be quite so docile once de Burgh's razor-edged tongue was on its way to England.

Chapter 3

Jasmine had heard Meg and the other girls giggling and whispering for a week and she had a pretty good notion what it was all about. May Day meant a celebration of spring rites that harkened back to pagan times and the old religion. However, Jasmine had been aware for years now that there was more to it than innocent maypole dancing in the village and choosing a May queen.

It was whispered that at Stonehenge, under cover of darkness, a bacchanalia took place. When Meg came to change her bed linen, Jasmine questioned her. "Meg, I wonder what it's like at Stonehenge?"

Meg blushed and said primly, "I don't know, my lady, I've never seen the goings-on."

"But you must have heard things," Jasmine pressed. "What goes on?"

"Well . . . 'tis said there is a feast and dancing. They light bonfires and dance about the flames."

"I should like to go," Jasmine said with conviction.

Meg lowered her voice to a conspiratorial whisper. "Me too, my lady. I'm planning to slip out and join in the fun."

Estelle was worried about the spring rites that took place amid the ancient Druid stones. She knew exactly what went on under cover of darkness, and the results would be a bumper crop of swollen bellies. The peasants could be counted on to obey their basest instincts, then come crying to her once the seeds had been sown. She sighed, knowing she could not turn the tide against human nature, but she would do what she could to prevent the young maids of the manor from attending the revels. She and Jasmine had taken part in the May Day holiday with the villagers, joining in the maypole dancing and crowning the buxom lass chosen as Queen of the May, but she whisked her charges back to the manor house before dusk had fallen and took Meg aside to give her extra duties.

"I want you to be sure to stay with Lady Jasmine until she falls asleep tonight. I think she has looked very peaked lately, and she is not robust at the best of times. Make sure she drinks lots of the mead and honey tonight. It is a potion that will make her glow with health and beauty."

Meg bobbed a curtsey, resenting the restricting duty with which Lady Estelle had charged her. She came tight-lipped to Jasmine's bedchamber and made a half-hearted attempt to set it in order as the long minutes stretched into an hour.

Jasmine had a difficult time concealing her amusement; she knew Meg had been sent to her as a jailer of sorts. Jasmine watched as the maid poured her a goblet of honeyed mead and held it out to her. Suddenly she became aware of an unusual aroma. She surreptitiously sniffed the mead and realized Estelle had laced it with poppy. A secret smile turned up the corners of her lips as a wicked idea came to her.

"You drink the mead, Meg. I know you're going off to Stonehenge in a little while and it will fortify you on the long walk." Meg needed little urging for mead was not often on the servant's menu.

Jasmine poked up the fire and watched in silence as first Meg yawned, then her eyelids drooped, and finally she slumped on the stool as Morpheus claimed her. Jasmine quickly changed into the servant girl's clothes, covering her hair with the rough linen coif, then she lay Meg in the bed and pulled the covers high to conceal her identity from a casual glance if someone opened the chamber door. With her heart beating wildly she donned Meg's shabby, dark cloak, pulled up the hood to doubly conceal her pale hair, and slipped from her chamber.

She walked briskly, lest her nerve fail her at the last moment, and hummed a happy tune to ward off the darklings. She took a black pony from the paddock beside the stables so that even the young grooms could not know of her departure. The moon seemed to keep her company as it sailed above her, disappearing beneath a cloud, then when the darkness made her heart thump, it glided from behind the cloud so serenely she chided herself for being a coward. She knew it was close on midnight and hoped she had not come too late for the revels.

Her excitement built as she neared Stonehenge. She realized there would be men there as well as women, but she intended to be very careful and observe only from a distance.

The great fire inside the circle of stones crackled noisily and lit up the sky. The revelers were making a great din, filling the air with wild laughter, shrieks, and screams. As she crouched behind a large boulder to watch the human forms dancing, she was shocked to her soul to see that the men and women cavorted naked! Mesmerized, she watched the naked bodies silhouetted against the flames and realized with horror that most of them were not dancing, they were coupling! She averted her eyes to stare across at the stark outline of the Druid stones. Her attention was drawn to a small group wearing hooded robes and became riveted upon a female figure that seemed to be carrying a baby. They walked toward a stone that formed an altar and the woman raised the child up to the sky, its white swaddling blanket clearly visible in the darkness, then she lay it down upon the altar. A man drew forth a long dagger and plunged it down into the baby.

Jasmine stood up and screamed, "No!" As fast as she could, she began running toward the stone altar.

* * *

Falcon de Burgh had made the journey of thirty miles from Berkley to Castle Combe in one day, and he hoped to better that distance on the journey from Castle Combe to Salisbury. He had not counted on the Cotswold Hills, some of which seemed more like mountains. He had had no word about King Richard and pressed his men as hard as he could so they would reach Salisbury without delay. If Richard died, the Earl of Salisbury would go to Normandy immediately.

When darkness overtook them, Falcon estimated they were still a good ten miles from their destination. They set up their tents on Salisbury Plain. As they did so, he noticed that some of the men were gathering in groups with worried faces. Ordinarily he would have consulted with his most trusted knight and friend Gervase, but he had not yet caught up from his journey to Mountain Ash.

Falcon went to the men who were tethering the horses for the night and asked bluntly, "Montgomery, what's amiss? Speak up, man!"

The knight glanced at his companion Fitzgerald and back to de Burgh. "Some of the men are afraid to make camp near Stonehenge."

Fitzgerald nodded, "Aye, my lord, 'tis a most unsettling place, haunted by ancient spirits."

De Burgh threw back his head in laughter. "God's bones, since when were Norman knights crippled by superstition?"

Montgomery offered quick denial. " 'Tis not the knights, my lord, but some of the men-at-arms who are from these parts. They say we are camping too close to Stonehenge for comfort."

"Rubbish! We're miles from the place. This is an excellent spot to make camp—flat ground, close to the River Avon. Tell them to stop their idle chatter and put them to work gathering wood for cooking fires." He grinned. "The fires will ward off the evil spirits."

Though the hour was late and most of the camp slept, the horses were decidedly unsettled. De Burgh heard their nervous whickering hour after hour and heard them milling about long after they should have quieted to rest. Perhaps there were wolves about or a wildcat come down onto Salisbury Plain from the mountains. He had been lying wrapped in a thick fur rug pleasantly conjuring up pictures of William's two daughters when a disturbing thought came to him. Perhaps the animals could pick up a strange unsettling atmosphere from Stonehenge. He shook his head to dispel such a ridiculous notion, threw back the furs, and stepped to the tent's opening. Was it his imagination, or could he hear chanting on the air? He stepped out into the darkness and listened. Faint cries and music were coming from a distance and the horses, with their keener hearing, were strangely disturbed by it.

He untethered Lightning and rubbed him behind his ears. Stonehenge was beckoning and his curiosity got the better of him. He mounted the destrier without a saddle and guided him in the direction of the singing.

The scene laid out before him angered him. Excess had always disgusted him. In any raid on castle or town his men were forbidden to rape on penalty of death. Self-discipline was a virtue he valued highly in himself and others. These people had no discipline and in fact were out of control. The veneer of civilization was so thin they reverted to savage, feral beasts at any opportunity.

He was appalled to see some hooded figures flee an altar, leaving behind a blood sacrifice of some sort. His sensibilities were affronted to see such an ancient and hallowed place as Stonehenge defiled.

As Jasmine flew to the altar like an avenging angel, her eyes fastened upon the tiny bundle swaddled in the blanket, the hooded figures melted into the darkness. Her hands trembled uncontrollably as she lifted the blanket. Her eyes filled with tears as she saw that it was a new-born lamb that had been sacrificed. Her sadness was mingled with relief that it had not been a baby. Suddenly fear gripped her. They were Devil worshippers. The sacrificial lamb had been used to conjure the Prince of Darkness himself.

De Burgh, towering above, his face dark with fury, saw the mutilated lamb and reached out a punishing hand to grasp her. She glanced up and shrank back in terror. It was the Devil! She had seen him before in the crystal!

Jasmine trembled from head to toe. Fear gripped her heart. Why had she so willfully disobeyed and come to this wicked place? Satan had caught her in a face-to-face confrontation. Quickly she covered her eyes so that he would not be able to look into her soul.

He took hold of her shoulder and shook her roughly. "Wicked wench, have you no shame? Look at me when I speak to you!"

"No, no," she cried, "if I look into your eyes you will be able to steal my soul!"

"What gibberish is this? You ignorant little peasant." He took hold of her hands and forced them down from her face.

She saw the Prince of Darkness in all his splendor. He was richly garbed in black velvet, the hilt of his dagger encrusted with blood-red rubies. He was a head taller than a mortal man and broader too. His face was darkly, wickedly handsome, and his eyes gleamed with green fire. They narrowed suspiciously as he felt her silken, soft hands.

"These are not the hands of a peasant girl." He pulled off the shabby cloak and looked at her closely. Though she wore the dress and rough linen coif of a servant, he knew she was no such thing. "You are a spoiled, bored lady come to amuse yourself in the guise of your servant," he accused.

Her throat constricted as half a scream was torn from her. With all his cosmic powers of darkness, he would identify her any minute. When he discovered she was a white witch who practiced only good, he would surely kill her. "Please don't kill me," she begged, terrified.

"I should beat some decency into you," he threatened. "You are a wayward little baggage, sneaking out at night for thrills. Your parents probably cannot do a thing with you."

The moon came from behind a cloud and bathed them in its silvery light. He realized suddenly she was hardly more than a child and that she trembled with fear. Instead of the saucy, pert features he had expected, he was looking into the face of an angel. Suddenly his anger melted and turned to amusement. Obviously this was the first time she had ever dared come to this place, and her encounter with him had really put the fear of the Devil in her. Well, before he was done with her, he would make certain she would never venture forth again in the name of temptation.

He held her hands fast so there was no hope of escape. "Why did you come here?" he asked.

She swallowed hard. Her heart beat wildly in her throat, choking her words. "I . . . was . . . c-curi-ous," she managed to gasp.

His eyes glittered with amusement as he accused, "You came to dance naked."

"No, no," she denied, shocked at his words.

Beginning to enjoy himself, he teased, "You came to find a man, a lover."

She shook her head in shocked denial, but words failed her.

"Well, you have found a man . . . you have found me."

Lurid snatches of folklore came to her about Satan having his way with human females. "Do not take my virginity, I beg you," she said, sobbing.

His lips twitched. "But surely that's what you had in mind when you ventured forth tonight? Surely, 'twould be a shame to come here and miss all the fun?"

"Fun?" she whispered in horrified fascination.

"Admit the truth and shame the Devil," he said, laughing. "If I hadn't caught you, you would have thrown off your clothes and danced naked round the fires." His fingers went to the buttons at the neck of her gown and deftly undid them. "Dance for me now," he invited, peeling the dress down to bare her shoulders.

She was experiencing firsthand the power he had over a female. The touch of his hands was strong and persuasive. "You cannot tempt me, Satan!" she cried. She felt dizzy, but knew if she fainted she was lost forever. The moment she swooned, he would deflower her. To be raped by Satan would be a worse fate than death! "Rape!" she cried hoarsely.

He laughed again. "Rape? Do you know the old definition of rape is to 'affect with rapture'?"

Her eyes closed with anguish and he took pity on the little maid. "Well, well, when a pretty girl is caught by the Devil she must pay some sort of forfeit. You have refused me your life and you have refused me your virginity, what forfeit will you pay?" he mused.

She had no money, she wore no jewel, her mind took a quick inventory.

"Let's see . . . you could dance naked." He hid a smile at her look of outraged innocence. "Or you could pay with a kiss . . . you choose."

"A k-kiss," she said quickly, willing to pay such a price to be rid of him. He smiled at her slowly and her heart turned over in her breast. He reached for her and she knew she would never be the same again. She had

never been kissed before. His mouth was warm and persuasive, inviting her to lose control of her senses as his
kiss took away her breath, her thoughts, her very will.
But in truth he was the one most affected. He could tell
she had never been kissed before, and her mouth was as
sweet as wild honey. Her fragrance filled his nostrils and
his head until he was dizzy with the scent and taste of
her. He realized in that instant that a virgin's kiss was a
thing to treasure.

His voice roughened with a peculiar protective need
she had aroused in him. "Begone from this place and
mend your wicked ways," he bade her, loosening his hold
on her shoulders.

She made the sign of the cross and flung herself back
from him into the deep shadow of a mighty stone and
sped off in the darkness to where her pony was tethered.
At that moment Lightning screamed and de Burgh, ut-
tering a foul oath of frustration, reluctantly tended to his
frightened war-horse.

Estelle, busy in the stillroom, kept glancing over at
Jasmine. She was very quiet and subdued this morning,
and her grandmother decided not to dose her again with
a sleeping draft of poppy. Estelle had made dyebaths of
marigold orange, day-lily yellow, and walnut brown, and
had picked dozens of early purple saffron crocus, one of
the world's best dye plants. She was busy dipping skeins
of yarn and lengths of cloth. Jasmine was silently occupied mixing the dyes and pigments into her paints, while
the air was redolent from boiling beeswax and bayberry
as Meg made candles.

A steward arrived from Salisbury Castle bringing a
cartload of supplies for the manor and wool freshly
sheared from the sheep to be expertly dyed by Dame
Estelle. He was bursting with the news that William was

returned from Wales because King Richard had been wounded in Normandy.

Estelle nodded knowingly. "So," she said portentiously, "it has begun."

Jasmine shuddered. She knew that when the steward had loaded his wagon with the things that were going back to Salisbury Castle, her grandmother would prepare to do magic this night. Usually Jasmine looked forward to participating in the rituals and spells, but to see what the future would bring would necessitate crystal gazing and suddenly she was afraid of a vision that had appeared to her twice. Once in the glass ball and once in living flesh and blood!

Jasmine made a special visit to the herb garden to gather plants to make herself a "tussiemussie." She would carry it as a talisman to protect her from all evil. She picked sprigs of sweet basil, wild thyme, rosemary, spiderwort, bloodroot, and tansy and bound them together with a red thread. Each was renowned for its protective quality and fragrance, which wooed the senses with an almost sacred promise.

Later, as the veil of darkness descended over the tower room, Jasmine was visibly relieved when Estelle said, "I will do the seeing tonight, child, but it is most important that if I go into a trance you must write down everything I say. My visions will need interpreting and every detail will be vital."

The circle of candles was lighted and Jasmine robed her grandmother in the black cloak covered with cabalistic symbols in silver thread. The old woman wore wide amulets of copper studded with amber and turquoise and anointed her forehead with sacred oil from an ivory vial. She stepped inside the circle of candles and with long, slim fingers crushed the herbs and set them to smolder. The air was filled with the scent of cloves as if the room had been suddenly filled with pinks and carnations.

Estelle took up the chalice majestically to drink the
wine and began her chanted command. "I call upon all
the Powers of the Universe to enlighten me tonight. Reveal to me the future." She caressed the crystal globe and
suddenly it began to swirl with brilliant colors. A stillness
came upon her as her concentration deepened into a
trancelike state. Her voice became urgent and husky as
she began to relay her visions to Jasmine, who sat with
quill and parchment at the ready.

"Animals . . . lions . . . three golden lions and a
lion cub with a crown. A great black oxen . . . the lions
flee in three directions, but the black ox tramples the first
lion to death . . . it seeks out the second lion and kills it
. . . now the third golden lion is trampled by the black
ox . . . a pig, no it is a wild boar, drags the cub into a
dark cave . . . now the boar picks up the crown where
it has fallen . . . the black oxen comes to trample the
boar but it swims across the water and escapes. The ox
submerges into the water to await the boar at a future
date . . . now comes a jackal to devour the dead lion. It
is not satisfied and seeks out another lion's carcass to
swallow it whole. The jackal has a pup to feed . . . they
seek out the carcass of the third golden lion and rend it to
pieces and devour it . . . still their greed is not satisfied
. . . they look toward the water and see the boar on the
far shore . . . yes, they are going after the boar. They
know it is weak and vain, caring for only the jewels in the
crown rather than the power the crown represents. All is
fading . . . come back, come back . . ."

Dame Estelle opened her eyes and shuddered. "Did
you take down everything I said?" she asked anxiously.
Jasmine helped her to a chair by the fire and handed her
the parchment. Estelle read it carefully, considering the
images she had spoken of. "I know what most of it
means, but I will sleep on it and my dreams will interpret

the rest. Tomorrow I will translate what is written and foretell the future."

"Is it good?" Jasmine asked hopefully.

The old woman shook her head. "It is like everything in life—good and bad, kind and cruel, happy and sad. However, in this case there will be a veritable surfeit of bad before the ultimate good."

Jasmine pondered her grandmother's words as she undressed for bed. There was only one question to which she desired the answer. Would she go to court? She shrugged philosophically; tomorrow may give her the answer. She picked up a large chunk of amethyst crystal quartz that contained all the cosmic energy of earth and heaven. She pressed it to her forehead and to her heart and made a wish. Before she got into bed she took Quill, the little hedgehog that was curled into a ball on the hearth, and put him into her slipper for his own safety. She did not want a red-hot coal from the fire to fall onto the little creature and singe him.

The beautiful May sunshine was in direct contrast to the fateful picture Estelle was painting. Jasmine set the dish of luscious strawberries aside as Estelle's words affected her appetite.

"The three golden lions are on King Richard's shield. As we all know, the black ox is the symbol of death. King Richard is already dead, it is simply that the news has not had time to reach England yet. The lion's cub with the crown is, of course, Richard's nephew, Prince Arthur, Geoffrey's son, who is next in line to be king. The wild boar who drags the cub into the dark cave and takes the crown must be Prince John of Mortain. The boar under cover of the dark cave must kill the lion cub in order to succeed."

"Grandmother, you are saying that John will murder Arthur! You did not see the wild boar kill the cub!"

"You are correct, I did not. A great mystery will surround the disappearance of the cub, and it will be a long, long time filled with rumor and disbelief before anyone has the courage to charge John with the heinous crime." Estelle took a deep breath and continued. "The boar takes the crown across the water, which means he will bring it to England and dwell here as England's king." She paused, hating to put the thought into words. "The jackal is Philip of France, his pup is his son Louis. By devouring the three lion carcasses they will swallow whole the Angevin possessions of Anjou, Bordeaux, and Gascony, then Brittany and finally even Normandy. Then because of King John's weakness they will covet England itself and eventually try to invade us."

Jasmine was shocked at the black picture Estelle had painted of John. After all, he was half brother to her father and thereby her uncle. According to Estelle's prophecy he was to be the new King of England. "Is he truly so evil?" she whispered.

Estelle's laugh cracked out. "Innocent one! All kings are evil. How else would they attain their high position and sustain it? Mayhap you have been kept too innocent for this world, child. You think a king would cavil at the stain of murder on his soul? There's never been one yet who has! How many deaths lie at the door of the bastard William the Conqueror, or for that matter Richard Coeur de Lion? How many bodies paved the road to Jerusalem and back? Not only the bodies of the enemy, I might point out. Nay, child, it comes with the territory of kingship."

Jasmine gazed with unseeing eyes at the red strawberries. "Will I go to court?" she whispered.

Estelle looked at her grandaughter long and hard, then said slowly, "I think perhaps you will."

Chapter 4

Falcon de Burgh became a little uneasy as his troop reached their destination. He was loath to receive bad news about the king, and truth to tell, he was more than a little apprehensive about meeting Ela and Isobel. Salisbury Castle, however, was another matter. The vast wooded hills and meadows belonging to the castle were rich with cattle and sheep. The castle itself with its Norman keep was fashioned entirely of stone. The rooms were enormous, with high-vaulted beamed ceilings rising to a full second story, all topped by towers and crenelated parapets. It was a massive fortress, enclosing bailey, courtyard, stables, and numerous outbuildings within a thick stone wall.

There were a dairy and stillrooms, a spring shed and a buttery, laundry, outdoor kitchens, and baths. Salisbury had its own blacksmith's forge and armory as well as tiltyards and gardens.

Walters, the steward and castellan of Salisbury, had obviously been told to expect de Burgh for in less than an hour he had taken charge of the produce and cattle brought from Berkley and Castle Combe, had shown the men-at-arms a fresh meadow by a stream where they could set up their tents, had settled Falcon's knights into the knights' quarters, and had shown young Lord de Burgh into the great hall where he was warmly greeted by William.

Instead of turning him over to a servant to show him his chamber, William put him into the tender care of his daughter Isobel. Falcon was startled at how lovely the girl was. All along he had been harboring a suspicion that William's daughters might be ugly or, at the very least, plain. The young woman who smiled warmly at him had expressive dark eyes that showed humor. Her hair was obviously dark, but it was seductively hidden beneath a wimple, and when his eyes dropped lower to frankly assess her figure, he did not find it wanting in any way. Though Isobel was tall for a female, she still had to tilt up her head to look the dark knight in the face. As she led the way to an upper chamber, his eyes were fixed upon the swell of her buttocks as they gently swayed up the stairs. After she ushered him into a luxurious chamber she said, "Father insists upon you having his room while you stay with us. Please don't protest, I assure you it pleases him to do this for you." She smiled at him, assessing him as openly as he had her, and she more than liked what she saw.

"Demoiselle, you are too kind. What can I say?" He bowed formally to her before looking about him. The floor was covered by a silken carpet, the walls by rich colorful tapestries, and the huge bed by thick furs. A massive wardrobe covered one wall, and the far wall was fitted with a stained-glass window that filled the room with colored lights when the sunshine filtered through.

"I am sure you will find everything you need, from wine and ale to quench your thirst to soft leather slippers to ease your feet. But I imagine you want nothing more than a warm bath to remove the stains of your travel and ease the ache of your bones."

"Demoiselle, my bones do not yet ache, thank God," he said, laughing, but he felt a definite ache in his groin at her mention of a bath.

"Please call me Isobel," she said rather breathlessly as his maleness filled the chamber.

"Lady Isobel, you are everything your father has told me," he said as formally as he could.

Her eyes sparkled with mischief. "Ah, save your com-

pliments until you have met Ela, I beg you, milord; her
virtues are outstanding."

The delicious play on words came back to him later
when he was introduced to Ela, for apart from an attractive face and prettily pouting mouth, her most outstanding feature was a pair of breasts that could only be described as breathtaking. Falcon's eyes sought out Isobel's
and they shared the humor with relish.

Ela had spent the afternoon with the head cook, Joan,
a formidable woman who held sway in the kitchens with
an iron hand and would have long since bullied William
Longsword and reduced his authority to that of a small
boy if it hadn't been for his capable daughters. The result
of the afternoon's running battle between Joan and Ela
was a culinary delight designed to seduce a man into
wishing for such domesticity that turned ordinary food
into manna.

The conversation flowed easily as they dined, showing
de Burgh how pleasant a meal could be in the great hall
of one's castle when a well-trained chatelaine was in
charge of a man's comforts. He learned that each daughter had been trained by their late mother to review the
accounts and inventory of the castle's provisions daily.
Controlling an enormous staff of strong-willed, capable
servants and cooks was no small accomplishment. When
necessary Ela and Isobel traveled from demesne to demesne gathering supplies needed for war, bullying the
bailiffs and stewards into supplying money, supplies, and
arms. They looked after the poor and set the moral stan-
dard for all the households on their vast properties.

"Father, enough!" cried Isobel, laughing. "I'm sure our
guest is not interested in how we check the salt meat for
maggots or the flour barrels for weevils or see that the
drains are running clear."

Falcon de Burgh put up his hand in protest. "Nay,
Lady Isobel, I am most fascinated to learn the role a

woman plays in running a castle. I had never given it a
thought before. Pray continue, I beg of you."

Ela looked at him with wide eyes. "We don't do the
work ourselves, milord, but rather must see that it is
done and done well. Cloth has to be woven and clothes
sewn. Leather has to be cured for shoes and tunics. Then
there is the laundry, the candles, the rushes."

Isobel picked up where Ela left off. "We look after the
sick and the wounded, select the seed and plan the gardens." The mischievous look came into her eyes again as
she added, "And tomorrow I was thinking about hunting
down a few wolves because so many of the new lambs
have been taken."

"Cry foul, Isobel," her father exclaimed, laughing.
"You must leave something for us poor males to take care
of."

"My men and I would relish a hunt tomorrow, milord,
if your time permits such indulgence," de Burgh offered
enthusiastically.

"I have some fine hawks and falcons I'd like you to try
out; to hell with the wolves," said Salisbury, who was
inordinately proud of his mews filled with magnificent
birds of prey.

Isobel refilled the men's goblets and the ladies left
them to their cups. Both girls were bursting to discuss
their visitor to find out exactly the other's inner thoughts
and share them.

Inside her chamber Ela hugged herself then pulled off
her wimple to let her chestnut hair come tumbling down.
"God's nightgown, I think I've died and gone to
Heaven!"

"Blasphemy, Ela?" Isobel chuckled, flinging herself
into the center of her sister's feather bed. "That tells me
exactly how deep your feelings are running at this moment."

"My feelings are indeed running," Ela said breathlessly. "I'm all liver and lights! Did you note the breadth of his shoulders?"

"I never noticed"—Isobel giggled—"nor did I observe the length of his thighs, the thickness of his wrists, the flatness of his belly, the bulge of his—"

"Isobel!" Ela cried in mock alarm.

"I was going to say bulge of his muscles, so that shows just where your thoughts are centered!"

"Do you know my legs are trembling? Oh, Isobel, I hope he chooses me, but if he chooses you I will try to bear it," Ela said with her usual generosity.

"He has no great rank, you know. Are you sure you wouldn't prefer an earl?" asked Isobel, trying to be practical and objective, though failing utterly.

Ela's nose wrinkled. "Remember the last earl who visited father? He ate like a rhinoceros with sore gums."

"How could I forget? But in all seriousness, Ela, we do have a large field to choose from and most of the eligible men father approves can be led by their pricks. Life would be easier wed to another. This one I think is dangerous and would be master in his own castle. He is not in awe of Father."

"I would give my salvation if he were masterful with me!" Ela sighed.

Isobel sighed also. "He looks fierce even when he smiles. Ela, my love, I give you fair warning—I want him. Lord, I could eat him whole!"

"I don't believe we'll trap him with the artful tricks of our sex, for women must positively hurl themselves at him. My guess is he wouldn't even consider taking a wife except for practical reasons," Ela warned.

Isobel, who considered herself slightly more clever than Ela, was often surprised by her sister's astuteness. "But we are equally competent as chatelaines, therefore it will be the one he most responds to physically who will win the prize."

* * *

Falcon and William sat late into the night drinking cup
for cup and matching tale for tale. Half drunk, William
became sentimental. "You need a wife, my friend, to bear
you fine strong sons. 'Tis what all men want above all
things. However, in my case it is perhaps a blessing in
disguise that I never had any. My father Henry bred a
pack of wolves who tried to bring him down like a hunted
stag. I'm the only sensible one he bred, but perhaps if I'd
had sons they would have been consumed by greed and
ambition. I blame Eleanor of Aquitaine for urging the
sons to destroy the father, but sometimes I wonder if they
needed much urging."

Falcon steered the conversation away from the crown
and back to the subject of wives when suddenly William
put the blunt question to him. "Would you have me for
father-in-law?"

Falcon clapped him on the shoulder. Though he had
not the slightest notion which daughter he would choose,
he was very sure of one thing. "I tell you true, William. I
will have none other for father-in-law!"

When they returned from a successful morning's hunt,
Falcon was relieved to see his squire Gervase had arrived
at Salisbury. On a pretext of showing him around the
forge and armory, de Burgh questioned him closely about
Mountain Ash and was satisfied with Gervase's detailed
report.

"You surely didn't expect trouble from the castellan
you appointed?" asked Gervase.

"Not before the head of the last castellan rots and
drops from its spike," de Burgh said with a grimace.

Gervase cleared his throat in hesitation then said,
"Morganna gave me no trouble, milord."

"Who?" de Burgh asked blankly.

"The female hostage you gave into my care," prompted Gervase.

"Oh, that one. God's spine, I don't know why I put you to all that trouble."

Gervase began to laugh.

"I amuse you?" asked de Burgh.

"You hardly remember her, yet she has set herself up as your mistress and has the servants running to obey her commands."

De Burgh flashed his wolf's grin. "She'll be in for a nasty shock if I bring a wife home."

"I can tell you have made good use of your time, milord."

"Both of William's daughters could run my three castles with their hands tied behind their backs. They have both been well and rigidly trained. Wait until you see them. I can't choose; I'll need your help in that direction."

Gervase's happy grin faded from his face and he hoped fervently that de Burgh was jesting with him, but nevertheless he observed the young women closely every chance he got.

William's daughters had trained the servants so well that the household ran smoothly as they went about their appointed tasks unobtrusively. Though Falcon de Burgh sought to find some flaw in either Ela or Isobel, he could not fault them in anything. They were efficient, industrious, courteous, full-figured, and each seemed willing, nay eager, to favor his suit.

As his squire inspected and cleaned every piece of armor in de Burgh's war chest, the two of them exchanged their thoughts.

"Since no news is good news, I suppose we can assume all is well with King Richard," said Gervase.

De Burgh frowned. "The uncertainty could spawn anarchy, especially with the northern barons. If England is

left long without authority, a wave of lawlessness will
sweep the nation." He flashed his grin. "It is good you
are keeping my armor at the ready. I don't like the men
to remain idle, so I've told William we'll hunt down his
wolves tomorrow."

"They are passing the time wagering which of William's daughters will become Lady de Burgh," Gervase
said with a familiarity de Burgh allowed no other man.

Falcon's eyebrows shot up. "And who's the odds-on
favorite?"

"I believe the betting runs in Lady Ela's favor, milord."

"They've undoubtedly discussed her fine points," Falcon said vulgarly. Gervase flushed slightly and laughed.

"I don't know," said de Burgh, "there's a lot to be said
for Isobel's humor."

"So you have made your choice?"

"Not really." De Burgh shrugged. "I don't suppose it
matters which. There is nothing to choose between
them," he said almost indifferently.

Gervase cleared his throat as he always did when he
was about to make a suggestion to de Burgh. "If it were
me, milord, I would find out which lands and castles each
lady will inherit and then make my selection."

"Splendor of God, and I thought I was a cynical bastard! Perhaps you've been my squire too long. I've tainted
you, Gervase."

Chapter 5

Dame Estelle Winwood decided that she owed it to William Longsword to warn him of coming events. The bad news would travel quickly enough, but if she could prepare him for the shocks that lay ahead she would not only feel a great deal of gratification but would entrench herself as infallible in seeing the future when messages confirming her mystic predictions arrived at Salisbury.

Estelle and Jasmine set out early on their relatively short journey. The sun shone brilliantly, warming the air delightfully even if a little unseasonably. Jasmine wore her prettiest gown for the visit to her father, a shell-pink velvet with a finely spun head veil fastened with silver hair ornaments. She rode a white palfrey and chose a fanciful, ornamented harness for her. Her grandmother prided herself on Jasmine's appearance whenever they rode out. She saw to it that the girl looked exactly like a princess from a fairy tale and smiled when mouths literally fell open as the virginal, ethereal vision of loveliness passed by.

They took no maids or attendants with them as Salisbury Castle overflowed with servants, but they did take two extra packhorses to carry their clothes and a goodly supply of herbs and electuaries Estelle had concocted especially for William's people.

After they had passed through Old Sarum, about two miles from the castle, Dame Winwood looked at her grandaughter indulgently and said, "Go ahead, child, I know you are longing for a gallop. If you contain yourself much longer spring fever will steal your senses. Just remember, not a word to your father. I want to find out

what he knows before I share my knowledge. Power
shared is power halved!"

Jasmine whispered softly to her palfrey and took a
handful of its long white mane to anchor herself for the
swift gallop. The wind soon took her filmy veil, and Jasmine tossed back her silvery-gold hair so that the sunshine turned it molten, surrounding her whole being with
a nimbus of light.

Falcon de Burgh and his knights had arisen long before
light of day to hunt down the wolf pack. It hadn't taken
Falcon long to detect the distant howling, then he easily
pinpointed their location by the clamorous yapping that
signaled the wolves had made a kill. The men were too
late to save a pair of newborn lambs, but they managed to
save the ewe from the jaws of death.

They were bloodied and de Burgh had a pair of wolf
carcasses slung across his saddle as they rode back to the
castle brimming with satisfaction that they had helped
repay some of Salisbury's hospitality. They suddenly
stopped in their tracks as a vision rode into the sunshine
from a small wooded area.

" 'Tis a unicorn!" Normand Gervase gasped.

"No such creature," asserted Falcon de Burgh, his
dark brows drawing together in sudden doubt.

The girl on the back of the unicorn took instant fright
at the party of mailed knights only a hundred yards off.
Dismay clouded Jasmine's delicate brow. She wheeled
her white palfrey and took flight back into the trees.

Falcon de Burgh issued a sharp command to his men.
"Stay! This quarry is mine."

As the great destrier closed the distance to the stand of
trees, Jasmine heard the hooves pounding the ground like
thunder. She felt like hunted prey. When she glanced up,
recognition hit her like a thunderbolt. It was he—the

Devil! He would devour her like a hound of Hell bringing down a white doe.

Falcon de Burgh grabbed her bridle and looked into her face. Fear clearly sketched its dark presence upon her lovely countenance. He was mesmerized at the sight of her. For one unreal moment he believed this beautiful creature riding the back of a unicorn was of another world. Such an exquisite vision could not be mortal. He was enchanted. The unicorn came to a halt and trembled.

The girl put up her small hands in supplication and breathed, "Ah . . . no! Whatever have I done that you must hunt me down and punish me?"

He was off Lightning in a trice. This close, he could clearly see that the "unicorn" was merely a white palfrey wearing a clever ornamental harness fashioned with a long, spiraled ivory horn. "Demoiselle, have no fear," he whispered huskily, wondering vaguely why his heart had stopped beating. Could this exquisite fairy princess, sprung from a legend, possibly be the same maiden he had encountered the other night?

Jasmine's eyes were wide. "Do not think to lure me with gentle words. I know who you are and I know exactly what you want of me," she said bravely.

He smiled at her youth and innocence. "Then yield it up to me without further protest," he teased. He reached up strong arms and lifted her down to him. She was all silver and pink and utterly delicious, like a bon-bon at a birthday fête.

His great hands encircled her waist and his thumbs were actually caressing the undersides of her breasts. She could feel him through the delicate material. Her breath caught in her throat. She had escaped him once, how could she do so again? She summoned all her courage and defied him. "I will never yield to you, my lord Satan!"

He did not know if he was amused or annoyed at her

words. "You live in a make-believe world. I am not the Devil; there is no Devil. Who has charge of you, that they have filled your head with fairy tales?" For the first time he saw a spark of anger in her lovely eyes.

"No one has charge of me. How dare you say my head is filled with fairy tales? Let me go at once or I shall scream!"

"You obviously live a fantasy that you are a fairy princess riding about the countryside on a unicorn. Are you escaping an ogre or a dragon? Are you fleeing from the wicked queen, your stepmother? How unfortunate for you that upon escaping your castle overgrown with poison vines you should encounter the Devil! Stop playing games. I am no more a devil than you are a princess."

She pulled away from him sharply. "You are the one playing cruel games. You know very well who I am. You know I am a real princess and I know you are Satan," she whispered, looking frantically about for some means of escape.

"I am a knight," he said flatly.

" 'Tis a guise. A knight in shining armor come to aid a damsel in distress."

The corners of his mouth twitched at the absurdity of it all. "Shall I slay the dragon for you and lay my heart at your feet, my princess?"

Her eyes were filled with dread. "What forfeit will you take to release me? Another kiss?"

"Since you are a thousand times more beautiful than you were the other night, I claim a thousand kisses." He pulled her against him, unable to keep his hands from her any longer. His fingers caressed her silvery, silken hair, then his lips covered the soft pink mouth whose taste he craved. With his mouth upon hers, he recalled that he had dreamed of her all night, and hot desire flooded his veins. The tip of his tongue tried to enter her delicious mouth, but she wrenched from him and gasped,

"You are the Devil!"

This time he took her mouth ruthlessly, invading the virgin territory. "Yes," he said in a hard, cruel voice. "I am the Prince of Darkness. I am here to carry you off to my underworld where I will ravish you nightly and keep you captive forevermore."

Jasmine gasped, alarmingly short of breath, then she slumped forward into a faint.

He caught her before she slipped to the ground. His face filled with awe as he drank in the beauty of his delicate burden. Never in his life had he been filled with such an intense need to protect and cherish. She was so small she seemed weightless. Her skin was like porcelain where the golden crescents of her eyelashes rested upon her cheeks. He held his breath in case she disappeared into thin air, then he found his chest so tight he could not take another breath. What the Devil was the matter with him? His head filled with the pretty scent of her until he actually felt dizzy. He stared at her in fascination, noting the delicious pinkness of her mouth, the delicate size of her wrists, which made her seem fragile enough to be broken into pieces if he grasped her too hard. Her hair was the color of moonbeams, and he shuddered as the silken mass fell over his hands. Lust hit him like a thunderbolt. A childhood legend fleeted through his head in which the beautiful princess could be awakened by a kiss. He shook his head, fearing he had been spellbound. He came out of his trance and realized that she was not going to revive and that he must get her to the castle.

He quickly tied the palfrey's reins to his saddle, ignoring the fact that the wolves' blood was making the small horse very nervous, then he swept the girl before him on his destrier and cradled her limp form with one strong arm. The great horse's hooves struck sparks on the cobblestones of the courtyard as he drew rein and swept his limp burden into the great hall.

Isobel saw him immediately and hurried forward. "Jasmine! Dear God, has there been an accident?"

"Nay, Lady Isobel, somehow I frightened her so much she has fainted," he said, trying to squelch his anxiety.

"Oh, poor little rabbit! I will take her to the women's quarters. Perhaps it was the heat." She quickly summoned two servants to carry Jasmine, and the serving women held out their arms expectantly.

Falcon was loathe to relinquish the delicate beauty, but under the circumstances he had no choice. Isobel followed the women up the staircase and said over her shoulder, "You had best beware Dame Winwood if she knows you have frightened her grandaughter."

He stood in the hall feeling almost bereft. Jasmine . . . her name was Jasmine. After a few minutes Ela came to keep him company and to reassure him that all was well.

"She will be fine, milord. The dear little lamb was frightened out of her mind."

"Who is she?" de Burgh asked eagerly.

"Well, she is our half sister." She lowered her voice to a whisper. "The poor little thing is illegitimate. She's never been very robust, you understand. The heat made her delirious."

He ground his teeth in mute rage at Ela's condescending tone, but she prattled on without heed. "Can you imagine, the silly child thought you were the Devil after her! That's what comes of leading a sheltered existence, isolated from men. Her maternal grandmother has charge of her. Oh, I must warn you about Dame Estelle Winwood. She is the most curious, eccentric creature . . . ah, speak of the Devil and she shall appear," Ela said with a giggle.

The small woman strode in as if she owned the place.

"Ah, Dame Winwood, how good to see you," Ela said courteously.

"Rubbish!" Estelle spat. "I hoped to be greeted by William." She gave the young woman before her a critical glance. "Ela, you are running to fat," she said flatly.

"We enjoy your visits so much," Ela murmured through tight lips.

The older woman swept de Burgh with a forbidding look. "Is that your great destrier outside? Brute almost nipped me, until I put my fist between its eyes!"

He was startled. Spine of God, it was a miracle Lightning hadn't bitten her arm off. "Excuse me, madame," he murmured politely, "I am bloodied from the hunt." He strode back to the courtyard to assess the damage to his poor war-horse.

William of Salisbury sat stunned as Estelle told him of her visions. Years ago he had scoffed at her predictions, but he had lived to rue the day that he had dismissed the things she told him. Older and wiser, he now knew better than to doubt the truth of her crystal gazing.

"Thank you for bringing me the warning, Estelle. It looks like I will have to go to Normandy."

She nodded her agreement. "The news will reach Winchester first, then the news will be brought to you tomorrow or the next day. Neither of us has any love for Eleanor, but I must admit I pity her losing her most beloved son Richard."

"Amen to that," said William, crossing himself.

"Perhaps this is not the time to speak of it, William, but when the time does come that a new king rules England and sets up a royal court here, Jasmine wants your permission to join that court."

He frowned and shook his head. "Court is too worldly for the child."

"She is a child no longer, William. Rest assured I would accompany her and protect her always," Estelle emphasized.

"We'll speak of it when the time comes, Estelle. I know you would protect her with your life. For now, make yourself comfortable. If there is anything you wish, you know you need only to ask. I must go to the chapel and pray for Richard's soul," William said with a catch in his throat.

Later, at supper, Falcon de Burgh looked in vain for Jasmine but of course she did not appear in the dining hall. William singled him out for a private word and told him of Dame Estelle's prophecy. Falcon was incredulous that a man of William Longsword's stature would place any weight on the words of a superstitious old woman. He tried to lighten William's somber mood and dismiss her as an eccentric, but William only shook his head sadly and said they would have confirmation soon enough.

De Burgh took himself off to bed where he would be free to indulge his fantasies of Jasmine. He wanted to pursue his thoughts of her, his mind lingering upon each remembered detail. His thoughts of her were persistent and involuntary. She intruded herself upon all his senses. When he closed his eyes, he heard her whisper his name. His recollection of the sight, smell, and touch of her were vivid and disturbing . . . physically disturbing!

He stripped and washed himself. The heat of the day had been oppressive, but as he stood before the open window a cold blast of air swept into the chamber, accompanied by a flash of lightning and healthy crack of thunder.

He opened William's massive oaken wardrobe and selected a handsome black, velvet bedrobe, then he stretched out full length on the bed to ponder the strange predictions William had foretold. Try as he might, he could not prevent Jasmine from intruding upon his every thought. Without his noticing, as darkness descended the room was periodically lighted with brilliance as the lightning flashed and the thunder crashed directly above the castle.

Suddenly the door flew open. "Father . . . I need your wardrobe," cried a lovely yet terrified female voice. All at once the lightning flashed its brilliance about the chamber and its occupants saw each other clearly. Jasmine looked wild-eyed at the black-visaged man before her and, opening her mouth, screamed her lungs out.

The crash of the thunder drowned out her scream, and once more the chamber was plunged into blackness. Falcon heard a door slam. By the time he had lighted the candles he found himself alone.

"Jasmine," he breathed. She had been so close and yet so far away. She had gone as quickly as she had come, and yet her presence lingered in the room in a most tangible form. Obviously she had come to her father's chamber for protection from the storm, not knowing that William had given his chamber to his guest. Regrettably her fear of him had been stronger than her fear of the storm . . . unless . . . he carefully opened the heavy wardrobe door a crack and looked inside. She was huddled in a white velvet bedgown with her arms wrapped protectively over her head. The lightning struck again and she screamed, "Shut the door!"

He slipped inside the massive wardrobe and pulled the door closed on them. Silence. Blackness. His excitement threatened to overwhelm him. Finally he whispered, "Jasmine . . . take my hand." Blackness. Silence. "Do not fear me," he commanded softly. "Whose heartbeat?" he asked, then answered, "It's ours," in wonder. He wanted to laugh at her for being afraid, but he could not. He wanted to carry her from the wardrobe and show her how irrational was her behavior, but he could not. He wanted her to talk to him so he could explain away her fears, but he knew she could not. Somehow without speaking they were communicating. Jasmine tried to recall Isobel's words about the dark knight. Hadn't she said she hoped to marry him? Obviously he was not the Devil. She had seen his face in the crystal because he was to be part of her family's destiny. Silence. Blackness. The minutes stretched out until the tension between them became unendurable, then suddenly he reached out decisively and a tiny hand was in his and he felt a ridiculous desire to stay thus handclasped through eternity.

"Jassy . . ." he whispered softly, his heart filled with tenderness.

"I'm sorry I called you the Devil," she whispered. "You must think me ridiculous."

He lifted her hand to his lips and bestowed a kiss upon it. She pulled away with a gasp. "We shouldn't be here . . . alone together."

"Why not?" He reached out to retrieve her hand, but instead he brushed across her breast and she jumped as if she had been burned.

"Because you are wicked . . . and because I am undressed. You've already forced me to kiss you . . ." She felt herself blushing profusely in the darkness. She cursed herself for a coward. If she weren't absolutely terrified of thunder and lightning, she would make a run for it from the wardrobe. The journey from Winwood Keep, the encounter with this man who had made her faint, topped off by the fierce storm had somehow exhausted her. Her legs felt weak and trembly and she was short of breath.

Suddenly he wanted to allay all her fears. "Little sweeting, don't be afraid. I vow on my knighthood I won't let harm come to you. Here, take my hands, share my strength." The long minutes stretched out, then finally she placed her hands in his and gradually she relaxed, closed her eyes, and drifted to the edge of sleep. They had been in the silence and blackness for almost two hours before he felt her hands totally relax into his and knew she was asleep. Very gently he lifted her from the wardrobe and tenderly placed her in his bed.

He was wildly curious about her, needing to know the color of her eyes, the feel of her skin, the size of her breasts. He had entered a sublime state where her image pushed all other thoughts out of his head. Being as quiet as he could, he lighted a bedside candle and sat down to gaze at her. She was so unearthly fair. Her silvery hair spread across the pillows was the most beautiful he'd ever seen. Of their own volition his fingers stole out to feel a silken tendril, then carefully he opened her white velvet bedgown to see what lay beneath. His breath caught in his throat. She was extremely slender and fragile, yet her breasts rose high and pointed, her tiny waist emphasizing their fullness. Her legs were slim and pretty and her tiny mound of Venus was covered with delicious golden ringlets.

His maleness throbbed with need. Lord God, he was hard. He wanted her, but knew that if he let his hands have their way she would awaken and scream. He could not dishonor Salisbury's daughter, yet he refused to give up the idea of possessing her. As he gazed at her he felt linked to her by an invisible thread. This was the one he would choose! Gently he drew up the furs to cover her nakedness and sat down in the chair to daydream of her becoming his bride.

When Falcon awoke it was full daylight and the huge bed was empty. For a moment he feared it had been only a dream, then with relief he realized that he would have awakened in bed if he had been dreaming.

He called for hot water to bathe and shave. He took great care in his dressing that morning, then with great deliberation he sought a private audience with William.

He waited until William's squire withdrew and even made sure the young pages were on the other side of the closed door before he spoke.

"William, perhaps my timing is poor when you are so worried about Richard, but I feel I must speak."

A slight frown creased William's brow at the young knight's serious tone. "What is amiss?"

"Nothing . . . I hope," said Falcon, gathering his courage. "William, I want to formally request the hand of your daughter in marriage."

William's face lit up. "My boy, it is exactly what I hoped for. Is it to be Ela or Isobel?" He beamed.

"William, I want to marry your daughter Jasmine."

William's brows drew together again. "Jasmine?" he said incredulously. "My boy, that is impossible. Jasmine will not inherit my lands or my castles—"

Falcon stopped him. "I don't want your lands or your castles, William, they are as nothing compared to my desire to have Jasmine."

William sighed. "You don't understand, my boy. She has not been trained to be a wife. Both Ela and Isobel have been in training all their lives to run many castles. Jasmine knows only music and painting and how to grow pretty flowers."

"I care naught for any of that. I will have stewards and castellans to run my households. I want Jasmine and no other for my wife," Falcon insisted.

William shook his head sadly. "She could never bear you strong sons . . . she is far too delicate. Let me tell you about her mother. I fell in love with her because of her fragile beauty, but my seed killed her! The baby was so puny she would have died also had it not been for the superhuman efforts of Dame Estelle, her grandmother."

As Falcon listened he realized incredulously that William was going to refuse him! This was a totally new experience for de Burgh and one that was just as totally unacceptable. He would have her!

He waited with quiet patience while William explained in detail why marriage to Jasmine was impossible, then he said straight out, "Jasmine came to me last night in the storm. She spent the night in my bed. I . . . comforted . . . her. I am sorry, William, but she is compromised beyond repair!"

William's first reaction was outrage, and yet it was tempered by the respect he felt for the man before him. De Burgh had wasted no time in coming to him and bluntly laying out the situation before him. His motive was obviously not greed; therefore his genuine affections must be involved. And, William grudgingly admitted to himself, it was almost always the female of the species who did the choosing. If Jasmine had stayed safely in the women's quarters, she could never have allowed herself to be compromised. The surprising element in all this was that Isobel or Ela hadn't gone to de Burgh nights ago. William sighed, letting his breath out in a rush of relief as he told Falcon truthfully, "It is not my decision to make. I gave Jasmine to Dame Winwood, her maternal grandmother, who saved her life and has had the responsibility of her." He pressed his lips and admitted grudgingly, "If it were my choice alone, I'd be tempted to give you the girl. I want a blood tie with you and if Jasmine is the price, then I'd pay it. But be warned, de Burgh, the dame will prove a worthy adversary even for one as strong as you. Never underestimate her power."

Falcon's brow cleared. "Then I have your blessing if her grandmother agrees to the marriage?"

William shook his head and chuckled. "Lad, ye make it sound like a fait accompli. Dame Winwood is impossible, implacable, immovable, impregnable; she's also a witch."

Falcon de Burgh licked his lips. He loved a challenge; besides, no woman had ever said nay to him in his life.

William laid his calloused hand on de Burgh's shoulder. "Whatever the outcome, will you look after things here for me? My ship is being readied in Southampton; I leave tomorrow for the coast. Once word is out that England has no king, lawlessness will reign here."

"I will keep Salisbury safe for you and yours, my friend. I agree with you that the barons think might is right and Richard's death will leave them free to rape the land."

Falcon de Burgh wasted no time seeking out Dame Estelle Winwood. He had decided to finalize matters before the Earl of Salisbury departed for France. However, he had reckoned without Estelle's habits and whims. She could not give him audience until after her ablutions, then of course it was time for her devotions. In quick succession followed her tending the sick, concocting her herbal medicines, and taking her exercise. The third time de Burgh went to her quarters to seek speech with her he was informed she was taking a bath. He took a threatening step toward the servant who dared deny him repeatedly and said firmly, "Then I shall see her while she bathes." The woman could see that the knight was easily capable of such outrage and fled the room.

Within five minutes the resolute figure of Dame Winwood confronted him, erect and unbending as a ramrod. "You have bullied my servant, but you cannot bully me, sir," she challenged.

"Dame Winwood, I am not here to bully you, my lady; rather I would beg you grant me my heart's desire," he began in what was for him an exceeding flowery speech.

"Ah, you need a magic potion for impotence," she stated with studied contempt.

For one brief moment Falcon saw blood-red fury, then he realized the wily old bitch was very deliberately goading him. So, he thought, what I am after comes as no surprise to her. She has sniffed what is in the wind. Without further preliminaries he stated his purpose. "I wish to marry the Lady Jasmine."

She laughed in his face. "As well ask of me the moon and stars. The answer is no; it is impossible."

"Nothing in this world is impossible, madame, to one as resolute as I."

Estelle changed her manner and spoke frankly as if taking him into her confidence. "Jasmine is too fragile to be wife to any man, let alone one as obviously virile as you. Frankly, sir knight, you would be too venal, too lusty, too demanding in bed for one so delicate."

Dryly he murmured, "A moment ago I was impotent." As they stared each other down, each knew they had the measure of the other.

"I need my grandaughter to carry on my work. She is a novitiate, a true adept. She must remain virgin so that her powers will be a hundredfold greater than mine. Your desire for her is totally selfish," she finished accusingly.

"So is yours," he stated bluntly.

They stood like two dogs with hackles raised, neither willing to back down by as much as a hairsbreadth. Falcon took the offensive, knowing no other way. "Her virginity is compromised since she spent the night in my bed, so her value as a 'white witch' or whatever it is you wish to exploit her as will drop considerably once the gossip starts."

"I believe her to still be a pure and innocent maiden in spite of the sojourn in your bed," hissed Estelle.

"Ah, but after laying eyes upon me, would anyone else?" he challenged.

There was a small silence while Dame Winwood gathered her scattered thoughts for a counterattack. "My answer is still no, and I have the support of her father to back up my decision."

"Au contraire, madame, I have William's blessing!" he pointed out.

"Why would he do such a thing?" she demanded in outrage.

"Perhaps so that no scandal will touch his daughter. An honorable marriage is infinitely preferable to the risk of producing a bastard child."

Estelle waved away the suggestion languidly as if it were no more trouble than a gnat. "I have a full stock of abortificants, so do not think to trap the girl that way."

They were at a stalemate. It was an even match— thrust and parry . . . parry and thrust. She decided to disabuse him of the notion that William would support him against her. "William apparently thinks the sun shines from your arse, but I do assure you my influence upon him is greater than yours. He will cast his vote with mine and they will both be an emphatic *no*. His lust killed my daughter and he has never forgiven himself; I rule William through his guilt!" Estelle decided to give him the coup d'état. "You are a most reckless man to tangle with me, young Lord de Burgh. My magic spells and curses are so powerful they make wise men tremble." Her eyes gleamed with triumph as she stood before him in all her majestic glory.

His dark eyes burned into hers a full five minutes. Then very deliberately he took his dagger from its sheath, laid it on the table between them and delivered his own ultimatum. In a measured voice he said, "Superstition and fear are unknown to me, madame. However, I too am capable of magic. If you deny me this marriage I will make you disappear from the face of the earth without trace."

As they looked at each other, she knew she had met her match. Grudgingly she admitted to herself that he was a magnificent man, and, God's nightgown, they were few and far between. It was a unique experience for her to encounter a male who did not fear her occult power. She saw that William was wise to align himself with a young man of such absolute strength of body and purpose. He would make a better ally than enemy, and a wise woman would use it to her advantage. Her agile mind took one step forward to offer a delaying tactic—a compromise. She could always retreat one step back if the opportunity ever presented itself. Estelle broke the pregnant silence. "A betrothal," she offered, and Falcon knew the magnitude of the sacrifice she was making.

"A betrothal," he agreed grudgingly.

Chapter 6

Because of William's imminent departure, he immediately drew up a betrothal contract under the close scrutiny of Dame Estelle and de Burgh in his small study off the solar. When the three interested parties were satisfied, Jasmine was sent for, almost as an afterthought.

When the servant summoned her to her father, Jasmine thought it was to bid him good-bye. She knew his ship was being readied to take him to France where great history-making events were taking place that would alter all their lives in one way or another. She hurried after the servant, but her step faltered as she entered the study and found de Burgh and her grandmother also there.

De Burgh was the first one in the room to become aware of her. As she hesitated upon the threshold, he feasted on her breathtaking beauty. His eyes drank in every detail of the exquisite picture she made framed in the doorway. She wore an underdress of the palest blue with silvery ribbons, her tunic embroidered with silver thread. She was as pretty as a confectionary atop a cake he had seen once at a wedding feast. He admitted frankly to himself that she had enchanted him. He sighed with a mixture of relief and satisfaction that the prize was his.

William cleared his throat, held out his hand for her to come forward, and began, "I . . . that is, we"—he glanced at Dame Estelle to give him courage—"have decided to betroth you to Falcon de Burgh."

Jasmine laughed. Falcon likened the sound to silver bells. Her grandmother gave her a small warning signal with her hand and said, "Your father is serious, Jasmine. The contract is drawn up."

Jasmine's mind was like quicksilver. She instantly assumed her half sisters had rejected his suit, and, clinging to any straw that would unite the ambitious de Burgh to the royal family, she was a poor third choice. Her eyes opened wide in mock surprise. "I had no idea Messieur de Burgh was an earl."

De Burgh stiffened. "I am not," he stated flatly.

"A baron, a lord?" she inquired prettily.

He almost flushed. "I am a knight, mademoiselle."

"A knight?" she repeated derisively. "A *knight* who fancies himself a *bishop* or a *rook* more like," she said, referring to the maneuvers of the chess game he thought to play. "You, sir, have mistaken me for a *pawn*, but let me disabuse you immediately." She drew herself up regally. "I am descended from *kings*. I am beyond your wildest dreams, sir. I have decided against marriage in general and against you in particular," she said. Calmly she took the marriage contract from the table and tore it cleanly in half, leaving the three occupants of the room stunned.

Her father was aghast. He'd had no notion the child could display such haughty willfullness. "Estelle, whatever has gotten into her?" he asked in bewildered amazement. It was as if the fairies had stolen away his sweet Jasmine and left a changling in her stead.

Estelle, barely able to conceal her admiration for her protegée, searched her mind for an explanation and was herself left speechless as Jasmine said coolly, "The reason

I have such an independent streak is that I was tempered and sharpened in day-to-day struggles for my own identity with my strong-willed grandmother."

Falcon de Burgh stared at the vision of loveliness through new eyes. What he had conceived to be a deliciously fragile and pretty toy had the spirit of ten headstrong men! It served only to whet his appetite. She was not yet a woman, but much more than a girl. Her exquisite skin was like ivory velvet, her gilt hair a cascading glory. Fair, innocent, pure, virginal. She was finer than other females—silkier, paler, slimmer. Her body was like a flower, her eyes clear and cool, her lips most inviting, her face delicate, her breasts luscious. Her qualities had allowed him to imagine himself domineering her. He would be dominant and protective at the same time. Now something irresistible had been added. Now between them was an unbearable sexual tension. The very look of her was an aphrodisiac.

"Hold!" he commanded her in a voice that brooked no nonsense. She turned and gave him a condescending glance. She saw that his hands resting easily on his belt were scarred and powerful. His voice was like the crack of a whip. "You may be insolent to me, demoiselle, without fear of penalty, but I cannot permit you to be insolent to your father. Beg his forgiveness!"

They stared at each other, their eyes flashing their challenge. She became an ice queen, her look freezing him with a coldness that penetrated his skull. He stared her down and at last in a quiet voice she said, "I beg your pardon, Father."

Then before she took another step toward the door, de Burgh said to Estelle, "Take her aside and explain matters to her. Explain that she's decided things long enough. From now on, I do it."

Estelle pushed Jasmine from the men's presence before she disgraced them all. Jasmine opened her mouth to demand an explanation but the words died upon her lips as she saw the fatality written plain on her grandmother's face. Suddenly, surely, she knew that the whole fabric of her life was going to be changed. The decision was going to be taken from her hands though she was unwilling to relinquish it.

Estelle said carefully, "A betrothal is not a wedding. Circumstances change, as they have today. The only constant thing in life is change. Life itself is not a straight line but a circle, or wheel. The wheel turns constantly from elation to despair to elation. Everything passes. The wheel turns. Life goes on."

Though Jasmine absorbed the wisdom of the words, she protested. "But I wished with all my heart to go to court!"

Dame Winwood's eyes hooded to hide her cunning. "Then bargain for it. If he wants you badly enough he will agree to anything you desire. A new contract must be drawn up anyway since you destroyed the first."

William, temporarily alone with de Burgh, explained, "She has been much petted and indulged. I fear she is poor wife material."

Falcon smiled at William. "She holds a special place in your heart. Never fear, I too am capable of indulgence, milord, though my fierce looks belie it."

William let out a sigh of relief and poured them both a horn of ale against the time the women would keep them waiting. "The barons to the north will have received the news of King Richard's wounding by now and some may come riding hotfoot to Salisbury. Tell them I could not wait, but extend them my hospitality."

"I shall, William, and rest assured if more than one shows up I shall keep the peace between antagonists."

"Aye, well, that's easier said than done, so don't hesitate to use the full weight of my authority."

The door opened and the women swept in. Jasmine did

not come meekly in submission, but rather she came as a general to parley. She looked at each in turn and said with quiet determination, "You thought you had a conspiracy of three, but I will be an equal partner in this or I will not play your game." She let the words sink in, then she picked on the easiest member of the trio. "Father, I am landless. I want an estate of my own that my husband, should it come to that, cannot touch."

William, guilty at never having deeded any property to his love child, immediately made amends. "You shall have Marlborough and Foxfield, the properties run together; each has a manor house and a village."

Her eyes widened in appreciation and spurred her on to face Estelle. "Grandmother, I ask that you impart to me all your secret rituals from which I have been excluded. I need your power."

The old dame closed her eyes in acquiescence. She had intended to impart the knowledge to Jasmine before she departed this earth, so no real harm could be done. Jasmine coolly appraised Falcon de Burgh. Everyone had agreed to her demands so readily that if he balked, he would appear surly and ungenerous. She smiled secretly, inwardly, for she knew she was winning this battle. "I agree to a betrothal if it be a *lengthy* one, and if you will allow me to take my proper place at court." She held her chin high and dared him to be ungracious.

He spread his scarred and powerful hands in a magnanimous and generous gesture. "I allow you to choose, my lady—a lengthy betrothal or court."

She fumed because he had effectively turned the tables on her. She would seem peevish if she insisted upon both. "Court," she said decisively, and watched as his bold mouth curved in satisfaction.

There was no betrothal ring, no kiss, but the documents were signed and sealed with his signet, which bore a great falcon. As she left the room she vowed, "You'll rue me, de Burgh." His eyes smoldered as he silently picked up the challenge she threw down.

Falcon de Burgh felt slightly uncomfortable the next day when he felt two pairs of reproachful eyes upon him. Ela pouted and kept stealing glances at him, while Isobel gave him a long look then averted her glance permanently. Thankfully, he escaped to the heavy burden of duties that demanded his attention in other parts of the vast Salisbury demesne.

Not a few of William's men had served de Burgh in Wales, yet he would not be satisfied until he had a workable acquaintance with all. Salisbury's fighting men had good captains for the most part so he made sure not to interfere or criticize when it was not called for. To keep idle men busy, de Burgh had set the knights to inspecting all weapons and mail in the armory. Almost every item housed there needed repairing, oiling, or the rust removed and then polishing. The blacksmith's forge was kept aglow night and day so that every war-horse could be reshod.

De Burgh worked alongside the men, knowing if he gave full measure of his strength, they could do no less. He was stripped to his leather breeks because of the blazing heat from the forge and well begrimed with sweat when he became aware of a commotion down by the bailey. Two men, obviously peasants, appeared to be angry and had come to the castle to seek justice from the Earl of Salisbury himself. They were directed to de Burgh, but he could not understand their shouts or wild gesticulations. "Calmly now," he admonished, "one at a time." He pointed to the first man to speak.

"Men-at-arms . . . a hundred . . . trampling the new crops . . . taking our fodder. Not Salisbury men. Be they yours, milord?"

Red-faced, the other peasant shouted, "To hell with the crops! They raped my daughter—"

De Burgh listened to no more. He was astride the destrier he had been holding and spurred it in the direction the peasants had pointed. Falcon thundered through the village toward the fields where the new crops of wheat, barley, and turnips were thriving in the April sunshine. He dragged on the horse's mane and slid to the ground when he saw tents being set up among the crops. He heard a woman scream and saw with his own eyes a knight take the female down by her hair and mount her savagely to ease his lust. Though he was weaponless, anything could serve as a weapon to de Burgh when he was this angry. He grabbed a spade from a gaping peasant and strode mercilessly toward the ravisher. He hit him such a sharp blow beneath the chin that it decapitated the man, covering the white-lipped girl with a gush of hot blood. As he turned, two knights rushed forward with drawn swords to cut down the half-naked savage who had just killed one of their own. De Burgh was vaguely aware that their accents were broadly northern as he rammed his elbow into the first man's throat and at the same moment wrenched his longsword from him. He cut a brutal swatch before him in the direction of the other knight and ordered, "Lay down your arms, whoreson. I command all Salisbury."

As the knight thought better of continuing the attack against the begrimed colossus, de Burgh ground out, "Where is your leader?"

"Yonder, at the castle," said the knight through his teeth, glad to let the Earl of Chester take care of the madman who fought and killed like the Devil.

As de Burgh swung up upon his horse, a company made up of his men and Salisbury's arrived at his back. He flung his orders. "Clear these planted fields of these *invaders.*"

* * *

Jasmine and Estelle, who had never been exactly comfortable at Salisbury, now found the atmosphere definitely unconducive to a long visit. Dame Winwood discovered her grandaughter packing her belongings.

"We are going home this morning," Jasmine said decisively.

"You will draw de Burgh's anger if you do not take leave of him," Estelle warned.

Jasmine's eyes flashed amethyst fire. "I am completely indifferent to de Burgh's anger," she said lightly, but Estelle knew this was an untruth. She had purposely picked a time when he would be occupied and unaware of their departure until after the fact.

"With a sweet tongue and kindness you can drag an elephant by a hair," Estelle reminded.

"A Persian proverb, no doubt. Grandmother, speak not to me of kindness. I have learned that the sensitive ones in this world can be eaten alive before they have time to grow an iron carapace!"

"You are heading for trouble; I know the road," warned Estelle.

Jasmine tossed her pretty head. "That which doesn't kill me makes me stronger! Please, let's not stand here all day exchanging proverbs. Oh, God, I hear horses below." She flew to the window and peered down. "It's not de Burgh," she said with relief.

Estelle peered over her shoulder, "Let me see if I can make out the device . . . ha! it's Chester. I should have known the wealthiest baron in England would be in the front row to see which way the wind was blowing. Well, he'll get nothing out of me. Too bad we didn't leave an hour past."

"We will leave now. Ela and Isobel will have their hands full with an earl to entertain."

Ranulf de Blundeville, Earl of Chester, was tall, spare,

graceless, with lank black hair and dark, hooded eyes. He had been trained by King Henry II in his ways and in his conception of administration, and the great king had rewarded him well. When Henry's son Geoffrey was killed in a tournament, his widow Constance of Brittany was given to Ranulf who could be depended upon to govern Brittany in the workmanlike way King Henry desired. Constance hated the union and God alone knows what had transpired between the couple, but the moment King Henry II died, she secured a divorce from the Earl of Chester, who returned to England and became its leading peer. He was enormously wealthy and carried a great deal of weight in the country.

Dame Estelle Winwood and Jasmine arrived in the great hall after Chester had been told that William of Salisbury had already left for Normandy. Chester had his squire and two knights with him, and Ela was serving the men refreshment. Chester recognized Estelle and greeted her warily. "Dame Winwood, I'm sure you will be able to furnish me with all the information I need."

"De Blundeville, isn't it?" She purposely omitted his title to annoy him. "We are just returning to Winwood Keep; unfortunately you catch me at an inconvenient time." She had the knack of putting his teeth on edge. His eyes caught sight of the beautiful girl who carried a bird cage containing, of all things, a sparrow. Bones of Christ, he thought, the women in this household are exceeding fair. With the exception of the old ratbag, of course.

Chester, usually a man sparing in words, said to Jasmine, "My men will provide you escort, my ladies."

Ela could not help comparing this man, this great earl, with Falcon de Burgh. His face was pitted by the smallpox and the beard he effected to cover the ugliness failed in its purpose. For all his wealth he wore armor covered by a plain green surcoat, and Ela hunched her shoulders slightly so that her breasts were not quite so much in evidence. After dreaming of the magnificently endowed de Burgh warming her bed, she did not relish Chester taking a fancy to her, for all his reputed riches. Isobel was about to send the servants off to prepare baths for their visitors when de Burgh strode into the hall.

He had washed the blood from his body at the horse trough and secured his leather jack before confronting Chester. He also had his temper under control, or so he thought.

Jasmine's heart thudded at sight of him and she moved closer to Chester as if to seek his protection. To explain the baggage the servants stood patiently holding, she blurted to de Burgh, "I am returning to Winwood Keep. The Earl of Chester is providing us with safe escort."

De Burgh swept the assembly with his crystal-green gaze. "I think not," he said crisply. "Knights who are allowed to rape peasant women do not escort *my* betrothed anywhere. Seek your room, mistress," he ordered with quiet authority.

Jasmine gasped at her dismissal, but he had already turned from her to Chester. The earl, sensing the authority and hearing the implication that de Burgh was to become Salisbury's son-in-law, nevertheless had taken the insult to his knights full in the face. Perhaps the young fool didn't realize whom he was addressing.

"I'm Ranulf de Blundeville, Earl of Chester."

"I know. That's why I could scarcely credit the actions of your men, sir. I am Falcon de Burgh, in charge of Salisbury until William's return."

Chester waved a dismissive hand. "If one of my knights has toyed with a maid, he shall be punished. It is hardly an earth-shattering offense."

"No need to punish him, my lord earl, he is dead. I decapitated him for the rape."

Chester stared in disbelief. Should he order his men to seize the young lout?

Falcon spoke again. "My men are assisting yours to camp farther afield where they won't trample our spring crops."

Something stirred in Chester's memory. This must be Hubert de Burgh's nephew, the one who had gained a reputation as the most skilled, cool-headed leader who struck with such passionate fury that he was sometimes called the "Rod of the Lord's Fury." The two men stood facing each other. Each recognized that he had just made a deadly enemy. Both anticipated with brutal relish the violence that was sure to come at a future date. This, however, was not the time.

Chester swallowed the insults. "Men need a strong leader in battle, to listen to crude jokes, drink wine cup for cup, chain them like the fierce hounds they are, and whip them when they misstep." It was a rather flowery speech for Chester, but it passed for an apology of his men's actions and an acceptance of de Burgh's execution.

Falcon's green gaze again fell on Jasmine, and without a word she did as he had bade her and sought her chamber.

Ranulf de Blundeville had been in a quandary when he had heard that Richard Coeur de Lion had been injured. He dismissed it lightly until his informants told him Richard's mother, Eleanor of Aquitaine, had left for Normandy the day she received the news. She was ancient and would not undertake so arduous a journey unless there was a chance the young king would die. There were two heirs to the throne. One was his close friend, John; the other was his ex-wife's son, young Arthur. There was no love whatsoever lost between Ranulf and Constance of Brittany, and he would do his damndest to see that she never became the exalted mother to the king. Constance would regret that she had never let the lad

come to England, because this would count against him.
As far as Ranulf was concerned, John would do very
nicely, thank you. Chester had hated to leave the north
for one reason only. The moment his back was turned,
the other rapacious barons would seize some of what was
his, especially since there was no crowned head in England. However, now that he had discovered Salisbury
had sailed, he made his decision. He looked at Falcon de
Burgh and said, "I'm sending my men home again, but
I'm traveling on to Normandy. Have you any knowledge
of Richard's condition?"

Estelle pressed her lips together. John would become
king and this man before her would rise even further in
power.

De Burgh, needing to be rid of him without delay,
shook his head, but added the spur. "William Marshal is
guarding the treasury, so all the important nobles are
there in case England's future needs deciding upon." De
Burgh read his mind as Chester silently added, They will
be when I arrive.

Chapter 7

It was early the following morning that the messages re-
porting King Richard's death arrived, just as Estelle had
prophesied they would.

Jasmine answered a low knock upon her chamber and
was disconcerted to find the powerful figure of de Burgh
filling the doorway when she opened it.

"May I enter?" he asked quietly as she made no offer
to invite him in. After a brief hesitation she stepped aside.

"May I sit?" he inquired politely as his large limbs bent toward a chair.

"No!" she screamed. He jacknifed out of the chair in reaction to her alarm. She ran to the chair and picked up a tiny bundle.

"It's Quill," she explained defensively. "You almost squashed him."

He looked at her as if she were mad. "A hedgehog?" he said with disbelief. "Is this another creature you use for your hocus-pocus?" he demanded, ready to forbid any further dabbling in her ridiculous magic.

"No, it is not. It is a pet. Betrothed to you am I not permitted even a pet?" she asked with loathing.

Irritated that she had put him in the wrong so quickly, he replied, "Of course you may have pets, but Prick won't last long if you let him up on chairs.

Jasmine blushed profusely. "His name is Quill, sir. Did you wish something in particular?"

"I know you wish to return to Winwood Keep, but I do not believe it is a safe place for two women alone now that we have received news that England is without a king."

"So, it is official that Richard is dead? You see, Milord de Burgh, my grandmother has seen the future. Now you have proof of what she foretold. John will be crowned king."

"I have no such proof. I put no credence whatsoever in Dame Winwood's prophecies, I assure you. King Richard received a fatal wound—it is as simple as that," he said flatly. She had given him no argument about returning home, and he was suddenly suspicious when he saw that her luggage was still packed. "It is agreed then? You will stay at Salisbury for now?"

"No," she replied stubbornly. "Must I stay here?"

"If I wish it," he answered.

She turned from him in anger, giving him her back.

His eyes traveled the length of her appreciatively, noting that her bottom formed a perfect heart. He felt himself harden. He longed to touch her.

"If John is crowned, then his wife Avisa will be queen." She turned to face him. "I wish to go to visit Avisa at Cirencester. I realize it is a great distance from here, but I wish to be the first to join the queen's court."

He thought, Cirencester is only forty miles from here, but I suppose to a young woman who has been pent up her whole life, it seems a great distance. "John is not the heir to the throne and Avisa is not queen. You have a female's illogic of facts."

"But Estelle—"

"Is a raddled old trout who has filled your head full of arrant nonsense," he finished.

Her hand swept back and flew forward at his words, but he grasped her fragile wrist and held it immobile. "Were you going to strike me, mistress?" he asked with disbelief.

"Let me free," she whispered.

He laughed at her. "You don't get things from a man by striking him."

"I want nothing from you!" she cried.

"Strange. A moment ago you wanted me to take you to Avisa at Cirencester. What will you offer me if I let you go?" He slanted an eyebrow.

"What do you want?" She had begun to breathe heavily with her agitation, and he watched in fascination the rise and fall of her tempting breasts.

"I want to dip my finger in your pot of honey."

She gasped; he grinned with delight. He unclasped his strong fingers from her wrist and she rubbed at the ache they left, backing away from him with untrusting eyes.

"You will learn that I do not like impudence, especially in a wife."

"You dream, de Burgh! I'm not your wife yet."

"Never use that tone of voice with me again, mistress, it pleases me not." His words were like the crack of a whip, and she knew she had gone far enough.

She lowered her eyes. Perhaps she would take Estelle's advice and use a sweet tongue to get her own way, for she was determined to go to Cirencester. "Milord," she breathed, and lifted her lashes to peep at him prettily. "If you should receive messages indicating that John is to become our king, would you then take me to Avisa?"

He was on the point of agreeing to accede to her wishes when she cooed a little too sweetly. "I'd feel so safe with such a strong escort as you, m'sieur."

He exploded, "I cannot be cajoled by flattery, mistress, it is a witch's trick. I am a busy man while your father is away. I suggest you occupy yourself learning how to run a household. According to all reports you are useless. You would do well to take lessons from your sisters." He strode from her chamber satisfied that he had put the little minx in her place. He reckoned without Jasmine. His words were like a slap in the face to her, comparing her so unfavorably with her sisters. Well, she would show him! She wouldn't stay there another day, no, not another hour. If he wouldn't escort her to Avisa, she would find another who would.

She waited until de Burgh had ample time to get back to his blacksmith's forge, then she sought out her grandmother in the stillroom. "Estelle, I have permission to visit Lady Avisa, soon to be Queen Avisa, at Cirencester. My things are all packed. Hurry and make ready. De Burgh is providing one of his men to escort us. Darling, you were right. A few sweet words and he was wax in my hands," she lied.

She hurried out to the stables and looked over the men as eagerly as they looked at her. She soon found her mark, a young squire of about sixteen, yet long-limbed and well muscled. He was in her father's service rather than de Burgh's, which suited her better. "Ah, you must be the young man Milord de Burgh described to me," she said airily.

"Me, my lady?" the lad said, blushing.

"Yes, you. What is your name?"

"David, my lady," he said, his heart hammering in his chest at her closeness.

"You are to escort my grandmother and me to Cirencester. When you have saddled our horses, you may come to the castle for our baggage. We brought our own packhorses."

He nodded that he knew which horses and packhorses had come from Winwood Keep, but he could not credit that he was to be entrusted to take the beautiful Lady Jasmine to Cirencester. "Perhaps it was not me Milord de Burgh meant, my lady," he said doubtfully.

"Of course it was you. He told me you were handsome and well made and I distinctly recall he used the name David. He has made a point of knowing all the men of Salisbury who serve my father. No one escapes his notice, David. He must be most favorably impressed by you to choose you for my escort."

"Thank you, my lady, it is indeed a great honor, one I'm sure I am most unworthy of," he said, dazed.

"Pooh," she said prettily, "don't stand about being modest. I wish to leave immediately."

In the courtyard, Estelle was busy giving David orders regarding her precious cargo and how it should be distributed on the packhorses. She never traveled without her magic paraphernalia and her apothecary case containing her potions, herbs, and elixirs.

Jasmine was in a panic to be gone, so finally she simply brought down her riding crop on her white palfrey's rump and it surged ahead, out of the courtyard, heading toward Salisbury Plain. David had no choice but to follow her leading the packhorses. As for Estelle, it took her quite some time before she was able to catch up with the little cavalcade. At least five miles had been covered before she came abreast of Jasmine. "Your wicked juices overflowed, did they not?" she asked with a shrewd glance.

"Oh, I'm sorry I was riding too fast for you, Grandmother."

"That's not what I meant, and well you know it. You took off as if the Devil was after you because you don't have permission for this little jaunt, do you?"

"Estelle, whatever makes you think such a thing?" she asked.

"De Burgh wouldn't let you travel with only one escort, and he certainly wouldn't have chosen a handsome youth like David to take you gallavanting across the country. He's like a dog with a bone."

"Estelle, I swear to you I asked his permission to go to Cirencester."

Dame Winwood let out a raucous laugh. "And he said *no*, didn't he? If you think he will release you because you lead him a merry chase you think wrong. Such a one as that would follow you to the ends of the earth."

By this time David had had a chance to gather his wits, and he had come to the same conclusions as Dame Winwood. However, he was caught between the kettle and the coals. He couldn't make her return to Salisbury and he couldn't abandon the ladies, ergo he must carry on with this journey and pray that nothing untoward befell his charges. Already the sweat trickled down his back at the thought of what de Burgh would do when he discovered her gone and caught up with them.

By the time they reached Marlborough on the great Roman road that ran east—west from London to Bristol, the sun had begun to set. Estelle, practical as always, decided they could go no farther. This main road had inns for those who traveled, and while they waited out-

side, she sent David in to secure them a room. They had
no money, so it would have to be procured on the
strength of the Salisbury name.

The common room at the White Boar was filled with
smoke, tempting aromas of food and ale, and a motley
collection of merchants, mercenaries, men of the cloth,
and thieves. David, desperate to find the ladies safe shelter
for the night, was a trifle loud in identifying his party.
Wishing to impress the landlord with the status of his
charge, he called, "The Earl of Salisbury's daughter
wishes shelter for the night." He certainly gained the inn-
keeper's attention, but unfortunately every other ear in
the place was pricked, most out of sheer curiosity, but
some out of pure greed. One man took a swift look at the
women as they entered and slunk off to make himself a
profit. He made straight for Hagthorn Castle where the
notoriously cruel and rapacious Roger de Belamé often
paid for information that would give him an advantage in
acquiring more of this world's goods than he had been
allotted.

At first the guard on the gate refused him entrance
because he knew the uncertainty of Belamé's temper
when disturbed at his dinner, but the fellow was adamant. When he divulged the Salisbury name, the guard
bade him wait at the entrance to the dining hall and
made his way to the dais. A pang of resentment stabbed
him as he saw his fellows were well into their wine cups
while he had the misfortune of standing guard tonight.
" 'Tis Ravener, milord, with some tale of Salisbury's
daughter staying at the White Boar. He's likely mistaken.
What would she be doin' in these parts?"

De Belamé put down his goblet and wiped his beard
with his sleeve. The workings of his mind were devious.
" 'Tis possible. She could be on her way to Castlecombe
to do the yearly tally. Tell Ravener I'll have a word with
him."

Ravener's thirst grew apace as he wended through the hall.

"How do you know it's Salisbury's daughter?" Belamé demanded.

"Her escort demanded a room for her. Said plain as plain it were fer the Earl of Salisbury's daughter."

"How many retainers?" Belamé asked.

"Only two . . . a man and a woman."

Belamé looked satisfied. "You did well to bring the information. Help yourself to some wine for your trouble."

Ravener blinked rapidly, getting up his courage to protest. "Milord, I was hoping for coin. I could have flogged their packhorses and made a tidy profit, but I chose to come all the way to Hagthorn."

Belamé considered for a moment before summoning the guard who was standing aside. "Put him in a guest chamber," he muttered.

It took Ravener only a moment to discern his meaning. Shit, he should have settled for the wine. Now he would spend the night below in a dank cell with rats for company. Fear rippled along his spine. Perhaps Belamé wanted no witnesses to what he was about to do. Ravener blurted, "I won't talk!"

Belamé replied, "You have the right to remain silent . . . forever." A bold plan was forming in Roger de Belamé's head. He got the idea from something another baron had already done. You needed permission from the king to marry an heiress, but since there was no king at the moment it needed only a forced marriage and consummation and the deed was done—the lands secured. Dawn would bring him a fine prize indeed.

When Falcon returned to the castle for supper, he was sorry that he'd spoken so sharply to Jasmine. She didn't show her face in the dining hall and he missed her. A mere glimpse of her brought him pleasure, and when he could contemplate her lovely face and form all through a meal it made it seem like a banquet. He would seek her in her chamber before he retired and tell her that she could go to Avisa if John was to be crowned king. He wanted to see the corners of her mouth lift when he told her. He wanted to kiss the corners of her mouth . . . For over an hour he savored the anticipation of being alone with her, knowing anticipation was sometimes more pleasurable than the reality. Falcon knocked low and, when she did not answer, thought she was asleep. He knocked again louder, then threw the door wide to reveal the empty room devoid of the baggage. He opened the inner door of the chamber, knowing he would find Dame Winwood's room empty also. He swore a fertile oath and kicked a stool across the room. The old bitch, aye, and the young bitch too, had gone home to the keep after he had told them plainly it was not safe.

It was full dark and the moon was rising as he strode into the knights' quarters. He picked three of his own and three Salisbury men to take with him to Winwood Keep. As he would leave them there as a guard, he picked older men who were veterans and could be counted on to defend a keep should the need arise. Within quarter of an hour they had packed their belongings and were in the saddle riding south.

Falcon de Burgh was stunned to discover that Jasmine had not returned home. That left only one alternative, which his mind almost refused to acknowledge. In all his life he had never had an order seriously disobeyed, and it had not occurred to him that he would ever suffer willful disobedience at the hands of a woman.

"She dared!" he said in amazement. "She actually dared." In that moment he knew that when he got his hands on her, he would beat her. "Sorry, lads," he muttered, "I'm afraid we'll have to turn about and ride north to Cirencester."

Not one man thought to grumble, though it would be tomorrow before they got out of their saddles, but de Burgh was angry for them. His men would miss their ale and their comfortable beds because of the whim of a willful wench. He would wash his hands of her! Then he grudgingly acknowledged that the very reason he was riding toward her, at once angrily and eagerly, was that he fancied she was the right wench for him.

Chapter 8

Daylight dawned very early on this May morn. Jasmine and Estelle did no more than wash their hands and faces. They broke their fast with bread and cheese left over from their supper and slipped down to rouse David who had slept with the packhorses for safekeeping.

The early mist in the hollows of the meadows would burn off once the sun was full risen. They were two or three miles past Marlborough when suddenly, from behind a copse of trees, four armed men bid them halt. David had his sword out instantly and was doing an admirable job of defending the women when one of the men who was not engaged with the young titan simply rode up behind him and stabbed him in the back.

Jasmine screamed, and just as she was about to slide from the saddle to the boy's side, she saw more men riding down upon them at full gallop. Her heels jammed into her palfrey's sides and the little mare sped away on fleet, slim legs.

De Burgh cursed and took after her. He was not sure

of the moment Jasmine realized he was her pursuer, but
he knew it was long before she brought her riding crop
down across his cheek, drawing blood. The mark would
leave a permanent white scar in his deeply tanned face.
"Seize her!" he ordered two of his men. He then wheeled
his destrier back toward the fleeing abductors. He relished the encounter that would provide him with the out-
let his violence needed at this moment. Unfortunately, his
men had left him only two to annihilate. The first he ran
through with his sword. The steel went so deep he could
not withdraw it immediately, so he unsheathed his dagger with his sword arm, dismounted on the run, and
pulled the last man still mounted from his horse. He
knelt on the man's throat, held the dagger at his carotid
artery, and demanded, "Who?"

The man felt fear like he had never felt it before. The
dagger pricked his neck eagerly. "Roger de Belamé . . .
Hagthorn Castle," he babbled, and then he felt nothing
really, just a mild sense of the fatality of it all as he began
his unplanned journey to eternity.

De Burgh turned and saw Jasmine struggling against
the hold of his men.

"Does it take two of your bullies to hold me?" she
demanded.

"It takes two of them to keep me from doing violence
to you." He pointed to David's limp form, which two of
the Salisbury knights were gently lifting. "He took that
wound defending you. It will likely prove fatal."

Jasmine sobbed. "Poor David, please let me help him,
he was so brave." Jealousy tore through Falcon like a
steel-tipped arrow. What was between these two?

Estelle looked up at de Burgh as she examined the
boy's wound. "It needs cleansing and binding immediately. He should also have a couple of hours rest before
an attempt is made to move him."

De Burgh nodded his agreement and said quietly,

"That suits my plans well, Dame Winwood. Take care of the boy while I take care of another."

For a moment Jasmine cringed, but then she realized she was being totally ignored. It was not a contrived ignoring for she saw clearly another matter consumed him. He left a burly knight to guard the women and mounted with grim determination.

The six knights strode into Hagthorn Castle with a sureness of purpose that forced aside any who would impede them. Roger de Belamé and his men had just finished breakfast and were still in the hall. Falcon de Burgh carried a long rope with a noose knotted securely at one end. Without preamble or a sidewise glance he strode to the dais and by dint of physical power forced the noose over Belamé's head. Four of de Burgh's knights held the gaping men at bay with their wickedly gleaming longswords while the fifth jumped onto the dais amid the leftover food and helped de Burgh throw the end of the rope over a heavy beam. They hanged Roger de Belamé on the spot before his impotent men. As they watched him dangling there, kicking until his face turned black, their desire for retaliation melted away, as each in his turn realized the inevitability of the retribution of a man who spread carnage and violence.

Falcon looked each man eye to eye before he said, "My name is de Burgh. I lay claim to Hagthorn." He spoke to his five knights briskly. "Stay here until I return from Cirencester. Bring some order to this place." He glanced with distaste at the hanged man and added, "Clean up the refuse."

Jasmine watched de Burgh ride toward her. He bore himself like a conqueror. He rode like a centaur, and she resented his dominance. Then he was close enough for her to see the bloody stripe she had put on his face, and she felt fear and excitement mingled together.

He ignored her and spoke to Estelle. "Does the boy live?"

She nodded in the affirmative, but said quickly, "He won't survive the ride back to Salisbury."

"How convenient that we are closer to Cirencester," he said dryly, aware that the two women had plotted and planned to achieve their goal. He'd taken the decision earlier or they would not be going, so he set about cutting saplings to make a horse-drawn litter for David.

Jasmine was filled with remorse that harm had come to the squire from Salisbury Castle, and she unpacked one of her cloaks and covered him with it gently. The tender look on her face made de Burgh say through set teeth, "Leave him, mistress, you have done enough."

The cavalcade rode north in silence until de Burgh finally said to her, "Have you any notion of what almost befell you back there?"

"We were set upon by thieves. David sacrificed himself so that I was able to escape them, until *you* caught me."

De Burgh was incredulous. "Are you so naive? Their prize wasn't packhorses; their prize was a kidnapped bride for their rapacious baron. They assumed you were your father's heiress." He hid a smile as he let his barb go in deep. "Think you when they discovered you were *worthless* it would have gone any easier for you?"

"Worthless?" she cried furiously.

"Priceless," he amended with irony. All too often it seemed to Jasmine that Falcon de Burgh got the last word.

As they neared Cirencester where Avisa, the Countess of Gloucester, had a magnificent manor house, he spurred his horse to a faster pace. Jasmine kept up with him and decided to pay him back for his cruel remark. Suddenly she jerked the reins on her palfrey so that she darted sideways into him, but his horsemanship was so superb that he simply maneuvered slightly without even glancing in her direction.

De Burgh could not hide his surprise when he saw Hubert de Burgh's men about the Countess of Gloucester's stables. "What are you doing here, Peter?" he asked his uncle's squire.

The fellow shrugged noncommittally and replied, "We are often here. I will inform Lord de Burgh of your arrival."

Falcon assumed his uncle had gone home to Dorset from Wales, but now he surmised he must be passing through Gloucester to his sheriffdom of Hereford. Falcon did not offer to assist Jasmine to dismount, thereby depriving her of an opportunity to spurn his help.

Hugh met them at the door and helped them lift young David into the entrance hall. Hugh asked, "What happened to your face?"

Falcon grinned and replied, "A love scratch."

Hugh grinned back, glanced at Jasmine, and said, "Yes, I heard all about Falcon's Folly. She is unearthly beautiful."

"What are you doing in these parts?" asked Falcon.

Hugh, evading an answer, said, "I could ask you the same thing. Looks like you ran into a little trouble getting here."

"Nothing I couldn't handle."

At this moment a lovely voice floated down the staircase. "Hugh darling, I believe we are about to have visitors." The voice and the Junoesque woman it belonged to stepped toward them and said, "Oh, dear, it appears I have let the cat among the pigeons."

Falcon's face certainly did not register the surprise he felt as he learned that his uncle was the Countess of Gloucester's lover; however, Jasmine could not conceal her shock. This was John's wife; he who would be king; she who would be queen!

Hugh, a little guiltily, said, "Thank God it is my nephew who has discovered us, Avisa. May I present Falcon de Burgh."

The countess, a tall, handsome woman, looked at the young de Burgh with appreciation. She was in her mid-thirties and had always had an eye for a powerfully built man. She held out her hand to welcome him and he raised it to his lips.

"A deep pleasure, your grace. May I present my betrothed, Jasmine. She is the youngest daughter of your brother-in-law, William of Salisbury."

Avisa swept the girl into a brief, warm embrace then set her away, saying "She is exquisite."

Falcon continued. "This is her grandmother, Dame Estelle Winwood."

Avisa's attractive face lit up with recognition. "I remember you from a visit we made to Salisbury when John and I were first wed." She spoke to Jasmine. "I remember your mother. She was as lovely then as you are now."

Such conflicting emotions were racing through Jasmine that she was at a loss for words. She was delighted that Avisa had known her mother, and she was wildly curious about this woman who was about to become England's queen, yet at the same time she was shocked that she was being unfaithful. She was embarrassed to have such knowledge and horrified that Avisa was slightly amused that she had been discovered.

Avisa had dispatched a servant to make ready a chamber for the wounded squire. Estelle picked up her apothecary case and followed the men who transported David.

"As you can well imagine, Dame Winwood, I am in need of a seer at the moment. Perhaps at supper you could foretell the future for me," Avisa said.

At this, both de Burgh men made a sound of derision.

Avisa looked archly at Hugh, daring him to openly scoff at such prophecies.

Jasmine had been ignored long enough. "Your grace, King Richard is dead and John will be crowned king. You will be Queen Avisa of England, and I have come to ask to be your first lady-in-waiting." A hush fell over the room. Avisa looked quickly to Hubert de Burgh and Jasmine glanced defiantly at Falcon.

Falcon said firmly, "Richard is dead, the rest is speculation from our renowned 'oracle.' " He inclined his head in Estelle's direction.

"Fascinating!" declared Avisa. "We shall dissect the possibility over supper." She picked up some of Jasmine's luggage. "Come, my dear, and we'll find you a pretty chamber." She towered over the petite girl, making Falcon think how incongruous they appeared. Jasmine had come to be lady-in-waiting to a queen, but it was the queen who was waiting upon his delectable betrothed.

When they were out of earshot of the men, Jasmine felt an explanation was needed. "When my grandmother saw these things in her crystal, I wanted to become a lady of the queen's court with all my heart. De Burgh forbade me to come to you here at Cirencester, so I simply left. Unfortunately, our escort David was set upon and stabbed in the back, and then de Burgh caught up with us and there was hell to pay."

Avisa smiled confidentially at her and whispered, "These de Burgh men are the very Devil, are they not?"

Jasmine opened her eyes wide solemnly and said, "I hate him. They betrothed me to him against my will."

Avisa was amused, though she had too generous a nature to let the amusement show. My God, how she envied this innocent the awakening the girl was about to experience at the hands and lips of Falcon de Burgh.

"Oh, my lady, this chamber is lovely," Jasmine exclaimed. "In fact, the whole manor house takes my breath away. I'm afraid Winwood Keep is a very rude place, and even my father's castle of Salisbury is poorly furnished compared to this."

Avisa said kindly, "I'm sure you'd like to bathe and rest after your wretched journey. Just pull the bellrope for a servant for anything you desire."

"Ah, I cannot take the time. With your permission, my lady, I should like to help Estelle nurse David."

When the two de Burghs found themselves alone, Hugh explained, "I had designs on Avisa for my wife many years ago. However, she was too good a catch for the likes of me—heiress of the Earl of Gloucester with huge estates in the west extending into Glamorgan. King Henry married her to his favorite son, John. After that, John's financial worries were over and it stopped people dubbing him John Lackland. When John made me his chancellor, Avisa and I spent a lot of time together."

"Aren't you risking your neck by putting horns on John? Christ, you know the Plantagenet temper borders on madness," Falcon said with concern.

Hugh shrugged his shoulders. "You know what a swine he is—faithless since his wedding night. He's never here nowadays. They live their own separate lives, thank God. I love her; what can I say?"

"More to the point, what does your wife Beatrice say?" his nephew asked. Beatrice was the daughter of the feudal head and great lord of the east, William de Warenne.

Hugh said defensively, "I'm a damned good husband to Beatrice. She's a happy woman and I have a great deal of affection for her, but this is different. I still dream that someday, somehow, Avisa and I will marry. There, I've said it, and don't let it go any further unless you want to lose a testicle." He shook his head. "God alone knows why we love one woman above all others. You yourself have chosen Salisbury's love child when you could have had a legitimate heiress."

Falcon grinned, then sobered. "Hugh, what if it comes about that John *is* crowned king?"

Hugh poured Falcon a hefty goblet of wine and shook his head. "I've always been a Plantagenet man. I almost worshipped King Henry, as I know you did when you were a boy. Then after his death it seemed natural to serve Richard. It's been almost a decade . . . where have the years gone? I don't want John as my king any more than the next man does. I know too many of his faults—I know more than I should, loving Avisa, but I'm still a Plantagenet man. When it boils right down to it, I'd far rather have John as my friend than my enemy."

Falcon drained his wine cup and said, "Well, the Plantagenets and the de Burghs have a lot in common. For a century we've been addicted to power. We've fought for it, blackmailed for it, betrayed for it, risked all for it, and we've never been able to get enough."

"Amen," said Hugh, setting down his cup.

Falcon said, "I'd better see how the boy fares, although from what Salisbury tells me Dame Winwood is an expert at medicine."

"You trust her medicine but not her magic, is that it?" Hugh laughed.

Before he ascended the stairs Falcon said, "I trust neither, but let's put it this way: I don't believe her curses could kill me; her poisons could."

David lay prone upon the bed, naked to the waist. His wound had been cleansed, poulticed, and bound. Jasmine sat at his bedside, holding his hand.

As de Burgh bent his head to enter through the doorway his eyes took in the tender scene. She hadn't even taken the time to change her travel-stained gown before she had rushed to the boy's side. His crystal gaze swept over her. "Seek your own chamber, mistress," he ordered quietly. "You will wish to improve your appearance before you dine with your future queen, I am sure."

Stung by his criticism, Jasmine gave Falcon a look that almost scorched his skin before she swept past him. Only the knowledge that David was on the way to recovery kept her from refusing to leave his side.

When Jasmine saw her reflection in the polished silver mirror in her chamber, she realized de Burgh's criticism was deserved. Perversely, hot hatred for him welled up in her. She purposely chose the loveliest gown she had brought. It was a deep peony-colored velvet. She was brushing her long, pale-gold hair when de Burgh entered the room with only a pretense at a knock. Avisa had placed her in the room, saying "Every woman should have a pink bedchamber . . . it's like being in the heart of a rose."

Jasmine made such a stunning picture that for a moment his thoughts scattered and he felt his heart skip a beat. Then he recalled the earlier scene and demanded, "What is between you and this David?"

"Nothing!" she flung vehemently, "Since he is a man. I *hate* men."

"What's wrong with men?" Falcon asked, surprised at the vehemence.

Her chin went up and she dug both fists into her bright-pink girdle. "The word men begins with 'me' to start with. All men are totally selfish. I've had a thorough education in the ways of men." She said the word with loathing.

Bemused, he asked, "What do you know of men?"

"I know they are hard to please and easy to displease," she flung at him.

"What else?" he asked in a warning tone that she completely ignored.

"I know that the last one wants to be the first one and the first one wants to be the last one."

He was angry that she had learned of sexual matters from Estelle.

"Go on," he said in quietly menacing tones.

"I have been warned about the devastating attraction of the 'lurking bastard' in men," she finished triumphantly.

He took her by the elbows.

"Let me go," she said furiously.

"Never," he vowed.

His nearness made her conscious of every pulse of her blood. The kiss was an age in coming. It started as a slow lazy thing with all the time in the world, then it strengthened until her slim body was crushed against his. She knew that he was taking, not giving. The kiss was so ruthlessly lustful it forced her to yield to his masculinity. When he let her go abruptly, she gasped for breath and staggered a little on weakened legs.

He had wanted to kiss her for so long, he had no idea what had kept him in check. Now that he'd had a taste of her, however, it wasn't nearly enough. He was in a reckless enough mood to see how far he could go. He took her chin in his hand and lifted her face to him again. Before his lips touched hers he stopped and said, "Every time you speak to me, mistress, you dare my manhood." He emphasized this last word by brushing it against her to show her how rock-hard he was. "That kiss was to warn you what will happen if you persist."

With the taste of him on her mouth and the feel of him against her soft belly, she could not disguise the fear she felt. This close she could not take her eyes from the wound she had inflicted upon him and they became liquid with apprehension. He relented a little. "Compose yourself and I'll escort you to dinner."

"I'll not dine with you," she stated.

The muscle in his jaw flexed. The moment he'd relented an inch, she had taken a mile. One hand slipped about her waist while the fingers of his other hand traced the neckline of her gown and began to stray toward her tempting breasts. "Is this your way of suggesting we retire for the night? Certainly it is the first time we have had a chance to be alone together. I too think we should use this night to become more intimately acquainted." His lips brushed the silken flesh where his fingers had played.

Her mouth went dry. He was deliberately misunderstanding her words. Now she wanted nothing more than to have him escort her to dinner. "I'm hungry," she said pointedly.

"But not for food," he whispered huskily, brushing the pale golden tendrils back from her temples and searching her eyes for a sign of awakening desire. He saw only stubborn resistance. He removed his doublet and stretched out upon the bed. "If we are ensconsed for the night, we might as well make ourselves comfortable. My boots, Jasmine," he ordered casually.

"You ill-mannered lout!" She choked. "Remove yourself from my bed and remove yourself from my chamber. You know we are expected downstairs. Avisa is preparing a special dinner. I have more manners than to flout her gracious hospitality." Jasmine grasped at straws. "If I don't go down immediately I'm certain Avisa will come to fetch me."

He chuckled. "Outraged innocence . . . I must admit you do that very well. Jasmine, you know as well as I that if we don't show up for dinner they will exchange winks and realize I have taken you up on your invitation to bed you."

"My invitation?" Further words failed her.

He was enjoying her discomfort immensely. He held out an inviting hand. "Why don't you remove that lovely gown before it gets ruined and join me on the bed, love?"

Tears of frustration sprang to her eyes. "De Burgh,

you are more wicked than the Devil. I swear you will plague me to death!"

He laughed outright. "Jasmine, for God's sake, unbend a little. Do you begrudge me a little teasing, a little fun?" He sat up and pulled her into his lap. She was furious to be handled so. He kissed the frown between her brows, then he kissed the tip of her nose and said quietly, "If you keep running off someone else will pluck the delicious fruit that is mine. My better judgment tells me to experience the joy of you now. After all, you are mine, we are betrothed, and none will really expect a bridegroom so hot to cool his blood until after the wedding."

She paled at his words and pulled herself from his lap on shaky legs. "My lord, I promise to be courteous and civil to you if you will escort me to dinner." Her lashes brushed her cheeks, hiding her defiance. "I know you are a most valiant knight who does not take his vows lightly. I am defenseless against you and beg you will be honorable toward me and wait for the wedding." She raised her lashes to peep at him and gauge the effect of her words.

"You are a little witch"—he smiled ruefully—"who knows how to wrap a man about your fingers!"

She held out his doublet to him and the corners of her mouth turned up prettily. "Come, you may escort me to dinner, my lord."

They dined intimately in a small room that personified Avisa's cultured taste. The furnishings were elegant rather than massive, the table was decorated with flowers, and they drank from Venetian glass. The quality of the food took precedence over the quantity, and Jasmine realized it was the first time she had ever been exposed to intelligent dinner conversation between men and women.

Her ignorance of history, politics, and the world at large was abysmal so she only listened and absorbed everything she saw and heard.

Hubert looked at Avisa and said, "So, there is a definite possibility that you will become the Queen of England."

Avisa made a little moue with her lips. "When they married me to John he received all my Gloucester lands, holdings, men, and monies. Combining everything I owned in Wales and England, it made him the richest peer in the realm. I, on the other hand, received nothing; not kindness, not fidelity, not even a child. Perhaps finally I am about to receive my reward." Avisa glanced at Estelle as if for confirmation.

After a moment's concentration Estelle said, *"Prince John's outstanding qualities were vanity, temper, lust, and greed. King John's outstanding qualities will be vanity, temper, lust, and greed. As before; so again. He will bring you unhappiness and grief."

Avisa smiled to lighten the mood. "We were ever a mismatched couple. I don't believe he ever forgave me for being taller than he."

Falcon said, "He was truly the runt of the litter. King Henry's other sons were as tall and broad as himself, and yet for all his shortcomings, John was always Henry's favorite."

Hubert spoke up. "Henry, now there was a man. He was the best king England will see in a century! After the anarchy and civil war of Stephen's reign, Henry strived for one law, one government, and national unity for thirty-five years. Do you realize that before Henry if you were charged with a crime you were given a trial of ordeal, or compurgation, or the outcome was decided by wager or battle?"

"Compurgation?" Avisa asked curiously.

Falcon supplied, "To purge or purify."

Hubert continued. "I know it was before your time, but really it was not so very long ago the law was settled by hocus-pocus." The three women exchanged amused glances that Hugh had come close to insulting Estelle and

Jasmine, but he didn't notice as he warmed to his subject of the late King Henry. "English law is now based on trial by jury of twelve men of high morals within the community," Hugh said with satisfaction.

Jasmine spoke for the first time. "A community would be hard-pressed indeed to find a dozen men with high morals."

Avisa's amused laughter spilled across the table. It was quite infectious, and soon the men joined in the laughter, even though the jest was at male expense.

Avisa said wistfully, "My father-in-law was a real man. Unfortunately, he bred sons who were like a pack of wolves or a skulk of foxes—save for your dear father, of course," she said to Jasmine.

Falcon raised his goblet in a toast to Avisa. "We would all dearly love to see you our queen, but if it comes to pass, England will rue John. History does not travel upward in a straight line; a single act of violence can destroy years of effort; hatred and fear cancel good works; life is absurd."

Jasmine saw an opening to shoot a small barbed arrow. "You live by violence and bloodshed!"

"I'm highly competitive, that's without question," he conceded with a dazzling smile, one black eyebrow contorting into a challenging arch. "But I'm perfectly happy to give the victory to anybody who can *take* it."

Avisa thought on first sight that he had enormous impact. He had a presence that was larger than life. She glanced at Jasmine, hearing the challenge the young couple sent each other. "So, you are to marry?"

Jasmine said, "We are only betrothed."

Falcon said emphatically, "Yes, we are to marry."

Avisa's eyes met Estelle's in mutual understanding. "Women marry men thinking they are going to change them, and they never do."

Estelle added, "Men marry women hoping they will never change, but they invariably do."

"Oh, how true," Avisa said, laughing. She arose from the table and her company followed suit. Discreetly the servants began to clear. "Thank you all for your company tonight. It was pleasant to play 'what if,' but it is William Marshal, Hubert Walter, the Archbishop of Canterbury, and your father, Jasmine, who will decide on the succession."

Chapter 9

In Normandy, Jasmine's father was indeed a deciding factor in who should be the next king. Urged on by the Earl of Chester, all the English barons present argued that the English would never accept Arthur as king. He had never set foot on English soil and because of his mother's influence he was no Anglophone.

The King of France was poised like a ravenous bird of prey to swallow Normandy, Brittany, and the Angevin possessions. If they crowned Arthur, a thirteen-year-old boy, he would swoop down and attack. Because of this, William Marshal and William of Salisbury favored John as the next king. Without exception, the barons of the continental dominions of Normandy, Anjou, and Poitou declared for Arthur. Hubert Walter, the aging Archbishop of Canterbury, also opted for Arthur because of a personal dislike for John and his abominations. In the end, however, he allowed himself to be swayed. He shook his head and said, "I promise you that nothing you ever did have you so much cause to repent of, as you will have of this."

To settle the matter, they issued a proclamation stating that Richard had named his brother John as his successor to the throne. He was to be crowned May 26, 1199. The most important men of the time were gathered for the coronation. The Archbishop of Canterbury, the chief justiciar, the constable, the marshal, the steward, the chamberlain, and the chancellor were the important posts, and the English barons vied with each other for appointments to the unfilled offices.

King John was surrounded by William de Warenne, William Earl of Devon, Ranulf Earl of Chester, Geoffrey de Mandeville, Robert Fitz-Walter, Saire de Quincy, Robert de Ros, William Mowbray, Meiler Fitz Henry, John de Courcy, and the de Lacy brothers, Walter and Hugh.

News of King John's coronation soon reached Cirencester. Falcon de Burgh contented himself to leave his bride-to-be with the new Queen of England.

He opened the door to the adjoining chamber Avisa had wickedly provided for the betrothed and held out his hand. "Here, take it!"

"What?" Jasmine demanded, angered that once again he had entered without permission.

"Your wretched hedgehog, Prick," he said with a grimace.

"You lout! Will you be told his name is Quill. You say it on purpose to provoke me."

He grinned because, of course, it was true. "No sweet words for me before I depart?" he teased. "No 'thank you, milord Falcon for allowing me to be lady to the queen'?"

"Allowing?" She almost choked on the word. "I am the granddaughter of a king. That same King Henry you de Burghs are forever extolling. I am a royal princess . . . I am—"

"You, my love, are the result of a night of illicit love, a roll in the hay, or fornication under a hedge perhaps."

"Oh . . . you . . . you . . . son of a whore," she blurted.

"And you, my sweet, are the daughter of a whore," he said with relish. "Can you be trusted among the young men who will be flocking to Avisa's court when they hear the news?"

Her mouth opened to indignantly protest her virtue when she suddenly changed her mind. "No, no, I cannot be trusted. I'll do my damndest to disgrace you. If you are stupid enough to marry me, milord, I promise all your children will be bastards, just like me."

He struck her then. She crumpled onto the bed, then raised tear-filled eyes and swore, "Whoreson coward!"

He took her by the shoulders and shook her. "I warn you that's enough. Persist in this and by God you'll drive me to further violence."

Her lips trembled and her eyelashes were spikey with tears, then she felt the rough sweetness of his kisses. He couldn't help himself. She was so desirable. She was at once earthy and ethereal, a combination guaranteed to drug him and become habit forming. "Jassy . . . Jassy," he murmured against her lips. "Let yourself go . . . let yourself float . . . sail away with me to another world." His hands were inside her bodice, cupping her breasts, squeezing them lightly, playfully, rubbing his thumbs gently over her nipples until they stood out like tiny jewels. The velvety caress of his tongue almost made her melt against his powerful chest, but she stiffened as she felt him quicken against the soft curve of her belly.

"Don't!" She pulled his hands from her breasts. "You think you can strike me one minute and rape my mouth the next. We are mismatched, unsuited . . . leave me at once!"

"Opposites attract!" he insisted. "For a man and a

woman to love each other, they don't have to be cut from the same cloth."

"Love?" She laughed derisively. "I'll never love you!"

He towered over her, his green eyes blazing with unquenched passion at the challenge she threw at him. "You shall," he vowed. "You shall!"

A shiver ran up her body. Wildly she wondered if it was fear or excitement. Disgust or anticipation? What was it about him that brought out the very worst in her? She had intended to ask him a favor regarding David, now she wondered if she dared. She had had to say a secret good-bye to the squire. When she told him how pleased she was that his wound was healed well enough for him to travel home to Salisbury, he had hinted that upon his return he would be punished by de Burgh for the part he had played in escorting her. "Do you think he will flog you?" she asked incredulously.

"Without hesitation," David said, confirming her suspicions of de Burgh's cruelty. Now she would have to risk a beating to help David. She'd just received proof that if she angered him enough he would strike her.

"I don't want David punished for my deeds; he was only obeying my orders. You have a cruel streak, and I fear for him if you intend to take out your anger on him."

"You affront me, mistress. I have a reputation for being a disciplinarian, but I also have a reputation of fairness toward men under my command. Why do you champion this David, what is between you two?" he demanded suspiciously. "Is he one of the long string of men with whom you intend to deceive me?" He lifted her in his arms and carried her to the bed. With sure hands he removed her shoes and reached up her skirts to peel the silken stockings from her pretty legs.

"My God, what are you doing?" she cried, shocked to her very core that he would be bold enough to reach up her skirts to disrobe her.

His passion was high, fed by his anger. "There is one way to make sure your first child will be mine. I will plant my seed deep within you here and now!" he vowed.

"I'll scream the castle down," she threatened.

"Little innocent," he said, caressing her thigh, his fingers seeking higher until they captured the delicious curve of her heart-shaped bottom, "no one would dare disturb us while I was making love to you. They would think you were crying out in passion."

Jasmine was by turns icy cold then burning hot. She shuddered as his hands roamed about her private places. Her eyes turned a dark shade of purple and she hissed at him through clenched teeth, "Falcon de Burgh, if you do this thing, I will never, ever forgive you!"

Falcon longed for her to be generous toward him. He would not see her for a long time, and already his body ached for her at the mere thought of the separation. He hesitated over taking what he desired by force, for he knew deep within his heart that if she did not give it willingly, it would be valueless. Slowly he removed his offending hand from beneath her gown and allowed her to sit up on the bed. He took her face in his hands tenderly and touched his lips to hers, gently, reverently. "Jassy love . . . give me something, anything to take with me to warm my heart. A kiss . . . a smile," he begged persuasively.

Silently she picked up the stockings he had removed from her and pressed them into his hand. She had decided it was best to let him go without another word. Distance between them was the safest, for whenever they came together it was like tossing a match into a keg of gunpowder.

The Earl of Salisbury sailed home the first week of June. He was surprised that Falcon de Burgh had had no trouble with the Salisbury knights, and his opinion of his future son-in-law's ability to handle men rose another notch. John had appointed his half brother William as head of his armies, no small responsibility with the King of France threatening war and the rebellious unrest always present in Wales and Ireland. To top it all off, King Alexander, the Red Fox of Scotland, was demanding the return of Cumberland and Northumberland as the price for maintaining peace and loyalty to newly crowned King John.

William regaled de Burgh with a description of the coronation and all who were present. Then he said, "I always knew John was jealous of Richard, but now I realize he must have hated him and coveted everything that was his. He has been waiting and plotting and planning for so long, he didn't wait to remove his coronation robes before he started issuing orders and bestowing honors upon his sycophants." William spread his hands. "Well, at least he recognized I'm a soldier and not a courtier. I'm head of the armies and over half of them are mercenaries, so we've got our work cut out for us." He paused. When de Burgh made no protest at the use of the word us, he went on. "I'd like to give you command of five hundred bowmen as well as Salisbury's knights and men-at-arms."

Falcon grinned. "Thank God you recognize that I too am a soldier rather than a courtier."

William cast an appreciative look about. The order de Burgh had brought to the well-stocked armory was evident. "Speaking of court, where is that little minx, Jasmine? I have arranged for her to go to court to be lady to John's new child-bride, Isabella of Angoulême."

"New bride?" Falcon asked with disbelief. "He's married to Avisa."

"John has put pressure on the church to grant him a divorce."

"He can't do that to Avisa!" de Burgh exclaimed, shocked.

"Falcon, he can do anything. He is the king. He intends to rule. He saw Isabella of Angoulême, a radiantly lovely child, vividly dark . . . only about fourteen years old. She was promised to Hugh de Lusignan, but John didn't give a shit about that. He abducted her, then said she agreed to become his new queen."

Falcon said, "He has no grounds for divorce."

William laughed though there was little mirth in it. "The divorce has been granted. They dragged out consanguinity again. Avisa's grandfather, Robert of Gloucester, was the illegitimate son of Henry I. Anyway, it's a done thing. Avisa will be well rid of him. Why so much concern for her?"

"Jasmine went to be lady to Queen Avisa," Falcon said lamely.

"I suppose that Estelle put her up to that?"

"William, I have discovered that Jasmine needs no one to put her up to things. She is capable of making her own mischief."

"What woman isn't? I'll send for her," said William.

"No, I'd better go and get her. Oh, hell, I might as well tell you the whole tale of her near-abduction before you hear of it elsewhere." When he had finished William roared with laughter.

"I fail to see the humor, sir," Falcon said stiffly.

William's eyes twinkled. "You took charge of hundreds of men without a problem, but one little girl leads you on a devil's dance."

Falcon grinned and rubbed the scar on his cheek. By God, wouldn't the sparks fly when he went to fetch her home. He could hardly wait! Yet he didn't relish a visit with Avisa. A woman who had just had a throne pulled out from under her would not make the best company.

* * *

Indeed, an air of unseemly haste pervaded the stately manor at Cirencester. All the barons and their wives who had gathered about Queen Avisa were leaving as quickly as they had arrived. The rumors of the divorce had flown as quickly as feathered arrows and the gentry were cutting their losses before matters became any stickier.

The Earls of Clare, Derby, Leicester, and Warenne and their countesses had departed that morning an hour before Avisa had received official letters and documents bearing the new king's seals. Only the Countess of Pembroke, the lovely Isabel, wife of the Marshal of England, intended to stay loyally by Avisa's side. Both Isabel and William Marshal were held in high esteem by their peers because their characters were almost too good to be believed.

The Countess of Warwick, a young widow, changed her mind about leaving the moment Falcon de Burgh arrived upon the scene.

Jasmine saw him and chose to ignore him, but she was annoyed when she saw that none of the other women did so. Elizabeth of Warwick clung to his arm, looking up at him as if she would like to devour him. "Falcon de Burgh, you are a sight for sore eyes."

"Hello, Bess, how's the prettiest widow in England?"

She pouted and whispered, "Worried to death!"

"About what, pray tell me?" he said, smiling into her dark eyes.

"I can't tell you here," she said, arching her eyebrows to indicate the subject was rather delicate. "Visit me tonight and I'll reveal all," she promised saucily.

Falcon de Burgh kept his face straight as he kissed her hand, then greeted Isabel, the Countess of Pembroke.

"Falcon, is there any news of William? He is usually so good at communicating with me, but I've heard nothing of his return."

"Perhaps it is because he doesn't expect you to be here at Cirencester, Lady Isabel. All I can tell you is that the Earl of Salisbury has returned. King John probably can't spare the marshal. As you know more than most, the work of ruling the realm falls to him rather than the king."

Isabel's lips tightened at the mention of John. She had been totally opposed to John becoming King of England, and she and her husband William Marshal had exchanged sharp words over it, but of course she would say nothing that would reflect upon her husband's choice in public. Her heart was wrung over this dreadful divorcing of Avisa. Good men did not sunder their marriages, whether they were made in heaven or hell.

Falcon extracted himself from the ladies to search out Hubert de Burgh. He found his uncle in his chamber reading royal dispatches that had been delivered within the hour. Hugh looked up from the parchment he held, pleasantly flushed from the contents of King John's letter. "Falcon, my boy, let me share my good news with you. John has made me custodian of the great fortress of Dover and warden of the Cinque Ports."

"Congratulations. With your own Castle of Corfe you will command the whole southern coast of England."

At that moment an unearthly wail caught their ears. "Noooo, oh, noooo." Hugh was on his feet and running the moment he heard it. "It's Avisa. Wait here for me, I'll be back as soon as I can."

Avisa's face was like a death mask as she paced her chamber, the paper clutched in her fist and pressed to her breast. Her eyes were hollow and terrible to behold. "Whoreson . . . swine . . . bastard . . . He is insane. No, not insane, clever . . . diabolically clever. He's known about us all along and this is his sick revenge."

"Sweetheart, what is it? Tell me!" Hubert ordered.

"Not enough that the pig divorces me, not enough that

the pig makes a fourteen-year-old child the queen, not enough that he keeps all my Gloucester holdings for his piggish, greedy self!"

She screamed and rent her garment across the breast.

Hugh grabbed her in strong arms. "Stop it, Avisa!" He took her to a large chair and sat down with her cradled in his arms. "Now, tell me!" he commanded.

"He's sold me," she whispered.

"What?" Hugh asked incredulously.

"He's sold me to Geoffrey de Mandeville for twenty thousand marks."

"By God's glove, de Mandeville is a dead man," vowed Hubert de Burgh.

Chapter 10

Falcon waited for almost an hour, then realized Hugh must have his hands full. He took his saddlebags to the room adjoining Jasmine's, which he had occupied before. He opened the door between and stepped inside. She was not there and yet her presence lingered in the room. His fingers touched the strings of a lute, and he wondered if she would ever play it for him, and if she sang. He wanted to know more about her. She had an elusive quality, revealing only surface characteristics, while keeping her deeper qualities veiled, hidden, mysterious.

His eye caught the scarlet velvet nightrobe on the chair beside her bed and he was unable to keep his hands from it. He stroked the soft velvet and the delicate scent of flowers assaulted his senses. A familiar ache suffused his loins and he swore softly. He caught his reflection in the mirror of polished silver. Suddenly he saw himself as Jasmine must see him. The high black boots and leather jack, the emerald earring to match the color of his eyes, the scarred hands and cheek, the deadly weapons at his belt showed him to be dangerous, selfish, worldly.

Suddenly he was covered with guilt. She was so young, so innocent, so delicate; he could not believe that he had actually struck her. He resolved to be more gentle with her from now on. The chirping of the little sparrow caught his attention and he went over to the wicker cage and said softly, "Feather? Pretty boy . . . pretty boy." He stuck his finger through the tiny bars and chuckled when it pecked him sharply.

"What are you doing?" an accusing voice asked angrily.

"Nothing," he said, turning toward Jasmine as she came into the chamber. The sunlight streaming through the window gave her the quality of luminescence. Her eyes, her skin, her silvery-gold hair surrounded her with a light-filled essence that took away his breath.

She examined Feather minutely with her eyes to discover some damage he might have inflicted then raised her eyes to his. "The rumors must be true about King John repudiating Avisa, else you wouldn't be here." She said it in an accusing tone, as if he had had some personal hand in the matter.

Remembering his resolve, he explained, "Your father is returned. King John has already divorced Avisa, I'm sorry to say. I've come to escort you home. You see now why you should not have come."

"Damn all men," she flared. "They always conveniently lay the blame at women's feet."

His resolve of gentleness flew out the window. "Must I remind you I advised you to wait until Avisa was crowned queen, but oh no, you had to go running off on a whim."

"Whim?" she spat.

He said mockingly, "You claim to see the future in your silly crystal ball. Why did you not foresee John making a child Queen of England?"

Jasmine's eyes widened. "I did . . . oh, indeed I did see the king and queen sailing on a vessel for England. Estelle . . . Estelle," Jasmine cried, going to the door.

Her grandmother came into the room and acknowledged de Burgh's presence with a brief nod of the head.

"Remember in the tower room when I gazed into the crystal and saw the king and queen set sail for England? I do have the sight, it's just that I haven't learned how to interpret it well yet."

"Hindsight is always amazingly accurate," Falcon said dryly.

Estelle did not contradict him. She should have foreseen that John would rid himself of an aging wife. She must advise Avisa before she left. All would be brought under the mailed fist of the crown whether they chose or not. Avisa must concede gracefully, or she would find herself imprisoned for years as John's father had done to his mother, Eleanor of Aquitaine.

Falcon said, "Be ready to leave at dawn. Your father has arranged a place at court for you as lady to the new queen."

"Think you I am so disloyal to Avisa that I would serve another?" she demanded incredulously.

He smiled. "For once we are in agreement. I'm sure you will be excused from your duties to take on the duties of a wife."

She had walked right into the trap he had set for her. However, the door had not sprung shut yet. Quickly she said, "On the other hand, a fourteen-year-old girl is still a child. She will desperately need someone a little older to help her adjust to a strange land. Queenship will overwhelm the little girl. I see my duty clearly." Her chin went up in defiance.

His eyes lingered upon her sulky mouth, which evoked such forbidden fantasies in him that his voice became husky. "You will sup with me tonight," he stated. It was not a request.

Hubert finally sought out Falcon. He had tucked Avisa into her bed, exhausted from tears.

"Is she taking it badly?" asked Falcon.

Hubert shrugged philosophically. "It is her pride that's in shreds. As for being queen—she cannot miss what she's never known. She knows that she is better off without John. She wouldn't have him back in her bed for a dozen thrones. But it rankles that he's to marry a beautiful young girl. She's devastated at the moment because John has chosen a new husband for her."

"Who?" asked Falcon.

"Obviously whoever offered the highest price. Geoffrey de Mandeville," said Hubert, his mouth tightening for the first time.

"What will you do?" asked Falcon.

"Sooner or later kill him, I suppose."

"It would seem more logical to me to kill John," Falcon said bluntly.

"It would of course, but I'm too bloody ambitious for that, so I'll substitute de Mandeville. I intend to be King John's justiciar."

Falcon looked at Hubert long and hard. He could not understand how he could take King John's preferments while John was venting his sick revenge upon the woman Hubert was supposed to love.

Hubert saw the look and said bluntly, "Wait, my boy— wait until you have a woman standing between you and power. See which one you choose."

"Well," said Falcon, putting the best face on it, "let's hope you get both someday."

* * *

Falcon ordered a brace of partridge, a compote of small buttered vegetables, and a strawberry torte for dinner. He went to the wine cellars himself and chose both a dry and a sweet chablis brought from France. Then he changed into a white linen shirt and left off the thigh boots in an attempt to look less threatening, less like a pirate looking for booty. He knew she would not come of her own volition, so once a servant brought the food, he tapped lightly upon their adjoining door and opened it.

Jasmine gasped. She was sitting clad in only her underdress, a filmy peach-color affair. The russet-color tabard that was to go over it lay draped upon her bed. He could not help himself. He went to her swiftly and put his hands upon her exposed shoulders. Her rustling garments had offered a whisper of invitation. Instant fantasies flamed up in him arousing such a desire that triggered forbidden taboos.

"Don't dare to touch me!" she cried.

He slanted an eyebrow. "You invite my fingers. You knew I would come for you to sup with me."

"I forgot," she lied.

He put his hand under her chin and tipped her face up. He looked into eyes shadowed by curling lashes. "You have a convenient memory." His eyes lingered on her soft pink mouth. "Am I permitted a taste?" he asked mockingly.

"No!" she flared.

"We are betrothed. You deny me?" he asked quietly.

"I would deny you even if we were wed!"

"Denial would avail you little," he said, amused. He cupped her face with his hands and reverently lifted it to his lips like a first communion.

The moment was shattered as Dame Estelle came in carrying her packed bags. "She draws you like a lodestone," she said with faintly concealed contempt.

"Is this how you gather your mystic knowledge, by listening at doors and spying through keyholes?" he asked with matching contempt.

"Sometimes," she admitted defiantly. "That way I found out John has sold Avisa to Geoffrey de Mandeville for twenty thousand marks."

Falcon wished Jasmine had not learned this ugly truth, but of course Estelle had been bursting to add fuel to the fire of Jasmine's hatred for men.

"Oh, my God, I must go to her," said Jasmine.

"You will not, mistress." His voice brooked no disobedience. He picked up the russet tabard. "Put this on before you drive me to the brink of madness."

Estelle helped her into the tabard and he held out a demanding hand for her to accompany him into his chamber.

Jasmine was afraid of the suppressed sexuality and violent danger that were just below the surface in this man. She thought him capable of any atrocity! In his chamber she strove to overcome her suffocating fear. Estelle had been carrying out her agreement and teaching Jasmine everything she knew. Jasmine called up her words to aid her in this intimate situation.

Estelle had shown her how to gain control over another. She had said that if you knew what people wanted, where they went to in their beds at night as they dreamed their wildest dreams, then you were well on your way to controlling them. Jasmine would watch Falcon closely and learn his deepest desires.

The food and wine were laid out on a side table. Falcon seated her in a comfortable easy chair and served her from the buffet. He poured her a chalice of the sweet chablis and set it at her elbow. Then he prepared a plate for himself and filled his own chalice from the dry wine. They began their meal in silence. Jasmine looked down at her plate, but her eyes strayed to his powerful hands. She studied him covertly, her eyes sliding from the very top of his dark head to his long muscled legs. She saw the material grow taut across his loins and her eyes darted to his in shock.

He had been watching the glow from the candles making light and shadow in her silvery curls and his fingers tingled to play with her hair. He never dreamed her eyes had been watching him harden, and to preserve her modesty he did not want to rise in front of her. "Would you pour me more wine, Jasmine?"

He could see rebellion clearly writ on her face, then very reluctantly she rose and took their goblets to the side table. He warned, "I chose the sweet bottle for you, the other is more potent."

Deliberately she splashed the dry wine into her own chalice and drained it then refilled it from the bottle he had first suggested. She took him his cup with an air of triumph.

He knew she hadn't wanted to serve him. "Thank you, Jasmine, I like a lady with fine manners."

"Fine manors, more likely!" she said tartly.

"Mistress, that is unfair. The Countess of Warwick has broad lands and fine manors and would favor my suit in an instant."

She caught her breath. What lies he told to suit his purpose, and yet . . . and yet . . . she had seen the way Bess Warwick had smiled up at him with open invitation in her face.

"All men are greedy. King John is to keep well over half of Avisa's Gloucester lands. You don't really expect me to believe you'd rather fight for your castles than have them given to you?"

"I am my own man, at my own cost," he said softly. His eyes devoured her, and she was left in no doubt whatsoever what it was he wanted. She again drank off her wine in a reckless attempt to become tipsy. If she became drunk, perhaps she would have the courage to strike a bargain with him. She stood up and walked about his chamber, coming to a stop in front of him, within easy reach if he stretched out a hand. She lifted her hair in a deliciously feminine gesture and let it fall about her shoulders. She ran a provocative tongue about her lips and swayed toward him temptingly. "Milord Falcon, if you will cancel our contract, I will give you anything you want."

He appraised her through narrowed eyes. "If you are offering yourself in return for releasing you from marriage, I do not bribe so easily. You look like a drunken lady of pleasure that I wouldn't bother to lay." His dark eyebrows drew together. "You are flown with wine, get to bed."

Her face flamed with humiliation, but with the pride of a lionness she walked toward the adjoining door. "Go to Hell, de Burgh, or better yet, go to Warwick!"

He bowed and drawled, "Your psychic power grows stronger . . . that is exactly where I am going."

She slammed the door and leaned back against it, panting. "He sent me to bed! Just like a child!"

Estelle sighed. Though Jasmine had no idea, her voice was tinged with regret.

Though de Burgh knocked softly on the chamber door only once, it was opened immediately as if he were expected. Although she wore her bedgown, the Countess of Warwick had not yet retired. She had dismissed her woman early in anticipation of his visit and ordered a large cask of wine. "Thank you, milord," she breathed, and taking his hands she drew him inside and closed the door.

She saw him comfortably seated with a large goblet of wine before she broached her subject. "Falcon, I've been doing a great deal of thinking while I've been at Cirencester this fortnight, and the conclusions I've reached frighten me to death," she said.

"What troubles you, my lady?" he inquired.

"Well, you know I'm a widow, and I make no bones about the fact I'd like to wed again, but I've been in no hurry. I've been taking my own sweet time because the second time a woman marries she should be free to choose so that she will receive some joy from the union."

Falcon kept a wise silence.

"While King Richard reigned he never exercised his royal prerogative over marriage. His permission was totally taken for granted, but now that John reigns, I believe all that will cease. He intends to live in England, and we all know how avaricious *Prince* John was to fill his coffers. *King* John will be twice as bad."

Falcon was wondering if she had heard about de Mandeville when she refilled his glass and confirmed his thoughts.

"I heard today that John has sold Avisa for twenty thousand marks. My God, if he will sell his own wife, it will be a nightmare in this country for an heiress. Women with any land, titles, or estates will be literally put on the auction block and sold and the money go straight into the king's coffers. He will sweep all legalities aside, as he must have done to obtain this divorce so quickly."

"I'm afraid you are right, Bess. Women will go to the highest bidders. You must choose yourself a husband quickly before John comes across the channel."

She sat down opposite him on the bed and as she crossed her long legs, her bedgown fell away to reveal her limbs. "Falcon, if the family of de Burgh united with Warwick, both would have twice its present holdings, twice the wealth, twice the power."

He moved over to the bed and put his arm about her. "Bess, your offer is most generous, but surely you have heard that I am pledged?"

"I've heard different rumors, Falcon. Nothing definite," she said, her mouth only inches below his.

"Then hear it from my own lips. I am going to wed Salisbury's daughter Jasmine."

"Ahhh," she said on a sigh tinged with deep regret for what might have been. "I do understand, Falcon, truly I do." She said it sincerely for she really did understand. Not only was it an exalted connection to link him to the royal family, she could see the irresistible attraction of the exquisite Jasmine for a man as virile as Falcon de Burgh. So fragile, small, and perfect. So innocent, pure, and virginal. Jasmine was indeed a delicate flower no male could resist.

Bess touched his mouth with a provocative finger to trace its outline. "Well," she said huskily, "we aren't going to let whomever we are to marry spoil what could be a very passionate night, are we?"

He flashed her a wicked grin. "Madame, we are not," he said, pressing her back on the bed.

Chapter 11

The next day Jasmine made a tearful farewell to Avisa. Gossip spread like wildfire at Cirencester, and a spiteful maid had made sure Jasmine knew where her betrothed had spent the night.

Hubert and his knights were departing for the Cinque Ports immediately so he could greet King John and his bride when they arrived at Dover. Falcon bade his uncle good-bye and led Jasmine, Estelle, and their packhorses south in the direction of Salisbury.

He was so used to riding at breakneck speed that he

could not adjust to the snail's pace set by Dame Estelle. Alone, he would have swallowed the forty miles to Salisbury without even reining in to give his horse a breather, but he could plainly see that even twenty miles before dark would be an accomplishment. This did nothing for his temper, and coupled with Jasmine's icy demeanor, his patience almost snapped.

The ladies were hungry, thirsty, and tired, but de Burgh's body was not weary, only his mind. He felt no desire for food, wine, or sleep. He craved action. The need for action pressed him on all sides.

Jasmine was determined not to appeal to him to stop. She'd be damned first. Dame Estelle was just about to suggest they find an inn or camp where they were, when de Burgh said, "We'll go to our castle of Hagthorn."

Jasmine and Estelle exchanged amazed glances. They knew they were close to the place they had been set upon and were wildly curious that de Burgh had a castle in the vicinity. Jasmine, however, would not give him the satisfaction of showing him her curiosity, while Estelle rode in silence shrewdly putting two and two together.

Hagthorn was a small castle yet it had rich herds of beef cattle and sheep grazing in the fields about the castle walls. At their approach the evening watch ordered the drawbridge lowered immediately, and the small party rode across the moat into the small bailey. Eager boys ran from the stables to greet the new lord, prompted by de Burgh's knights who were quartered at Hagthorn.

Jasmine was assisted from the saddle with much bowing and scraping. An amused de Burgh took in the attitude of deference. His men had wrought a great change in the place, and he soon realized this had been easy to accomplish because the people of Hagthorn had been cruelly oppressed and were hoping for better treatment from their new master.

The cooks began to rush about preparing a worthy

meal and the servants all flocked to the entrance hall to greet their lord and lady, hoping to get a good look at them and judge for themselves whether their lives would be markedly improved.

Jasmine was pleased to receive such attentions, for at Salisbury she was usually ignored. Three female servants took her luggage and ushered her upstairs, exclaiming over her pretty clothes and exquisite hair. They fussed over whether the master bedchamber was suitable for a lady, to which she quickly pointed out that she was not Lady de Burgh and would require a separate chamber. The women were so visibly disappointed at this disclosure that inexplicably she found herself saying "I will be Lady de Burgh, we are just not married yet." Their smiles returned and she was struck with a disturbing thought. How many female servants were twittering over de Burgh at this moment as they ushered him to his bedchamber? Women, it seemed, were attracted to him as if he had a damned magnet in his chest, she thought with disdain.

Estelle also was receiving her share of attention. Men were coming with hot water to cleanse the dusty travelers and other servants brought clean linen and wood.

One of the women asked shyly, "May we know your name, my lady? We know the new lord is called de Burgh, but we do not know your name."

"My name is Jasmine of Salisbury and this is my grandmother, Dame Estelle Winwood. You say he is the *new* lord? How long has Hagthorn belonged to him?"

"Since the day he stormed the castle an' hanged that wicked Baron Belamé on a beam over where he sat at table. Between one mouthful an' the next! Heavensent he was, like an instrument of God."

A shy young woman carrying wine knocked on the door politely then entered and said hesitantly. "Welcome, my lady. I am Joan. I was married to one of de Belamé's knights until the early spring, but he was killed in a raid."

"Oh, I'm so sorry," said Jasmine, noticing that the woman's clothes were shabby. Indeed all the people at Hagthorn were poorly clothed, the servants clad in no better than rags, in spite of the fact that the castle was well appointed.

"Oh no, my lady, I am happy to be widowed by such a man. I was terrified that I might be taken by de Belamé or another of his knights, but since your great lord's knights have been in charge here, our lives are improved in every way. Milord de Burgh's knights are truly chivalrous. They live by the vows they took."

When Joan and the servants finally withdrew, Jasmine said to Estelle, "Can you believe it? He took possession of this place that day we were set upon. He told me there was a plot to abduct me and force me to wed for my father's money."

Estelle said, "He took a swift revenge. Never underestimate him, Jasmine; he is tough, damned tough."

Jasmine said in awe, "But he stormed a castle and hanged its owner and returned to us in little over an hour. I wonder if he is a warlock?"

"He never misses a chance to scoff at witchcraft, and yet . . . he may have the power and be unaware," Estelle mused.

Jasmine stared at Estelle wide-eyed and whispered, "He has always reminded me of the Devil. You don't suppose he is in league with Satan? He seems to have a power over women."

Estelle said dryly, "Except the one he desires over all others."

"Perhaps that explains why he wants me so much. I'm a witch and a virgin. If he gets power over me, his strength and powers might increase tenfold."

Estelle looked at her for long moments and said cryptically, "Ah, child, if you got him in your power you might control the world, as we know it."

Two hours after their arrival a feast was served them in the dining hall. Falcon and Jasmine sat on a high dais. Directly in front of them at the head table sat Estelle and Falcon's knights. A young man with a harp asked permission to sing a ballad he had composed, and Jasmine was delighted that they were to be entertained. The Countess of Gloucester always had troubadors, jugglers, or dancers in the hall, and Jasmine decided she would have the same when she became chatelaine. The young minstrel sang a praise to de Burgh of his gallant feats, likening him to a falcon who had swept down from the skies upon wings of vengeance and in a single swoop vanquished the evil that had threatened their lives for so long. Then he sang a romantic ballad about Jasmine's ethereal beauty, and though she realized it was a song from his repertoire that could be adjusted to praise any lady present, she clapped with pleasure when he had finished.

Falcon whispered to her, "You look so happy tonight. I hope you won't be disappointed to learn that we will have to stay an extra day. There are so many things that need my attention."

She was surprised at his thoughtfulness. Usually he simply issued her orders or didn't consult her at all. She thought she could afford to be gracious for once. "I don't mind at all. What things are so pressing?" she asked politely.

"There are so many disputes, I'll have to hold a court of law tomorrow. The shepherds and the cowherders are disputing territory. There are prisoners in the cells below whose fates need deciding upon, even servants inside the castle are vying for positions they held before de Belamé replaced them with his own slime."

"I see," she replied.

"Would you like to make some of the decisions, Jasmine?" he asked generously. "This is our castle, not just mine. You sit in judgment on the problems of the castle servants and I'll take care of the rest."

"Oh," she exclaimed, surprised that he was giving her the responsibility. "I will do it!"

"I also must decide which one of my knights to make castellan here," he said as if voicing his thoughts aloud.

Her eyes went to the head table and for the third time during the meal she watched as glances of admiration were exchanged, showing a strong attraction developing between Joan, the young widow she had met, and one of de Burgh's knights. She leaned toward de Burgh and murmured, "Are you considering the tall, fair-haired knight with the mustaches?"

His eyes held hers as he wondered if she had singled out his man because she was attracted to him. He answered somewhat guardedly, "I can see how Sir Rolf would appeal to a woman."

"So can I," said Jasmine, teasing him.

His brows drew together and he deliberately chose the ugly knight sitting next to Estelle. "Rupert there might be the best choice."

Jasmine's eyes danced with amusement as she went on to explain her choice. "I think with a little encouragement on your part Sir Rolf would take to wife the young widow he is so hot for. That way you would not only get a good castellan, but I would get a good chatelaine for Hagthorn in my absence."

His brow cleared and he shot her a guilty grin that acknowledged he had been jealous. "Thank you for your advice, chérie. You are most perceptive."

"The people here are very grateful that you and your knights have treated them kindly."

"We are civilized, my lady, in spite of your misgivings about me," he said, smiling. "I am pleased you have been listening to them. You know the old saying, 'The castle that will parley and the woman who will listen—surrender.' " He took possession of her hand, his strong fingers curling around hers.

She stiffened immediately, withdrew her hand, and turned to ice. "Please don't touch me, it disturbs me."

He laughed and mocked, "That is no way to hold a man off, telling him his nearness disturbs you. Rather it would make him come much closer."

"I never intend to surrender, Falcon de Burgh. You will have to conquer me."

"I have already killed for you," he said, looking intensely into her eyes. "I intend to have you at any cost."

She was the first to lower her gaze. "I am tired. Leave me be, de Burgh."

He arose from the table, stretched, and said mockingly, "Ah, chérie, would you like me to carry you to bed?"

She stood so quickly her chair almost fell backward. "Good night!" she said, her voice dripping with ice.

His hand shot out to take her wrist and hold her beside him. He murmured, "Lady, you will not rush from my side with contempt before everyone in the hall. You will act like a lady, *my* lady, or I will warm your backside here and now. They seemed to enjoy the entertainment with their meal. Would you like to be the encore?"

She stopped dead in her tracks and grew pale. She wanted to throw the contents of her goblet into his face, but dared not. He was far too reckless and thoroughly capable, even willing, to carry out any threat he made.

"Smile at me," he ordered.

Slowly, stiffly, she complied, and he escorted her from the dais with a possessive hand at the small of her back. At her door he left her with a parting shot. "Sorry I cannot come in, but I have an assignation with another."

She opened her mouth and closed it again in frustrated

fury. She flung into her chamber and slammed the door. "I could kill him!" she said through her teeth.

"Admit the truth and shame the Devil," said Estelle. "You enjoy sparring with him."

"I'd enjoy it better if I ever got the last bloody word!" she shouted, taking off her shoes and flinging them across the chamber.

Falcon had purposely misled her about the gender of the one he had an assignation with. In actuality, it was with his knights, to tie up the ends of the business of running Hagthorn.

Rolf spoke up quickly. "I tracked down the priest. He had been hiding in the village with one of the serf's families since de Belamé took over eighteen months ago."

"Good. See that he's moved into the castle quickly and begins his duties immediately. We want to restore the moral tone of Hagthorn as quickly as possible," replied de Burgh. "Which brings me to another point. Rolf, if you fancy the young widow you are bedding you can wed her and become castellan here. But if you would rather escape her toils you may return with me. The choice is yours."

Sir Rolf spoke up eagerly. "I'll stay!"

"Good. I'll also leave Rupert and André here and take you other two back with me. Tomorrow I want you to begin recruiting men-at-arms from Hagthorn and training them in earnest. I may have need of them shortly. William of Salisbury has been made head of the armies and intends to place five hundred mercenaries in my command. No doubt they'll require a deal of training also before they measure up to my standards."

Rupert announced, "We hanged three cohorts of de Belamé. The people came forward and accused them of such horrendous crimes, we had no choice, but there are others whose fate we left up to you. One of them, the old

castellan, swears he has information with which he will
be able to buy his life from you."

"Did you find de Belamé's coffers?" asked de Burgh.

"We looked high and low but found nothing," replied
Rolf.

"Then the old castellan must know where the monies
are hidden. I have legal jurisdiction to hold a baron's
court tomorrow. I'll decide everything there. I bid you
good night." He winked at Rolf. "I wish you joy of her."

Jasmine awoke eager for the day's events. She summoned every servant in the castle to attend her in the
hall. Clad in her richest gown and bolstered by Dame
Estelle and the crystal ball, she climbed the dais to hold
sway. She liked the feeling it gave her. Every eye was
riveted upon her, every ear pricked to catch her words.
As the cook related the event to her husband later that
night, she said, "The room was so quiet, you could have
heard a cockroach fart!"

Jasmine, after a cursory glance into the crystal ball,
held up her hands and said, "I see a wedding celebration
soon. The lady Joan will marry one of my future husband's knights and you will take your directions from her
in my absence."

Estelle whispered, "Are you guessing?"

Jasmine's eyes sparkled. "You taught me one of the
strongest tools of witchcraft is the power of suggestion. I
have sown the magic seed." She raised her voice. "Let us
proceed to the first dispute."

Two enormously fat women stood before her, their
faces bright red from the strength of the emotions involved. They were head cooks by profession and, as custom dictated, their bulk attested to the quality of their
culinary ability. The first one spoke up. "My lady, I was
head cook of Hagthorn before the evil de Belamé came
here and set *her* up in the job." She felt confident that she

would be restored, as practically every other server of the dreaded de Belamé had already been deposed by the new knights.

Jasmine turned her attention to the other fat woman to hear what she would say. "I do my job well, my lady. I am a better cook than her. In fact, I could cook better than her stood on my head with my hands tied behind my back!"

Jasmine saw the graphic picture she painted and could not conceal a peal of merriment at so fat a woman in so ridiculous a position. "The meal we had last night was excellent," decided Jasmine. "I see no need to replace the present head cook."

At her words, one red face beamed, the other looked as if it would burst. Jasmine added quickly, "I have, however, a most important post to be filled and feel you are an excellent candidate for the position." She inclined her head toward Estelle. "Dame Winwood knows the magical properties of all plants. Go to the stillroom with her now and she will instruct you in herbal medicine so that you will be able to minister to the health and welfare of all at Hagthorn." She had said the words that enabled the second red face to beam.

Jasmine passed judgment on all the other disputes of the castle servants, most of which dealt with the pecking order. When all was decided, she held up her hands again for silence. "Which of you women are good seamstresses?" she asked. Half a dozen stepped forward and then four others hesitantly held up their hands. "I have noticed that all who serve at Hagthorn would benefit from new clothes." There was a murmur of delight as she continued. "I should like all those who serve in the hall to wear a livery in a cheerful color, perhaps yellow or green, definitely not brown." She had gotten the idea of livery from the Countess of Gloucester, whose servants were all uniformed. "Anyone who has a messy job to perform shall receive a smock as well as a new outfit of clothes." She smiled at them knowing she had won their hearts. She decided that at the royal court she would assist the little queen to make decisions. Jasmine was acquiring a taste for power.

That night the meal served surpassed the one the night before, and at table Jasmine told Falcon of her day's decisions. Somewhat hesitantly she added that she had promised all the castle servants new clothing.

He silently appraised her and when she thought he was about to refuse the money to purchase the cloth, her stubborn chin went up, her eyes flashed, and she said, "De Burgh, you are a s—"

He leaned close and murmured a warning, "Make your words soft and sweet, chérie, in case you have to eat them."

". . . you can be a generous and understanding lord when you choose. I hope you will not disappoint these people."

He grinned at her, knowing she would like nothing better than to slap him. He said quietly, "It's a good thing I discovered a treasure trove of gold last night the way you have squandered my money today. Just think, if I'd allowed you to tempt me into your chamber last night, I might never have uncovered the hoard."

He was baiting her into a sharp retort, but she was aware of his intent and sighed prettily, "Ah, milord, my loss was your gain."

His teeth flashed. He was pleased that she joined his game. He bantered, "My gain could be your gain. I also discovered a jewel or two secreted away. One in particular would match your beauty. 'Tis a flower of diamonds and sapphires on a fine chain." He paused and whispered suggestively, "You have a jewel I desire . . . we could come to some arrangement perhaps."

Her eyes flashed with silver ice, then she quickly veiled

them, her lashes brushing her cheeks as she murmured, "Ah, Sir Falcon, my jewel is more precious than yours."

"What if," he said boldly, "your jewel is a myth like that unicorn you ride? Things are seldom what they appear. You look so pure and virginal and yet I know I spoke to you at a bacchanalia at Stonehenge once."

Her eyes flew wide. Why was he himself there unless he had been practicing Devil worship? She shivered as a thin thread of hatred ran through her. She put up her chin and said, "I grow tired of being pricked by your words."

"When I prick you with my weapon your virginity will be proven," he said mockingly.

She was damned if she would let him have the last word this time. Her wicked juices bubbled over and she said cruelly, "I hope I am barren; I think I would hate your child as much as I hate you."

The banter and mockery were gone. His hard gaze bored into her, while at the same time his hand crushed down over hers. "Apologize!" he commanded.

She thought he might crush the fragile bones, yet still she was reckless enough to fight him. "I'm sorry, milord . . . I'm sorry I will hate your child."

Suddenly she felt herself swung up into his arms like a piece of Viking booty. He strode from the hall, leaving the onlookers agog with their mouths open. Tonight he did not stop at the chamber door, but swung inside and slammed the door loudly to warn Estelle he wanted no interference.

He dropped her onto the bed. "Your backside needs warming. A damned good thrashing followed by a good bedding will go a long way to curbing your impudent tongue." He sat down quickly beside her on the bed and dragged her facedown across his hard thighs. He pulled up her dress and shift, yanked down her drawers, and

brought his hand down in a stinging slap on her bare
flesh.

Jasmine cried out, but he brought his hand down again
a second time. She was very frightened. She knew he
hadn't the faintest notion of how much the slaps had hurt
her. She twisted over in his lap and flung her arms about
his neck. "No please, I beg you, don't beat me, milord.
'Twas only a game to see who could make the cruelest
remark."

"You are very deceiving, Jasmine. You appear to be
soft and sweet as an angel, yet your tongue can be as
cutting as a sharp sword. You dazzle a man's eyes and
wits with your ethereal beauty, but the moment he is
drawn close to your warm glow, you turn to ice and
freeze his blood in his veins. Because you are small and
pretty you have been used to having all your own way.
Well, I see through your lovely façade. . . . I know you
are headstrong as ten men. You are all sweetness and
light so long as you are getting all your own way, but the
moment someone comes along with a stronger will than
yours, you turn mean as a spoiled child who refuses to
play anymore."

"You paint a very flawed picture of me, sir. Too bad
you haven't as clear a picture of yourself!" she said
boldly, removing herself from his lap. "Why, you are
more used to having your own way than I am. Because
you have never encountered another who was stronger or
more dominant than yourself, you overrule everyone. Because you are a natural leader of men and because every
slut who sets eyes on your physique falls on her back for
you, you think you have the God-given right to take me
and bend me into anything you desire."

He appraised her through narrowed eyes. Her breasts
rose and fell temptingly with her agitation. His desire
could not be held in check much longer. "When we are
wed, Jasmine, I will be your lord and master and I will

have the God-given right to take you and bend you into anything I desire."

Her anger flared at his ruthless male attitude. "Some women may enjoy being treated like dirt, but I am not one of them. 'Tis a strange wooing where you try to win my affections by comparing me to a spoiled child each time we meet."

"A better analogy would be a spirited, unbroken filly. The trick will be to tame you without breaking your spirit."

She gave a little shriek. "Now I'm a filly! You'll have me eating out of your hand in no time."

He pulled her hard against him, anger and lust flaring up until he was crazed with the desire to make her submit to him. His hands stroked down her back to the base of her spine, then very deliberately he took hold of her buttocks and rubbed her body against his hard, pulsing erection. His hot mouth moved up her throat. "Jassy, yield to me!" His mouth was on hers, forcing his entrance between her soft pink lips. As his tongue plunged into her, she knew his shaft would soon be ravishing her other soft pink lips. Desperately she reached down and put her hand over his arousal to shield her mons from its onslaught. As he felt her hand enclose him, he took in a ragged breath and groaned aloud with pure pleasure. The moment his hands slackened she pulled from him and ran across the chamber.

"Why do you run from me?" he demanded, closing the gap between them in three strides.

"Because I fear you. Because you struck me before and would do so again if the whim took you. Because I'm smaller, weaker, softer. Because I have no weapons, no strength, and cannot defend myself in any way against you!"

At her words his heart softened, yet he was disgusted with himself that he had failed to properly teach her a lesson. He said almost contemptuously, "You're too delicate to beat and too fragile to fuck! I'd have to restrain myself too much." He slammed from the room and though she was relieved, she was also very stung by his contempt and angry that once again he had had the last word.

Chapter 12

King John would rule from London, and that is where the royal court would reside. People were flocking there from every corner of England, and Jasmine was deep in preparation for her journey. She was going with her father's blessing and Falcon's grudging permission, and she needed a sumptuous new wardrobe as befitted the niece of the king. Naturally Estelle would accompany her, and the older woman was having new clothes of her own fitted. Although she would never have admitted such a thing, the new garments were a source of pleasure. Estelle was also distilling a large supply of potions and electuaries. She compounded medicines and simples and gathered roots, seeds, flowers, leaves, and barks to take with her to London.

Jasmine had come to the stillroom for some rose petals, lavender, and cloves to pack between the layers of her new dresses. She was still tender from Falcon's spanking and could still feel the impression of his hand against her bare flesh. Her grandmother said, "Tomorrow is the twenty-first day of June, the summer solstice. We must go to Stonehenge. Every year I have gone alone, but this year I will let you have the life-giving magical power. When the first summer sunlight shines upon you through the great arch of Stonehenge, you will be surrounded and protected by the great white light of the universe for one whole year."

Falcon de Burgh passed by the stillroom window and heard Jasmine's silvery laughter. He heard her say, "If we ride out, we are sure to be followed. Why don't we take the little boat on the Avon to gather cattails and waterlilies? None will suspect us of going to Stonehenge."

On the spot he decided that he would take the time to be at Stonehenge before them. He hoped that Jasmine was not involved in live sacrifice. The practice went against his nature and was most distasteful to him.

It was still dark when Falcon de Burgh tethered his horse in a copse at least a mile from Stonehenge. His long legs carried him to the ancient Druid circle before the first light of dawn, and on impulse he scaled the side of one craggy rock and lay down atop the flat stone arch. The sun was just climbing above the horizon when he spotted the two women. His high vantage point allowed him to watch them walk all the way from the river.

Estelle wore a strange garment decorated on the front with the four elements of the natural kingdom—human, animal, vegetable, and mineral—and upon the back with the four elements—earth, air, fire, and water.

Jasmine wore a loose robe embroidered with sunflowers. The sunrise was a spectacular one, bathing everything in a light of pure gold. Falcon watched as Dame Winwood positioned Jasmine in what seemed to be an exact and predetermined spot, then to his amazement Estelle stepped away and took Jasmine's garment from her.

Jasmine stood naked, motionless, waiting for the Divine Power. Falcon was entranced. She was the most beautiful vision he had ever beheld. His gaze was riveted where her thighs joined her belly. Just above the pubic area on either side of the curls of her mons venus were two identical small, black beauty marks. They were symmetrical and had a mesmerizing effect, for whenever his eyes lifted to devour the rest of her, they were pulled back irresistibly to the intimate triangle. He knew such beauty spots were sometimes called witches' marks and Jasmine had not one, but two.

Suddenly the rays of the sun shone through the arch of the Druid stones, bathing her with an unearthly, ethereal luminescence. Her hair, falling to her hips, looked like pure molten gold that was somehow on fire.

He heard Estelle's voice chanting.

"Harness the power—a golden opportunity—bright with promise. The sun is the most important life-sustaining element on earth, bringing growth, attainment, success, joy, and happiness."

To Falcon's eyes, Jasmine glowed with a light-filled essence that made the air about her take on a sheen. She was bathed in sunlight so that her own aura and that of the sun were joined. Then the sun moved higher in the sky, and immediately Estelle pulled Jasmine away and wrapped her in the sunflower robe before she could be touched by the stone's great shadow.

Falcon lay atop the great slab long after they had departed. Jasmine was different from all other women. Special, pure, angelic, perfect. He dreamed of her almost every night and fantasized about her every day. She triggered sensations in his body and mind. Between her legs was like a flower blossom; making love to her would be like penetrating the lotus and discovering precious jade. The anticipation of waiting for her carried an unbearable tension. He was constantly in a state of physical arousal these days. Everything that subtly reminded him of her sent desire flaming through him. A scent, a voice, a thought. His bed had never been so empty, and yet the very feel of the sheets upon his body was like an aphrodisiac. Somehow, he knew that with her, sex would be magic; sex would be supreme power.

* * *

It was the longest day of the year, and after dinner Falcon asked Jasmine if she would walk with him in the gardens. She had known, of course, that before she departed for London he would insist upon being alone with her. She anticipated that his masculinity would force him to lay down prescribed rules of behavior for her to follow during their long absence from each other. Jasmine was determined to keep her temper under control. She would be amenable to his suggestions, silver-tongued in her answers to him, and try to look poignantly regretful that they were parting. Once she was in London, of course, she would do exactly as she pleased.

Twilight lingered long in the garden at Salisbury. The shadows gathered under the trees, the swallows swooped low to catch the last insects before dark, and the fragrance of the night-scented stocks stole to them from the borders at the edge of the lawn. Her nearness affected him physically, as it always did, and he crushed down the urge to lay her in the cool grass.

They stopped walking and faced each other. There were a million things he wanted to say to her, a thousand love words he wished to murmur, a hundred kisses he longed to steal, a dozen places he yearned to touch, but in the end he said, "Court is a worldly place, Jasmine. Don't let its evil touch you. It pleases me that you have known no men." He reached out and took a tendril of her hair between his finger and thumb and quivered at the silky, sensual feel of it. He cupped her face with his hands and dipped his head to brush her soft pink mouth with his lips.

She fought the urge to stiffen and resist him, and after his persuasive mouth had possessed hers for a full minute she managed to melt against him, reasoning that it could not hurt to thaw toward him a little in face of the long spell of freedom she would be able to enjoy after that night.

He lifted his mouth from hers but held her captive against his heart. His scarred thumbs brushed the lovely curve of her cheeks. The magic of the garden enfolded them in a perfumed paradise. He breathed, "Ah, Jasmine, you are fairer than any flower that blooms here tonight. You beg to be plucked, but should any hand but mine reach out to take so fair a blossom, I hope you would tear it to shreds with a multitude of thorns." He took both her hands into his and, lifting them to his mouth, dropped a kiss upon each dainty wrist. Then his arms encircled her in a captive embrace.

She could feel the heat of his hands on her back through the material of her gown and for a fleeting moment imagined his hands on her bare flesh, beneath her back, as he would lie with her in the marriage bed. She shuddered as his tongue invaded her soft mouth and knew not if it were in repulse or response. She was agonizingly aware of the peril she was in. His physical response to her was overwhelming him, and soon he would overwhelm her. She gasped softly. "No, Falcon, no." She was smothered by his nearness and could not breathe. She struggled against the close contact of his hard, muscular chest. "Let me go!" She trembled and pushed with all her might against his wide shoulders.

Suddenly he swept her up into his arms, one arm beneath her knees. Greatly alarmed, she cried, "Where are you taking me?"

He buried his face in her hair and murmured thickly, "I'm carrying you up to my bed, sweet, I can wait no longer."

"Falcon, don't spoil this beautiful last night in the garden for me. I want it to linger on in my memory, unspoiled by your forcing my body to satisfy your quickly aroused lust," she said on a rising note of panic.

Reluctantly Falcon withdrew the arm he had beneath her knees, allowing her feet to touch the grass again. As she tried to pull away from him, she was mortified to see that the material of her bodice was snared upon a fastening of his doublet and had torn to expose one of her breasts. He groaned and his lips immediately sought the tempting swell of the round globe.

"My lord, you mustn't do such scandalous things," she choked. "I must bid you good night."

A strong hand kept her anchored close to him. "Does it not excite you to do scandalous things?" he teased.

"No! I must go now," she insisted, "for 'tis plain you cannot keep your hands to yourself."

"If I promise not to touch you further, will you stay with me longer?"

"Why?" she asked, not trusting him.

"I get pleasure from just watching you, looking at you," he said, drawing her toward a bench in a secluded garden alcove.

She laughed nervously. "You will soon tire and grow bored watching me, I am sure."

He sat down and drew her down beside him, occupying his hands with hers so they would not wander to more intimate places. "I could watch you all night. I want to watch you sleep . . . I want to watch you dance . . . I want to watch you bathe . . . I want to watch you dress, for the sheer pleasure of undressing you so you will have to start all over."

"You mustn't say these things to me, it is most unseemly!" she protested sharply.

"Jasmine, I want to be unseemly with you . . . I want you to be unseemly with me. Just think of all the lovers who have sat here in this garden before us," he murmured.

"We are not lovers!" she pointed out.

"We could be, sweetheart. Yield to me, Jassy," he whispered urgently.

She tried for a light note to escape his intense purpose. "Ah, milord, a year will pass so quickly and then you will have your way and drag me off to your Mountain Ash and I will yield to you."

"A year?" A look of thunder descended upon his brow and his voice was like a whiplash. "Three months, mistress. Make no mistake, you will be wed to me in three months unless I'm in Hellfire!"

She watched him stalk off, his cloak swinging to his heels. He had delivered his ultimatum, as usual giving her no room to argue her case. He went directly to her father and told William he would let Jasmine play lady-in-waiting until the autumn and then they would wed. Finally he sought out Dame Winwood and issued her a list of dos and don'ts concerning Jasmine and her safety, which almost made the old woman's head spin.

William of Salisbury escorted his daughter to the City of London where King John and his child-bride, Isabella of Angoulême, had arrived and taken up residence at Westminster Palace. At first sight, Jasmine was awed by its size, but she noted Dame Estelle calmly took it in stride and so she tried to do likewise. She reasoned that if she felt intimidated, how much more so must the little Isabella feel?

Jasmine and Estelle were given rooms on different floors at Westminster since Jasmine had been chosen to be a lady of the bedchamber and Estelle's status had not yet been established.

William went off to closet himself with John while Estelle unpacked and Jasmine tried to make Feather and Quill accustomed to their new home. She met the two attendants Isabella had brought with her from Angoulême and felt sorry for the two little mites. They were hardly more than children and both had tear-swollen faces from homesickness. A few motherly women had been appointed to guide and advise Isabella at Westminster Palace in everything from dress to religion, but rumor had it that the little queen had taken one look at them and dismissed them immediately, likening them to a flight of bats.

Jasmine was slightly shocked that such a young girl was not heavily chaperoned, especially since she was in the delicate position of being married but not yet old enough for the marriage to be consummated. She felt protective toward the young girl before she had even met her.

Isabella occupied a large suite of rooms that adjoined the sumptuous suite chosen by King John. Jasmine tried to close her ears to the gossip concerning the king, which flew fast and furious about the royal halls of Westminster Palace. She had been warned that court was a cesspool of venomous gossip and discounted every lurid thing she heard. Such things couldn't possibly have any truth in them anyway. Jasmine was about to experience a severe shock.

The first morning she was on duty, she arose at dawn. She sang happily as she bathed and dressed in a white silk underdress over which Estelle helped her don a tunic embroidered all over with pink and golden thread. She had been given strict instructions that the queen liked to sleep late and did not want to arise before ten o'clock. At that precise hour Jasmine took the queen's breakfast tray from a servant, knocked lightly, and entered the bedchamber. She set the tray on a side table and drew back the heavy drapes from the tall windows. Light flooded in, revealing the untidiest room Jasmine had ever beheld. Clothes were strewn about everywhere and the bed was in tumbled chaos. A small, dark head emerged from the disarray to demand, "Who are you?"

Jasmine stared at the vivid beauty of the child-woman. Her eyes were large, black, with great fringed lashes, her head was a mass of tousled black silk curls, and her luscious mouth was red as a strawberry.

Jasmine curtsied gracefully before the young girl. "Queen Isabella, I am Jasmine, daughter of King John's brother, William of Salisbury."

The little girl clapped her hands. "Good! I like to have royalty about me." She sat up and stretched like a cat. She threw off the bedclothes, totally unmindful of her nakedness, licked her fingers, and thrust them between her legs, manipulating herself furiously.

Jasmine was so horrified at the self-abuse she cried, "Queen Isabella, you must not do that!" as if she were addressing a naughty child rather than the Queen of England.

Isabella's fingers slowed in surprise. She was torn between anger and amusement. Finally her sultry laughter bubbled out. "Why not? It feels delicious! I do it every morning. Aha, it must be true what they say about English girls being frigid as icicles." She stroked herself again and said, "Don't you do this, English?"

"No!" Jasmine gasped.

The girl laughed again. "Why not?"

Jasmine's face was crimson with her embarrassment. How could she explain to the little queen that she would damage her maidenhead; that when she matured to womanhood and the king consummated the union he would think her unchaste if she did not bleed. Finally with Isabella's dark, amused eyes upon her, she said simply, "It is bad!"

Isabella was off gasping and rolling about the bed, doubled over with laughter. "I love bad things. That is why John is insatiable for me!"

Jasmine ceased to think. A veiled curtain was drawn across her mind as stiffly she took the tray, laid it upon the rumpled bed, curtsied low, and walked from the chamber. She walked rapidly, not caring where she went. All she knew was that she must get outside for some fresh air.

Gradually in the courtyard amid the bustle of castle life she became aware of her surroundings. The place was alive with merchants, servants, clergy, guards, dogs, horses, carts, and wagons. She walked on to seek a more secluded place to rearrange her thoughts and came to a herb garden with apple and quince trees. The color in her cheeks subsided and she reached up to pick an apple. Suddenly a hand was there before hers. It deftly plucked the fruit and held it out to her.

"Oh!" she said breathlessly.

"My lady, I did not mean to startle you," said the polite young man. "You are Jasmine of Salisbury, I know your father William. Permit me to introduce myself. I am Will Marshal. As is yours, my father is rather important," he said with a faint, deprecating smile.

"I am lady-in-waiting to the new queen," she said quietly.

"Poor lady," murmured Will. "I am one of King John's squires. I've served him since I was a small boy and he was still Prince John. I take sanctuary in this garden also." Their eyes met. Each knew the other had been besmirched by the one they served. She wanted to ask him so many questions, but of course propriety forbade her. He wanted to warn her of the corruption she must witness, but found it impossible to defile her ears with even a hint. Finally he touched her hand comfortingly, they smiled at each other, and departed.

Her father sought her out before he left London. Already the realm was in an uproar and he was deeply concerned, but he tried to look carefree as he bade the two women farewell.

Dame Winwood was too shrewd by half and soon had him voicing his concerns. "The King of France is ambitious to extend his power over the whole of that country and is naturally taking full advantage of the hostility to John of the barons of Normandy, Anjou, and Poitou."

"The barons who wanted Arthur for their king?" asked Estelle.

He nodded. "King Louis has summoned King John to attend a feudal court made up of the dukes and counts of France. Naturally John has refused. I go now to recruit the northern barons of England for war."

Jasmine asked, "Does de Burgh go north with you?"

"Yes, thank God. He's the best leader of men I ever saw."

"Does John go with you?" asked Estelle.

"No," said William. "He needs money and he will go about the business of getting it." He looked grim. "He's the best usurer I ever knew. God help us all," he murmured.

The vast dining hall at Westminster Palace was hot and overcrowded. Estelle and Jasmine joined the throng of diners and got their first glimpse of the new king. Jasmine was startled by her uncle's appearance. Her father was a big, bluff man with fair hair who bore a slight resemblance to his late brother Richard, who had been a large man with red hair. John was under medium height and extremely dark. He was so handsome that his face was almost beautiful, but he was vain to a fault, strutting and posturing in an exaggerated manner. He was flamboyantly dressed in brilliant colors with many jewels and even wore his crown to dine. His voice was loud, his laughter bordered on manic, and his language was most profane.

He had surrounded himself by sycophants who laughed every time he said a filthy word. He taunted the servants with his power and enjoyed their cringing. Isabella sat beside him, mimicking him in everything. It was plain to see she was a vain, self-indulgent, precocious *enfant terrible* who had fallen in love with herself at an early age and would never get over the infatuation. She carried a hand mirror on a long chain and glanced into it constantly.

Apparently both king and queen cared only for pleasure, as dozens of minstrels, jugglers, acrobats, and dancing girls performed continuously among the diners. Ribaldry and coarseness were the order of the day at the royal court of King John and Queen Isabella.

Suddenly King John stood and raised his goblet. "My father used to offer this toast to my mother after he had imprisoned her: "The pox, blue balls, and lice, I've had 'em all, by Jesus Christ. But there's no soap this side of Hell to wash away that fishy smell. Gentlemen . . . the queen!"

Jasmine and Estelle exchanged glances of distaste. Estelle murmured, "I must find a vulnerability in him that I can exploit to give me some measure of control. It is certain we don't want to be in his power. Remember, Jasmine, one of the tenets of witchcraft—in any encounter between two people, one is dominant, one submits. The difference is fear!"

Tonight the heads of all the great London guilds were being entertained, but the reason for King John's hospitality became clear midway through the meal when he revealed that he expected a huge contribution from the guilds to the crown. The men became highly indignant at the sum suggested, and one even went so far as to voice his opinion that there was a difference between gifts or contributions and outright bribes.

Easily angered and always on a short fuse, King John gave vent to the infamous Plantagenet temper, which quickly rose to fury and rapidly escalated to violence. It was a performance that outdid any juggler or acrobat. He went red in the face, shouted and gesticulated wildly, made insane threats, then fell to the floor and bit the rushes. His closest adherents closed ranks about him, though not too close, as those who were accustomed to King John's rages knew there was nothing to do but wait them out.

Estelle clutched Jasmine's wrist and whispered, "My God, the Plantagenet temper brings on fits. He has a form of epilepsy and doesn't even know it." She smiled with satisfaction. "Here is John's vulnerability handed me on a silver platter!"

"A distillation of lily-of-the-valley taken in wine will control it," said Jasmine, as if reading from her herbal.

"Exactly," said Estelle. "Run quickly and fetch some from my medicine case, but tell no one the magic potion we use on him."

Dame Winwood elbowed her way through the circle of attendants. Acting with supreme authority, with great confidence she took up a silver spoon from the table, knelt at the king's side, and slipped the handle of the spoon crosswise in his mouth. The people crowding about were in awe of her for having the courage to touch John when he was in one of his rages. The whispers began that this was the witch with such strong magic powers they'd heard about.

Jasmine returned and emptied the distillate of lily-of-the-valley into the king's wine cup and handed it to Estelle. After only one mouthful she noticed that John's heels ceased to drum upon the floor and after the second his color receded from an alarming purple to a flushed pink. Suddenly John was on his feet as if nothing had happened. The London guildsmen hastily agreed to pay their tributes and the servants rushed in to clear the tables.

Though no words were exchanged, Estelle caught

John's gaze and held it for a full minute. A small part of his mind was now hypnotically under her spell. Before he retired for the night, Estelle was summoned to his private apartments. When they were entirely alone he said, "My brother William has told me of you, Dame Winwood, and how you predicted that I would become the next king. You have the sight, and you have the knowledge and power that go with it."

Estelle sent William a silent thanks and offered her services to the king. She dwelled at great length upon his favorite subject, himself. With the shrewdness of one who has lived a thousand lives and experienced everything all down through the ages, she held John's attention. "I know your secret," she said simply. This covered the gamut of sins he had committed since boyhood. She stripped him to the core of his black soul with those four words, and she did so with such total conviction he was left speechless. Having reduced him to less than nothing, she began to build his ego again. "Many great leaders and rulers of the world have been afflicted as you are. Alexander the Great—Julius Caesar—Charlemagne."

He was riveted to her words now. She had her hook well into him, now all she had to do was make herself totally indispensable. "Your seizures set you apart . . . make you unique. There is, however, the danger of death everpresent with this royal affliction, so it is imperative you always have the distillate and someone who knows how to administer it."

"Dame Winwood, you have wisdom that goes beyond the ordinary. I make you privy to my person at all times of the day and night, and of course you will always be part of my entourage when I travel."

Estelle was satisfied she had convinced him that he could not do without her.

Chapter 13

Jasmine made sure that she was not the one to awaken the young queen in the mornings. She arrived in time to aid with her toilet, help her to dress and to put the queen's elaborate clothes away in an orderly fashion.

When she heard the little queen squeal, she came out of Isabella's closet and once again received a great shock. Apparently King John had come to visit the queen's bed-chamber. The moment he had come through the door Isabella jumped upon him, squealing. She wrapped her legs about his back and he swung her about the room laughing until they were both breathless. They fell upon the great bed and Jasmine was stunned to see Isabella reach out to massage the bulge between John's legs. "Mmm, is that big, hard weapon for me, your High-ness?" teased Isabella.

John's face was tight with lust as he pulled the little girl atop of him and said, "Come and fellate me, Bella."

Jasmine left the room quickly and quietly. In her haste she almost bumped into young Will Marshal who was just quitting King John's private apartment.

"Are you all right, Lady Jasmine?" he asked, concerned.

"Yes, no, I . . . oh Will, I had no idea they cohab-ited."

He said quietly, "You are shocked because he is thirty-two and she is only fourteen, but really, my lady, age has little to do with it. They are voluptuaries; two of a kind. They are like two peas from the same disgusting pod." He led her away from the royal apartments. "Let's take a walk under the quince trees. There is little that is evil in a garden."

"Will, what does 'fellate' mean?" she asked quietly.

He shook his head. "I would not soil your ears with an explanation, my lady. But I am happy when he sleeps with Isabella for she cannot be corrupted. She is wiser than Eve in the ways of men. He likes young girls, virgins; he enjoys the fear on their faces. Their cringing and pitiful cries excite his lust."

"He does these things with you as witness?" she asked, shocked again.

"That part he really enjoys. I was brought up so respectably. My father and mother set such store in strict moral conduct. The king enjoys my discomfort. It is his only way of getting at the great Marshal of England, even though he does it vicariously through me, his son."

"Your father would run mad if he knew what you were exposed to," she said.

"As would yours. Never be alone with King John, my lady."

As Jasmine took leave of young Will, her mind was filled with Falcon de Burgh. He would be outraged when he discovered what this court was like. He would physically remove her from the place. The whole court was contaminated. The evil lurked in the collective consciousness, threatening, insinuating. There were subterranean undercurrents, the vibrations tangible enough to smell and almost taste. All seemed shrouded in shadowy mists of dread.

That night she visited Estelle in her chamber and finally summoned enough courage to ask, "What does 'fellate' mean?"

Estelle looked long and hard into her eyes, then sighed. "Come and sit down while I explain these things. You know of the sex act that takes place between a man and a woman. I told you of it when you had your first flux. I did not tell you of other things men like. Probably the most erotic act a woman can practice on a man is fellatio.

You go down upon his shaft with your mouth and bring him to climax by sucking him and licking him with your tongue. It is a whore's trick. Most men must pay a whore for this service because they wouldn't ask it of their wives. Peasants and men-at-arms prefer their sex straight, it is only the nobility who indulge in these practices. There are many other perversions. I suppose I had better educate you for your own protection."

As Jasmine listened to Estelle's lurid accounts of men's sexual appetites and the lengths to which they would go to appease them, she became quiet and subdued.

She shrank from being Isabella's lady-of-the-bedchamber and resolved to do something about it. As Estelle had used her wits to make herself indispensable to the king, so would she, Jasmine, make herself indispensable to the queen in a way that would remove her from the intimacy of the bedchamber. She discussed her plan with her grandmother and listened to her shrewd advice.

"Now that I have been endorsed by the king, I can make myself a small fortune at this court. When I am too old and tired to practice my craft I will be able to afford to live out the rest of my days in luxurious comfort. I shall charge a high price for my spells, potions, charms, and predictions. If I sold only aphrodisiacs, abortificants, and cures for impotence I would be a rich woman, and I need only give exactly the same as I gave the villagers at Winwood Keep."

Jasmine said, "Isabella is so totally absorbed with thoughts of herself that I can make a full-time job for myself simply reading the tarot cards for her, or gazing into the crystal ball and predicting her future. I think I should have another talent that will amuse her, such as palm reading or astrology."

"Astrology is very involved and convoluted, and I believe I heard that the king has his own astronomer from the days when he was prince. Palm reading, on the other hand, would be very simple for one with your perception. Here, let me show you."

The two women sat up until the small hours, honing their magic skills layer by layer, knowing instinctively that the allure of the unknown and mysterious added a forbidden yet irresistible desire to indulge in the occult. Isabella would easily fall for the witch's trick—Jasmine would get her hook in to capture her interest immediately, then she could tell her any yarn. People, especially queens, never tired of hearing about themselves.

King John went from rage to rage at the news he was receiving from the Continent, so Estelle had her hands full. Since the king had refused to attend the feudal court to which the King of France had summoned him, Louis now declared King John's territories were forfeited by feudal law. He had already marched into Normandy, Anjou, Maine, and Poitou and taken them immediately into his own hands. John had not the guts to sweep across the channel and challenge him. Instead he sought money with which to pay mercenaries to do the job for him.

King John had a backlog of thousands of cases of law to be settled by the king's court. He gave his new justices orders that people could buy their way out of punishment by paying large fines. Every dispute over land was settled in favor of whoever gave the king the biggest present of money. He decreed that all heiresses needed his permission to marry and sold them as he had Avisa, to the highest bidder. If he heard a widow had no wish to marry, he dug up a husband for her so she would pay him to leave her in peace. Even cities were expected to give bribes. Finally, his baseness knowing no bounds, he ordered that all Jews be arrested and imprisoned; they would be freed again only if they paid the huge sum of ten thousand marks apiece.

John was making a mockery out of the fine system of

law his father had spent a lifetime establishing. The barons were already outraged and, it was rumored, were holding secret meetings. Their worst fears had been confirmed. King John was untruthful, dishonest, and treacherous. He was also profane, tyrannical, and violent.

Jasmine liked her new role at court decidedly better than the old one. Queen Isabella was intrigued by the idea of having her tarot cards read every day. Since no cards were to be found at Westminster, Jasmine was designing and painting Isabella her very own set of cards. The deck contained seventy-eight cards, twenty-two in the major arcana and fifty-six in the minor arcana. She wisely painted Isabella's likeness on to the faces of the four queens and the empress and used her own countenance for the card known as the high priestess. She painted John's likeness onto the four kings and also, to amuse Isabella, she used John's likeness for the Devil.

So eager was the young queen for Jasmine to finish the cards, she often hung over her shoulder as she sat with her brushes, painting the brilliant mystic symbols. Isabella's face was always vividly eager, lighted with laughter. Giggling, she referred to the cards as the Devil's pasteboards. Isabella was too impatient to wait until the cards were ready to learn her future, so after much pressing and veiled threats Jasmine reluctantly agreed to perform the ritual crystal gazing. The performance was set for midnight in the queen's bedchamber. The maids were pressed to find thirteen green candles, and Estelle produced a silver wine goblet a foot tall, embossed in gold with a lion and a unicorn rampant.

Each passing day had brought more nobles to court petitioning John for lands, titles, and castles. Their ladies came with them, agog to see young Queen Isabella, the child-woman with the reputation of a voluptuary.

As midnight approached, Isabella allowed only a handful of ladies into her chamber—the ones who heaped flattery upon her vain head or gifted her with expensive jewels. Dozens of others who were excluded started vicious rumors of what was actually to take place in the queen's private bedchamber, and inevitably the whispers reached King John's ears. He would wait until half-past midnight, then force the door to the queen's chambers to see for himself the vice in which Isabella indulged.

With an air of solemnity Jasmine lighted the thirteen green candles and glided into the magic circle. The candles' glow made her transparent silver robe shimmer about her nakedness. With a grace and leisure that made it appear that a trance had already transported her to another plane, Jasmine lifted the wine chalice and held it high. Her voice was like chiming, silvery bells as she chanted: "Earth and Water, Air and Fire, Wand and Pentacle and Sword. Work ye unto my desire, harken ye unto my word!"

An eerie silence descended upon the room as all held their breath to hear the words. Jasmine knew the high drama she created and stretched the dramatic silence to its limit, then she quaffed deeply from the magnificent wine goblet and stretched her fingers wide over the crystal ball. As the inside of the ball began to glow and swirl with smoke, a collective gasp was heard about the room. Then she began shrewdly, carefully omitting any specific names.

"The most beautiful woman in this room has left behind her a broken heart. I see a handsome young nobleman who sits with saddened countenance because his heart is weeping with tears of blood." She paused dramatically. She would make the picture beautifully poignant. "He is a man of honor, a true knight with a pureness of soul seldom found in men. He will never forget the woman he loves. He will hold her in his heart forever. He will never marry another, but will remain true to the memory of this woman whose beauty stands out above all other women."

Jasmine stopped speaking and in the hush that fell one woman sniffed, one sighed deeply, another sobbed, and there was not a dry eye in the room save that of the queen. Isabella's eyes glittered with excitement as the image of Hugh de Lusignan materialized clearly in her mind. He was a man of honor who had been waiting for her to grow to womanhood before he would dream of touching her. How cruel Fate had been to poor, dear Hugh. How could she have helped it if a king had stolen her to be his queen?

Jasmine began to speak again as the smoke inside the glass ball cleared. "The greatest woman in this room is a queen, but the magnitude of her greatness will not come to her because she is queen . . ." Jasmine paused, heard gasps of apprehension that something dire might be predicted, then she finished boldly. "No, her years of glory will come to her in the future when she is the mother of a king. He will be named Henry after his grandfather and will go down in history as one of England's greatest kings. While he is a young man, his mother will have supreme power in the land."

Jasmine thought she had fed Isabella's ego enough for one night and finished on a lighter note. There had been rumors that the king would travel north, so to ensure that Isabella insisted she go along, Jasmine said, "I see a great journey of more than two hundred miles. It will be filled with happiness and adventure. Every castle will vie for the honor of entertaining their new queen and showing her the beauties of this new land she has come to rule. Every baron who sees her will lose his heart to her. The crystal grows dim, I can see no more."

The chamber door was thrown open forcefully as King John, flanked by two burly guards, strode into the room. His steps halted as his eyes were drawn to the illuminated figure in the center of the room. She seemed bathed in a pure light from Heaven as if she were an angel. Her pale golden hair fell to her waist, and it too radiated a glowing nimbus. Her aura was innocence; the contrast between his dark, sensual wife and this maiden was so marked, he felt his shaft fill to bursting.

Estelle saw the raw lust in him and was alarmed.

Isabella's loud laugh rang out as she jumped up and ran toward her husband with outstretched hands to draw him to the center of attention. She was sly enough to trivialize what they had been up to yet at the same time feed his insatiable vanity. "We have been having a little game of trying to foresee the future."

John dismissed the guards with a gesture and, licking lips gone suddenly dry at the sight of the seminude goddess, he came all the way into the room and stopped just outside the circle of candles. He looked into Jasmine's eyes and asked, "What did you foretell for me?" His eyes coveted her openly and a great fear was born within her.

She wanted to scream "Death! Death is what I foretell for you!" but Estelle's training had been so rigid, she lowered her lashes to her cheeks and said, "A son . . . an heir." As she stood before him almost naked, she was aware of his greedy eyes feeding on her.

John felt consumed by his desire for her virginity. "I would know more," he stated. "Tomorrow night you may attend me in my chamber." He glanced a challenge at Isabella, daring her to object, but she was too wise to worry about John's infidelities; they were legion. She cared for nothing save that she was the queen. If the predictions of the white witch were true, she would outlive him and her son would be crowned king while still a child. John's days were numbered.

Chapter 14

Estelle made Jasmine get into bed and brewed her a posset of chamomile to calm her and help her sleep. "Tomorrow night I will go to John in your stead. Somehow I will find the words to keep his lust at bay."

Jasmine's fear receded only slightly; in the end, John was the king and the king must be obeyed. The chamomile finally made her drowsy, and her thoughts began to float all about her. If John managed to get her alone, what things would he command of her? She had evidence of the lurid sexual appetite he indulged with Isabella, and suddenly she wished that Falcon de Burgh was close at hand. Falcon would let no man touch her. He was the most physically powerful man she had ever seen, and even a king and his commands would mean nothing to him. Sleep overtook her and with a last incoherent thought she said to herself, "I will go to Falcon in my dreams; he will keep me safe."

Falcon de Burgh was far away to the north, close to the border of Scotland. Salisbury had made Eustace de Vesci captain of the northern fighting forces. Eustace was married to Margaret, an illegitimate daughter of the King of Scotland, and he was therefore most useful in negotiating a treaty for peace between King John and the Red Fox of Scotland.

Falcon had been wined and dined at Eustace de Vesci's great castle on the border, but he had refused the offer of a comfortable chamber and a plump maid to ward off the chill, preferring instead to sleep in the field with his men. The scarlet silk tent provided all the comfort the hardened soldier required, but as he lay in his furs oblivious to the rigid earth beneath him, his senses were filled with an unendurable longing for Jasmine. His fingers tingled with the need to touch her. He would play with her nipples, then fill his palms with the heavy fullness of her luscious breasts. His hands would sweep lower to be filled with her delicious heart-shaped bottom, then he would part her soft thighs and let his fingers play to their heart's content. First he would wet the tips of his first two fingers in his mouth . . . or hers. Then he would make contact with the marvelous slippery flesh at the front of her mons. He would not probe or press, but wait for her response. When she gave it he would move his fingers down to her opening and gently enter so just the pads of his fingertips would be inside. He could feel himself filling now, until he was hard as marble and throbbing. He could taste her mouth as his tongue deeply explored it, and his nostrils were filled with the scent of her womanliness. He actually felt himself shudder as he imagined her hair brush across his face.

Now he would sensually flutter his fingers to give them more penetration. With his other hand he would gently play with her little erect bud while his other two fingers were inside her. He would not jump on her when she was ready, but stay with it at least another ten minutes. When Jasmine began to beg and told him she had to have it, he would not give it to her. He would tease. He would make her want it as she'd never wanted anything before.

Jasmine's dream began with King John. He held out imperious hands to her as he lay in the royal bed. "Come and fellate me!" he commanded. She turned and fled. She did not stop until she reached Falcon de Burgh's scarlet silk tent. There she felt safe, secure; there nothing could harm her. Falcon de Burgh lay on the ground and beckoned to her. He did not speak. No words must disturb the magic. She knew he was naked beneath the furs. Slowly, like the rising sun, the realization of what was happening to her dawned on Jasmine. His eyes bored into

her, understanding her arousal, slightly mocking it but at
the same time encouraging it. Whatever deed would be
done, she had silently agreed to it. She was a gift, a divine
sacrifice to his passion. Her beautiful virginity was wide
open, there to be taken. Her lifelong innocence had
primed her for this headlong descent into abandonment.
She heard herself begging him as she slipped inside the
furs, "Please hold me, my love! Please never leave me
alone again!" Then in blissful collusion she allowed him
to ravish her.

The sound of her own sobbing awoke her. She sat up
shivering, trying to blot out the wicked things she had
urged him to, but her body felt pleasurable sensations in
all her most intimate places. She hugged her knees to her
breasts and vowed with clenched teeth that she would
never be wanton, that she would never, ever beg him to
touch her; she'd die first.

Falcon de Burgh came awake with a violent start. He
was covered with a light perspiration though the night
was chill. He cursed under his breath at whatever had
awakened him, for it had put an end to the unbelievable
magic of the erotic dream he had just had about Jasmine.

Estelle did not wait until the hour of midnight the
following night, but knocked upon King John's privy
chamber at eleven. He was clearly annoyed at her intrusion. He wore a flamboyant, rich bedgown embellished
all over with rampant stags. A warm supper sat waiting
beneath silver covers along with an infinite array of wines
from the provinces of France.

Estelle's mouth quirked with a slightly derisive sneer
as she looked pointedly at the crown he wore. Even when
he intended seduction he needed the added confidence
the symbol of the crown lent him. Dame Winwood began
her denunciation of his intentions without preamble. "A
man burning with desire wonders why he should not give

full freedom to his sexual desires. But if he is unchecked by custom, morals, or laws he will never understand that sex is a river of fire that must be banked and cooled by a hundred restraints if it is not to consume in chaos both the individual and the group."

He refused to be thwarted. "I thirst for her!"

"Jasmine's magic powers as a white witch are unlimited because she is a virgin. If you destroy that power because of your selfish lust, you are playing with the will of the gods and could bring Hellfire down upon your head."

"Think you I'm afraid of Hellfire?" he asked, laughing.

"Possibly not, your Majesty. But if you have any common sense at all you will be afraid to call down Salisbury's wrath upon your head when he commands all your armies. If you defile his love child, it will set his sword against you. Moreover, it would be an act of incest, which carries with it, as you know, an ancient curse."

These words had the desired effect to cool his ardor. His eyes hooded. He would bide his time. As an unmarried maiden she was under the dominion of her father, Salisbury, but what if he found a husband for her? Then she would be the property of her husband, and every husband at court was willing to share his wife with his king, if he so desired her.

Estelle knew her stronger will had prevailed . . . for the moment. She hoped she wouldn't need to take stronger measures and brew him a potion that would render him impotent, or worse.

In Scotland, Eustace de Vesci had managed to negotiate a treaty of peace with King Alexander. England would promise to control her northern barons from raiding across the borders from their castles in Cumberland and Northumberland and in return Alexander, the Red

Fox, was to relinquish his claim on those lands. Alexander had finally agreed to the terms of the treaty less because Eustace was his son-in-law than because England's armies sat on his doorstep.

King John was to travel north to sign the treaty, yet he feared to travel through the land of his own northern barons even more than he feared the French. Salisbury had to send a company of one hundred knights and two hundred mounted bowmen to accompany the royal court north. Even then King John refused to go farther than Eustace de Vesci's stronghold on this side of the border. He would leave the queen and court at the great fortified castle of Nottingham, where he commanded that the entire army be on hand to accompany him north to sign the treaty.

Estelle and Jasmine were now in fashion. The women clustered about them like puppies at a bitch's teat. Jasmine noticed a beautiful young woman who always hung back shyly, yet she could tell the girl was bursting with unasked questions. She took her aside the day before they were to travel north and asked simply, "What is it you wish to know?"

Mary-Ann FitzWalter, who had accompanied her father to court to settle a dispute of land, blushed to the roots of her hair as she explained the unhappy situation in which she found herself. "Oh, Lady Jasmine, I am so far gone in love there is no help for me. His name is Robert, Lord of Huntingdon. We were pledged until one day I was riding in Barnisdale Forest and Roger de Longchamp, a friend of King John's, abducted me. Before he could force marriage upon me, Robert rescued me. He is the strongest, bravest man in England and I will love him till I die!" she cried defiantly. "Robert slew Roger de Longchamp, and the king declared him outlaw and took his lands and title. Now even my father forbids me to see my love." A tear stole down her cheek and her throat was so tight with unshed tears, she could speak no more.

Jasmine was amazed at the similarities of their abductions, yet de Burgh had gained by killing de Belamé, while Robert had been declared outlaw. Jasmine took the velvet cloth from the crystal and gazed into it for long minutes. "Mary-Ann, let your heart be light, for you will see your Robert when we arrive at Nottingham Castle. You need have no worry for him. He is fearless, strong, and before he is done his name will be legend. Your path will not be smooth, but good will triumph over evil. It seems that you are not the only one to have affection for this man. He draws friends like a lodestone. He is a great leader. Mary-Ann, never refuse to do as he asks. He will protect you with his life."

"I know that, Lady Jasmine. I would do anything for him. For just one more kiss I would gladly die. I melt the moment he touches me."

Jasmine's thoughts flew to her dream and her cheeks stained a delicate pink. What must it be like to be deeply in love? Pray God she never found out if it brought her to Mary-Ann's besotted state.

In spite of her silliness over a man, Jasmine liked this girl. They were both out of place at this court where the queen's vicious words were as sharp as any dagger and all around were her allies, the cunning tongues of her ladies. "Ride beside me tomorrow when we leave for Nottingham?" Jasmine suggested, and Mary-Ann quickly agreed.

The servants had been up all night readying the king and queen and their entourage for the trip north. The courtyard at Westminster was a seething mass of humanity. The master of household was trying to create order from chaos as he organized the baggage train, which would stretch out over a mile. Grooms stood trying to calm the horses as the people traveling with the court came from the castle to mount the animals they would ride north.

Jasmine had chosen a cloak of ruby velvet for traveling. She saw Queen Isabella surrounded by men and women who shouldered each other for position and quit the vicinity as quickly as she could. She could find neither Estelle nor Mary-Ann FitzWalter, but she saw a groom lead out her white palfrey and with light steps she ran across the yard toward it.

Suddenly she was aware of eyes upon her. She looked up quickly and was horrified to see none other than King John leering at her. He was surrounded by men who were also stripping her with their eyes. Each had acted as procurer for John at one time or another. They were making suggestive remarks, each trying to amuse the king with his ribald banter, but John had the dirtiest mouth in the realm and none could top him.

They formed a half circle about her that she could not penetrate without coming into physical contact with them, and she realized how very foolish she had been to choose the ruby-red cloak. With her silvery hair about her shoulders she would stand out in any crowd, especially once she was mounted on the white palfrey. As she pushed between two men her gown brushed against them and John said, laughing, "You can rub up against my leg anytime, kitten."

Suddenly she couldn't believe her eyes as Falcon de Burgh's long strides brought him to the king. She flew to his side immediately, looking up into his face with pure joy. "Falcon, how glad I am to see you!"

He blotted out the king and the other men. The plumed helmet made him tower over her, blotting out even the sun. He knew instinctively she had flown to him for protection. Something had frightened her or, more likely, *someone!*

"Jasmine, my love," he said, his deep voice carrying a

message to all that this woman was his possession and God help any who forgot it.

King John's eyes narrowed as de Burgh cupped the beautiful maiden's face and bent to claim a kiss. Jasmine tried to resist, but he forced compliance with possessive arms. When he released her she was flying the flags of her anger in her cheeks. She demanded so none but he could hear, "Must you paw me in public?"

"It seemed the quickest way to brand you as mine," he murmured simply. He gently set her aside and saluted King John, handing him a sealed paper.

John took it and read Salisbury's giant scrawl. "I send you the best captain you or I have ever known. You may safely place your life in de Burgh's capable hands."

So, John thought, this is the man my brother has chosen for his precious daughter. Suddenly he laughed aloud as a most diabolic thought struck him. "Take charge, de Burgh. I expect to see Nottingham two days hence."

De Burgh nodded. "My knights will ride ahead of you, your Majesty, my bowmen will be solidly at your back."

King John's eyebrows rose and he rebuked lightly, "*My* knights, de Burgh . . . *my* bowmen."

Falcon bowed to the king, put one large hand at the small of Jasmine's back, and propelled her forward. He took the bridle of her palfrey from the groom's hands and without a word lifted her into her saddle. Mounted, she was on eye level with the tall, powerful knight. She had been grinding her teeth in mute rage since he had spoken of branding her as his property. She lifted her chin and appeared to be a cool vision of poised womanhood. "De Burgh, you will never own one small part of me."

Stung, he joined the battle at once as he always did. "I may never own one small part of you, but be assured I will have the use of it."

She gasped at his vulgarity and turned aside from him. So, he thought, the warm greeting was a little perfor-

mance she had been acting out for the benefit of others.
She had wanted to show the king and his men that she
was under Falcon de Burgh's protection. All he had to
learn now was which man she feared. He knew instinctively in his bones that it was John.

Chapter 15

De Burgh moved his knights out immediately, and King
John and his party took their place at the center. The
queen and her attendants fell in line behind. Falcon put
one hundred bowmen at their back and the other hundred at the rear of the packhorses and baggage train. He
would set no breakneck pace. Such a large party of
women and packhorses could be expected to cover only a
certain number of miles per day regardless of when the
king wished to reach Nottingham.

The travelers were fed at the king's castle of Berkhamsted, twenty or so miles from London, and then the journey was continued until nightfall. Arrangements had
been made to house the king and queen at Northampton
Castle. The Earl of Northampton's hospitality was evident in the sumptuous meal and the entertainment he
had provided for the entire court, which numbered over
one hundred. The three hundred knights and bowmen set
up their tents in the surrounding meadows, but were provided with food and fodder for the horses.

Dame Winwood was as stiff as a corpse by the time
they arrived at the castle. Once inside their cramped
room, she imperiously bade Mary-Ann FitzWalter rub
her back with oil of wintergreen and sent Jasmine running to the kitchens for a restorative julep of fennel. As

the girl carried the steaming basin toward the women's quarters of Northampton Castle, she was encompassed by the unmistakable aroma of licorice.

Young Will Marshal took her aside for a word of caution. "Lady Jasmine, I overheard the king say he fancied his palm read tonight. That he was in sore need of a certain fair maiden's magic touch. I believe he will dispatch a servant for you after dinner."

"Oh my God, no." Jasmine gasped. Her finely arched brows drew together as anxiety gripped her. Hazard or haven . . . her choice was simple. She would seek out Falcon de Burgh. She found him with his knights, but she was shocked to see the number of women who had sought their company. De Burgh was being offered food by two and ale by another and aught else he desired by all three! Falcon saw the fear and weary fatigue in her at once. He felt an urge to carry her to his bed and hold her cradled against his heart all night. He begged a favor from the serving women and pointed out his crimson silk tent in the meadow beyond.

"You hunt women more than you hunt the stag," Jasmine accused.

"Untrue, chérie, 'tis they who do the hunting," he said with a guilty grin.

They stood looking at each other. Jasmine could find no words to convey that she sought his protection.

Finally he said, "Will you come to my tent, my lady?"

She dropped her eyes shyly from his and nodded her head. His strong fingers curled about her small hand and his warmth crept up her arm. The only thing she needed from him was his strength. At this moment it was a relief to drop the rigid guard and become the soft, dependent woman.

When they entered the tent, Gervase, who was just lighting the lamp, turned and could not help his jaw from falling open. He went to de Burgh to relieve him of his armor but Falcon shook his head. "My lady will help me," he said.

Her eyes flew about the tent, taking in its sparse furnishings. It contained only his war chest, a lamp and brazier for light and warmth, and the thick fur skins upon the floor, which was carpeted against the damp earth. She stood before him perplexed by the trappings of his hauberk, gambeson, and chain mail. "Where do I begin?" she asked, puzzled.

He laughed at her. "My mail is far too heavy for you to lift . . . I just wanted Gervase to leave us private."

"You think me useless!" she flared.

"Useless?" he said, drawing close. "I could think of so many uses for you it would take a lifetime to fulfill."

She ignored his meaning and climbed nimbly upon the war chest to undo the fastenings at his wide shoulders. Just then two women carried in a wooden washtub and the third emptied the hot water buckets into it which she carried on a shoulder yoke. They had thought the bath was for him, of course, when he had made his request, but when he tossed them silver they were happy enough to let him share it with his pretty little whore.

With the straps undone, the armor fell away, leaving him clad in a linen shirt. He turned to face her where Jasmine stood, still up on the war chest, his hands slipping about her tiny waist, his eyes on hers, dark and smoky with desire. His heart was thudding. She could feel the echoing beat inside her breasts as she hung over him, a tumult of sensations racing through her. He brought his mouth close to hers but did not quite touch her lips as he whispered, "Are you a generous little wench or a selfish one?"

"S-selfish!" she breathed.

"May I share your bath?" he teased.

"No!" she cried, aghast.

He allowed his lips to brush hers. "May I bathe you, then?"

"Absolutely not!" She struggled to free herself but it was in vain.

He brushed her lips a second time, then sighed with resignation. "Alas, I must content myself to merely watch you."

He removed her ruby-red cloak, then his eyes examined her matching gown to learn the secret of its fastenings. His fingers deftly undid the buttons and slipped the velvet down to bare her shoulders.

"What on earth do you think you're doing, sir?" she demanded.

"Undressing you for your bath, you said I might watch you. Or did you intend to bathe with all your clothes on?" he teased.

"De Burgh, I did not say you might watch me . . . you made that outrageous suggestion if you will remember."

"Did I? I make so many." He grinned, giving the velvet gown a sharp tug so that it fell to her ankles. She was clad in a short shift that completely revealed her pretty legs.

"You horsefaced lout!" she spat. "I come to you for protection only to have you molest me."

"Ah, now we are getting to it. Protection from whom, Jasmine?"

She blushed. "It was nothing, just a silly fancy really."

He cocked an eyebrow. "A silly fancy that sends you rushing to my arms? You risk your reputation and your precious maidenhead to come to my tent where you know I may do anything I please with you?"

"I most certainly would not have come if I had known you would strip me and make me pay a penalty!"

"A small price to pay for my protection, Jasmine," he teased. "You are welcome to seek another's protection, since you seem to hate me so much. Perhaps you would seek King John's protection?" he asked lightly. He felt her begin to shake.

"No . . . Falcon . . . I seek your protection."

"Then you didn't come to seek me out because you love me. I'm merely the lesser of two evils," he accused, knowing if he raised her temper she would forget her fear. "What's the matter with your legs?" he asked, looking down with a slight frown.

"What do you mean?" she said, glancing down at her bared limbs.

"Is one fatter than the other or do they have that peculiar look because of your uneven knees . . . one is higher than the other?" He lifted her down from the chest. "Walk about for me so I can have a good look." Stung by his criticism, she paraded before him in her shift to show him his error. He repressed the urge to tell her how exquisite she was. A young woman who had been told of her beauty every day of her life did not need compliments. To tease her he kept a critical look on his face as he judged the fine points of her legs. She was disturbed that he found her flawed and some of her confidence evaporated.

Finally he conceded, "It must have been a trick of the lamplight, they seem quite passable now I observe them more closely."

She caught the amused gleam in his eyes and her anger rose immediately. "Only passable?" she demanded, hands on hips as she stood before him.

He reached out for her and pulled her against him. His lips brushed hers. "Vain little wench. You know your legs are absolute perfection. Does the rest of you match?" he whispered huskily as he caught a soft, round breast and cupped it in his palm.

She shivered at his touch and said sharply, "Stop playing this cat-and-mouse game with me, de Burgh. Whatever it is you intend, do it, and have done!"

"You mean get it over with quickly while you close your eyes and grit your teeth? Ah, chérie, you haven't the faintest idea about lovemaking, have you?" His powerful hands caressed her silken shoulders. "A night of love can have no time limits imposed upon it, no barriers of any kind can come between two as they merge and become one." He stroked the back of his hand down the swell of her breast. "The whole night is separated into delicious phases, each uniquely enjoyable. There is the time before love"—his lips brushed her temple—"the time during love"—his lips brushed her again—"the time between the first and the second loving"—his fingers slipped the chemise off her shoulders—"and the time after love." He kissed her eyelids. "The overture, the prelude, the performance, and the cadence."

When she opened her eyes she saw he had her naked. Without another word he lifted her and sat her down in the water. She gasped as his hand dipped beneath the surface to grope about for the soap. She was trembling visibly as he lathered his hands and soaped her breasts erotically.

"Falcon, I came here to you so that I would not be seduced. I think of you as my protector," she said in a small voice filled with trust.

At her soft words an aching tenderness began in his heart and spread throughout his chest. He knew he would shield her their whole lives if she would let him. He stood up and said gruffly, "Have your bath, love."

He walked his usual rounds, checking on men and horses, then stood outside his tent until he saw her silhouette emerge from the tub and pull on her shift. As he lifted the tent flap and entered he saw her shiver from the cool night air. She moved the small brazier, which gave off little heat now, closer to the war chest and sat down primly, clutching her cloak. She felt his bold eyes caress her body like a physical fondling. The bath had relaxed her and after the long day in the saddle she wanted nothing more than to go to sleep. She hoped he would be gentleman enough to give her his furs and bed himself down elsewhere.

"Have you ever slept on the ground?"

She sat up very straight and shook her head.

"Don't worry," he said softly, removing his shirt, "I will cushion you against its hardness."

Her eyes flew open in indignation. "Are you hinting, de Burgh . . . are you dreaming? Please disabuse yourself of the notion I am about to share your bed!"

"Jasmine, you know if I decide to have your body tonight, you will have to do as I say."

Her eyes were fixed on his hands, on the long slim fingers that had the strength to kill. "You have the strength to force me to your will!" she accused bitterly.

He shook his head regretfully and murmured, "Jasmine, when I make love to you . . ." He didn't finish the sentence, but his words implied that it wouldn't be under these circumstances.

She gave an inward sigh of relief and pulled her cloak tighter about her chilled body. He shrugged as he removed the remainder of his clothes and slipped under the furs. "Suit yourself," he said, hiding amused eyes from her.

She sat for a whole hour without moving. Each minute seemed longer than the last. De Burgh was obviously sound asleep from the deep even breathing that came from the warm furs. Damn him to Hell, she was freezing! The last coal in the brazier had cooled and blackened long ago. How could the day have been so hot and the night so cold? she wondered wearily. What if she froze to death . . . while the author of her misery was totally oblivious to her dire peril? Did she dare to steal his furs while he slept? She heard a rumble in the distance which her terrified mind identified as thunder. The next instant she slipped under the furs beside him as quietly as she possibly could. His whipcord arms were around her instantly, pulling her head down onto his shoulder. "Jassy . . ." he murmured softly as his lips brushed her temple, "have no fear."

Instinctively she knew she was safe from everything in the whole world. His warmth became hers as she melted against him and sleep claimed her. Of course Falcon could not sleep, for the night held magic for him. He lay in exquisite torture, needing her more than he had ever needed a woman before, and yet his need to protect and cherish were greater than the demands of his body. He knew a deep, satisfying pleasure that she was here beneath his hand, trusting him implicitly. With the scent of her filling his head, he allowed his imagination full rein to run riot and indulge every fantasy as his blood ran like fire along his veins, pulsing his shaft until he thought the ache would kill him. He caressed a handful of her pale golden hair, kissed it, smelled it, tasted it, then bound it about his neck, chaining them together. He lifted the furs slightly so he could see her delicate pale breast through her shift pressed against the dark tan of his chest covered with the mat of black hair.

Their bodies made such a contrast it sent a deep thrill through him. He promised himself he would furnish their bedchamber with a very large mirror so he could watch their bodies when they made love. He rubbed the tip of his arousal against the silken skin of her thigh and shuddered at the feeling of pleasure it brought him. She turned toward him in her sleep and her soft breast thrust against his hand. He cupped it gently and dipped his head to taste its sweetness. He had to stop himself from sucking hard on the tempting, erect nipple, for it would surely waken her and she would withdraw from him.

He knew a need like he had never known before. It was an unbearable torture for him not to take her there and then, but he had promised her she would be safe with him. He would wait for their wedding night, but his willpower was not strong enough to forego the sensuality of touching her from head to toe. The deep need to feel her beneath him, between his thighs, overpowered him, and he straddled her carefully. Then he slowly crouched above her and let the silken head of his hard shaft slide across her breasts, up the valley between them, then he dared to proceed until it was a hairsbreadth from her lips. He was so sensitized there that when he felt her faint warm breath against the tip he thought he would go mad. He had thought he could stop at any time, but now he realized he had reached a point where he was out of control. Crouched above her, he fought a battle with his white-hot senses. He closed his eyes to blot out the enticing pale loveliness that provoked his manhood. His mind and his body were at war. It was slow, painful torture, but finally he forced his fiercely demanding flesh to withdraw and he lay back down beside her and willed his blood to cool. He couldn't move; he was too weak with lust.

Just before dawn he slept. The change in his breathing pattern made Jasmine awake. She was covered with blushes as she untangled her hair from his possessive fingers and slipped from the furs.

Mary-Ann FitzWalter's eyes were misty as Jasmine slipped into the small room Mary-Ann had shared with Estelle. "Oh, Jasmine, you spent the night with your lover. I am so happy for you, but oh how I envy you." She sighed.

"Mary-Ann, Falcon de Burgh is not my lover! Our betrothal is a temporary arrangement I intend to get out of as soon as it is possible for me to do so." Jasmine glanced quickly at Estelle, expecting an attitude of outrage that she had slept in de Burgh's tent, but Dame Winwood's attitude toward Jasmine marrying the strong knight was undergoing a change. She saw the malignancy of the royal court. King John's evil was pervasive and would contaminate almost everyone it touched. Jasmine would be better served as the cherished and protected wife of the powerful de Burgh. She had been kept safe so far, but Estelle knew of John's insatiable appetites. He thought sex was power and as well as indulging in corrupting practices with his child-bride every day and night, he needed the venal conquest of every female who crossed his path. It was common knowledge that the wives of his closest sycophants and his nobles were his for the asking, and now his eyes were falling on their daughters as well. At first the men were outraged, but John had no conscience. He bribed, he deceived, and he threatened. They soon discovered his threats were not empty—he was capable of any atrocity and gave proof every day of his reign.

Berkhamsted Castle had made the Plantagenet king welcome not only because he owned it, but because they feared the rumors that were more numerous than whores on a Friday night in London. Since arriving seemingly exhausted, the shrewd Dame Winwood had gathered in the rumors from the lowest servant to the highest-ranking duchess in residence at Northampton as she had at Berkhamsted where they had lunched.

The clergy were absolutely outraged at King John's sexual excesses, but the thing that really stuck in their ecclesiastic craws was that he was a law unto himself, reducing the power of the clergy to naught in church and in legal matters. Sin of sins, he was helping himself to their vast wealth.

They asked Hubert Walter, the Archbishop of Canterbury, to issue King John an ultimatum and bring him back under the church's thumb, but the archbishop was old and ailing and nothing official was done. Various churchmen spoke out against him, namely Geoffrey, the Archdeacon of Norwich and the Bishop of Worcester. Only John's personal friend the Bishop of Lincoln stayed loyal to him. However, the weight of these churchmen was not as significant as Canterbury's would have been, and John thumbed his nose at their condemnation and marked their names well for retribution.

The baronage was also on the verge of revolt. Their lives and possessions could be forfeit on a whim. John demanded money, he insisted that they ready themselves for war on a moment's notice, and he demanded their sons as hostages for their good behavior. His strongholds of Corfe, Carisbrooke, and Windsor and Dover castles held the sons of England's wealthy and powerful aristocracy as a safeguard that they would not revolt. It was an ancient custom and up until now an honorable one, but Hubert de Burgh had confided to his adored Avisa that John had gone too bloody far when he had asked him to blind his young nephew Arthur, so that he could never be brought to the throne.

Avisa, who hated John with a passion, now had her weapon. She opened her mouth to tell the tale to everyone who would listen. She added fuel to the fire by embroidering and exaggerating the things her lover told her in confidence. She said that Arthur, the rightful heir to the throne, was mysteriously missing and that some people even went so far as to accuse King John of disposing of his own nephew.

She filled the ears of her very good friend Matilda de Braose, the Lady of Hay, who, scandalized, passed the stories on to her husband William, a baron who owned much land in Wales and Ireland. The de Braose family was related to the powerful Lacys through marriage, and King John had asked for sons and grandsons from both families. Because of the rumors of John's vile character, his barons began to plot secretly.

Falcon de Burgh had the royal court and his three hundred escort on the road headed for Nottingham before eight bells. The previous night he had dispatched riders to Leicester Castle, to notify them to be prepared to feed four hundred people and five hundred horses. Everything seemed to be going along well, thanks to de Burgh's total command, until the unwieldy party was readied for the last leg of the journey from Leicester to Nottingham.

With a smirk marring his darkly handsome features, King John summoned de Burgh and drawled, "Escort Jasmine of Salisbury to me, de Burgh. I fancy her company on this long ride. My beautiful young niece and I share many common interests." He paused for emphasis and added, "She would do anything to please her uncle the king, I am sure."

De Burgh saluted him smartly with a totally impassive face, then wheeled his great destrier to search out his sweetheart who had lain against his heart all night.

She blushed hotly at his approach and her lashes brushed her cheeks as she lowered her eyes from the intense greenness of his.

"Lady Jasmine, King John asks that you ride at his side."

Her eyes flew to his in anger. "You are jesting, sir. I would not have believed such cruelty even from you!" she snapped.

"I wish with all my heart that it was a jest, my lady. But I beg you have no fear. Put your trust in me as you did last night and you will come out of this unscathed." He grinned wickedly and she remembered the warm scent of his body beneath the furs. He had smelled of sun, horse, and sandalwood all mingled together, and a shiver of excitement rippled along her spine. More likely it was fear that once again the king had singled her out, only this time there was no escape. She rode forward beside de Burgh with her head held high. A cool remoteness came over her as he led her to the left side of King John. Her stirrup grazed the king's and she glanced down, realizing his legs were as short as her own. Her mind, unbidden, immediately began making odious comparisons. De Burgh's legs were long and strong, almost like tree trunks. His iron-thewed thighs were as high as her waist. Her mind snapped back instantly as John said, "Tell me the secret thought that just crossed your mind, lady fair."

She lied blatantly and added, "It is kind of your majesty to take a fatherly interest in me."

"Mmm, a father-daughter relationship is a pleasure I have yet to experience. Daddy's little girl . . . mmm . . . most tempting." His conversation was leading down a path Jasmine did not wish to explore further, and it was with an enormous sigh of relief she saw de Burgh ride up escorting Queen Isabella.

"I'm sick of eating your dust. I have decided to ride on your right-hand side. Is it not fitting that a queen should ride with a king?" she bantered. If Isabella was angered by her husband's interest in Jasmine, she was not in the business of showing it.

John threw a malevolent look at de Burgh, who had outmaneuvered him for the moment. He said, "Do you not envy me such a wanton little bedpartner? She cannot get enough of me, day or night."

De Burgh bowed formally to the vividly lovely child-queen and said, "She is a jewel in the crown of womanhood, sire."

"Ha!" John said lewdly, "She could suck the brass off a doorknob!"

Isabella's eyes glittered and she licked her lips as she raked her eyes down across de Burgh's loins.

Falcon glanced at Jasmine and was relieved to see that the crude sexual comments had gone completely over her head. Not a hint of a blush showed, proving she had not understood the king's words. Her eyes held Falcon's for a moment, however, as she gave him silent thanks for bringing the wretched little queen to her rescue.

"Tomorrow night, John, before you go running off to Scotland, we must have a great feast," Isabella said. "I'm dying to meet your wizard or astrologer or whatever he is, who resides at Nottingham. You know, the man named for the great star, Orion." Her eyes flashed a challenge at Jasmine. "I will give you until tomorrow night to finish painting my tarot cards so we can all have our fortunes told."

John's smile, which always resembled a leer, licked over Jasmine. "What other specialties do you perform? Perhaps something in private, one on one?"

Jasmine answered in a cool, detached voice. "I can read palms, sire, but my time belongs to the queen and I'm sure she would never spare me for private consultations with another, not even the king."

"Ha! John, so do not try to lure her behind my back as you were doing when I came upon the scene. I forbid it!"

"Forbidden fruit is always sweeter," he said, laughing.

"So you showed me this morning. 'Tis a good thing I'm mounted today for I could hardly walk when you left my bed, you brute!"

Jasmine had quickly learned how to block unpleasant words. It was a trick of the mind. Quite simple really. Her ears heard nothing, her mind freed itself to wander in a far-off place. She was present only in a physical sense. Mentally, emotionally, and spiritually she had withdrawn to a private place of her own. A secure and protected place where nothing and no one could touch her. She heard, saw, smelled, and felt nothing in her immediate environment.

A light drizzle began in the late afternoon, turning the landscape to a dreary gray-green. It made the travelers irritable and nasty-tempered, which quickly sapped the energy of master and servant alike. It seemed the day would have no end when at last the weary party sighted the high turrets of Nottingham Castle and man, woman, and horse dragged in wet to the bone.

It was well past midnight by the time all were fed and bedded down in exhausted, dreamless sleep. Dame Winwood's services had been imperative to control one of King John's bouts of temper or "madness," as Estelle called them, and she hurried off to the king's bedchamber —The Lunatic Asylum, as she dubbed it.

Falcon de Burgh had bribed the castellan of Nottingham to make sure Mary-Ann FitzWalter and Jasmine shared a chamber. He bit off a foul oath, however, when his betrothed was nowhere to be found. The weather had had no effect on a hard-bitten soldier like de Burgh, but it doubled his burden of seeing that dry tents were set up for his men and that their mounts and the packhorses were well rubbed down before being bedded for the night. The last of the wagons were being unloaded in the bailey when, incredibly, he caught sight of Jasmine.

"Splendor of God!" he exploded. "What in Christ's name are you doing scrabbling about the wagons in the middle of the night?" Sometimes he had the urge to put his hands about her beautiful little neck and throttle her, so maddening could she be.

"Oh, milord, please don't be fierce with me," she begged. Her lashes were spikey with rain and tears and her voice was husky with emotion.

He wanted to carry her to bed and warm her with his body before she caught her death of cold. His hard eyes raked her, noticing how the wet material of her gown molded her thighs, belly, and breasts, and the hard little nipples were erect with cold. Her physical impact on him was immediate and pronounced as his shaft lengthened to a solid nine inches.

"I can't find my hedgehog!" she explained.

"Is that what this is all about? That damned vermin-ridden bit of trash you call Prick?"

"His name is Quill," she corrected with a sob in her voice.

He took her shoulders in hard hands and pulled her to him. "I've paid good gold coins to keep you safe this night and here you are like a common camp follower where any man could rape you." He shook her roughly until he noticed her teeth were chattering from the cold dampness. He bent his head to cover her cold lips with his hot mouth. For a moment she melted against his warmth, then tried to push him away with her pitiful last ounce of energy. As usual the aching tenderness began in his heart and spread throughout his chest and he began to question the thing he had denied for so long. Was he beginning to fall in love with her? Nonsense, he told himself firmly. He was in passion, in desire, in lust all right, but in love? Never! He reached down between his quilted tunic and hauberk and pulled out a warm, dry, prickly ball. "Here!" he said, thrusting it into her hand.

"Oh, milord, thank you from the bottom of my heart. 'Tis the most precious gift you could ever give me," she said softly. Though he knew he could allot not one more minute of the fast-disappearing night to her, he swept her into his arms and carried her up four flights of stone steps to the chamber he had secured for her.

Chapter 16

Nottingham Castle. The centerpiece of England. It seemed the world and its mistress were gathered there. It was a vivid, swirling crush of humanity . . . very much like Hell must be.

Earls were more plentiful than fleas on a dog's belly. Either there already or expected at any moment were the earls of Nottingham, Derby, Leicester, Warenne, and Chester. Each was accompanied by his countess, except of course Chester, who was divorced from King John's sister-in-law.

Mere lords and their ladies were as commonplace as caterpillars on cabbages, and abbots, friars, and prelates rubbed elbows with sheriffs, bailiffs, justices, and knights. Wandering minstrels, jongleurs, and entertainers for miles around had been drawn to Nottingham as if it were a lodestone, and each meal was eaten while watching acrobats, rope dancers, wrestlers, or trained dogs. Mingling among the crowds were those who lived by their wits and whiles alone, such as beggars, pickpockets, and prostitutes. Many pretended to be what they were not: prostitutes who pretended to be fine ladies and, paradoxically, ladies who tried not to show that they were whores.

Dame Winwood's lips twitched with amusement as she overheard a snippet of conversation between one couple. "You can't introduce yourself as a count," protested the man's wife, to which he replied quite truthfully, "This lot couldn't tell a count from a bucket of shit!"

Jasmine was busy in the chamber up on the fourth floor of the castle painting the last of her royal tarot cards. Suddenly a man on a rope swung into the room and landed on his feet, lithe as a panther. Jasmine, too surprised to even scream, blinked several times, utterly amazed that a man could climb through a window four stories from the ground.

"Forgive me, demoiselle, I thought this was Mary-Ann's chamber." As he spoke he removed a hooded cowl from his head. He was easily the most attractive man Jasmine had ever beheld. He had thick curly brown hair, merry blue eyes, and the loveliest white, even teeth that flashed in a smile that made a maiden's heart turn over. He was well muscled and his skin was as tanned as a rich brown nut. He wore boots, tight breeches, and a sleeveless vest all made from soft doeskin. Slung across his back was a longbow and a quiver of arrows.

"You're Robert—Lord Huntingdon!" exclaimed Jasmine, delighted to make the acquaintance of Mary-Ann's beloved.

"My lady, I am an outlaw now. There is a price on my head."

"Oh, my lord, you are in grave danger. King John is here and the place is bursting at the seams with lawmen and soldiers."

"I know," he said, grinning. "I can smell them."

She giggled.

"I have no right to put you in jeopardy, but if you would bring Mary-Ann to me, I will repay the debt someday."

"I will go and find her, but please, milord, conceal yourself before you are arrested."

Jasmine found Mary-Ann with her family. Her uncle Robert FitzWalter of Dunmow had just arrived with his wife and daughter. Mary-Ann introduced them all to Jasmine, saving her young cousin to the last. "Jasmine, this is Matilda. She's twelve today. She wanted to celebrate her birthday by coming to see the king and queen."

Matilda was one of the most striking girls Jasmine had ever seen. Her hair was her crowning glory. It was red-

gold and hung in natural ringlets to her waist. She was so
small with such an abundance of curly hair she looked all
hair and eyes. Her skin was like white porcelain, un-
marred by the usual freckles that plagued most redheads.
Jasmine looked over the child's head into Mary-Ann's
eyes and formed one silent word with her lips, "Robert!"

Mary-Ann bobbed a little curtsey to her aunt and said
breathlessly, "I must run and see if I can find you a
bedchamber. Nottingham Castle is very big, but before
long I swear people will be standing on each other's
shoulders."

Mary-Ann literally ran up the four flights of stone
steps and did not stop running until she was in the arms
of her lover. Jasmine felt very shy to hear their exchanged words of love, and yet she knew she must hover
at the door to warn of any approaching danger. She
heard Robert say "Ralph Murdach, the Sheriff of Not-
tinghamshire, has put a price on my head. I'm telling you
this, sweetheart, so you won't be upset when you hear
about it. They don't know my real identity. They haven't
connected me with Robert, Lord Huntingdon. I'm an
outlaw they have dubbed Robin Hood because of the
hooded cowl I and my men all wear."

Mary-Ann clung to him. "Please, please, Robert, go
from this place. King John is rumored to be so cruel he
likes to watch men tortured for the sport of it."

Robert laughed. "I'll not forgo seeing you, my darling.
The risk is slight in this crowd."

"No, no, love. Don't come to me, I will come to you.
Perhaps Jasmine will ride out with me early each morning. I know we would be safe in the forest . . . 'tis your
kingdom and you rule all who go there."

"And very profitable it has been of late. Each traveler
who comes to Nottingham must pass through one of the
great forests—Ettrick, Derby, or Sherwood." He put his
arm about her and led her to the window embrasure.

"Ride yonder toward the River Trent, then go north into Sherwood Forest and right into my arms."

"Godspeed, Robert," Mary-Ann said with stars in her eyes.

Jasmine was putting the finishing touches to the tarot card she had left until last, the wheel of fortune. Sitting on top of Ezekiel's wheel was a sphinx, to the left a serpent, and to the right the Egyptian jackal-headed god. Each of the four corners depicted a living creature—an angel, an eagle, a lion, and a bull. Each had a set of wings, and it was these feathered wings that Jasmine found hardest to paint.

Mary-Ann rushed over, the stars in her eyes replaced by tears of sorrow. "Oh, Jasmine, I want to die!"

"Whatever is wrong, Mary-Ann?" she asked urgently.

"I am caught between two loyalties, two loves . . . I'm being torn apart!" She threw herself onto the bed and sobbed into her pillow.

Jasmine moved to the bed and smoothed the girl's lovely chestnut hair. Mary-Ann's muffled voice said, "While I was sneaking up here with Robert, the Sheriff of Nottingham took my father into custody to question him of the identity and whereabouts of the outlaw Robin Hood, because he had been seen on numerous occasions near our manor of Malaset. My father managed to convince the sheriff he knew nothing and had been with the king's court in London these past weeks, and so he was released. But of course my father knows his identity, knows that it is the former Lord Huntingdon who was courting me. Jasmine, I cannot go to meet Robert tomorrow because we are probably being watched. The sheriff wants to be able to deliver Robin's head on a platter to King John."

"I will go tomorrow," Jasmine said with quiet resolution. "I will warn him."

"Oh, Jasmine, what if you are caught? What if you are
tortured? I cannot ask it of you!"

"Rubbish! Get up off that bed and do something about
those red-rimmed eyes. One look at you and they will
read guilt and despair writ plainly on your face. You
must be merry tonight at this feast. Mask your fears and
think of celebrating your little cousin Matilda's birthday.
I will brew you a posset that will make you carefree."
Jasmine's mind leaped apace with her nerves. She knew
her talents would be on display this night when she read
the queen's cards. One missed step, one tiny miscalcula-
tion as she diced with danger could jeopardize her own
future.

The vast dining hall with its open fireplaces had big
square candles known as quarions held in iron brackets
along the walls. As well there were hundreds of wax tapers in iron candelabrums hanging from the ceiling. The
serving people were staggering about under heavily laden
platters, dodging cuffs from the guests who were trying to
keep food splatters from their best clothes.

Jasmine wore one of her new gowns her father had
provided for her stay at court. It was made from the
softest lambswool in a shade of pale lavender. It clung to
the curves of her figure, outlining and emphasizing
breasts, waist, and hips, then fell in full folds to the floor.
A silver-gilt girdle went about the waist, crisscrossed at
the back and tied again at the front just above her pubic
bone. Unknown to Jasmine, the glittering V attracted every eye. She was partnered by Dame Estelle who was
adorned in her cabalistic robes. That attire set her apart
and above everyone gathered. Jasmine saw coming toward them an extremely tall, thin figure adorned in skull-
cap and flowing gray robes. His beard and bushy eyebrows were the same gray color. He looked exactly as she
imagined Merlin would look had he sprung from the

mists-of Avalon. His nose was long and sharp and turned slightly to one side as if he had used it unwisely.

Estelle had been watching him for some time holding court beside King John and Queen Isabella. Around had clustered a dozen ambitious courtiers, wrapping their tongues about shameless compliments like ass-licking parasites. A feeling of exhilaration coursed through Estelle as she anticipated firing the first shot in a long, cruel campaign that would establish the pecking order of the purveyors of magic to their majesties.

The Countess of Nottingham said, "I must introduce you to Orion, the king's astrologer and a known wizard of renown."

Orion looked down at Estelle and said from his great height, "I hear you dabble in the occult?"

It was meant to be a sneering putdown, but Estelle laughed and in a loud, carrying voice, said, "Orion? Orion? More likely O'Ryan from the sound of that common Irish brogue!" All those present at the opening skirmish agreed that Dame Winwood had won the first round.

Jasmine and Estelle moved forward to make their obeisance to the royal couple. Isabella eyed the pale lavender gown with envy, but she knew it would have done nothing to enhance her own beauty. She had chosen royal purple to show off her dark, vivid coloring, and for adornment had chosen a diamond and amethyst necklace to attract every eye since she was still too young to have anything but the slightest breasts. John also ogled Jasmine, his eyes bulging almost as much as his codpiece. He was annoyed that the old woman watched her so vigilantly, her hooded shrewd eyes reading his every thought. He asked sarcastically, "Are you two joined at the hip?"

Estelle's quick tongue was more than a match for him. "No, I am connected to her by blood alone, as are you, your majesty," she said to shame him for lusting for his brother's child.

"Are the pasteboards ready?" asked Isabella, her eyes glittering with anticipation.

Jasmine nodded. "Yes, your majesty. The paint is drying on the last card."

"Excellent. You can be part of the entertainment. After dinner Orion is going to perform some wizard's tricks for our amusement, then you may read my cards to climax the evening. Orion has declined to read horoscopes." Isabella licked her lips in excitement as a child would do. "Would you like to entertain us instead, Dame Winwood?"

Estelle drew herself up to her full five feet, which on her was intimidating and menacing. Her haughty look quelled the queen as effectively as she could subdue a village maid. "I never abuse my special power by using it to entertain. I am an adept, not a charlatan with a bag of tricks." She swept past, taking Jasmine along with her. "A bitch doesn't stand a chance against a witch, remember that, Jasmine."

Above the heads of the crowd in the minstrel's gallery Falcon de Burgh stood where he could observe the whole panoply without being seen. His squire Gervase had reported that he had seen a man climb from the window of Jasmine's chamber just after dawn. When pressed to describe him, Gervase had compounded de Burgh's jealousy by saying he was well muscled and lithe as a panther.

Falcon didn't believe she had a lover, but the hall boasted a dozen men at least who fancied themselves in that role, from the king down . . . or up, depending on your opinion of the monarch. His eyes narrowed as he saw the Earl of Chester greet the king. The physical contrast between the two men was marked. Chester was tall, stark, graceless while the king was short, flamboyant, al-

ways laughing over some crudity while the jewels on his
fingers flashed as his hands gesticulated. Yet the two men
had a great deal in common. Both loved power and
wealth and cared not a fiddler's fart how they came by
either. De Burgh admitted to himself that it was a Norman trait; he was power-hungry himself, but the difference was *honor*. Some men were honorable and some
men were not. Why couldn't the crown go to the most
honorable man in the realm? he mused. Like William
Marshal? Now there would be a king! Instead, England
was ruled by a pricklouse—an insane pricklouse, to boot.

His eye caught sight of the most mercenary of the
king's mercenaries, Falkes de Bréauté. Falkes was a captain like himself, a hardbitten soldier who was a savage
fighter, who neither gave nor asked for mercy for himself
or the men whom he led. He too was cursed with the
Norman ambition for power and money, and by the looks
of it he was halfway home to filling a dead man's bed. He
had his arm about the widow of the Earl of Devon, who
held castles all through the Midlands. She rubbed herself
against Falkes like a bitch in heat. Christ, women were
faithless! De Burgh mocked himself for the thousandth
time that his heart was ruling his head in his choice of
women. Before his eyes was an example of how an ambitious man could feather his nest and get his acquisitive
Norman fingers on castles and land. All he had to do in
return was marry an old earl's widow and screw her
brains out!

The instant he saw Jasmine his breath caught in his
throat. She was utterly lovely, without flaw. The unique
pale-gold hair set her apart from other women. She was
like a vision, a princess from some mythic tale. Delicate,
ethereal, desirable. Splendor of God . . . what the hell
was she wearing? Her gown clung so lovingly to the
curves of her body, she might as well be naked, and what
was worse she actually wore some sort of gilt girdle that

outlined her mound of Venus, framing it, emphasizing it. By Christ, if this was meant for some lover's eyes, he'd thwart her plans instantly, and tonight if the lithe panther returned, he'd find himself dead meat—skewered on de Burgh's longsword.

Falcon left the gallery and sought her immediately. His methods had always been direct. He stopped directly in front of her, his wide shoulders effectively blocking out the rest of the room. His green eyes swept down her body in disbelief, then he looked directly into her eyes and asked grimly, "What the hell is this display in aid of?"

She refused to answer when spoken to in such a fashion.

"Well, is this a dumb show; are you deaf?"

"I am neither deaf nor dumb, milord, I simply do not understand what you mean," she said in a cool, controlled voice.

"You are a little liar. You understand exactly what I mean. Your gown and girdle were designed with one purpose in mind. It was meant to arouse a man's lust. You will go upstairs and change into another and you will never wear it again except in the boudoir for me alone!"

She gasped in outrage at his autocratic commands. As always, she was more than prepared to accept the gauntlet. "Issue me no orders, Lord Dogdung, I'm in no mood to obey them!"

"Mood or no mood, madame, you will change that gown," he said grimly.

"I will not!" she said, emphasizing each word of defiance. Then she deliberately spun about to walk away from him. With horrified dismay she felt the material of the gown being torn from her body. She looked down in disbelief and saw that he had merely placed one great boot on the hem of the delicate cloth and allowed her to do the rest. The gown was rent from armpit to hip and she desperately sought to cover her dishabille.

"I warned you . . . you heeded me not. Go and change into something that makes you look more like a maiden and less like a strumpet."

Her eyes blazed their anger. She wanted to scream, Go to hell, de Burgh, but her revenge would be more subtle. She gathered the torn material in one hand and walked away from him, her small steps sure as a prideful cat.

Chapter 17

In her chamber she knew exactly where to lay her hands on a gown that really was outrageous. She had set it aside when she had unpacked, thinking it could not be worn, for it was only one piece of a two-piece outfit. It was an underdress of white silk; the red velvet tunic that went over it had somehow not been packed. The silk was so fine it was almost transparent, and if observed closely the flesh of her limbs could be discerned. She twisted the gilt girdle about her torso in exactly the same way it had been tied before, making a V of gold that pointed to her mound of Venus.

She had done this thing, but now that she had returned to the hall she was afraid of the consequences. She had been determined to defy him, and yet in the end the fact remained that he had made her change her gown. He was perfectly capable of carrying her kicking and screaming from the hall. She must circumvent him from another confrontation.

Dinner was about to be served and the king and queen climbed to the dais. Jasmine quickly chose a seat directly in front of the dais in full view of their majesties. Even de Burgh would be loathe to make a scene where every word

would be overheard. She had no doubt that he would be
enraged with her, but he would have to wait for a private
moment after the dinner and the entertainments, and that
would be hours away.

She glanced across the table and was amused to see
Estelle sitting between the Countess of Devon and the
Countess of Warwick. Both were widows but were solicit-
ing Estelle's help for opposite problems. The king had
dug up a husband for Warwick's widow named Geoffrey
de Serland of Lincoln. Her first marriage had been arranged, and she had had no say in the matter. True, Warwick had left her a wealthy widow, but this time she
wanted a husband of her own choice, someone she could
enjoy in and out of bed. She'd heard rumors that de Serland enjoyed an occasional boy and the very thought of it
made her flesh creep.

Devon's widow, on the other hand, had had her eyes
and other intimate parts on Falkes de Bréauté. She knew
he was ambitious enough to covet the castles and land
Devon had left her, but she didn't think the mercenary
captain had enough money to pay John the high price he
would set for her.

For Estelle the two problems were simply solved. All
the Countess of Warwick had to do was offer John a
thousand pounds and a dozen or so of the famous Warwick white stallions to allow her to refuse Geoffrey de
Serland, then she could take her sweet time in choosing
her own mate. The Countess of Devon simply had to give
Falkes de Bréauté enough money to buy her. However,
Estelle would not dispense the wise advice until she had
extracted a generous fee from each woman.

Ranulf, Earl of Chester, sat on the dais at John's right
hand. The two men were thick as thieves. For ten full
minutes Ranulf hadn't lifted his eyes from the vision who
sat down directly in front of the dais. Finally he turned to

John and said, "Your brother's daughter is a very desirable piece. How much will you take for her?"

Inwardly John was frustrated. If he couldn't have her, he was damned if he wanted Chester between her legs. He temporized. "Do you mean one fuck or had you something more permanent in mind?"

The pockmarks on Chester's cheek whitened slightly at the crude remark. "I have marriage in mind. I would have spoken to Salisbury, but he'd just betrothed her to young de Burgh."

The workings of John's mind were so convoluted that he was immediately at war with himself. Obviously Chester was ensnared enough to pay any price. John coveted the girl himself, yet his palm itched for the riches Chester could pour into it. Then his mind walked down another path and he knew he could have both. He'd make a secret pact with Chester. Implicit in the deal, however, would be that once she was a wife and no longer under his brother's authority, he would be free to enjoy her sexual favors.

Toward the end of the meal, the comfits were passed round and fresh hogsheads of wine and ale were rolled in for the fun part of the evening. Isabella clapped her hands in excitement as Orion stepped to the center of the hall. An accomplished magician, he plucked a rose from thin air and, with a flourish, presented it to the queen. Then he walked along the row of diners at the front table and seemingly pulled brilliant silk veils from the left ear of every person at the table. The astonished antics of those who had imbibed too much added to the laughter and enjoyment of the room at large, and suddenly each victim Orion chose for his next magic trick became the butt of the jokes of his fellow diners. Amid oohs and aahs, Orion lifted his arms high and a white, fan-tailed dove flew from each upraised hand into the rafters above.

John leaned across Isabella to question their host, Nottingham. "Don't you have any of those dancing girls who walk on their hands and show off their legs?" he asked restlessly.

Nottingham shot an embarrassed look at the queen and apologized for the lack.

Next came the trick where Orion turned objects to stone. Isabella had been anticipating this for days, ever since she heard he could perform such feats of magic. He asked his audience to give him objects they carried on their person and he would turn them to solid stone before their eyes. Dozens of hands held out a variety of objects. One by one he selected a ring, a knife, a goblet, even a shoe as he intoned an incantation: "By all the might of Moon and Sun, cast the spell and it is done!" He then handed back a stone ring, a stone knife, a stone goblet, and a stone shoe.

The audience was spellbound. Jasmine's eyes were filled with wonder as the spoon she had given Orion was handed back to her turned to stone. "Isn't it amazing?" she said to the table at large.

Estelle sniffed loudly. "There is a limestone cave just a few miles off, this side of Sheffield. People leave objects inside the cave and the walls and ceiling drip, drip constantly with limestone, which coats all the objects. Orion, or O'Ryan as I call him, simply took the spoon you gave him and switched it for one he retrieved from the cave!"

The Countess of Warwick laughed richly. "Are you sure?"

"Of course. You'll notice he only picks very common objects that are certain to be handed to him. Demand he turn something unique into stone and he'll be stumped. The King's crown," Estelle suggested in a loud, carrying voice.

Orion cast her a look of malice while pretending not to have heard the suggestion.

Now the audience was in stitches as others took up the

cry, "My wife's mother," and from the back of the hall, "My husband's tool!"

As he heard the tone of the group degenerate, which it always did sooner or later when the ale and wine flowed, Orion held up his hands to quiet them. When he had their attention he said, "If you wish me to turn your stone objects back, simply bring them to me and I will give the counterspell."

Estelle mocked, "By the power of Land and Sea, as I will, so will it be!"

The Countess of Devon said, "Estelle, stop before I pee myself!"

Isabella, childlike, had thoroughly enjoyed herself. She stood now and the diners quieted to catch what she said. "Jasmine of Salisbury is going to read my tarot cards now, which will fascinate all the ladies. I give my permission for the gentlemen to play dice or other games more suited to their tastes."

Many of the men in the hall rose and stretched and refilled their goblets preparatory to an hour's gambling— all the men with the exception of King John and the Earl of Chester.

John jumped down from the dais and took Jasmine by the hand. He led her to Chester, lifted her in his arms, and handed her up to Ranulf's waiting arms. "Priceless!" John said with a wink.

Ranulf grimaced. "Not to the wealthiest man in England," he said with meaning.

De Burgh ground his teeth in mute rage as they handled his betrothed. Jasmine had exchanged one provocative gown for another simply to inflame his temper—at least he hoped her defiant action had been done with him in mind. His dark brows drew together in a frown as he recalled the man who had scaled walls for her before dawn. He glared down the hall. At least one thing was certain, it hadn't been Chester. Though the earl was un-

doubtedly strong, his arms and legs were overlong and
lanky; he could never be described as lithe as a panther in
a million years. Falcon's ears picked up snatches of conversation from his own knights, from nobles who had
traveled to get here, and from Ralph Murdach, the Sheriff of Nottingham, who was weary from listening to complaints. All the talk, it seemed, was centered on an outlaw
in these parts who had taken over the forests. Men were
flocking to him by the hundreds, according to rumor, and
even though there was a price on his head, none would
turn him in to the king's bailiff. Falcon heard Murdach
excusing his inadequacies as sheriff for the tenth time at
least. "My men are outnumbered. I intend to petition the
king for more men to rid the forests of this scourge."

De Burgh curled his lip in contempt. A few peasants,
freemen, and farmers were making a laughingstock of
Nottingham. What the hell would the man do against
enemies like the Scots and Welsh, fiendish plunderers,
wild and fierce and cruel as mountain cats who came
ravaging and burning? Falcon dismissed the talk of
Sherwood's outlaws with disgust. He shook his head
when his knights offered to hazard the dice with him and
made his way down to the dais where Jasmine was dis-
playing the beautiful but absurd occult cards she had
painted for Isabella.

Estelle rose from the table anticipating difficulties for
Jasmine if the queen's layout should be a bad one. De
Burgh slipped into her vacated seat between the two widows and shot Chester a warning look cold and hard
enough to freeze a man's soul, but now that Isabella was
monopolizing Jasmine, the king and Chester left the dais.
Nottingham followed like a trained hound. De Burgh realized with a shock that the ladies were very excited over
the fascinating, mysterious tarot cards they had heard so
much about. Why were women so ridiculous? he mused.
What made them so gullible? They were ready, willing,

even avid to be deceived. He proved to himself within five minutes that it was so. By dividing his attentions equally between the widows, he ascertained that each was willing to provide him with bedsport this night. Now all he had to do was decide which one he wanted.

Isabella, drawing as much attention to herself as possible, shuffled the large tarot cards, made her wish, then choose to lay out ten cards. As each was revealed, Jasmine became more dismayed. Though unbelievably accurate, the cards were anything but flattering to the queen. Isabella would probably have Jasmine executed if she read their true meaning before the assembled women.

Then her panic receded. She was playing a role. She had already rehearsed her attitudes and her lines if the cards were lethal. She glanced down from the dais and saw de Burgh. His gaze was detached and impersonal as if he found nothing to distinguish her from others. She saw the females flanking him and hated them on sight!

Jasmine gave the cards her undivided attention and began her interpretation. To de Burgh's ears her voice was like silvery chimes, clear, pure, elfin. He glanced at the other women and knew he wanted neither. He wanted Jasmine, exactly as she was. Damn her to hell, the maddening little witch was too exactly the way he would have her.

"The queen of pentacles is your first card and therefore represents you, your majesty," said Jasmine. The card meant a woman who was selfish, exhibitionistic, avaricious, bedecked in jewels, who cared more for luxury than love. The throne she sat upon was covered by symbolic figures of Cupid, ripe fruit, goat heads, and a rabbit, which of course represented sensuality.

"This card simply means a woman who will have every luxury in life," said Jasmine, which was true enough.

"What does the rabbit mean?" asked Isabella.

"All the symbols indicate that you will be fruitful and bear many beautiful princes and princesses."

Isabella looked pleased, then pointed to another card, the king of swords, and said, "There is John!"

Indeed it was John personified. A short, very dark man who inflicted verbal and physical abuse on children and women. A mean man, a bully and a tyrant who abused his position of power.

"Yes, your majesty. The king of swords represents a very dark man in highest office. A military man, as you see by the unsheathed sword."

"What are all the dark clouds gathered about his head?" asked Isabella.

"Just decoration," Jasmine lied.

"Why isn't his card beside the one that represents me? Who is coming between us?" Isabella demanded.

Jasmine was dismayed that it was the high priestess, which she had painted in her own image. The queen could clearly see that Jasmine stood between her and her husband. Jasmine did not like the implication at all. Not only was she between them, but the queen's hand had laid her card below the queen and king, and this clearly meant that they intended to step on her.

"What is the meaning of that card?" Isabella demanded.

"Subconscious knowledge, intuition, inspiration, occult wisdom, hidden mysteries, inner resources, the power of the subconscious mind to effect change and healing in one's own life, the ability to get to one's own inner center and function as a creative, life-affirming human being," Jasmine interpreted truthfully.

Isabella, consumed by thoughts of herself, thought the card referred to her, and she looked even happier. Next to the card representing John, the queen had placed the Devil. Jasmine thought perhaps she could get away with describing the card and its symbolism without directly connecting it to the King. Of course everyone in the room would think it most apt.

"This horned Devil with batlike wings sits on a throne. Chained before him are a naked man and woman. This card represents evil. Hedonism is not freedom to do whatever one wants, but slavery to one's desires. This card means self-indulgence, sensuality without sense, animallike conduct. It means someone practicing malevolent magic, satanic or Devil worship."

"Whatever does that card have to do with me?" demanded Isabella, her eyes sparkling dangerously.

Jasmine soothed, "The card is simply a warning to eliminate undesirable elements and not be chained by materialistic values." All the women in the room exchanged meaningful glances. They knew the card had hit home about the royal couple.

"The three of cups reversed, and the three of swords next to the Lovers is a most unusual layout," said Jasmine. "The three of cups represents a bride, a happy fulfilling card denoting joy in anticipation of marriage, but reversed and next to the three of swords it means a broken betrothal, interference of a third party who imposes himself between the lovers to break up a romance." Uppermost in Jasmine's mind was the fact that Isabella had been betrothed to Hugh of Lusignan and that King John had broken her betrothal and stolen her from Hugh.

Isabella, however, was thinking along very different lines. She knew Jasmine was betrothed to Falcon de Burgh and the cards were foretelling that she would be the third party who would break up their romance. What great fun. Such a diversion! And the girl had predicted it herself!

"Next to the lovers is the moon." Then Jasmine hesitated.

"Oh, I know . . . that must mean honeymoon," offered Isabella, showing her cleverness.

Jasmine grasped at the straw thrown to her. "Yes, how wise you are," she lied.

The moon had a crab, a dog, and a wolf baying beneath it. It warned Jasmine that she had secret enemies who would conceal something vital from her. There would be underhanded deals made and she would be surrounded by deception. Jasmine bit her tongue as she almost blurted that moon meant Lunatic, from the Latin word *Luna*. Now Jasmine realized this reading touched her as well as the queen. Jasmine found this woman and her court distasteful. The very air was filled with mists of dread and lurking undeniable evil. Perhaps she could influence Isabella to change things for the better. She recalled tales told her of the old queen's court, Queen Eleanor of Aquitaine. She recalled the very things that had awakened her desire to become a lady of the court.

The next two cards were disastrous: the ace of swords and the tower. The ace was a death card, which warned to expect the worst. It meant interference in one's plans, being blocked and thwarted, fearful anticipation, sadness and woe. Coupled with the moon it meant underhanded activity, using deception and trickery. Jasmine took a deep breath and plunged in. "The ace of swords is a very powerful card. It shows that the person can influence a great many people, as did King John's mother when she was queen. Her court of love became renowned. It was always filled with color, laughter, and music. Open lust was distasteful. Men did not approach a lady of the court in brutal fashion. Men were encouraged to treat women as ladies. They used flattery, wit, and elegance. It encouraged young men to sigh over other men's wives, and it was fine for the ladies to smile kindly upon them, but it was most innocent and harmless. The court encouraged musicians, poets, and the arts. The court had an ambience of romance and the hall rang with the tales of great love affairs, such as Tristram and Isolde, and Lancelot and Guinevere. Pages, knights, and minstrels fought for the honor to serve the ladies at table." When Jasmine glanced at the queen, she realized her words had had the wrong effect. Isabella did not like to be compared with Eleanor of Aquitaine and come up lacking. The queen looked down at the last horrific card the tower and swept it from the table. "I tire of this game," she said petulantly.

Jasmine looked from the dais to where de Burgh had been sitting but the table was empty. The queen, her mind already busy with a wicked plot, said cruelly, "Young widows are formidable competition with their knowledge of what men like best. Two bitches fighting over one bone." Isabella laughed at her own crudity. "Who knows, perhaps the bone is big enough to satisfy both."

Jasmine was seething inside. Whenever she had to spend time close to Isabella her nerve endings screamed their protest, and then to add insult to injury, the man who was supposed to be betrothed to her had offered her a public insult. Well, if he thought he could ride roughshod over her, he was sadly mistaken. She'd go to his tent this minute and catch him in the act. She'd make a scene that would disrupt the entire camp and castle. She had warned him once that he'd rue her. Well, tonight was the night! She'd sully his name and tell him flatly that by his venal, carnal indulgences he had broken their betrothal. She'd shatter his composure into a thousand pieces. Tonight would finish it!

Fearless as a tigress, she reached up to snatch a torch from its wall bracket as she left the castle and stalked through the bailey toward the meadow where the scarlet silk pavillion stood. As she neared the tent she could see the shadows of the couple inside. "Don't do this thing," whispered her better self; but her worse self threw all caution to the wind and plunged in.

Chapter 18

De Burgh and Gervase were talking seriously. Falcon looked up startled as Jasmine flew through the entrance as if the hounds of hell were nipping at her heels. Alarmed, he asked, "What's amiss, sweetheart?"

She blinked stupidly, then stammered, "N-nothing!" For once she was truly at a loss. She swallowed the accusations she had been about to scream and they almost choked her.

Suddenly he knew exactly why she was there. She had seen him leave with the women and had come to make a scene. Keeping his face straight, he came to her, took the torch from her hand and gave it to Gervase, then whispered, "Sweetheart, you came to share my bed again." The emphasis on the last word made her blush and Gervase flush.

"I did no such thing!" she denied hotly.

"Gervase will tell no one you came to me in your nightrail," he cooed.

"Nightrail? Nightrail?" she parroted.

"Well, that's what this transparent thing is, surely?" he asked smoothly, lifting the thin white silk with his strong fingers.

Gervase fled the tent before the approaching storm erupted.

"Under ordinary circumstances I'd be happy to accommodate you, my love, but I must inform my men that the stag hunt tomorrow has been changed to a manhunt."

"You conceited, vain, insufferable lout, you should have been drowned at birth!" As his words penetrated, a cold fear touched her. "Manhunt?" she whispered.

He said with contempt, "The king's sick idea of sport. Tomorrow we rid the forest of outlaws."

"Ah, no," she breathed, her hand going to her throat. She would go to the trysting place and warn Robert, but would she be in time?

In the flickering torchlight she looked fairylike, fey. Falcon forgot he had been teasing her as desire rose up within him, filling his head with her fragrance. "My love, I'll be as quick as I can with the men. Wait for me?" he implored. He cupped her face in his hands and lifted her mouth to his.

With his hot demanding mouth on hers, his powerful arms encircled her and pressed her to his hard length. Locked in his embrace, it was as though she lost separate identity. He overpowered her. She was conscious of every pulse of her blood. She was also terrified. He was too much . . . too big, too hard, too male, too hot, too driven by lust.

He swept her up in his arms and took her to the furs. Suddenly she knew without doubt that all the women in his varied past had been obligingly willing. He carried her with such practiced ease, accenting the power of his hands and his body. He laid her on the furs and looked down at the lushly carnal picture her silken-clad body made. He towered over her, clothed and booted, as dark as Lucifer. She felt as if his strength and size had already invaded her.

She lay obediently passive, hoping he would trust her to stay once he was gone. He bent to quickly remove his boots, threw the impeding cloak back over his shoulders, and lowered himself to the furs beside her.

"No, Falcon, women come too easily to you. You have been utterly spoiled where women are concerned. Your looks are so darkly beautiful and dangerous, they are all avid to have you make love to them. You must realize I'm different!" she cried.

"It's not the looks, darling," he demurred, "women simply want what they can't have. I'm a challenge to them." His intense eyes were iridescent in the lamplight. "I do realize you're different, Jassy darling . . . *you're* a challenge to *me*." He brushed her cheek with his fingers and immediately felt the blood drumming in his fingertips, his throat, even the soles of his feet. These, however, were nothing compared to the blood-throb of his erection. It was wildly alive and seeking the hot place it longed to plunder mere inches away. Through his soft chamois breeches she felt him rigid just above her mound of Venus and quickly put her hand down between their touching bodies to shield her private part. The effect on Falcon as her hand came in contact with him was overwhelming. He became almost orgasmic and knew if he didn't swiftly focus attention from the hot core of his manhood to the hot core of her womanhood, he would disgrace himself.

He reached up under her silken gown, sliding his hand up her leg, inside her thigh, dislodged the protective hand she was using to cover herself, and with one swift rip tore her undergarment so that it no longer covered her between her legs. As she gasped, he sighed with satisfaction that he now held in his hand the jewel for which he'd lusted so long. Easy, easy, man, a voice in his brain warned, don't deflower her with greedy, impatient fingers! More than anything on earth he wanted her to stay with him this night, yet his duty demanded that he leave her for a short time. His male arrogance told him that the only way to keep her in his bed was to arouse her desire to such a fever-pitch, she would wait all night for him to return and give her the bliss of fulfillment.

He was monumentally aware of her virgin state, knew she'd be sensitive in the extreme to plundering fingers, and therefore he would have to use the magic of his lips, first on her mouth, then lower as her fever built. "Sweet,

sweet," he whispered huskily as he brushed his lips across
hers, then entered her fragrant mouth with his tongue.
He gasped. "Can you die of pleasure?" Then his mouth
returned to hers, but it was out of control, plundering her
in a barbaric invasion. Jasmine had no choice but to yield
to his overpowering onslaught. A small measure of control returned to him as he began the delicate business of
her first orgasm. Experience had taught him that it was
entirely possible to bring a virgin to climax without tearing the hymen, but it called for a certain amount of very
gentle and delicate manipulation. How to manage touching her with the strokes of a butterfly's wings when all his
urges demanded he be a battering ram?

His mouth was dry, his manroot throbbed with bursting blood; he thought he could taste the blood in his
mouth. The pad of one fingertip gently traced the hot,
dry lips between her legs. He felt her shudder . . . or
was it he who shuddered? He stroked her gently, softly,
over and over, holding his breath, waiting for a tiny drop
of wetness on his finger that would be the signal for him
to proceed. She was fever dry, so different from any other
woman he'd ever touched. By now most females would
be slippery with desire. Some he knew would be spilling
their love milk onto their thighs in anticipation.

He increased the pressure of the pads of his fingertips
and increased the speed of his rubbing friction. "Do you
like me to touch you here, darling?" he whispered.

She squeezed her legs together tightly to prevent his
fingers from their erotic teasing. "No!" she said fiercely.

As he held her cupped in his hand, his fingers curled
ever so slightly inside her, he felt her heat until she
burned him. He could not help imagining what his shaft
would feel like if he plunged into her this moment, and a
low moan escaped from his throat. This was a new sensation for de Burgh. Up until now, sex had been a playful
diversion, a sport that brought pleasure, a casual game.

Now it was driving, urgent, his body demanding, clamoring, starving for her.

Try as he would, he could not control his lust; rather it controlled him. He told her in heated detail what he was going to do to her when he returned, how many times he would love her, and how she'd feel when he did those things. "Sweet, sweet, wait here for me; promise me you won't move? The first thing I want to do when I come back is give you your first kiss."

"Don't be silly, de Burgh, you've been kissing me all night," she said, gasping.

He chuckled. "Sweet innocent, I mean kiss you down here." His possessive fingers curled inside her. "Darling, when I take your virginity it will hurt you. My shaft is very large and will stretch you to the limit. I know you want to wait until we're married for the consummation, but starting tonight I'll make love to you with my mouth. By the time we are wed you will be more than eager to try something longer and harder than my tongue."

She was shocked to her soul. Not really comprehending fully, she whispered in disbelief, "You would kiss me, there?"

"Like this, darling," he said raggedly as his mouth took hers and he used his tongue deeply, intrusively, filling her totally with thrusting, dominant possession.

Her woman's cunning was the only thing that saved her. "I don't know how to do anything," she said softly.

He smiled down at her and slipped his fingers from her delicious heat. "By morning you will, darling."

"If you don't hurry, morning will be here, Falcon," she said breathlessly.

He rose from the furs and pulled on his boots. "Sweet, sweet, I'll hurry," he swore.

She was afraid to move until she was very sure he had gone, then she threw back the furs and stood up. She swayed dizzily, as she realized her legs had turned to water with fear. Fear of de Burgh, fear for Mary-Ann's lover Robin, fear of the morrow's manhunt.

De Burgh cursed silently as he moved about the camp. Because of the Sheriff of Nottingham's incompetence, compounded by exaggeration of the outlaw's daring deeds against the crown, his men were committed to take part in this travesty. He'd been ordered by John himself. When he learned that Chester, Nottingham, and Falkes de Bréauté were taking part, he had protested that it was superfluous to add his knights and men-at-arms to hunt down a few freemen, farmers, and peasants who used the forest for their refuge, but John had been adamant. John himself wanted to enjoy the manhunt and would feel safer with de Burgh's men about him. It wasn't that Falcon minded ridding the area of outlaws—he was in the business of killing—but somehow it seemed obscene to him to make a sport of it.

He spent longer with his men-at-arms this night than he did with his knights, for he knew common soldiers had a dread of the uncanny and the forests around Nottingham were legendary for their tales of the brotherhood of little people, of Mount Folk, Stone Folk, and Tree Folk who were supposed to rule the greenwood. Tales abounded of high mounds in the lonely deep forest where you could enter into entrancing lands of green twilight where lovely fiends dwelled and dreadful wizards worked their soul-snatching wiles and enchantment.

When Falcon returned to his tent he was sorely disappointed that Jasmine was not there awaiting his return, but he was not surprised. He had known somehow that she would flee the moment he left her. He knew she would have to be a wife, decently wed, before she gave herself to him. Even then it would be a reluctant mating on her part. He sighed. She was innocent, unawakened. No burning of the flesh, no hot desires, not even yearnings to be held in strong arms and stroked plagued sweet Jasmine.

He groaned aloud as he slipped inside the bed where her lingering fragrance clung to the furs. He closed his eyes and willed his demanding body to take rest while it could. His hot blood coursed through his veins, throbbing incessantly, making the heavy ache in gut and groin almost unendurable. He asked the impossible of himself. How could a man as hot and lusty as he rest at ease in a bed where his heart's desire had just been lying almost naked? He made an endless night of it, his body's frustration keeping him tense, aware, demanding. His thoughts prowled like a foraging wolf. Gervase must have been mistaken about the man. It may have been a thief climbing from a window, or some young squire scaling the wall on a dare, or the man could have sought a damsel other than Jasmine. His seeking mind went over the unlikely alternatives. Finally he groaned, gave himself up to the agony of her lingering presence, and buried his face in the fur's female fragrance.

Dawn had not paled the sky when he arose. His mind and body demanded action and his men were probably in like case. A stag hunt would have been an ideal remedy, but the abomination that was planned for that day presaged a bad feeling inside of him. He made a quick decision and started to waken his men to give them their orders, beginning with Gervase. "Anyone spotted in the forests, round them up and take them prisoner. I don't want a wholesale slaughter. No bloodshed unless your life is at stake."

The breakfast fires were lighted and the men were arming themselves and readying their horses. De Burgh mounted and rode off toward the River Trent. Perhaps if he doused himself in the cold river water, he'd be able to shake off the dirty feel of contamination. As he rode to-

ward the river the sky began to lighten imperceptibly and
for a moment he thought his eyes were playing a trick on
him. Damn it all to Hellfire, it wasn't his eyes that were
playing tricks, it was the wench he'd almost given his
heart to who was playing the tricks! She had just emerged
from the forest, riding directly in his path, and he had
seen her before she had seen him. The moment she spotted him, she jerked on the reins, then wheeled her mount
back into the trees. He touched one knee to his war-horse
and its powerful muscles gathered then surged ahead,
overtaking the smaller horse in less than a minute. He
reached out one long arm and snatched the reins from
her, bringing her palfrey to a quivering halt beside the
heaving, dangerous destrier. He was on the ground before
the horses stopped, quickly looping their reins to a tree.

Jasmine lifted her riding crop, but he gave her no opportunity to bring it down. He reached up and wrenched
it from her hand with such force she lost her seat and
came tumbling down to him in a flurry of skirts and
petticoats.

His emerald-green eyes were blazing with anger. He
slashed her short, heavy whip against his boots to release
some of the anger he felt, for before God he needed all his
willpower to keep from striking her. She had been to
meet someone—a man—and by the divine power of St.
Jude he'd know his name *now!* "Whom do you secretly
meet?" he demanded.

"I was out riding, I saw no one," lied Jasmine.

"That is an outright lie. Whom did you meet?" He
slashed his boot again and the sound of the whip was
ominously threatening.

She turned her face from him and caught her breath on
a sob. Cruel fingers took a firm grip on her chin. "You
will look at me when I speak to you. Whom did you
meet?" he shouted.

"No one," she denied, her face drained of color.

"Don't impugn my intelligence by treating me like some gullible fool. 'Tis obvious you've just come from a tryst. Have you been out all night? Did you leave my bed and go straight to his arms?" The questions came swiftly. He took her shoulders in his hands and began to shake her like a rag doll. "Answer me! Have you no brains? Don't you know these forests crawl with outlaws?"

At his last word her fear became so palpable that suddenly he knew. "Splendor of God, that's who it is! You lured the information from me last night and you've been to warn him! You treacherous little bitch." He snatched his hands from her as if he could not bear to touch her and she fell to one knee. He taunted, "I had no stomach for this hunt, but suddenly it's an event I'm anticipating with relish. I hope you measured him for his shroud last night."

"De Burgh, please," she cried, "you don't understand."

A jealous anger shot through him. "You plead for him?" He laughed. It was a bitter sound. "I understand, all right. You once told me my children would be bastards . . . like yourself!" he couldn't resist adding.

She recoiled from his words. If she had been afraid for Robin Hood and his men before, it was nothing compared to the fear she now felt for him. De Burgh would have no mercy. Robin had not even taken her warning too seriously. He had laughed and told her to stop worrying. "The forests of Sherwood, Ettrick, and Sheffield cover more than a hundred miles. They won't find hide or hair of us," he had boasted, but stacked against de Burgh's fury and determination they would go down like trees before the ax, like barley in a hailstorm.

Suddenly Falcon heard the king's hunting horn sound and knew he could dally no longer. He snatched Jasmine up and set her in her saddle.

"Get to the castle. Seek your chamber and remain there!"

He had tucked her whip into his belt and as he untied her reins, she reminded him, "My riding crop, de Burgh."

"I'll return it tonight, after I've flogged you with it!" He gave her palfrey a resounding smack across the rump almost to show her what she could expect at their next encounter.

The day turned out to be a nightmare of frustration for the hunters, and at its end, after crashing about the vast, deserted forests, a good majority of the men believed Robin Hood to be nothing but a myth. Others, like de Burgh, had different ideas. There had been an uncanny atmosphere present, as if every move they made had been watched.

There were inevitable casualties, poor devils who had been in the wrong place at the wrong time. The bodies were tallied at day's end. An old woman who had been gathering wood. A freeman farmer searching for a lost sow and a young boy who had been setting snares for rabbits, but nary an outlaw had been spotted, let alone bagged.

At twilight just as the hunt was about to be called off, de Burgh had felt the presence of death's angel. At a cry, he turned swiftly in time to see Gervase fall from his horse with an arrow in his back. It had punctured his squire's protective mail, proof that the arrow had been shot at very close range by a powerful longbow. De Burgh knew the arrow had been meant for him, and he gnashed his teeth to think that Jasmine's outlaw lover had almost eliminated him by superior stealth, cunning, and marksmanship. He was off his horse in a flash, kneeling beside his loyal squire. He thanked all the saints in Heaven Gervase had not fallen on the arrow to ram it deeper into the pierced flesh. The arrowhead was barbed, and Falcon knew he needed better light to extract it cleanly from the mangled flesh. The lad was unconscious, saints be praised. Now if he would just live until de Burgh tended him. He snapped the arrow's shaft in strong fingers as gently as he could and stuck the feathered half into his own quiver. Perhaps it would provide a clue to its owner's identity, though he was already convinced who wanted him dead.

He lifted his friend Gervase in his arms, held him secure against one broad shoulder, and mounted his destrier. The other horse followed as he walked his mount carefully back to the castle. He scribbled a hasty note to Dame Winwood, stamped the wax with his falcon seal ring, and dispatched it with a young page.

The boy found the frightening witchwoman scolding two young women who sat huddled miserably on a tester bed. Their eyes were liquid with apprehension as they awaited the day's outcome. This greatly puzzled the page, for the young queen and the other noble ladies had spent the day playing and laughing and dancing.

Estelle read the note quickly. "De Burgh asks my help . . . an arrow in the back. Mmm. I'll need alkanet and rue," she said to herself as she took out the box containing her medicines and ointments, "and borage for the fever that will come in the night."

Jasmine's eyes were wide with the unasked question. She opened her mouth, but the words would not come out.

Estelle looked at her wisely. "Nay 'tis not de Burgh who took the wound."

Mary-Ann's tongue was loosened by this information. She grabbed the sleeve of the young page and demanded, "What news of the manhunt?"

The page giggled. "It was a mixed bag—a pig herder, a rabbit catcher, and an 'owd woman. If you ask me there's no such man as Robin Hood!"

"Well, we didn't ask you," Estelle said sternly. "Get to the kitchens and get me a jar of vinegar. Take it to Lord de Burgh's tent and don't dally or I'll have him deal with you."

Relief had washed over the two young women, leaving them almost limp, but Jasmine didn't want to examine her relief too closely. From the sound of things the manhunt had been a colossal failure, almost a joke, and they thanked God and St. Jude that Robert had heeded the warning and fled.

Jasmine had dreaded the moment de Burgh would search her out to carry on where he had left off this morning. Though one of his men was wounded and he was busy at the moment, she didn't delude herself into thinking he would not return, perhaps on the morrow, to give her the beating he had promised.

When Estelle arrived at de Burgh's tent, he had already had a bed set up in it for Gervase and was in the process of removing the barbed arrowhead from the mangled flesh. The wound was swollen and angry and oozed blood rather than spurted it profusely.

The young man had regained consciousness for a while, but the pain when de Burgh drew out the offending lump of metal had rendered him unconscious once more.

De Burgh looked into Estelle's eyes. "Thank you for coming," he said evenly.

"I want something in return," she said shortly, brushing aside his thanks.

The page came in with the jar of vinegar. She took it from him and dismissed him sharply. Such sights were not for the eyes of babes. "Hold him while I cleanse the wound with vinegar," she directed.

"He's unconscious," Falcon pointed out.

"He won't be," she promised.

De Burgh held Gervase prone on the bed, pressing down upon his shoulders. As Estelle tipped the whole jar of vinegar into the wound, Gervase rose up like a rearing horse, screaming his pain.

"Vinegar has anesthetic qualities. It hurts only in the beginning," she soothed. "Dry it with the linen while I get the alkanet ointment. It will draw out any poison."

"Good God, you don't think the bastard used poisoned arrows, do you?" Falcon asked with alarm.

"Nay, I meant the body's poison that forms in wounds." She spread a thick coat of the ointment, which was made from the red flowers of the alkanet and had an almost pleasant odor. "His kidney has been damaged. Don't be alarmed if there is a lot of blood in his piss." She pointed to the brazier. "Boil some water and wine and I'll put borage in for the fever he is sure to produce in the night. In a couple of days we will change the ointment to rue. It has a strong, unpleasant odor, but it heals wounds with hardly a mark."

"Then you think as I do, that he will recover?" he asked gravely.

"Only because I'm here to tend him," Estelle said pointedly.

"Will you stay all night?" he asked quickly.

She looked at him with her shrewd, hooded eyes and wondered why he asked her. She knew he was capable of nursing his own squire. It must be something very important he had to do to keep him from this duty. "I'll stay. But, de Burgh, if the king goes on to the border shortly, you will have to leave him here. His kidney won't heal if jarred constantly in the saddle."

"Of course," agreed Falcon.

"I had heard you expected superhuman endurance from your men."

"I expect every last ounce they are capable of; no more, no less." He brought the borage mixture to the bed and touched it to Gervase's lips. "This will be bitter," he warned gently. Then he looked across at Estelle. "You said you wanted something in return."

She stood up to her full height. "When we first met you know I was set against your marriage to Jasmine. I have changed my mind. I want you to marry her and get her away from this court."

His nostrils flared. "Perhaps I have changed my mind," he said stonily.

She looked a question. He flung out his arm to Gervase. "I've had enough hurt from her."

Estelle wondered how Jasmine could have anything to do with the squire's wounds. "I thought her beauty enchanted you as no other had," she said quietly.

"She is exceeding beautiful, but still a woman and therefore treacherous."

"We are still the better half of the human race," Estelle said staunchly.

"Then may God help us," he said bleakly.

Chapter 19

The last thing Falcon de Burgh wanted to do was leave his faithful squire now, when he was sorely needed. But something inside him knew what he must do. He knew in his bones that the outlaw would risk all and come tonight. The lure of Jasmine would be irresistible. Wherever she went, he would follow, drawn against his will by the exquisite face, angel's hair, and tantalizing body. She had a magic power about her that was a siren song. Well, tonight it would literally lure a man to his death, he thought grimly as he found a concealed niche beside a stone archway.

He drew back into the shadow silently and prepared himself for the long wait. His mind darted about, touching upon one thing, then another. Why had Estelle changed her mind about him? Perhaps she hadn't really, perhaps he was simply the lesser of two evils. Jasmine . . . Jasmine . . . he had tried to understand that the delicate girl brought up to abhor and despise men would be cold to him, but with patience and determination he had thought she would have warmed toward him. His mouth formed a grim line as he fingered the scar her whip had left on his face. This morning when he caught her sneaking back from her rendezvous with the outlaw she had raised that whip again.

His blood ran cold when he thought of the outlaw. He swore an oath to avenge the wound Gervase had taken for him. His mind conjured a picture of the king and he spat upon the ground. This realm was in trouble. He'd sounded out men belonging to every northern baron and had not yet found one who had any loyalty to John. They had loyalty for their own barons, as he had for Salisbury, but he didn't believe there was a man left breathing in England who didn't despise and hate John for the weak coward that he was. He had inflicted private injuries on many of the barons and members of their families and Falcon sensed revolt coming, perhaps even civil war. The thing he found difficult to stomach was that he'd be on the wrong side in any conflict. Mayhap he'd hand the precious Jasmine back to Salisbury and be finished with the Plantagenets. Mayhap he'd go to Wales or Ireland.

It was three o'clock in the morning before he detected movement high on the wall. His quarry had arrived and was scaling the sheer stone wall of Nottingham Castle with the stealth of a cat. Falcon grunted his satisfaction as he slowly straightened from a cramped squatting position. He need not hurry, he would have plenty of time.

Let the lovers compromise themselves. That way it would be a most interesting *coitus interruptus.*

Soundlessly he made his way up the four flights of stone steps to the chamber he had paid for in gold. What a fool he had been! De Burgh fingered the knife at his belt with grim satisfaction. He would try to hold onto his temper so that he didn't kill the bastard. He would take him prisoner, prove to the crown that Robin Hood was no myth, and collect the reward. He would have to forgo the pleasure of gutting him in front of Jasmine. Pausing outside the chamber door, he noted the light streaming from beneath it. He unsheathed his knife, feeling a satisfaction at the weight of its haft, and burst through the door.

"De Burgh!" cried Jasmine, quickly putting herself between him and the couple behind her. He swept her aside with his free hand and advanced upon the man before him who was far too good-looking for his own health. He saw that Mary-Ann FitzWalter was present; he had forgotten he had ordered the two women to share the chamber.

The outlaw had kicked de Burgh's knife from his hand in a movement as lithe as a dancer and had drawn his own knife to attack. The two men grappled with each other. De Burgh held his assailant's wrists in a vicelike grip in a grim struggle to keep from being stabbed. They rolled to the floor of the chamber oblivious to the cries of the women who were begging them to stop.

With superhuman strength, de Burgh pinned his opponent, just long enough to put unbearable pressure on the other's wrist and force his fingers to release the deadly weapon. Now they were both unarmed, and the struggle grew in intensity. Fists smashed into jaws and cheekbones with sickening frequency. Neither man ducked the blows, preferring to take the punishment then give it back. They were almost enjoying it! De Burgh felt a grudging admiration for the other man and knew they were equal in strength and fighting ability. There was one big difference, however. De Burgh had sworn an oath to avenge himself for Jasmine and Gervase.

A scarlet blur of anger blotted out everything in the room until Falcon had his enemy under his control. Then he took the rope the intruder had used to climb in the window and trussed him like a haunch of venison. Falcon's eyes gleamed their victory. "Robin Hood, I arrest you in the name of the crown!"

Mary-Ann fell to her knees before him, beseeching, pleading, begging. "Lord de Burgh, I beg you to listen to me." The tears streamed down her face and fell onto her hands, which were clasped before her as if in prayer.

De Burgh blinked and glanced at Jasmine who stood by horrified with a look of total condemnation in her eyes. Mary-Ann was almost incoherent. "If he dies, I don't want to live. I love him, please, de Burgh, help us for pity's sake."

In a blinding flash it dawned on Falcon that the outlaw of Sherwood was Mary-Ann's lover, not Jasmine's. A wild elation ran up his spine, filling his head and making him dizzy with relief.

Jasmine knew that Mary-Ann's pleas would avail her nothing. If anyone on earth could sway de Burgh, it would have to be her. She went to him, placed her hands upon his broad chest, and looked up into his battered face. "Milord," she said softly, all woman, a supplicant to his strength, "I would ask your permission to speak."

"I will listen," he said evenly, his heart doing crazy things inside his chest.

"This is Lord Robert of Huntingdon. He and Mary-Ann were pledged. Then exactly the same thing happened to her as happened to me. She was abducted by a man called Roger de Longchamp while riding in Barnisdale Forest. Before he could force marriage upon her,

Robert rescued her and killed de Longchamp, as you killed de Belamé."

He glanced at the man he had trussed and said with disgust, "The king has made it fashionable to abduct young women."

Jasmine touched Falcon's bruised jaw with a tender finger. "Our stories are very different from this point on. Milord, you gained the Castle of Hagthorn by ridding the world of such scum, but Robert was stripped of everything—his home, his lands even his title—because de Longchamp was friend to the king. He was declared outlaw and put to the horn, but men will not turn him in for the reward. Rather they flock to join him by the hundreds. He has total rule in the forests."

De Burgh accused, "I knew you were there watching everything. I could feel your presence. You shot my squire by mistake when I was the one you intended to kill."

"Nay," said Robert, shaking his head in denial. "The arrow was not mine. Examine these in my quiver. I make all my own arrows from larchwood. The tips are weighted with lead. The feathers from wild birds."

De Burgh examined the arrows and knew the man spoke the truth. "Did you see who shot the arrow?" he demanded.

"It was a man belonging to the Earl of Chester. I know not which."

Jasmine stood on her toes in an attempt to look into de Burgh's eyes. He looked down at her. "Falcon, please, for me, let him go?"

The whispered request hung in the air for long minutes. It was the first time she had ever said his given name with tenderness. Implicit in the request had been a half promise. He made his decision swiftly and acted upon it immediately. He picked up his knife from the corner where it lay and severed the ropes that bound his prisoner.

The legendary outlaw said, "Someday soon perhaps I may be in the position to do you an equal service." He rubbed his wrists, then drew the tearful Mary-Ann close against him. "Come with me," he urged. "Let us be wed."

"I will! I will come!" she cried without hesitation. Happiness shone from her face, turning an ordinary girl into a radiant beauty. Robert put his finger to his lips to silence her, then opened the chamber door a crack to make sure no danger lurked outside. It would be easier if they crept down the four flights of stone steps, but de Burgh was sure in that moment that if there had been no other way out, the man would have taken his beloved down the walls on the end of a rope.

"My God, what a foolish girl," cried Jasmine.

Falcon took her by the shoulders and pulled her hard against him. "Why? Because she went with a man who had nothing to give her but his love and his strength?" he demanded. "She's not foolish, she's courageous. A man would give all for a woman like that," he said with admiration. His arms tightened and she felt all the strength of his body, the heavy shoulders, the powerful legs. He lifted her in his embrace so that her feet swung clear of the floor. Then he kissed her. Slowly he let her slide down his body until her feet touched the carpet and his hands drew aside her bedgown to take possession of her delicate breasts.

"Don't!" she cried, shocked.

"Sweet, sweet, there's only an hour left till dawn. Let me love you. Don't turn me away again." He felt her resisting him. "You don't have to give me everything until we are wed, but damn it, give me something." His lips touched her throat and traveled lower toward where her heart fluttered erratically.

"No, no, de Burgh, don't do this to me," she cried.

"Jasmine, you asked me for something and I gave it, now I am asking you for something."

"You are not asking!" she hissed. "You never ask. You order, you command, you take, but you never ask."

"I ask, Jasmine, I asked just now, but I won't beg, I won't grovel. I'm a man!" He spread his arms wide. "What is it you want from me?"

"You ask that as if you would give me anything I desired."

"I will," he promised. "What do you want?"

"Nothing!" She laughed, deeply satisfied. He had offered her anything and she had refused.

He almost struck her. She goaded him to the edge of violence, daring his manhood. He took hold of her roughly and crushed his mouth down on hers. He relished the pain it brought to his swollen jaw, and he needed to give her a little pain. With hurting hands he felt all the private places of her soft body. His mouth effectively silenced her cries. The kiss was ruthlessly lustful. Abruptly he let go of her and said with deadly intent, "You accuse me of taking . . . so I shall!" Deliberately he fastened one scarred hand into the neckline of her bedgown and tore it assunder.

"My God, my beautiful clothes! You destroy everything I own, you must be mad!" she cried, kicking the tatters from her ankles and crossing her arms protectively across her bared breasts.

He ground out, "I owe you one bedgown and one damned good beating with your riding crop." He snatched it up from the stool where it lay and Jasmine turned and fled. His anger was immediately replaced by lust as he saw her long, pretty legs and the opulent swell of her bare bottom. She ran into the far corner of the room then turned with fear-wide eyes, expecting him to bear down upon her with the cruel weapon in his grasp, but his only intent was to introduce her to the ways of love.

He lifted her up so that he could kiss her, but his mail crushed into her upthrusting breasts and she cried out. He lifted it off, dropping it to the floor with an ominous clang of metal which rang in her ears. Before he seized her up again he undid his breeches so that his great weapon sprang free. She dared not look at it and lifted beseeching eyes to his face. She saw only lust written there as his dark brows slanted above his deep-set, sea-green eyes.

Pressing her up against the wall, he bent his knees so that he would be able to support her when he thrust upward and entered her. Poised on the brink, he felt the thrill to the tip of his toes.

She needed a weapon to defend herself but had only a cutting tongue, sharp nails and teeth, and her wits. She tried out the first. "You sicken me! You are an uncivilized, brutal savage. You are driven to madness by your lust! You don't give a damn for anyone but yourself! Your squire lies near death, but all you can think of is fucking!"

He was shocked back to reality by the filthy word his beautiful Jasmine had just uttered and also by the truth she threw at him. Falcon de Burgh in that moment experienced shame for the first time since his early youth. Abruptly he set her feet to the floor, picked up his chain mail, and quit the chamber.

Jasmine fell back against the wall, bruising her thigh. She clenched her fists and swore an oath. "By God, de Burgh, before I'm done with you, I'll make you beg, I'll make you apologize for every insult you've flung at me!"

As Falcon approached his tent, he heard Gervase babbling nonsense and knew he was delirious with fever. He lifted the flap and entered just as Estelle was giving him another drink of bitter borage. Her shrewd eyes took in his bruises and his anger as he entered, then watched it disappear, replaced by anxiety for his squire. "I'm glad you are back," she said. "Very shortly his fever should break and he will be soaked with sweat. You can help me change him and change the linen."

He nodded. "I appreciate what you are doing, Dame Winwood."

"Have you been fighting over Jasmine?" she asked him bluntly.

"I thought I was, but I was mistaken." He shrugged. "I've fought all my life . . . it's fight and survive or fight and die."

"De Burgh, you have royal blood, do you not?"

"Aye," he acknowledged. "We de Burghs are descended from William the Conqueror's brother, Robert of Mortain."

"Too bad. It is too, too bad that the royal throne of kings did not come to a man like you. Instead through an accident of birth we have scum, that piece of offal to rule us." She sighed. "Ah, well, the only thing in life we can be sure of is change."

He said evenly, "Let's hope when it comes it is change for the better."

She looked up at him in surprise, then realized he didn't have the gift of second sight as she did. "No, de Burgh, things are going to get worse, much worse, before they get better."

They worked over Gervase for two hours, bathing him and changing the linen, then finally, mercifully the sweating ceased and he fell into a more peaceful sleep. Estelle began to gather her paraphernalia and said, "I'll go and get some rest now. In the afternoon I will return and dress the wound with rue."

"Estelle," Falcon said quietly.

"Yes?" she asked, pausing at the entrance.

"When I return from Scotland, I will marry Jasmine and take her from court."

Poor devil, she thought, he hasn't the vaguest idea that he's far gone in love with her. He still thinks he's in control. "Good night," she bid him.

Chapter 20

The next morning King John decided to continue his journey to the border to sign the treaty with King Alexander. Isabella and the court would stay on enjoying Nottingham's hospitality until John returned. Since Chester did not accompany the king, John had a word with him before he left. "Ranulf, about the secret matter we discussed . . . I believe Isabella has some fine ideas about the whole thing. She loves secrets. She'll plan everything down to the last detail. Put your heads together and we'll all come out of this with something we consummately desire," he said, winking.

"Remove the old woman for me, she is a bloody impediment," said Chester.

John chose to take offense. "Have a care, Ranulf. Dame Winwood is indispensable to me. I wouldn't consider such a lengthy trek without taking her with me. Her apothecary skills are unmatched. My physician is a butcher compared with her."

Estelle, however, was furious when she learned she must accompany John. She disliked riding and actually protested to the king on the grounds that her old bones would not take kindly to a trek that would take them over three hundred miles there and back.

The king dismissed her protest instantly. "Estelle, cut out the crap, you are as tough as old boots."

She had no option but to pack her apothecary paraphernalia and hope that Falcon de Burgh would not set a murderous pace. At first de Burgh was annoyed that Gervase was not healed enough for the journey, but upon reflection he felt it might not be a bad idea to leave a pair of "eyes" behind.

"Gervase, I have reason to believe the arrow you took was intended for me," he told his squire. "I suspect Chester wants me dead. Watch him closely for me. Don't trust him; he's far too clever to have only one scheme in his head. Since the king is taking your nurse with him, I'll have to ask Jasmine to dress your wound for you."

Gervase actually blushed, and Falcon realized she'd snared another heart. Was there no end to the little witch's conquests?

Falcon sought her out at the very last moment. Much to his irritation, he found her in the castle garden walking with Will Marshal, the king's squire who was about her own age.

"I hoped you would be too busy to bid me good-bye," she said cruelly.

De Burgh said pointedly to the squire, "Attend the king, he is ready to depart."

"No, Will!" cried Jasmine. "Stay by me lest he brutally attacks me again."

De Burgh took a step toward Will and winked broadly. Then he said in a deliberately harsh voice, "Begone, Marshal, I want no witnesses to what I am about to do to her."

Will grinned and sprinted off to find his groom who would be waiting with his horse. Jasmine glanced at de Burgh and noticed his battered face was healing well and was almost back to normal. "I warrant I've more bruises than you, you brute."

"I have little desire to hurt you, Jasmine, but I warn you now, wench, that if I continue to find you with men, I will give you a hard slap or two."

Her eyes flashed fire and she said regally, "I came to the garden for fresh air. Please be good enough to leave me, sir."

He couldn't resist. He set his hands to her waist and lifted her up to him. She had no choice but to cling to his wide shoulders for support. Then he brought his mouth to hers and kissed her. It began with the sweetest tenderness, his lips holding hers captive for long lingering minutes. The sound of her heart leaping about in her chest alarmed Jasmine. Her wicked juices began to stir, and suddenly her sharp little teeth bit into his bottom lip.

He set her to the ground with a look of surprised disbelief.

"Oh, I'm so sorry, Falcon, I was carried away," she said with the innocence of an asp.

His blood surged with anger and lust, the deadly combination. He pushed her into the deep grass and fell on top of her. One bold hand reached up her skirts to fondle her bare thighs and his fingers sought the tiny jewel nestled deep inside the exquisite flaxen curls.

As she desperately sought to squeeze her thighs together to prevent him from plundering her, she knew she had goaded him beyond control.

Young Will Marshal was astonished to see the couple in the grass. He had had no notion that de Burgh would bid her adieu by making love to her on the ground. He had not been jesting when he had winked and said he wanted no witnesses to what he was about to do to her. Though he was embarrassed to do so, Will had no choice but to interrupt their love play. "M'Lord de Burgh," he called, "the king commands you attend him, sir."

Jasmine gasped as he held her pinned long minutes with both his hands and his crystal-green gaze. Finally he said, "When I return, I'll finish what I started and that's a promise!" He left without a backward glance.

Later that day it was reported that Mary-Ann FitzWalter had gone missing. Jasmine tried not to laugh when a search party was organized and men were sent along the banks of the River Trent and into the fringes of the forest for sign of foul play. At last Mary-Ann's father must have guessed where she had gone and tried to downplay her disappearance. When they discovered that her young cousin, the red-haired Matilda, was also missing, they decided the two girls must have gone home to either Malaset or Dunmow.

Estelle was never more relieved in her life to see the high turrets of Pontefract Castle looming in the distance. De Burgh had bidden one of his men ride at her side and assist her to mount and dismount. She was thankful for the strong arm to lean upon as he helped her into the women's quarters and carried her boxes for her. She ordered a tray for herself, for there was no way she was going to drag herself to the hall to sit through a three-hour bout at table with the king and his host. She put on a warm bedgown, for the autumn nights this far north had a definite nip to them, and fell asleep almost instantly.

She blinked owlishly as a young page shook her awake. "Dame Winwood, please awaken, the king has need of your services, ma'am."

"Damn the king!" she said, visibly shocking the young errand boy. "It must be close on midnight, what the hell can he want at this hour?"

"I don't know, ma'am. I was told to sleep outside the royal chamber. All at once King John came out and kicked me awake and told me to hurry and fetch you."

"Well, mayhap he's had a fit," she murmured to herself." Then she added, "And by God if he hasn't, I'll give him one." She took out a bottle of distilled lily-of-the-valley and said, "Lead the way, lad, then get to bed. A child should be in his bed at this hour, not sleeping in doorholes."

She found the king's chamber locked, so she rapped lightly. The door was opened a crack. "Are you alone?" asked John.

"Of course I'm alone. Who else would be about at this ungodly hour?" she demanded.

He opened it only partway and said, "Come inside quickly."

She scrutinized him and saw that although he wasn't in a fit he was deathly pale and extremely agitated. There was definitely something odd about a man who would wear a bedrobe and a crown.

He jerked a thumb toward the great bed. "Something has happened to her . . . you'll have to revive her."

Estelle could see no one in the great bed. She went closer, then turned back the cover. "Mother of God," Estelle cried, crossing herself, a thing she seldom did. The small, naked body of the twelve-year-old Mathilda FitzWalter lay whiter than death. In contrast, her brilliant red hair spread across the pillows as an omen of what Estelle would see when she pulled the covers down all the way. Crimson blood pooled the bed where the child had hemorrhaged. Her thighs ran with it and a pillow had been stuffed between them in a futile attempt to stem her life's blood.

John wrung his hands. "Give her something to restore her."

Estelle's accusing eyes burned into his. "I work miracles, but I do not resurrect the dead!"

"She's not dead, woman, she's not dead I tell you!"

"She is dead. You have killed her." It was a dangerous moment for Estelle. One missed step, one word wrong as she diced with death could seal her doom. She quickly told herself that in any encounter between two people, one is dominant, one submits. The difference is fear and John was certainly afraid.

"We'll have to get rid of her," he said, linking her to the conspiracy. "What will we do with her?"

"It's best you don't know. Leave all to me," she temporized. This was one body that was not going to be conveniently disposed of, Estelle decided. She would send it home for burial. She thought of de Burgh, then dismissed the name instantly. She didn't want him connected to this. Likely he would never compromise his integrity and could lose his head as a result.

She washed the small body until it was free of blood, then she gathered the sheets and pillow and took them to be burned. "Don't open this door to anyone until I return," she instructed the king.

He nodded solemnly and fingered his crown nervously.

She hurried along the hall to Will Marshal's room and drew him outside into the hall. "I want you to get a wooden box with a lid and fetch it to the king's chamber," she told the young man.

He looked puzzled. "How large?"

"Large enough to hold the body of a child," she said softly. "Take it home to the FitzWalter family at Dunmow."

Will closed his eyes. "Sweet Mary and Jesus." Then he added, "I'm going to tell my father what he's done. I can remain silent no longer. I'll never be back, Estelle."

She nodded her head. "William Marshal is the only man who would dare call him to task. When a child's life has been frittered away the heart cries out for justice, justice."

John spent an unquiet night. He wished he'd brought along Orion to cast him a new horoscope. Surely his Fate was not taking a turn for the worse? By morning, however, he had a firm grip on himself and the incident was forgotten, at least by John, as more urgent matters plagued him.

All the way north he had sent recruiters ahead of the party to gather support for his armies. The men had fanned out reaching into every northern county and shire held by his barons. None had escaped the king's request, be they vast landholders or owners of a single castle. He needed the support of his northern barons if he ever hoped to regain what had been lost across the sea. He needed it to keep peace in Scotland and Wales, and when he thought of the savages in Ireland who knew only tribal patriotism, he ground his teeth that anarchy ruled.

Although the barons' service was supposed to be assured to the king, one by one the answers were coming back *no!* The northern barons were not willing to have their knights and men-at-arms sacrificed by an ineffectual leader who could have nothing but losses against a king as strong as Philip of France. They could not help but compare John to his great father and to his brother Richard, and he came up sadly lacking in all things. One baron put it rather aptly when he described the king as all cock and no balls.

When they reached their destination, Falcon de Burgh was glad to be quit of John. He looked at his friend Salisbury, amazed that the two men were actual brothers. He did not for one minute doubt that the Earl of Salisbury was Henry II's son, but doubt began to creep in about John. Had Eleanor of Aquitaine palmed off a bastard on an unsuspecting Henry? Poor Henry must be writhing in his grave to think that his favorite youngest son was squandering everything he had strived for in his lifetime.

The host, Eustace de Vesci, who had gone on crusades with Richard, did not quite know what to make of this king. John openly coveted his wife Margaret and did not even try to keep his hands from her. At first Eustace pretended to laugh it off and treat it as a joke, but when John made it plain that he expected Margaret would be his bed partner, Eustace stopped laughing.

Margaret had retreated to the women's quarters of the castle, but she knew full well that when a king commands, a subject obeys. Eustace came to her there in a high temper, venting it on any hapless female within earshot. Dame Winwood, seeing Margaret burst into helpless tears, offered the couple a little advice. "These parts are famous for a very strong liquor they brew, are they not?"

"Aye, 'tis a liquor distilled from grain and malt, but I don't believe ye'd care for it, dame, 'tis not exactly a lady's drink. One swallow steals yer brains, two swallows steal yer legs, and a whole cup knocks ye on yer arse!" Eustace exclaimed.

"King John likes his drink," she said smoothly. "If you plied him with enough, you could easily put a substitute for Margaret in his bed and him be none the wiser."

Eustace hurried off to find a large keg, while Margaret took herself off to the knights' sleeping quarters in search of a whore.

Dawn's light brought a courier with a message that knocked all prurient thought from John for days. Old Hubert Walter, the Archbishop of Canterbury, was dead and the canons in England who had seen the teeth drawn from canon law wanted more power. Without consulting the king, they chose from among their own ranks Stephen Langton and sent him to Rome posthaste to be consecrated by Pope Innocent. John became so angry he fell to the rushes and had a seizure. Estelle was sorely tempted to dose him with a substance that would worsen his condition. She had an almost uncontrollable urge to see him suffer, but common sense prevailed. All knew she medicated John, and if anything befell him, the finger would point to her. Throughout history since the Garden of Eden men had put the blame for misfortune upon women. No, if she ever gave John a potion she would make sure it was a lethal one, for his revenge was terrible.

John ordered Falkes de Bréauté to Canterbury to seize the estates of the archbishopric and the land of all the other bishops of the province of Canterbury.

He ordered Salisbury to go to Rome to "straighten out the Pope." William was horrified at the prospect. "John, I'm no churchman. To me the Church is all bells and smells and popery! I'm a plain soldier. This delicate business calls for a diplomat such as William Marshal. I'll go immediately to Chepstow and brief the marshal. You may trust him to do the right thing."

"Let's get this damned treaty signed so I can return south. I don't trust anyone with a northern accent," urged John.

"I'll leave Eustace de Vesci up here to see that the peace is kept, and don't forget you are taking the two little princesses of Scotland to ensure their brother Alexander keeps his word," Salisbury said.

"Ha! They don't call Alexander the Red Fox of Scotland for nothing! How far can I trust him?" asked John.

Salisbury grinned. "About a tall man's pissing distance!"

John said, "I'll have his sisters hostages. I'll take them to Nottingham."

A warning bell went off in Salisbury's head. Estelle had told him straightforwardly why John was not to be trusted with little girls. William cleared his throat and said firmly, "These are such important hostages, John, I think they should be entrusted to Hubert de Burgh, who does such a fine job with all your other political prisoners. I'll send young Falcon de Burgh with them for safekeeping until he puts them into his uncle's custody. He'll need only a few of his men for that; the rest can give you safe escort again to Nottingham."

"And by the bones of Christ I'll need it in this unfriendly northern clime. So far every northern baron has refused me service, so instead I'll command every last one of them to pledge me a son as hostage for their good behavior."

Salisbury thought this a bit drastic and tried to lighten John's heavy hand. "In faith, you'll have to give Hubert de Burgh more castles to house them all," he said, laughing.

"He has Corfe, Sherborne, and Wallingford as well as Dover and the Cinque Ports. I gave him the Roumer lands and Causton in Norfolk before I was ever king," John pointed out.

"I was jesting," said William. "Don't be so serious. Go to Nottingham and relax."

"I'll not stay in Nottingham, 'tis too damned far north for my liking. I won't rest easy until I'm on my own broad acres in Gloucester."

William kept a wise silence, but inside he chuckled to himself. "You'll be looking over your shoulder, terrified, every step of the way."

Chapter 21

Queen Isabella had developed an amuse-me-or-else attitude. As a result, Jasmine and Orion were hard-pressed to trot out every skill they possessed in connection with the occult.

Today Orion was describing the personalities of those born under various signs of the zodiac. Isabella naturally insisted he begin with Leo since it was her sign, and Jasmine had to hide a smile behind her hand when she heard him try to be diplomatic and not give offense. It was a tricky business trying to please a vain, childish girl who had the power of a queen.

What he said was "You are the center of your universe and attract many people to you. You have considerable ability and power to influence others and have them carry out your ideas. You have very little fear in your nature and you can present a forceful, dynamic, and commanding attitude when necessary. You have a great amount of pride. You must guard against your temper, but you have good willpower and an independent nature when it comes to doing your own thinking and working out your own ideas. You have quick perception, which allows you to grasp facts quite rapidly."

What Orion did not say about Leo was "You will achieve personal success no matter whom you have to step on. You are too egotistical and self-important, you can be rash, sharp-tongued, and unpleasant. You indulge yourself in all things. You are stubborn, obstinate, and headstrong. You are prejudiced in your views, narrow and intolerant."

Isabella was pleased with what Orion said and did not say. "Now tell me the character of one born under the sign of Scorpio," she bade.

Orion, no fool, knew she had King John in mind. Again he chose his words carefully, sticking to the truth but eliminating all that was negative. "Scorpians can be attractive, magnetic, and dynamic, but they are sometimes difficult people to understand. This is because they have a tendency toward being secretive. They are capable of influencing others to a great degree. They are consumed by desire for the luxuries of this world and must guard against overindulgence. If the Scorpios exercise proper control, they will attain great success in life. At times they can be generous, loyal, and will receive many appeals from people for understanding when they must face situations and personal problems. Their powers of observation are keen and they will not take another's advice. They have a most powerful will and determination."

What Orion left unsaid was "There is no fury like a Scorpio temper. They not only get angry, but are extremely obstinate and headstrong with it. They speak bitterly and cuttingly. No consideration is given to others. They are cynical, self-willed, and selfish. They will be the cause of their own downfall in life. They are temperamental and highly nervous. They have intense emotions, which can cause them to lose all self-control."

Isabella had stopped listening. Her whole attention was now taken by a monkey on a chain who was trained to do little tricks such as beg with its little hat in hand and play dead.

On impulse Jasmine asked Orion to tell her the personality of one born under Aries. The moment the words were out of her mouth, she wondered why she had asked such a thing. Just because she knew Falcon de Burgh's birth date did not mean that she had any personal interest in the man. But perhaps she would learn something to help her with him should Fate frown upon her and make him her husband. "Orion, do not leave out the bad traits; I would know all," she said.

Orion rubbed his nose hard, and Jasmine thought perhaps that was why it almost turned a corner. He said, "Aries is the first sign. They are the leaders of the world because of their active and dynamic personalities. They are very fond of being looked up to by others. They are courageous to the point of daring. By nature they are restless and fond of all sorts of activity. They should guard against engaging in risky and hazardous adventures. They can be affectionate, courteous, and generous, but they are also quick-tempered, and if crossed they can hold a grudge until they are able to take their revenge. They are aggressive and determined and have the personality and temperament that will make or break their own destiny. They are very impatient and in a hurry about everything. They live for and love action and follow their own judgment. Their mental capacity gives them the ability to grasp a situation before others have even thought about it. They have excellent coordination between mind and body, and they usually enjoy a lifetime of action and accomplishment. However, those about them often wish they would not try to impose their strong will quite so often."

He has described Falcon exactly, thought Jasmine. Impulsively she asked Orion, "What mate is best for an Aries?"

"There is only one true mate for an Aries, and that is a Sagittarius. Their life together will not be smooth, rather it will be an invigorating tiger ride, a clash of brilliant personalities; sometimes dangerous and frightening, but always exhilarating. Both will strive for the upper hand so that sometimes you are the driver and sometimes you are driven. But in the end Sagittarius will submit to the stronger Aries."

Surprise etched Jasmine's lovely features for she was a Sagittarius. Quickly she chided herself for being a fool. This astrology stuff was all nonsense, or was it? "Thank you, Orion. Tell me, which of the twelve signs produces the most perfect personality?"

"Ah, child, that is an easy one. If you need a friend choose one born under Cancer. Cancers exert a very fine soothing influence upon others. They are never egotistical or vain. They are very deep thinkers with a true depth of feeling. They are sensitive and easily hurt, but they hide this well from others. They have the ability to make other people happy. They are straightforward, generous, upright, and very loyal to friends or causes that interest them. They can be trusted with important secrets and you can totally rely on them for any duty, commission, or work. They dislike any small or petty act. They view the people around them with a maternal or parental attitude as though they were children, and in their noble yet silent way they guide them. They are sympathetic, understanding, and very practical. They have keen powers of observation and enjoy reviewing facts, ideas, and theories in their reflective minds. They are meditative with unusual powers of concentration, and there is very little that escapes their attention. They are cautious and prudent and analyze thoughts and impulses. Their faculty of imagination is very active and they enjoy musing about the past. They have the ability to improve everything they touch."

Jasmine smiled at him. "You yourself were born under Cancer?"

He pretended astonishment at her perception. "However did you guess?" he replied, twinkling.

The next day it was Jasmine's turn to use her talent to amuse. She decided she would do a little palm reading. Her audience numbered so many overeager ladies who sat with their hands spread out before her awaiting her revelations that it took her hours to explain the meaning of the myriad lines and signs on their palms.

When she had finished Jasmine drew a deep breath and turned to see if Isabella was pleased or displeased. However the queen, like everyone else in the hall, was peering into her hand with a puzzled look of concentration upon her countenance.

Suddenly a male hand was thrust before her eyes and a persuasive voice said, "Princess Jasmine, what do you make of this appendage?"

She turned to see Chester towering at her side. "My lord earl, I have no such title," she protested, unsure of his motive.

"You are Henry II's granddaughter, are you not?" he asked quietly.

"Yes, milord," she said softly.

"Then you are a princess. Would you like me to tell you of your grandfather?" he offered.

"Why, that would be most kind of you, milord. Did you know him very well?"

"Come, let us walk while I tell you of him," he said, formally extending his arm so that she could place her hand upon it. "Henry considered me one of his bright young men. He was like that—he took a keen interest in those who served him. He trained me himself in his ways and in his conception of law administration. Henry was a generous man to those who served him well. He gave me Brittany to govern; he rewarded me well for my loyalty. I am the last survivor of the aristocracy of the conquest. Bloodlines are very important to me, Princess Jasmine."

"Oh, please call me Jasmine."

"If you will call me Ranulf?" he asked.

"Ah, milord, I could not," she protested.

"You will in time," he said gently, happy that she was in great awe of him.

"The rewards from your grandfather have made me the wealthiest noble in the realm," he said with pride, "and yet I am a plain, blunt man. I do not parade my wealth upon my back like some of the flashy peacocks at court. I have no claim to beauty, and yet I appreciate beautiful things more than any man I know."

Jasmine wondered why he was telling her these things. "Everyone speaks so well of my grandfather, and yet because I am a woman I find it incomprehensible that he would imprison his wife."

"Ah, it was her vast power as queen that he had to contain. She bred him four sons and then used those sons like young wolves to pull down an old lion, so that hers was the power and the glory! Eleanor was very strong and willful and grew ever more so with age. That is the reason he turned to your grandmother, the beauteous and gentle Rosamund Clifford. Now, there was a love match."

Jasmine deliberately insulted him. "Ah, I had no idea you were so old, milord earl, you must be senior to my father." She looked at him with pretended innocence and saw that his eyes were remote and malignant, and she shivered as if a goose had walked over her grave.

"I am not yet forty years old, mistress," he said bluntly. "Your grandfather insisted I marry into his family. He always intended I should have a wife with royal blood," he added pointedly.

Jasmine could not quite bring herself to insult him about the royal bride who had divorced him as soon as she was able.

Ranulf de Blundeville's eyes dropped to her breasts and he said thickly, "I once spoke to your father William about needing a young wife."

Jasmine knew they were on dangerous ground indeed, so she again deliberately misinterpreted his words. "Perhaps one day we shall be related through marriage then, for I have two sisters who are not yet betrothed. Excuse me, sir, I have duties that cry out for attention."

"We will be related through marriage all right," he said under his breath, relishing the thought of having the exquisite, delicate body at the disposal of his own body's demands.

Chapter 22

As the days stretched out, Jasmine found that Isabella was throwing her and Ranulf de Blundeville together on the flimsiest of excuses. Jasmine began to miss Estelle's support and wise words of advice and longed for the older woman's return. Of course this also meant King John's return, but it would almost be worth it to have the security of her grandmother's presence.

King John's foul reputation preceded him, once Mathilda FitzWalter's still body was returned. The gossip and rumors spread like wildfire and were on every tongue until a pall hung over all Nottingham. Whispered plots of revenge were overheard and hushed up, and the ranks began to thin out. It became dangerous to venture anywhere near the forest lest a terrible accident befall those connected to the royal court. Wives urged their husbands to put a distance between them and the king and return to their own safer castles.

The Lady of Hay, Mathilda, was outraged and insisted her husband William de Braose leave Nottingham immediately. They would return to their own estates, which bordered those of her good friend Avisa, and wouldn't she have a thing or two to pour into her ears. John was a cold-blooded child murderer. Hadn't he disposed of his own nephew Arthur because he posed a threat to the throne? Something must be done, she told everyone she encountered.

It did not take King John twenty-four hours in Nottingham to learn which way the wind blew. He ordered the queen pack up the royal household to remove to Gloucester and gave her one day to accomplish the impossible. He insisted that he wished to be in Gloucester by September. If she was not ready, he informed her, she would have to follow, but it would be at her own peril because he needed his soldiers at his back and was willing to spare her a mere token escort.

John sat down with Ranulf for a serious tête-à-tête on their favorite subject, money. De Blundeville offered him a hundred thousand crowns for Jasmine. John promptly accepted and invited the earl, his best friend, to accompany the royal party to Gloucester where Isabella would be able to indulge herself planning a secret wedding.

Estelle sat in a bath of Epsom salts, bewailing the fact that she had no nipbone plant to add to the water. A quiet knock on the chamber door sent Jasmine quickly to stop any from entering while Estelle was naked. She opened the door a crack to see a young page. "The court is ordered to Gloucester. You have one day to ready yourselves," he piped.

"God's love." Estelle moaned. "I'm tempted to poison all the horses. My arse will never be the same again."

"Why don't you ride in a litter, Grandmother?" Jasmine asked with concern.

"What? And admit I'm an old woman? 'Tis a good thing my backbone is stronger than my backside."

Jasmine couldn't hide a smile. Pride kept Estelle in the saddle. Pride was what she herself had inherited from Estelle. Pride was a luxury that came with a high price, but oh, how she scorned those without it. "I've warmed this towel at the fire. Let me dry you and you can slip right into bed," soothed Jasmine.

"Thank you, darling, but it can't be done. I have to go down to the tents and give Gervase a sealed message from de Burgh."

"Didn't he return with the king?" Jasmine asked, surprised.

"No. He took the Scottish princesses to his uncle, Hubert de Burgh, for safekeeping."

Jasmine didn't know if she was relieved or disappointed. "Well, that's good. The wretched man is forever threatening me with marriage."

Estelle began to dress. "There are men about far more wretched than de Burgh."

"I know," admitted Jasmine. "I hope Ranulf de Blundeville goes back to Chester."

"Don't count on it," advised Estelle. "He and John are close as copulating dogs."

"Grandmother!" Jasmine exclaimed, shocked at her language. "Don't be obscene."

"I abhor obscenity!" said the old woman. "Bar this door while I'm gone."

As it turned out, Queen Isabella was nowhere near ready to depart at the end of the twenty-four-hour ultimatum John had issued. Thinking only of himself, as he was wont to do, he left for Gloucester, taking the lion's share of the knights and men-at-arms. The Earl of Chester was stuck escorting the queen and her ladies. This, however, gave him ample time to discuss the plan for the secret wedding. Isabella was extremely excited by her own cleverness for she had thought of the perfect cover to blind everyone to her plotting.

It was the upcoming wedding of Falkes de Bréauté to Joan, the widow of the Earl of Devon. Joan had provided the thirty thousand crowns King John demanded for her hand in marriage, and the wedding was to take place as soon as de Bréauté reached Gloucester after he had done the king's dirty work of dispossessing the bishops of their Canterbury holdings. So all the talk was of "the wedding."

Much to Jasmine's annoyance, Chester seemed to enjoy her company. For the most part she remained silent while Ranulf impressed upon her his exalted ancestry, his importance to the realm, the number of cities and towns he ruled, the jewel of these being Chester, an ancient, walled Roman city.

When the weather turned cold and nasty for traveling, which was unusual for autumn, he described the sun-warmed coast of Brittany around the Gulf of St. Malo, an area he had governed for her grandfather. She knew the stark and graceless earl was wooing her. She tried being cold and distant, but he did not seem to notice. Next she told him pointedly, "My lord earl, I do not think it is wise for us to be seen so much together. I am promised in marriage."

He was amused. "No man is more aware than I that you are promised in marriage," he said enigmatically.

She relaxed a little, offering a silent prayer for Falcon de Burgh. He served as a powerful barrier between her and men's unwanted attentions. But Ranulf de Blundeville seemed impervious to the implied wrath of her betrothed.

To Jasmine the journey seemed endless as mile after weary mile they walked their horses at a snail's pace toward Gloucester. She was tired, irritable, and a small knot of apprehension was growing inside of her because of Chester's insidious presence. She was picking up vibrations from the man that frightened her. He was almost like a predator circling his prey in ever smaller circles, and she had the feeling that she might be trapped if she didn't proceed with caution. At last the spire of Gloucester Cathedral could be seen in the distance. It had taken them over three weary weeks to make the journey.

Falcon de Burgh and a dozen of his best fighting men were playing nursemaid to Alexander of Scotland's two little sisters and their personal servants. The hard-bitten Norman soldiers had set out with tight-lipped anger and disgust at their assignment. Everything that could possibly go wrong had done so. The little girls cried because they were leaving their dogs and pets behind, then their horses became lame and de Burgh had to purchase new mounts for them at Newcastle.

The children and their servants spoke with such a thick Scots' burr that communication was almost impossible, resulting in one misunderstanding after another. The weather had a will of its own and chose to be perverse until de Burgh's men were at their wit's end. Finally the whole debacle degenerated into farce. Falcon was relieved that his men's high spirits broke out in hilarity. The horseplay and heels-in-the-air laughing fits were infinitely preferable to a volcanic erruption of frayed tempers.

They jousted and pushed at each other with their rough hands when they mounted, played devastatingly cruel jokes on one another, and seemed to exult in the inclement weather. The more bitter the wind, the more they threw off their hats and opened wide the necks of their leather jacks, laughing boisterously. It was as if the wind lifted their wild spirits. And indeed to men who lived by the sword, this was like a holiday, sauntering from castle to castle along the east coast. The little girls were tucked in their beds by suppertime, leaving the long evenings free for the men to laugh and drink and gamble and tell tall tales, each outdoing the one told before.

The next night, spent at Folkingham Castle, turned out to be the most miserable experience of the whole wretched journey. It was pouring cats and dogs, the heavens chucking down everything they had. The place was in such disrepair they spent the night in the leaky stables with their mounts, vying with one another for piles of moldy, wet hay.

Tempers frayed somewhat around midnight with curses and accusations of "witless bastard" and "weak-livered whoreson." A voice said, "Horse shit's supposed to be lucky, stop whining." Another voice answered, "Lucky for me, unlucky for you!" This was followed by the sickening thud of a fist in a face. When the gray wet dawn arrived at least half of de Burgh's men sported black eyes and sheepish countenances.

After an hour in the saddle, both children were sneezing and coughing and their servants were almost useless. De Burgh realized that winter had arrived early and no more warm autumn days would be forthcoming. He made a quick decision. Instead of going directly south from Spalding, he turned east, skirting the wash, and rode into Norfolk.

The de Burghs had vast holdings in this part of England. Hubert's Castle Rising was a snug, well-appointed place where the children could be put to bed until they were well and Falcon and his men could lie before roaring fires, eating and drinking their heads off if they so chose.

The hour was late when they arrived at Castle Rising, and Falcon was surprised to see that the stables were almost full. He glanced up in the darkness and saw that the de Burgh flag was flying, indicating that Hubert was in residence. They clattered over the drawbridge and rode under the spiked portcullis to the inner bailey where he left his men to deal with their charges. He walked through the passageway with guardrooms on either side filled with men at their evening meal.

Hubert's face split into a broad grin. "Falcon, lad, well met. Is Salisbury here?"

"No. I've only a dozen of my men with me, but you're the one man in all England I'm glad to meet up with tonight."

"Why's that?" Hubert asked suspiciously.

"I'm escorting the Scots' princesses to you for safekeeping and I'm glad to be shut of them," he said, grinning. "We don't make very good nursemaids."

"Shit, that's all we need," Hugh exclaimed, looking decidedly uncomfortable. He indicated the man sitting on his right. "Falcon, this is the Bishop of Norwich."

"Yes," Falcon said, nodding, "I've known the bishop since I was a lad in these parts."

"Aye, well, that's why I rode up here to get his advice about how to proceed with the news I received from the latest ship." Hubert hesitated, then plunged in. "Pope

Innocent has excommunicated John. The shit will really fly when he finds out."

Falcon removed his damp cloak and ran his fingers through his hair. "That's why you hoped Salisbury was with me."

"Aye." Hubert nodded. "In Greece they used to kill the messenger who delivered bad news . . . but I figured even John wouldn't kill his own brother."

"Don't count on it," Falcon said grimly. He turned to the bishop. "What will this mean?"

The Bishop of Norwich puffed out his lips. "It will all blow over as soon as the king accepts Stephen Langton as Archbishop of Canterbury. Then the Pope will reinstate him. In the meantime, John won't be able to attend church or receive the sacrament. While he is under the ban of excommunication, any religious service he attends will be invalid."

Falcon said carefully, "And if the king refuses to obey the Pope? Where do you stand in this?"

"Of course he will obey the Pope. We all must obey the Pope, for his is the higher authority. I shall certainly obey him."

"You may, my lord bishop; the king may not. What then?"

"It would be anathema. The Pope would lay England under an interdict. All religious services would be ordered to be suspended. No burial services, no wills probated. We would cease to be a Christian land. With a papal ban the Pope could curse King John within and without, sleeping or waking, going and sitting, standing and riding, lying aboveground and underwater, speaking and drinking, in field, in town . . ."

Falcon beckoned Hubert with a jerk of his head. What he had to impart could not be said before the bishop. Hubert rose from the table and said, "I'd better take a look at the little princesses. Special quarters will need to be plenished."

When they were alone Falcon said, "John has sent Falkes de Bréauté to confiscate all the lands of Canterbury. Salisbury is on his way to dispatch William Marshal to Rome to read the Pope a tirade. John is a bloody fool! He has no support from his northern barons, but thinks he can rule without it. Now he makes war against the church. If he thinks he can rule without the support of the church, he is wrong, dead wrong."

"Christ!" said Hubert, shaking his head. "No wonder he was afraid to stay in the north and returned to Gloucester. Salisbury's gone to Chepstow, ye say? My men will have to escort the princesses to Corfe. Tomorrow I'm on my way to Chepstow. Perhaps Salisbury and myself with William Marshal's help can bring John to his senses. Will you ride with me?"

"Only as far as Gloucester. I'm getting married, remember? Then I'm going to my own castle in Wales at Mountain Ash to sit out the winter. John is unstable. I can smell civil war on the air. What the hell would I do if he ordered me to ride against Nottingham or Lincoln? Do you think I'd sacrifice my men in a civil war?" he said with disgust.

"Your men worship you," his uncle pointed out.

"They wouldn't for long if I ordered them to fight their brothers."

"Those who stick by him will get preferment, rewards," advised Hugh.

"Oh, aye, next time I see you, you'll likely be justiciar." Falcon flashed his wolf's grin, then shook his head. "The price is too high for me," he said honestly.

Chapter 23

Gloucester Castle was the most well-appointed and comfortable stronghold Jasmine had ever seen. No wonder the king had kept it in his possessive Norman fingers when he had divorced Avisa. The household chamberlaine ushered her to her own spacious room, high in the castle with a breathtaking view of the Black Mountains of Wales. Behind these rose some of the highest peaks in the world, the Cambrian Mountains.

She hung Feather's cage by the window and gave Quill a little pan of water and an old slipper. It was only after she was unpacked and settled in that she learned her chamber was just a short distance from the apartment occupied by the Earl of Chester. She decided that on the morrow she would have a word with the chamberlaine and demand a room close to her grandmother.

Estelle needed to replenish her supply of medicinal herbs and reasoned that she would be able to find most of them close by along the banks of the great River Severn. Also Joan of Devon wanted to learn how to make scented candles. Rushlights, torches, and quarion candles, which were widely in use, smoked and stank. Estelle had spoken of using beeswax mixed with the oils of flowers, and the bride-to-be was quite taken with the idea.

Jasmine was trying to decide what she would wear to the wedding, which was only three days away. It must be something demure, modest, perhaps even prim to discourage men's eyes from feasting upon her, especially those of Chester and the king. The trouble was that Estelle had always seen that she was dressed like a fairy princess. She thought perhaps she would wear the shell-pink velvet because it was plain and cut with a high square neckline. Of course the underdress that went with it was delicate as a spider's web, embroidered with silver threads. She sighed, realizing no matter which she chose, she would stand out. The contrast between her dresses and the queen's was very marked, since Jasmine's were all in pastel shades to complement her flaxen tresses, while the queen wore jewel-bright tones that showed off her vivid darkness and the ladies of the court all copied the queen's fashions.

Next morning Jasmine chose a pair of boots and a warm cloak so that she could go out with Estelle to gather plants, but before she left her chamber, a young page brought a summons from the queen. Jasmine was puzzled that Isabella wanted to speak with her privately, and assumed it was in connection with some card reading or magic she wanted her to perform at the wedding celebration.

Isabella was still abed though the bedcurtains had been thrown back to let in the pale wintery sunshine. Jasmine noticed immediately that the queen's eyes were unnaturally bright—shining and glittering with suppressed excitement. She licked her lips with anticipation before she spoke. "I want you to prepare for a wedding tomorrow. Do you have a suitable gown, Lady Jasmine?"

Jasmine was slightly confused. "I thought the wedding was two days from now, your majesty. Has the date been changed?"

"I am referring to *your* wedding, Lady Jasmine," Isabella said, the corners of her mouth lifting with delicious malice.

"My wedding?" Jasmine repeated blankly.

Isabella's eyes glittered with mischief. "The king has decided to honor you with a great marriage. He has given your hand to Ranulf de Blundeville, the Earl of Chester. The wedding will be tomorrow night."

Jasmine was stunned. "Your majesty, that is impossible. I am betrothed to Falcon de Burgh."

Isabella waved her hand in dismissal. "The king has decided upon a more fitting match for one with royal blood. He has considered the matter carefully, and if he searched the length and breadth of the kingdom he could not find a wealthier or more powerful baron for you. You should be highly honored."

"I am not honored, I am dishonored to be used as pawnbait! My father William of Salisbury contracted me to Falcon de Burgh. I will not marry the Earl of Chester!"

Isabella's eyes flashed dangerously and her mouth turned sulky and cruel. "My husband is not asking you to marry Chester, he is commanding you to do so. Must I point out to you that Salisbury is nothing more than a bastard? John is your king! Seek your room, mistress, you will need to prepare yourself for this wedding."

Jasmine was so angry she wanted to slap Isabella silly. A petulant, spoiled, child-bitch was trying to ruin her life on a whim. "I will speak to the king," Jasmine said coldly.

Isabella laughed. "He and Chester have ridden out somewhere. Do you not recall you predicted all this yourself, Lady Jasmine, when first you read the tarot cards? I remember your words exactly. 'The three of cups represents a bride, a happy fulfilling card denoting joy in anticipation of marriage.' It was reversed and you said that meant a broken betrothal. So it all came right from your own mouth."

Jasmine cast her mind back. It had meant interference of a third party to break up a betrothal. She remembered that her card had been placed slightly beneath those representing the queen and king, which indicated that they would step on her.

"Tomorrow evening you will be wed. You are dismissed."

Jasmine whirled about and ran from the room. She did not stop running until she was safely inside her grandmother's chamber. There she flung off the cloak she had been wearing. Her blood was high at the moment, she needed no cloak to keep her warm. "Estelle, I knew they were up to something! Isabella has just informed me I'm to wed the Earl of Chester tomorrow evening."

"By the rood, the bastard has bought you from John! His pride never recovered when the king's daughter-in-law divorced him. Now he takes his revenge by marrying another with royal blood."

"There will be no marriage! John cannot do this, can he Estelle?" she cried.

"John can do anything he fancies," Estelle said quietly.

"Where the hell is de Burgh when I need him?" Jasmine cried in anguish.

"I will speak to John. I know something terrible about him I can use to coerce him."

"Isabella said he and Chester have ridden out," she said helplessly.

"Then I will see Isabella," Estelle said firmly.

Jasmine shook her head, "No, Estelle, it is pointless to try to reason with that evil little bitch. She took too much enjoyment in telling me. She was in an ecstasy from the torment she inflicted. It is an amusement for her. I am a gift . . . a divine sacrifice to her gods of passion," said Jasmine bitterly. "I will speak to Chester, explain how the thought of marriage repels me. Perhaps he will listen to reason," she said with faint hope.

Estelle took her hands. "I've had a vision. I have reason to believe John and Ranulf belong to a secret group of Devil worshippers. The vision was filled with chant and counterchant, sacrifice, robes, masks, drugs, sex, phallic symbols. They marched in patterns, holding banners, they carried crosses upside down. Once they step through the secret door everything in life is reversed. Wrong becomes right, evil becomes good, hate becomes love."

Cold fingers of dread gripped Jasmine's heart. "What am I to do?" she whispered.

"Gervase must ride out to bring de Burgh hot spurred."

"But we don't know where he is. Estelle, do you have the power to locate him, do you really have the power?" she beseeched.

They held their breath as a low knock came upon the door. Both women were relieved to see Gervase slip inside quietly, although they could see concern written in every line of his face. "Lady Jasmine, Dame Winwood, I am charged with keeping my eyes and ears open regarding Chester. I do not wish to alarm you unduly, de Burgh would not be pleased, but if I failed to warn you of real danger he would never forgive me, nor would I forgive myself."

"Tell us what you have learned, there is not a moment to spare," ordered Estelle.

"Chester tried to kill de Burgh. I took the arrow that was meant for him. Now I know why. I overheard his men speak of his plan to wed tomorrow and I fear you are to be the bride," he said.

"The queen has just informed me that I am to be given to Chester tomorrow. It won't happen, of course. I'll be long gone. I'll seek my father at Chepstow," Jasmine cried. "Try to get me some boy's clothes, Gervase, and give me your hat to cover these telltale tresses."

Estelle spoke quickly. "Don't waste time looking for clothing, I'll see to that. You must find de Burgh."

"He could be anywhere in England. I will try my damndest but it could take weeks," Gervase said practically.

"Attitude is everything. Do not give the idea of failure headroom. Be positive! You *will* find him because you *must* find him," Estelle commanded. "I will consult the crystal. Jasmine, your powers are stronger than you think. Our powers combined may be enough. If you have a psychic bond with Falcon de Burgh, he will receive your message that you are in danger. Concentrate, Jasmine! Your soul must call to his."

Gervase eyed the two women doubtfully. He had been trained by de Burgh to be practical and straight thinking. Did these women really think they could perform a magic trick and pull de Burgh from a hat as if he were a rabbit?

Jasmine's eyes were closed, her lips moved silently as if she were in a trance. His eyes turned toward the older woman and he saw she was in a different sort of trance. Concentration upon the crystal orb brought sweat to her brow, and she chanted strange cryptic words.

"There! I see a castle," cried Estelle. "By the color of the stone it would be near Norfolk," she said with conviction. Her brows drew together as she sorted out the vision. "The castle is in the air, I don't understand. It moves slowly upward from its foundation and sits in thin air. There, it is rising again."

"Castle Rising!" Gervase almost shouted, suddenly catching Estelle's determined enthusiasm. "Hubert de Burgh owns Castle Rising in Norfolk."

"That is where Falcon de Burgh is. Jasmine, your thoughts must compel him to leave now and come this way. Gervase, you must leave immediately. It is all the way across England, but you must believe strongly enough that you will find him and he will come in time. You must visualize it to its conclusion, no matter how impossible it seems!"

He was dimly aware that they had seduced him into their way of thinking. They were white witches, convinced of their own power. A lifetime of scorn for such hocus-pocus could not be altered in the space of a minute and he knew how wildly improbable it was that he would find Falcon de Burgh, and yet he must try. He had no alternative.

At Castle Rising that morning uncle and nephew had almost come to blows. "Christ Almighty, Falcon, take a damper. Unlike you, I'm a mere mortal. I can't sit up half the night and be in the saddle before daylight. That Spanish rubbish we were drinking produces the worst hangover in the world."

"It's not the quality of the stuff you drank, it's the bloody quantity! Why did you have to get paralyzed when you knew we were leaving today?"

"Have ye no vices at all, ye intolerant young swine? Just because your prick's itching for that fancy piece of yours, we all have to burn leather."

"I'm off," Falcon said with finality. "You're nothing but an old woman. No wonder John picked you to nursemaid all his hostages."

Hubert, eyeing Falcon and twelve men, booted, spurred, saddled, and waiting, speeded up his preparations to leave. "Falcon, lad, let's not come to blows over this. Give me a minute. I don't know what's your infernal hurry, but you're acting like a bear with a sore arse."

Falcon sighed. "I'm sorry, Hugh. It's just that I have this feeling I can't put a name to. The back of my neck is prickling, like hackles on a dog that senses danger. I feel if I don't hurry I'll be too late." He shook his head. "I must go, I'm compelled."

Hugh almost taunted him for his silly fancies, but Falcon flashed him a dark forbidding look as he wheeled his destrier and set his spurs to its side.

* * *

Estelle soon put her hands on a smallish pair of riding breeks and a padded doublet. She told one of the stable-boys to ready Lady Jasmine's palfrey and went in search of one of de Burgh's men-at-arms. She had no authority to recruit one of his men, but of course a thing like that never entered Estelle's head. "The future Lady de Burgh must get to her father William of Salisbury. She needs a man she can count upon to escort her safely to Chepstow. Are you that man?" she challenged.

"I am, madame. Whenever my lady is ready." The soldier grinned to himself. The dung would fly if de Burgh turned up and found she had run back to her father, but he had more brains than to refuse help to the lady who would wed his lord. If he knew aught of brides, she would have supreme influence over his life and every other man belonging to de Burgh, especially those with Plantagenet blood.

Jasmine's heart was racing as she pulled on the leather breeks and fastened them securely with a black sash. She pulled on her riding boots, all the while issuing orders to Estelle and at the same time bidding good-bye to Feather. Excitement was building inside her. She scooped up her beautiful hair and tied it severely with a leather thong, then crammed the brimmed hat over it and pulled it low across her brow. Her nerves were so highstrung, she felt like laughing hysterically when she thought of the faces of the ones she was tricking. The look of neat spite would be wiped from Isabella's face. But underneath, Jasmine was driven by fear. She knew that thwarting the monarchs' evil plans was a dangerous, almost insane thing to do, and if her escape didn't succeed the conse-quences would be terrifying and swift, not only to herself but to her beloved grandmother. Tears sprang to her eyes, blurring her vision, and the lump in her throat threatened to choke her. How could she leave Estelle?

Estelle saw her tears. "Jasmine, stop thinking of me and think of yourself!"

"Promise me you'll slip away from here somehow. I'll send Father's men back to help you. My God, it seems you've sacrificed all your life for me."

"And that is precisely why you must get away now, before it's too late!"

Jasmine bit her lips to stop a sob from escaping. With shaking hands she drew on her gloves and picked up her small riding whip. She opened the door and stopped dead. There on the threshold were two very large guards. "Let me pass," she commanded.

"We have orders. You cannot leave, my lady."

"Whose orders?" she demanded hotly. They remained silent. She took a chance and darted between the pair, but immediately they grabbed her and shoved her back inside the chamber, none too gently.

"Unhand my granddaughter, you vile lout, before I curse your soul to Hellfire!"

"Dame Winwood, we have orders to escort you to your chamber, where you must remain."

"Have you no fear of my dark power?" Estelle demanded with all the force she could muster.

"Aye, Dame, but we fear the king more than the Devil himself," said one while the other pleaded,

"Don't curse us, Dame Winwood, we are only carrying out our orders."

"I shall curse you and your offspring unless you take me to the king."

One looked at the other and he nodded imperceptibly.

"Go back inside, Jasmine, and lock the door until I return," she said.

The minutes crawled past so slowly, Jasmine thought she would scream. She took off her gloves, flung the hat across the room, and began to pace. The minutes stretched into hours. The pacing had worn off her nervous energy. Slowly her anger and frustration were replaced by fear. She sat down upon the bed and for the first time her imagination began to skirt about the odious idea of them actually wedding her to Chester. The thought was unendurable, and she tried to push it from her. Black shadows stretched from the four corners of the room to unnerve her further. What if Estelle had tried to coerce the king and she had been arrested? What if Gervase was not able to find de Burgh? If by a miracle he did, would there be enough time? Would de Burgh care enough to come to her rescue? What chance did he stand against such invincible power as Chester and King John?

She could throw herself on the king's mercy—if she begged him he might not give her to Chester—but she knew John's price. She knew he would take her himself for bed games, and she shrank more from him than she did from Chester.

Perhaps her only hope was to throw herself on Chester's mercy. Though she shrank from the idea, she was becoming desperate. In the small hours of the morning she lay down wearily upon the bed and slept.

She awoke with a violent start. She realized it was late even though the morning was dark with a sky heavy with rain. Her stomach rolled like an empty drum and she felt sick with dread as her thoughts flooded in on her. This was the day her life would be ruined. This was the day her future ended. This was the day that would end in a nightmare.

She flung open the chamber door. "Where is Dame Winwood? I demand you take me to her."

"She's in her own chamber where she belongs. You need have no concern for her safety, her door is well guarded."

The two guards were different men. If they had changed the guard there was little hope of their falling asleep, she reasoned. Then she saw that they wore the badge of Chester. "Take me to the Earl of Chester, his apartment is just down this hallway."

They looked at each other. She pressed. "If you do not I shall scream my head off and claim that you assaulted me." She opened her mouth to scream. A big hand was clamped across her mouth, "All right, my lady, don't force us to hurt you. We wish you no harm, especially on your wedding day." They escorted her down the long hallway. As one reached out to knock, she threw open the door and sped inside, slamming it behind her.

Ranulf de Blundeville sat at breakfast in a velvet bedrobe. Jasmine leaned back against the door jamb panting. He rose immediately and came toward her. Chester in a bedrobe was more threatening than Chester fully clothed, and her knees turned to water. "My lord earl," she breathed, "please help me, you are the only one I can turn to."

"What in the name of God are you wearing and what have you done to your hair?" he demanded.

"What do my clothes matter," she flared "when my life is about to be destroyed?"

At the insult, his jaw clenched and the pockmarks on his face stood out in patches of white. He reached up a hand to undo the leather thong. As he removed it her pale silken tresses tumbled down and he let out a hiss of relief through his teeth. "When I purchase an *objèt d'art* I do so for its esthetic beauty."

"My God, you are not listening to me," she cried. "I do not wish to marry any man, least of all you!" She had not meant to tell him in such an insulting fashion.

High on his cheekbones, twin spots of red began to spread like bloodstains. "You offend me, mistress, as does this male attire. Remove it!"

"I will not," she said flatly.

The vein in Chester's forehead began to pulsate. His hands grabbed the neck of her doublet and jerked it viciously apart. She wore only a thin shift beneath it. She felt the color drain from her face as her heart stopped. Her breasts rose and fell before his hooded eyes and in that moment he reminded her of a snake. One that was ready to strike.

"Why must I marry you?" she pleaded, whispering the words piteously.

"Because I have paid for you," he said bluntly. He took a soft breast in each hand and squeezed cruelly. "I have paid for these . . . and this!" He grabbed her between the legs, a feat made easier by the breeches she wore. Her breath came out on a sob and he took his hands from her.

"I will send women to bathe and dress you as befits the bride of the greatest earl in the realm. The wedding will be at six o'clock in the chapel of Gloucester Cathedral." His eyes narrowed. "Make very sure you are beautiful for me." He opened the door and thrust her at the two guards. "Return her to her chamber until it is time to escort her to the chapel."

She stumbled back to her room, devastated by men's rapacious duplicity.

Chapter 24

Gervase cursed the heavens that were responsible for the continual downpour that began before his horse had covered ten leagues. After three hours he was forced to slow his breakneck speed for fear of breaking his stallion's legs in the slippery, oozing mud its hooves churned up. There was no point in changing to dry clothes for he was already soaked to the skin, and would be again in a matter of minutes. He did not carefully reason out the route to take, he more or less went by instinct and left it to Fate, always keeping in a northeasterly direction. He knew Northampton was just short of the halfway mark and he need not pick his route too carefully until he was past that point. Then he would have a difficult decision to make, but for now he put it off as long as he could.

The de Burghs decided to ride as far as King's Lynn then head southwest to Peterborough. The weather was foul enough to make any God-fearing man stay home by his hearth, but Falcon de Burgh pressed on, oblivious to the elements. At King's Lynn the bridge across the River Ouse had been washed away. The great river was swollen and angry from the torrential downpours of the last few days and it had flooded its banks.

Falcon made a swift decision. They would ride south along the river to see if they could cross at Ely, if not they would go on to Cambridge, where the river joined itself to the Cam and there was more than one bridge across.

When Gervase reached Northampton it was past midnight and his horse was floundering. He knew it needed food and rest or it would be unable to carry him the rest of the way. He stopped at an inn called The Hole in the Wall and paid the hostler for a stall in the stable and a feed of oats. He rubbed down his animal with dry straw and took himself off to the common room to fill his own growling belly. He could not spare more than a few hours and knew he must be on the road again by four o'clock.

A traveler who had come from the east told him with graphic descriptions how the River Ouse was impassable. It was swelling wider by the hour and taking out the bridges as if they were made from matchsticks. At four in the morning Gervase stirred and stretched. His bones ached from the damp and from sleeping in wet clothes. He wondered briefly if he would be plagued by rheumatics now he was getting older. Then he laughed at himself, for he was only twenty-one. He swung into the saddle, encouraging his mount to take heart as they once more headed out into the rain. It was a deluge no longer, but had settled down to a steady drizzle that he knew would last all day.

He pondered which route to take. The fastest was straight east to Cambridge, but that would mean he would have to cross the River Ouse twice because it twisted back on itself. If he rode as far north as Huntingdon he would only have to cross the river once. Should he toss a coin? No, he thought, I will choose Huntingdon because Robin Hood was Lord Robert of Huntingdon and perhaps that was an omen.

He circled around Huntingdon before he saw the river, then he thought perhaps he had made a mistake. The river was angry and swollen and dangerous. He followed its east banks, which had overflowed, and wondered where the closest bridge was. His mind seemed numbed with the cold and the wet. It seemed to have penetrated to his very brain. Was there a bridge at Ely? He couldn't remember. He knew there was a town and a cathedral, therefore he reasoned there must be a bridge. He pressed on but he was filled with doubts. By the feel of his hungry gut, the hour must be midday. Even if he met up with de Burgh now there would not be enough time for Falcon to reach Gloucester and stop the wedding.

He stopped his horse to look across the raging river. Surely he must be at Ely or very close. He thought he had begun to hallucinate, for there across the angry torrent, fifty feet away across the river, was a group of riders. The men and mounts were familiar and their leader sat his horse like no other man in England. He shouted, "De Burgh!" He did not know if they would hear him above the roar of the raging River Ouse but his voice carried clearly across the water, as sound always does, and the men waved to him. He shouted the bad news across to de Burgh. "Chester weds your lady!"

Falcon looked at Hubert. "I'm swimming."

"You're mad! Keep yourself safe, lad."

"Keep myself safe? You're making noises like an old woman again." He dismounted and removed his doublet, boots, and chain-mail vest and shoved them into his saddlebags.

Hubert shivered as he watched his nephew bare his flesh to the freezing elements. Falcon half turned to his men and shouted, "Mountain Ash!" They understood. Then he wrapped the leather reins of his war-horse about his forearm and went into the river.

Hubert looked at Falcon's men and shook his head. "The young stallion is hotheaded and impatient, but his steady nerve has no equal in England!"

De Burgh was a very strong swimmer, but even so the current took man and horse and swept them into a swirling maelstrom neither could control. Both man and beast thrashed with powerful legs and with a supreme effort managed to keep their heads above the muddy, debris-strewn waters. They pitted their full strength against the current and slowly began to gain on the far bank.

Filled with dread, Gervase watched in agony as de Burgh went under and surfaced at least half a dozen times. Then he held his breath as unbelievably Falcon regained control. The horse was the first to strike the shallow bottom, and it scrabbled up the bank with a surge of power, spurred on by fear.

De Burgh had the presence of mind to unwind the leather reins from his arm before he was dragged beneath the flailing hooves. Then he grabbed onto a tree root and slowly hauled himself from the torrent.

The great black destrier snorted and sprayed water

from his nostrils then stood quivering, waiting impatiently for his master's next move.

"Did you say Chester weds my lady?" Falcon demanded incredulously.

"Aye, tonight at Gloucester. She planned to get away disguised as a boy and ride to her father at Chepstow, but I wouldn't underestimate Chester and that bastard John. They won't let their quarry slip through their fingers."

"Ride to Cambridge and take rooms at the Crusader Inn by the stone Bridge of Sighs. Hubert is with the men and that's where they'll cross the river. We'll meet again at Mountain Ash," de Burgh ordered.

"Aren't you coming to the inn to get dry clothes?" Gervase asked incredulously.

De Burgh shook his head impatiently. "No time, but you get there, you look like hell. You and your horse are about finished, man."

Gervase nodded wearily. De Burgh didn't need his squire to hold him back; his part in this drama was finished.

In midafternoon four female attendants went to Jasmine's chamber to prepare the bride. They carried in a bathing tub and plenty of hot water and liberally poured in her own precious oil of jasmine Estelle always made for her. She protested as they began to remove the boy's disheveled clothing she still wore. "Where is my grandmother? She is the only attendant I require."

They shook their heads, claiming no knowledge of Dame Winwood's whereabouts. Jasmine had no choice but to submit to their ministrations as they washed her hair and bathed her. They placed soft pads of linen soaked in witch hazel upon her eyelids to erase the tear-swollen puffiness. They murmured amazement at the silkiness of her white skin and lavished praise upon her for the way her newly washed hair formed a cloud of pale silvery gold about her shoulders.

A wedding gown had been provided by the earl, and while the women were in transports over its loveliness, Jasmine sat tight-lipped, consumed with loathing. A white lace underdress with long, delicately trailing sleeves went on first with no shift beneath it. It was fine-spun and almost transparent. Her round breasts with their pink thrusting nipples could clearly be seen through it. Over this came a white satin tunic, slit up each side and with a low-cut square neckline edged with white ermine fur. A silver girdle encrusted with pale mauve amethysts was fastened about her hips and a simple wreath of tiny white rosebuds was pinned to her hair.

It had just struck the hour of five, time to leave for the chapel, when the door opened to admit Chester. The women cried out that it was bad luck for the groom to see the bride before the wedding, but he quickly dismissed them and came toward Jasmine holding a luxurious white ermine mantle. His eyes swept over her with lascivious appreciation; he knew there had never been a more beautiful bride.

She faced him defiantly. "I'll never wed you. When it is time to make my responses I shall not take the vow. I shall appeal to the bishop to stop the wedding!"

One powerful hand closed into a fist, crushing the fur he held. "I wouldn't advise it," he said ominously. "I have Dame Winwood locked safely away. She has had no food or drink since yesterday. Her guards are instructed to give her water only after we are safely wed," he said with satisfaction.

Jasmine felt the blood drain from her face as she struggled to make sense of the earth-shattering knowledge that she must go through with it. Dimly, through mists of horror, she began to comprehend the enormity of it all. She realized how much he had in common with John.

They were bullies to the core, and there was nothing they enjoyed more than exploiting weakness.

He wrapped her in the ermine and called for the guards. Like a sleepwalker she allowed herself to be ushered from her chamber, down the long hallway past his apartments, and down the winding staircase of Gloucester Castle. Although the cathedral was adjacent, it still required a long walk in the cold evening air. Darkness had arrived early on this late autumn night. The wind ruffled her furs, yet she felt nothing.

She was taken past the magnificent arched entrance to Gloucester Cathedral and taken by a side entrance into the smaller chapel. There were perhaps two dozen people present. John and Isabella occupied the front-row private pew. Only high-ranking nobles and their ladies had been invited to the secret wedding.

Jasmine lifted her downcast eyes only once as she was escorted to the front of the chapel. Her eyes met Isabella's neat smile of spiteful malice, and she quickly lowered them again until her lashes swept her cheeks. She heard the Bishop of Gloucester chanting in Latin, she smelled the nauseating incense that covered the acrid smell of the burning candlewax, and she felt the lace of the hated underdress chafe cruelly against her tender nipples. She could smell, see, hear, and feel, but she could not think.

She dared not think of Estelle, she dared not think of the night to come, and so her mind had withdrawn and gone blank. She did not make her responses until she was prompted to do so, then she parroted the unctuous tones of the Bishop of Gloucester.

"Who giveth this woman to be married to this man?"

Jasmine was startled to hear the king say "I do," and knew she was lost. All hope was gone. She felt dead inside. Then Ranulf was kissing her, and she was his in the eyes of God and man.

There was a great blank space after that. She could not

remember going from the chapel, the cheering outside, the showers of rice and rose petals, entering a private dining hall in the royal wing of the castle, or eating the wedding supper. She became aware of her surroundings amid uproarious laughter.

The king was on his feet giving a speech. "And now at great expense to the royal exchequer I have had our wise wizard Orion prepare an aphrodisiac to ensure a night of wedded bliss."

Chester good-naturedly went along with the ribbing but protested, "I need nothing to speed me up, rather I need something to slow my ardor."

There was a great fanfare of trumpets then Orion appeared through an arras in a cloud of green smoke. He held aloft a great foot-high silver chalice and bore it to the new bridegroom. "Drink this magic elixir made from powdered pearls, rubies, sapphires, and amethysts. It also contains emerald dust and finely ground gold."

The guests sent up an "Ahh" of wonder at the costliness of such a rare brew.

Orion chanted, "Sip the sorcerer's philter from a silver chalice of ecstasy and your virility will gain in strength like unto a magnificent stag."

Jasmine's face was whiter than her gown. Ranulf took her hand and dragged her to her feet. Then he picked up the chalice in both hands and quaffed deeply.

"The bride, let the bride drink," came the shouts.

Ranulf handed the tall goblet back to Orion. "Nay, I will do the awakening. I possess a more tried and true weapon to arouse her lust than any aphrodisiac."

The laughter and ribald shouts increased as they imbibed drink upon drink. The toasts descended from risqué to ribald, then degenerated from bawdy to obscene.

Jasmine yawned. It was not a sign of boredom, it was a sign of extreme nervous tension.

Chester swayed on his feet as he announced, "My bride longs for her bed, I think it is time to bid you good night."

"A bedding! A bedding!" went up the demand, and the king, urged on by Isabella, lurched to his feet and cried, laughing,

"You don't think you're getting off that easily do you, you randy old goat!"

The men surged forward and lifted the couple aloft. They were all quite drunk and fumbled and staggered so that they all but dropped the bridegroom, but undeterred they hoisted him high again and carried them to the other side of Gloucester Castle where Chester's apartments lay ready to receive the newly joined couple.

At the heavy oaken door studded with brass, the terrible reality of Jasmine's situation swept over her. She did not know how she would get through the next few minutes, never mind the rest of the night. She glanced across at Chester and the look in his eyes terrified her. Her knowledge of men was limited, but she knew that lust brought out the most unpleasant characteristics a man had and very shortly she would be forced to submit to whatever it was men did with women.

They set her on her feet and began to strip off her wedding gown. She gasped to the nearest female. "I cannot bear all these leering men to see me naked."

Joan of Devon's heart went out to her. She had endured it when she was married the first time and would have to do so again tomorrow to a much larger audience than this. She was to be married in the cathedral proper, with hundreds of guests.

Isabella's spiteful voice came at her clear as a bell. "You ought to be proud to prove that you go unblemished to your bridegroom. Are you marked in some way?"

Jasmine stood completely naked as eager hands pulled

off the lace wedding gown. She held her hands in a way that covered the two tiny beauty spots that made a triangle with her golden mound of Venus. Jasmine trembled visibly as they turned her about before the men, lifting her silvery tresses to reveal her satin-perfect back and legs.

She stood naked with downcast eyes, yet she was acutely aware of the greedy eyes that fed from her. Chester had been stripped almost naked before he insisted enough was enough and urged the drink-sodden guests to quit the room so he could get down to work. Only the king remained. He leered at his friend, "Ranulf, I believe I will claim the *droit du seigneur.*"

Chester's eyes narrowed dangerously. "How long do you think you could keep such a tale from her father?" he pointed out. "Be patient, John. The marriage is not legal until it is consummated. Then she is *my* property to do with as I wish, not her father's."

Jasmine's eyes fastened upon the king and she turned cold as ice inside. It was not Isabella she should blame, nor even the Earl of Chester, for if the king, her uncle, had one shred of decency she would not have been sold. It was John's innate evil and greed that were responsible for her plight, and she swore an oath in that moment to be avenged for this night's work.

She closed her eyes and swayed with dizziness. Ranulf caught hold of her to steady her. John threw back his head in uncontrolled laughter. "Have at her then. Some night soon we'll exchange bed partners and you'll see for yourself how hot and hungry Isabella is for a well-endowed man."

Chapter 25

Chester threw the bar across the door, turned, and came toward Jasmine. The last thread of her courage fled. She backed away from him, but he went after her and dragged her back to stand before the fire. "Please, milord . . ." Her voice disappeared.

He took her chin between his finger and thumb and forced her to look at him. "You will call me Ranulf, do you understand?"

"Yes, milord . . . Ranulf. Please, have you sent word to the men who hold my grandmother?" she whispered.

"You are now the Countess of Chester. You have more important things to worry about than your grandmother. I would advise you to worry about pleasing your husband. Your maiden's shyness pleases me, but I will brook no disobedience from you. I will not indulge and spoil you as your father has. I will school you to do your duty by me. If you do not please me in every way, I shall punish you."

She stood trembling.

"Do you understand me?"

"Yes, Ranulf," she murmured now on a half sob.

"Now come here to me," he ordered softly, and his hand covered the creamy swell of her breast.

De Burgh arrived in Gloucester at ten o'clock. He had gone beyond weariness. His body demanded action. He sought his own men immediately. They filled him in on what they knew but it wasn't much. The wedding had been secret with only a handful of Chester's most trusted men knowing of it.

"If Chester has married my lady I intend to challenge

him. I need your help. When Chester calls for his men I want them to be incapable of responding. This night's work will be remembered a long time by Chester and by King John, so if you want no part of it, speak now and I will release you."

No man spoke.

"At midnight get the hell out of here. We will meet again at Mountain Ash. Pass the word to every de Burgh man." He chose two he knew he could trust with his life. "Montgomery . . . de Clare . . . attend me. Montfort, look to my destrier. I stabled him. See that he is warmed and fed. He'll only have a short rest, I'm afraid. I'll need another strong horse and a couple of packhorses made ready. I also want my lady's palfrey saddled."

The next stop he made was at the residence of the Bishop of Gloucester. He was informed by a servant that the bishop had retired for the night and could not be disturbed. By this time de Burgh had little patience left. One strong arm forced back the door. "Stand aside, man, if you know what's good for you. He'll be disturbed by what I have to tell him, I'll warrant."

The servant was reduced to a handwringing subservient as he followed the three men down the hall to the bishop's private study. De Burgh offered the token of a brief knock before he entered.

The Bishop of Gloucester, a beefy man with a round, ruddy face, quickly set his drink aside and was on his feet to challenge the intruders.

"Did you perform a wedding tonight between Ranulf of Chester and Jasmine of Salisbury?" demanded de Burgh.

"I did. Who are you and by what right are you here?" the bishop demanded fearlessly.

De Burgh's hand swept his question aside with an impatient gesture. "Did the king attend the wedding ceremony?" he rapped out.

"I'll answer no more questions until you identify yourself, sir, and I learn if your business is legitimate!"

De Burgh clenched his fists in fury, then schooled himself with a great effort to patience. "I am Falcon de Burgh. The Lady Jasmine is my betrothed. I have a valid contract with her father, Salisbury. If the king attended the wedding ceremony tonight the marriage is illegal—null and void."

"Illegal?" echoed the bishop, thinking his authority was being challenged.

"Pope Innocent has excommunicated the king," de Burgh said simply.

The words took the wind from the bishop's sails. "By all that's holy, is this true?" he asked, overawed. The news was devastating, but if he was honest with himself he knew that John had asked for it, deserved it.

"Who will tell him?" he asked quietly.

"Have you the courage?" de Burgh asked sarcastically. "Or is it more expedient for you to ignore Rome and take the side of the king?"

The bishop sat down as if his legs had collapsed. "I cannot do that. My duty is clear-cut; I must uphold the excommunication or Rome will issue an edict against the whole realm."

"Just so," said de Burgh, satisfied the bishop was not weak-livered. "If King John took the time to read his dispatches from Rome, he would know of this. He would have known his attendance at the religious ceremony of a wedding would invalidate it. Get dressed, my lord bishop, you have a wedding ceremony to perform."

The bishop paled visibly.

"Courage, man. John will have drunk himself into a stupor by now. His brother Salisbury, William Marshal, and the justiciar will deal with the king in a few days." De Burgh was finished with explanations. "Hurry, man, if Chester has consummated this marriage, I won't be responsible for my actions."

Ranulf was busy inspecting his merchandise. He was savoring his acquisition, running his hands over every inch of Jasmine's creamy satin skin, letting his fingers play with her pale silken mass of hair that fell about her shoulders like a silvery waterfall. His palms cupped and weighed each perfect breast, then he let his mouth suck and taste each taut, pink nipple.

Jasmine stood before him like a cold statue of marble. She had withdrawn to a place apart, a place of the mind, not of the body. A place where Ranulf's avid fingers could not touch.

He removed the last of his clothing and Jasmine's eyes looked at his body impassively. He was not an attractive man. Though he was tall, it was his body that was long rather than his legs, and though he had no belly, his torso was the same width from shoulder to hip and his muscles had a knotty appearance. His body was devoid of hair except his groin, and this was covered by the same lank, black hair that covered his head.

He reached for Jasmine's hand and brought it to his swollen member, which had been in a semiaroused state since he had seen her in the pristine white wedding gown.

Jasmine's small hand lay unresisting in his own. When her fingers did not eagerly close over him, he bent to cover her mouth with his. He forced her lips apart and thrust his tongue deeply into her mouth. She went limp as if she would swoon, and he gave her face a small, sharp slap. "Respond to me!" he ordered.

Suddenly there was a heavy crash upon the door. The bar splintered with a loud crack and Jasmine's eyes flew open. Were the Powers of the Universe she had begged for help coming to her rescue?

Three heavy shoulders applying their power in unison

had battered down the door. De Burgh murmured, "I'll do this alone," and the two men who flanked him backed off and took the Bishop of Gloucester a discreet distance down the hall.

Falcon, like an avenging bird of prey, swept into the room. Naked, without a weapon, Chester knew he was trapped. De Burgh stood with one hand on his sword hilt, the other held his dagger. He was dressed from head to toe in black. His black leather boots reached up to his thighs and he had casually tucked his black leather gauntlets into the cuff of his boot. He wore a flared hat to shield his eyes, and only the slant of his scarred cheek and jaw were visible.

Chester threw back his head and bellowed, "Guard! Guard!"

One of de Burgh's men came to the door. Chester cried, "A hundred crowns if you seize him!"

Montgomery laughed. "I wouldn't piss for a hundred crowns," then retreated down the hallway.

De Burgh spoke for the first time. His voice was quietly menacing. "Don't move unless you want to lose a testicle." He was trying to control a terrible bloodlust, and he found it the hardest thing he'd ever had to do.

Chester argued, "You're too late to do anything about it . . . we are wed."

"In that case I'll have to make a widow of her," he threatened with relish. The vein on Chester's forehead began to pulsate with fear. De Burgh towered over him, an unforgiving mountain of hatred. Chester took an involuntary step backward.

Jasmine stood rooted to the spot. De Burgh hadn't spared her a glance. It was obvious he was more interested in taking his revenge on Chester than rescuing her, and in that moment she hated him. She darted to the bed and snatched up the ermine mantle to cover her nakedness. Chester looked quickly over to her.

"Keep your eyes to yourself, man," ordered de Burgh, the fury inside him still threatening to spill blood.

Jasmine's eyes were wide with horror. She knew de Burgh's temper, knew his reckless daring. Any second now he would murder the man who had dared take what was his. The naked steel would plunge in and come out covered with bloody entrails. She saw her two tormentors through blurred, tear-filled eyes. "Devils!" she sobbed, "savages!"

De Burgh looked at her directly for the first time. "Me? I abhor violence," he said.

Jasmine had an uncontrollable desire to laugh and cry and scream and curse. It all came out on a sob.

De Burgh advanced upon Chester. He saw clearly that he had gone pasty gray and was convinced he'd drawn his last breath. "Take her," Chester offered desperately. "I renounce all claim."

De Burgh was amused. A great bark of laughter rang out. "I intend to take her. You never had a claim. Your dear friend King John is under excommunication. His attending the ceremony made it illegal and invalid."

A great relief rushed over Chester. His strength was sapped; his knees buckled.

Jasmine looked upon him with contempt. "Where are you holding Estelle?" she demanded.

"I am not holding her," he denied quickly, fearfully. "I never harmed her. She left Gloucester—ran off somewhere."

Now it was Jasmine's turn to be weak with relief.

De Burgh gagged Chester, then trussed him up so tightly he looked like a boar ready for the spit. Then he looked at Jasmine. "You've had the mock wedding, now we'll have the real one." He was a frighteningly potent image, one of real flesh and of real blood. Falcon de Burgh wasn't used to the passive role. From the moment he had set eyes on the enchanting girl, all his keenest instincts as a hunter had been aroused. Her heart started its wild war dance as he reached for her, but he simply ushered her through the door with a possessive hand at the small of her back.

In the hallway he beckoned his men. "Put this door back on its hinges and make sure it will take a great effort to reopen it." He looked down at Jasmine. "Where is your chamber?"

She was trembling and could not find her voice, so she pointed to a door farther down the hall.

"Here is the good bishop risen from his bed just to perform the ceremony," he said silkily.

"Falcon, no, I've been through so much," she cried.

He said ominously, "You've been through nothing yet." He led the way to Jasmine's chamber. The Bishop of Gloucester followed on his heels thinking irreverently that the bride was already conveniently naked beneath her fur.

De Burgh's strong hand kept her at his side. "I'm sorry to press you, my lord bishop, but I'm afraid our time is running out. Say the necessary words, then you can get back to your safe bed."

Jasmine glanced up at de Burgh. His face was as hard as granite. The dark arrogance lay on his face as if his very soul was fierce and wild. It was his arrogance that always unnerved her. The thin white scar from brow to cheek gave him such a slanting, devilish look.

It was as if he read her mind. "You put it there," he pointed out.

The Bishop of Gloucester aided them in exchanging their vows. Jasmine felt she had as little choice now as she had had earlier in the evening.

"We'll need witnesses," reminded the bishop.

De Burgh opened the door and called to his men who had just finished securing Chester's great studded door.

"Do you want witnesses for what comes next?" Montgomery asked with a good-natured leer.

De Burgh flashed his wolf's grin. "I don't want you watching, but you can listen if you've a mind to. I'll need you to stand guard at the door."

All the necessary signatures were obtained, including the Bishop of Gloucester's, then at last Falcon was alone with his bride. She clutched the ermine wrap about her desperately as he began to divest himself of black cloak and doublet. He removed the heavy chain-link vest and finally his lawn shirt. Stripped to the waist, he advanced toward her.

"Jasmine . . ." He put his finger under her chin. "Look at me while I explain things. There is no time for pretty speeches. You deserve to be wooed with a flower, a poem, a sigh . . ." His thumb caressed her cheek. "A stolen kiss . . . a soft embrace . . . but you will have none of these. Jassy, forgive me for what I am about to do to you. It seems like all my life I've had to do the expedient thing, and tonight I'm again forced to be strong, decisive, practical, and unfortunately for you, quick!"

"Falcon, please." Her hands came up to his chest in supplication.

"This marriage must be consummated, and consummated now. It must be made legal so that none can take you from me, do you understand?" he demanded harshly.

She looked into his eyes and saw only green fire and knew that he would not relent. She nodded mutely and her lashes swept down to her cheeks.

"Your eyelashes are thick as feathers," he murmured as he reached out a firm hand to take her wrap. It fell to the carpet and he kicked it aside. For a second or two he feasted upon her, his devouring eyes sliding all over her flowing body. Then he swept her up in powerful arms and took her to the bed.

She turned her face from him as he stripped off the rest

of his clothes and towered above the bed. He closed his eyes momentarily and offered thanks that the flower he so desired had not been plucked by another, then he opened his eyes, expecting to fill them up with the lover's vision of a lifetime. The bed was empty. Jasmine was kneeling on the floor on the opposite side of the bed, her hands pressed together, her eyes closed as she begged her god to deliver her from men's evil. His blood ran hot in his veins. His emotions swung wildly with unrequited desire. He had wanted, nay, craved her for so long, banking the fires that had threatened to consume him for months. He had snatched her from the arms of another man and now instead of sweetly yielding up her prize to him, she was invoking the power of God against him.

He bit back an oath and vaulted across the bed to stand before her. She opened her eyes, saw his bare muscled legs inches from her face, and closed them again, sobbing "No, no!" He reached down strong hands to clasp her sweetness to him, but the moment he touched her she screamed and he realized this deflowering would be no easy task.

Still on her knees, she turned from him and rolled herself into a ball with her arms crossed tightly about her body. She was so tightly coiled he feared there was no time to coax her into a loving response, but he knew he must try. He desperately wanted to make her first time good for her, but he knew the precious minutes were ticking away. He deeply regretted that he did not have all night to make love to her, to arouse her, to play with her. This was no game. This consummation was an absolute necessity for her own good, her own safety. He knelt down behind her and lifted the silken mass of her hair to his face. His rigid, throbbing shaft pulsed against her back, and she bit down on her lips to stop herself from screaming. He swept aside her mass of hair to kiss the exposed nape of her neck. She knew the closeness of their naked bodies and the warmth of her smooth perfumed flesh was driving him to such a pitch that he would soon be out of control.

"Jasmine, I want you to like it when I caress you, I want you to like it when I kiss your lovely breasts, I want you to like it when I make love to you."

She raised her head from her knees. "I don't like it, I hate it!"

Still on the floor, he lifted her into his lap, his back resting against the great bed. "My little flower," he murmured huskily, "unfurl your petals for me." He knew that the nipples of her breasts could be made erect for he had done it before. He dipped his head and caught the tip of her left breast between his lips. His tongue caressed it and circled it slowly, then he sucked hard, hoping this would stir the tiny bud between her legs to awaken and ache to be stroked.

Her sobs had subsided to little mewling cries, so he lifted her buttocks to allow his erection to slide along the cleft between her legs. She was so sensitive she could feel his heartbeat through his hot maleness with each and every pulse of his blood. She reached down frantically to dislodge his weapon before it sheathed itself inside of her, and she gasped with renewed terror as she realized its size. Falcon gasped also as her tiny hand closed over him. The intensity of his pleasure almost tumbled him into the sensual abyss.

She stood up and tried to climb upon the bed to escape him, but as she did so the golden curls of her mons brushed across his cheek. In a flash he had her soft thighs imprisoned in his hands as his hungry mouth covered the secret place for which it had hungered and thirsted for what seemed like a lifetime.

Jasmine was appalled by his animal maleness. Everything about him was hard as iron. His arms, his chest, his legs, even his thighs were corded with rigid saddle muscles. She experienced none of the first delicate moments of the journey to intimacy when everything is new, veiled in mystery and promise of the passion that was sure to come. Desperately she struggled to free herself from his hot, possessive mouth. Finally she knelt upon his shoulders and climbed onto the bed. He was upon her instantly.

"Falcon, stop now . . . please stop now, or I will hate you forever."

He said regretfully, " 'Tis a pity, darling, I must force you, but I cannot stop now. I know what is best for you. Please, love, try to understand you won't be safe unless I make you my wife completely." The words he spoke were the truth, but he couldn't have stopped himself from making love to her in that moment if his life itself was the price he'd have to pay.

She sobbed her fear. "Don't . . . don't . . . oh, please don't," but he didn't even hear her. One powerful hand held both her arms above her head and he kissed the intimate hollows under her arms. His lips covered her breasts roughly, wantonly, then became more gentle as they nibbled the silken flesh beneath each breast, sending wave after wave of pleasure surging through him as his mouth took possession of places it had never traveled before. The taste of her, the fragrance of her heightened the sensations until his very blood sang with the joy of her.

"Jasmine, open to me," he urged.

"No, no . . . I cannot . . . I cannot." She honestly believed that if he impaled her, he would kill her. She was crying hard now, her face buried against his chest, her tears bathing his heart.

Falcon felt he was being patient in the extreme. If they had had all night, he would have given her more time, but he did not. He went up on his knees to straddle her. After forcing apart her soft thighs, he placed one of his knees between them to keep them apart. With firm fingers he separated her pink center covered by the tight golden curls and plunged down. He felt the hymen of her maidenhead give way and heard her terrible scream.

He quickly covered her mouth with his and thrust himself up as hard as he could as he pulled her down. At last he was buried to the hilt, and no force on this earth could have prevented him from carving out his place inside of her.

He was acutely aware of the tremendous contrast between their bodies. His great size emphasized her delicate smallness. His hardness made her all the softer. His powerful strength showed her fragility. But the greatest contrast was in their coloring. He was so dark, his tanned body half-covered by crisp black hair, while she was so pale and fair, her silvery gold tresses spread out in a tangle across the pillows. From above it must have looked like the Devil was ravishing an angel.

For him, magic danced in the air. His powerful hands held her imprisoned and immobile beneath him as he stroked in and out ruthlessly. She was the smallest woman he had ever made love to. She was unbelievably tight, and each time he thrust inside her, he had to stretch her anew. He knew that his first assault was hurting her, but he also knew that would change perhaps the next time he made love to her. He watched her face through half-closed eyes as he moved himself back and forth upon her. He was a skilled lover and knew just how far he could drive her. Each time she tried to cry out he covered her mouth with his. Finally in desperation she bit down savagely on his bottom lip with her sharp little teeth and he lost control. His erection erupted into climax, spurting his burning seed deep inside her.

It had been an experience like no other because he had been aroused to the point of madness before he had allowed himself fulfillment. Falcon also knew he'd never have enough of her. Nothing would ever be the same again. He felt different; he thought differently. He felt fully alive for the first time in his life. Everything was heightened and he knew at his heartroot that she would belong to him forevermore.

For Jasmine, death would have been preferable. He rolled off her to catch his breath. She lay still like a crumpled doll. Falcon felt a great surge of power. He was triumphant, invincible as a god. She felt like a doe whose flesh had been torn and impaled by the hunter's arrow.

He came up from the bed and she saw the small pool of blood upon the white sheet. She watched in fascinated horror as he dipped his great seal ring into her blood and stamped the sheet in half a dozen places with a crimson falcon. He was leaving his unmistakable, indelible mark showing the king, Chester, and the world that he had claimed the prize.

Chapter 26

Jasmine closed her eyes, too fatigued to keep them open longer. His kisses had been so demanding she throbbed all over.

He dressed immediately, urging her to rise and do the same, but his words merely floated over her. He came around the bed and, kneeling down beside her, touched her cheek. *"Pouvre petite,* did you receive no pleasure at all from it?"

Pleasure? her stunned mind echoed. She lay limp, unmoving, pale, lifeless.

By God, he'd have to kindle a fire in her if they were to escape this place. He knew he'd have to make her angry.

She had a fiery temper when roused. He set about deliberately to infuriate her. He slapped her across the bare bottom and said, "Get up from there. I'll give you two minutes to get dressed." He flung open her wardrobe and rummaged through her clothes. He pulled out a woolen gown and threw it at her. She ignored it and let it lie upon the bed. He realized it would take stronger medicine than his orders to arouse her temper. "If you are lying there in an attempt to lure me back to bed, it won't work. God's love, but you're not much use to a man yet. Next time . . ."

She was off the bed in a flash, hands on hips, teeth bared. "Next time? Next time?" she repeated like a demented parrot. "There will be no next time, Falcon de Burgh!"

He hid a smile.

She panted with hatred of him. He had acted like a brutal savage. Well, no matter how big his weapons she would find a way to return a more stinging fire.

"Will you hurry, woman," he urged.

"Woman now is it, you silver-tongued devil? How I resisted you for seven long months is a mystery to me," she flung sarcastically. "Now that we are wed the prize becomes the possession. You expect unconditional surrender. You, milord, are in for a rude awakening!"

He was rummaging among her silken hose looking for a woolen pair. "Perhaps you should put on two of everything. You can take only what is on your back."

"Where are you taking me?" she demanded.

"Mountain Ash, of course," he replied.

"You're dragging me off through those godforsaken Black Mountains I've been staring at all week? In that case I'll need everything." She threw open an enormous traveling trunk and began to pack her dresses.

"Jasmine!" he protested.

"Lady de Burgh, if you please," she replied.

He tried to hold his patience as she threw everything she could find into the trunks. He said furiously, "You do realize we are trying to escape with our lives? Must you act like a spoiled child?"

"Yes, I must," she retorted maddeningly. "I'm silly, spoiled, pampered, and what was it you said: *not much use to a man.* Well, more fool you for marrying me."

He picked up the ermine fur and she recoiled. "I'll not wear that. I never want to see it again."

Forcibly he wrapped her in it. "You'll be damned glad of that when the snow howls down the passes into Wales."

She stood facing him, her color high, he noted thankfully. She scooped up her hedgehog and said, "Don't forget my pets."

His mouth fell open. "You're jesting. Honey love, we can't take Prick and Feather," he said.

"If they stay, I stay!" she announced imperiously.

He threw open the door savagely and thrust the bird cage and the prickly ball at Montgomery. "Wipe that bloody grin off your face. De Clare, fetch that trunk."

About one hundred de Burgh men had gathered under the trees outside the stables. They held the horses their leader had ordered ready. They stared in amazement at the beautiful creature with gilt hair, wrapped from head to foot in white ermine. Each and every man wondered what use the exquisite little plaything would be to their master. Each and every man would have exchanged places with him.

Falcon helped Jasmine into her saddle, secured the packhorses, and called, "Away, lads, 'tis past midnight!"

"Nay," came back the reply, "we'll stay another hour to safeguard your back."

De Burgh's authoritative voice rang out. "Then we'll meet again at Mountain Ash. Watch your own backs, men."

De Burgh set a steady pace for he knew Jasmine was at the limit of her endurance. Remembering his ordeal of the previous day, he hoped fervently that the River Severn just to the west of Gloucester had not damaged its bridges. Once they crossed the great river, he decided against riding directly west into the mountains, but thought he would go to William Marshal's castle of Chepstow on the Welsh border. With any luck Hubert and Salisbury would be there, and he would tell them plainly what he had done this night.

The Severn seemed as it had always been and they followed its winding course for an hour. Falcon kept a close eye upon Jasmine, wondering at the pride that kept her erect in the saddle. The long day and night were beginning to take its toll on him but he knew he must keep moving. He stopped only long enough to reach up and lift her in his arms, then, holding her securely in front of him, he remounted and wrapped his dark cloak about them both.

She did not speak one word to him, but neither did she make any protest. Gradually he felt her relax against the warmth of his body. Though she would have died rather than admit it, she was grateful to drop the role of Amazon, to lean back against his broad chest and draw from his immense strength. She resented that he was so unwearied, yet at the same time it made her feel safe and protected for the first time in weeks. She closed her eyes and drifted off. Before sleep claimed her totally, she knew she would never make the mistake again of underestimating him. He had come for her, after all. He had kept his promise to wed her if he wasn't in Hellfire.

To de Burgh's ears came a faint sound that he had both dreaded and expected. The galloping hooves gained on him. He could tell there were at least twenty on his tail who had been ordered to ride him down. The road ahead forked in two directions, and he knew he had no choice but to try to outrun them. Neither he nor his black destrier could be seen in the darkness, but he cursed Jasmine's white ermine in that moment, knowing the impossibility of their remaining unseen. And sure enough, a hue and cry went up as they were spotted. One way the road lay open, unimpeded. De Burgh knew he could make better time if he rode it. However, at the last minute he swerved to the right toward Deerhurst Forest where he hoped he might lose his pursuers among the densely growing trees.

De Burgh gripped Jasmine tightly with one hand and she opened her eyes and cried out. His arm came up swiftly to keep a low-hanging branch from raking her face, while at the same time his iron-muscled thighs guided his destrier through the trees. The score of riders were so close he could smell the leather of their saddles and the heavy male sweat of their bodies, then to his utter amazement and relief he saw men swing down from the great oaks and elms onto the backs of his pursuers.

He turned briefly but the darkness blanketed the furtive action behind him, although he could hear the screams of men and horses clearly enough. He did not allow Lightning to lessen his speed until they were in the very heart of the forest and all about them was silence. De Burgh's knife was already in his hand when Jasmine cried out in alarm as a man stepped forward into the clearing.

"Sheath your weapon. It is I, Robin Hood," a merry voice rang out.

"Robert!" cried Jasmine, sagging with relief against de Burgh's chest.

"How did you find me?" asked de Burgh, amazed.

"My men have been tracking you for days, across the breadth of England," he explained.

"Why didn't they make themselves known to me?" de Burgh demanded.

"Until now you needed no aid." Robin shrugged, laughing. "Come, we have your packhorses safe. There's a cottage through the trees and a warm bed waiting."

"We should press on," said de Burgh.

"Rest, if only for a couple of hours. I know how long you've gone without sleep."

De Burgh nodded and Jasmine heaved a great sigh of thanks.

"Mary-Ann!" she cried as the door to the rustic wood-cutter's cottage was thrown open and the light from the welcoming fire spilled across the threshold.

"Are you Lady de Burgh?" Mary-Ann asked anxiously.

Jasmine nodded, but the situation seemed unreal as a dream. She swayed on her feet and de Burgh swept her up in his strong arms.

"We have two beds," Mary-Ann said happily, "though there's little privacy, I'm afraid."

De Burgh grinned at her. "Since we're all married here, there's no need for privacy." He lay Jasmine on the narrow bed. She was trembling uncontrollably from the ordeal of the past hours. He took off her boots and rubbed her small feet vigorously. Mary-Ann brought her some warmed mead and she drank it down gratefully.

Robin and Falcon each shared a horn of ale and de Burgh thanked him gratefully for his help. Robin shook off the thanks and urged him to join Jasmine in the narrow bed. "I'll wake you long before dawn," he swore.

Though Jasmine was exhausted, she lay rigid in the bed. The room was bathed in firelight, and she could hear Robin and Mary-Ann murmuring softly in the other bed. Each time Robin and Mary-Ann's eyes had met, it was like bound lovers claiming each other. Why couldn't she have found a love like that? Finally it was all too much for her and the tears came unbidden. Falcon gathered her in his safe, protective embrace and allowed her tears to run their full course until she slept against him in exhaustion.

It seemed to Jasmine that no sooner had she closed her eyes than de Burgh was shaking her rudely awake. The two couples shared ale and oatcakes and the girls made their tearful good-byes to each other.

Jasmine whispered to Mary-Ann, "Have you no regrets?"

The girl shook her head. "I've never been happier in my whole life! Falcon will make you happy too, Jasmine, if you will give him the chance." ·

De Burgh refused to let her ride her own mount, but ordered her up before him. She raked him from head to foot with a disdainful, black scowl and complained, "Robert always treats Mary-Ann with infinite gentleness!"

De Burgh hid a grin and said, "That's because he loves her. I hope I'm never fool enough to let love besot me."

"Oh! You are an uncouth beast!" she cried, and vowed she would not speak to him the rest of the day.

Falcon held to a relentless, slow, steady pace throughout the whole day. He did not rest his mount until early evening. The sky was pewter-colored with heavy gray clouds. The bad weather and cold rains that heralded winter were following them west and would shortly overtake them.

He hated to disturb Jasmine's slumber, fitful as it had been, but he knew it was necessary. When he eased from the saddle she opened her eyes, startled momentarily at her whereabouts. He held up his arms to lift her down and everything came flooding back to her. She raised her arm and threw aside his hand. Falcon had the ability to infuriate her between one heartbeat and the next. All it took was a word, a gesture, or even a look.

He bit his lip to prevent a fertile oath from slipping out and went to gather wood to build a small fire. Jasmine sat

down upon a fallen log, her teeth almost chattering from
the chill evening air. Falcon fed the horses, rearranged
the loads on their packhorses, then took his saddle from
his tired destrier and put in on the extra horse he had
brought along, a chestnut stallion of good height. He returned to the fire to add thicker branches when Jasmine
said in a reproachful voice, "I'm hungry, but I suppose a
mere woman must take second place to your horses."

He kept his face perfectly straight and said, "You are
the woman, that's your job."

She flared up. "Where in the world am I supposed to
find food in the middle of nowhere?"

He threw out a casual hand. "There is game in the
woods, fish in the river."

She looked at him incredulously. Surely he didn't expect her to help feed them? She opened her mouth to
retort, then closed it again.

"There's food in the saddlebags," he said casually.

"Oh," she said, rising uncertainly.

"Don't bother, Lady de Burgh, I know how useless
you are." Her bottom lip thrust out and he dipped his
head to kiss her. Desire raged within him instantly, but
he held it in check. There was barely time to eat, no time
whatsoever for dalliance. But he remembered every intimate detail of their consummation. What a sensual delight Jasmine had been the night before! Once he had her
safe from danger he would indulge to the full the sensuality she aroused in him. He anticipated hours of pleasure
when he would teach her all the ways a man and a
woman could love each other. He would not be satisfied
until he had taught her to have erotic demands of her
own, until he lighted a flame within her that burned with
the need to love and be loved. He lifted his mouth from
hers and nuzzled her ear. "Useless now . . . but I intend to change all that," he promised.

When they had finished their meal, she refused to ride

in front of him, and insisted on mounting her own palfrey. They stayed in the saddle until midnight, when Falcon saw her slip to one side in exhaustion. He lifted her down and lay her on the ground. She was fast asleep. Then he covered her with his cloak and sat down wearily to watch over her, his back resting against the bole of an oak tree.

They were no sooner in the saddle the next morning than the heavens opened and the rain poured down. Doggedly they rode on, sloshing their way mile after wet, cold mile. Jasmine was numb with fatigue. She hoped he would take mercy on her and let her rest every few miles, but he seemed never to look back at her, he just kept riding for seven more hours.

Actually, he was sick with dread for her. She was delicate as a flower and had been soaked through to the skin since early morning. What if she took an ague or lung fever from being wet and cold without proper rest or nourishment? Worriedly he glanced back and saw that her palfrey had come to a stop. Falcon spurred his horse back to her and saw that she wept helplessly. His heart ached for her. He had driven her so hard because he knew it was possible that day to reach William Marshal's resplendent castle of Chepstow, which offered every amenity. He was certain they were within a mile or two; he could not let her stop now.

A leader of men all his life, he knew there were weakening words or there were strengthening words to urge people on to achieve an impossible goal. He reached into the saddlebags and pulled out one of his cloaks that was merely damp and dismounted. He stood beside her stirrup and scrutinized her face closely. He saw the purple smudges of fatigue beneath her eyes, her bloodless lips, the heartrending droop of her shoulders. He forced amusement to his face. "I've never seen anyone so forlorn over a little drenching."

She lifted her whip to him, but he reached up and gently took it from her numbed fingers. He lifted her into his arms and stood cradling her, then he wrapped her in his big cloak and carried her to his horse. Again he took her up before him and pressed his knee to the side of their mount. As it moved forward steadily, he murmured in her ear, "Sweetheart, just a couple of miles farther is Chepstow. You'll be able to see your father and I think you know Lady Marshal. She is a fountain of kindness and hospitality. You'll be tucked up in a warm bed before four o'clock this afternoon."

She looked at him incredulously. "Truly?" she questioned between sobs, not at all convinced such a miracle was possible.

"Close your eyes and when you open them we'll be there," he soothed. She rested her head beneath his chin, her cheek against his heart and fell instantly asleep.

In the vast courtyard at Chepstow they had all come outside to receive and welcome the newlyweds. Lady Isabel Marshal and two of her maids were fussing about Jasmine, who looked like a little drowned cat.

Falcon lifted her down to Isabel, a truly wonderful, kind woman. "Can you put her to bed for a couple of hours, my lady? She hasn't had an easy time of it."

Isabel was always happy to have company. She was delighted to have the newlyweds for a couple of days. Lady Marshal, in her late thirties, was still beautiful, but she was also very maternal. She was in her element the moment she saw Jasmine needed a little mothering. She took her upstairs to the best guest chamber and ordered a fire be lighted immediately. Jasmine let the maids strip off her soggy garments and wrap her in one of Isabel's bedrobes, then they turned back the covers on the big bed and helped her into it.

Isabel came to the bed with a goblet of mulled wine.

"When you awaken I'll have a bath ready before dinner. Then you will be able to have a lovely visit with your father and tell us all about the wedding."

Jasmine drank down the warm spiced wine. It went to her head immediately. She held up two fingers. "Two weddings, Isabel . . . two husbands. I was married twice."

"Whatever do you mean, child?" the woman asked, amazed, but Jasmine was fast in the arms of Morpheus.

A hot bath was prepared for Falcon in the bathhouse, but he quickly dismissed the two maids who came to help him as Salisbury, Hubert, and William Marshal entered the room.

"You don't mind an audience, do you? We can talk up here," said William.

Falcon grinned as he picked up the soap. "I'm highly honored to have the marshal of England, the justiciar, and the sovereign's brother watch me bathe."

Salisbury slapped him on the back. "I'm proud to have you as son-in-law. Welcome to the family."

Falcon held up his hand. "Save the welcome until you've heard what I've done. When I arrived in Gloucester I found her already wed to Chester. I dragged the poor bishop from his bedside to confirm that John had attended the ceremony. I told him the Pope had excommunicated the king and that made the marriage he'd performed in the presence of the king null and void. Then I forced him to wed Jasmine to me. I left Chester trussed like a haunch of venison."

"By Christ, what takes possession of my brother to do these things?" Salisbury demanded with impotent fury. Then he answered his own question. "The whoreson did it for money, of course. He sold her to the highest bidder. At least Chester did it for lust, but John did it just for the money!"

Falcon cut in. "John lusts for Jasmine as much as Chester. I had to remove her from his grasp."

William Marshal was disgusted. "We have to put a stop to it. His lust knows no bounds. If he sees any woman he desires he takes her. If she is unwilling he simply has her abducted. Sometimes with fatal results."

Hubert brought the conversation back to Falcon's plight. "How did you escape?"

"My men stayed behind so that we could get away safely. My men-at-arms will probably stay in the king's service, but I know most of my knights will follow me into Wales. They will go straight to Mountain Ash. They'll make short work of Chester's men if they are attacked. The king will order my arrest and come after me, but with any luck it will soon snow and the passes into Wales will be effectively blocked for the winter."

William Marshal poured Falcon a horn of ale. "The king has far too many problems on his plate to worry about you, although he doesn't have the brains to know it. When we confront him in two or three days' time it must be forcibly brought home to him that he must settle his differences with Rome. If I have any say in this, I will insist he lead a more circumspect life. It is time he started being faithful to his wife the queen and begetting sons."

Falcon didn't want Salisbury to think he had deserted the army. "From Mountain Ash I will patrol the Welsh Marches and keep the peace."

Salisbury replied, "I think it prudent you are putting a distance between yourself and the king. After the winter has passed and tempers have cooled, will you be willing to fight again in the king's cause?"

"I will, providing it isn't a civil war," Falcon answered bluntly.

"Aye," replied William Marshal, "that's what we must avoid at all costs. If John was well beloved by his barons, he could afford to thumb his nose at the Pope, but with support of neither church nor barons, he cannot rule."

Salisbury shook his head. "There is an imbalance of mercenaries in my army. I don't like it."

Falcon said, "They are great fighting men, but they are in it for gain alone, not for any loyalty to England."

Hubert spoke up. "Falkes de Bréauté will control the whole of the Midlands when he marries Devon's widow."

Falcon stood up in the wooden tub and William Marshal handed him a towel. "That wedding will have already taken place." He grinned. "I bet John was conspicuous by his absence so there would be no doubt of its legality."

"God's bones, I'd like to be a fly on the wall in Gloucester Castle right now. John's excommunication being shouted from every pulpit, Chester the butt of everyman's jest. You must have sat the whole place on its arse!" said Salisbury, laughing.

"You must be dead on your feet, man," said William Marshal. "Hubert has told us how you swam the river."

Falcon donned dry garments provided from the marshal's resplendent wardrobe. "Hugh, how did you get here before me?" asked Falcon.

"We crossed the bridge at Cambridge, changed horses at Tewksbury where your men and mine parted company. I arrived this morning and missed all the heavy rain."

William Marshal said, "We'll get some hot food into you and let you get to bed."

Falcon glanced up in time to see the three men wink at each other.

Chapter 27

"Jasmine dear, your bath is ready," said Lady Isabel, shaking her gently. Jasmine opened her eyes and yawned.

"Oh, I so hate to disturb your sleep but I know you will want a bath before you go to your bridegroom tonight," Isabel said, hanging Feather's cage by the window.

Jasmine was on the point of asking her to find de Burgh another chamber when Isabel clasped her hands together and said with shining eyes, "Oh, 'tis so exciting for me to have a new bride here, and since this will be your first night together, I mean in a real bed—oh, you know what I mean—I've ordered a special bridal supper, but after the toasts I promise you I won't let the men keep Falcon at table."

"Thank you, Isabel," Jasmine said faintly, unable to spoil the woman's obvious enjoyment.

Isabel helped Jasmine into the steaming water and liberally lathered her flaxen hair with soft soap. " 'Tis easy to see he fell in love with your great beauty. Well, he won't be disappointed tonight when he sees how utterly lovely you'll look."

Jasmine, realizing she had no alternative but to share the bed with de Burgh, said, "Isabel, may I borrow a night rail from you?"

Isabel laughed. "Oh, you are shy of him seeing you nude. I bet he's an outrageous rogue who has you in a continual blush. How I remember my wedding night. I was like you, I had no experience of men. I lived in Ireland with my parents until my father's untimely death, then I was cloistered here at Chepstow and finally taken to the Tower of London for safekeeping so no man could

abduct me for my vast land holdings. They married me to
the marshal of England and I was terrified of him until he
took me to bed and worshipped me. Even though I have
grown children, I'm still in love with my husband."

"You really love him?" asked Jasmine in disbelief.

Isabel nodded happily. "He still makes me breathless
with desire when he gets that speculative look in his eyes.
We are lucky, Jasmine, there aren't too many love
matches, you know. Hubert told us how magnificently
heroic Falcon was when he sensed you were in danger.
All the bridges had been swept away over the Ouse River
and he plunged into the raging waters, risking his life to
reach you in time."

Jasmine looked at her strangely. Isabel sighed. "You
must be very much in love." Jasmine stepped from the
tub and stood by the fire to towel her hair dry. Isabel
lifted the lid of Jasmine's traveling trunk and took out the
pink velvet. "I'll just warm it to take the dampness
away," Isabel said, draping it over a brass fireguard. "I'll
go and get you that nightgown for later. If I can put my
hands on it, I have the most alluring black négligée William brought from France a few years back. It will be
shockingly delicious for a wedding night!"

Jasmine wished she'd never asked for it. The maids
came in to remove the bath and then they put scented
satin sheets upon the bridal bed at Isabel's insistence.
They brought a good supply of wine and sweet cakes for
the bridal couple and saw that the fire was well banked
with plenty of wood and coals in a brass holder.

"Your son Will was very kind to me at court, Isabel.
He was one of the few friends I made."

Isabel sighed. "Will and his father had the most awful
fight when he left court. He urged his father to turn his
back on King John, but William said that would be like
turning his back on England. Loyalty, I'm afraid, comes
very high on William's list of virtues. Men are quite silly

really. They have this wretched code of honor. They chose John for king and they will stick by him to the end, no matter that he's the worst king that England has ever known. Women are far more practical than men with their high ideals. We see men as they really are."

Jasmine grimaced and said, "I don't even know where my poor grandmother is, but she always says men only sweat, fart, snore, and shout."

Isabel's laugh rang out. "Oh, Dame Winwood is so outrageous, but if we don't go down to dinner soon that's just what they'll be doing!"

When Isabel entered the private dining room with Jasmine on her arm, all the men in the room stood and gave a collective sigh. Never had there been a more beautiful, feminine bride than Jasmine de Burgh.

Her father came forward to take her in his arms. "My little darling, you've had quite an ordeal, I hear."

She looked up into his kind eyes and marveled that he could possibly be John's brother.

He patted her head as if she were a little girl. "Never mind, you have Falcon to look after you now. I knew what I was doing when I betrothed you to the young devil, you know."

Jasmine's eyes flashed. If they had been alone she would have told him exactly what he could do with the *young devil,* and would tell him so the first chance she got.

He took her to Falcon and placed her small hand in his. Falcon looked amused. Jasmine looked daggers!

Lady Isabel Marshal was a magnificent chatelaine. Her servants were trained to be unobtrusive as well as efficient. As she had instructed they had set up a twelve-foot refectory table to seat six. It was laid with cream linen and Venetian crystal. Dark russet chrysanthemums decorated the center along with slim tapers of purest scented wax. She sat Jasmine between her husband and her father, and Isabel sat between her own husband and Hubert de Burgh.

William shook his head in wonder as he gazed across at Jasmine. "So fair, so small. Are you sure this child is old enough to be wed?"

"She is nineteen, William." Isabel spoke up. "Exactly the age I was when we were wed. Do you remember?"

"Remember? I remember details I can't recount in company, but I'll remind you of them later when we are alone."

Isabel said laughing, "I told you he loves to make me blush."

They were served clear turtle soup laced with cream, followed by plaice, which the chef had properly calvered for the guests. An abundance of oysters set the men to teasing Falcon as they pressed him to a second helping. Jasmine did not quite understand the innuendos and the men looked on her with approving eyes. Innocence was a desirable quality in a bride.

There was heron in Burgundy sauce, piles of rice colored by saffron accompanied by all the vegetables of late autumn. The pièce de résistance was a crisp saddle of mutton with mint. After the main course came meringues filled with apples, nuts, and whipped cream and a great wheel of cheese decorated with ripe pears. There was the choice of many drinks: old ale, cider, and both red and white wine, brought from the marshal's vineyards in France two years back.

Each in turn offered a toast to the bride. Falcon thanked them on her behalf and offered a toast to their hospitable host and hostess, but when Jasmine held her goblet up for the servant to refill, Falcon refused the wine for her.

Hubert spoke up. "Maybe the lass wants some more."

Falcon said firmly, "Lady Jasmine wants what I want."

She clenched her fist under cover of the table and thumped de Burgh's thigh. She gave a little yelp of pain as her hand felt as if it had struck iron. Her cry drew all eyes and she took advantage of the situation to lie, "My husband pinched me."

"Can't keep his hands off her," said Hubert, laughing.

"Well, I think we can excuse these young people. After all, it is their wedding night," William said indulgently.

Isabel rose from the table and drew Jasmine with her. She looked at Falcon with sparkling eyes and said, "Just give us a few minutes, milord."

Isabel fussed over Jasmine's preparation for bed, as excited as if she were the bride. Finally her pale golden hair was brushed, perfume was applied, and the sheer black nightgown, gathered beneath the breasts with pink ribbons, was donned. Isabel wished her joy of her wedding night and at last departed. Within two minutes Falcon opened the chamber door.

He stood transfixed by the transparent black garment, which was designed to reveal rather than conceal Jasmine's exquisite form. He had been exhausted, yet suddenly the need for sleep vanished.

She ran to him quickly with her fingers to her lips. "Hush, we will have to whisper. I don't want Isabel to hear us fight like cat and dog. She has gotten hold of the notion that this is a great love match and we are deep in love with each other."

He tried to take her by the shoulders. "I don't mind pretending for once . . . just to please Isabel," he whispered.

"Don't touch me!" she hissed.

He took away his hands so quickly she almost fell. His voice was a savage whisper. "Do you expect me to ask politely each time I touch you? It's getting to be a wearisome affair having you always deny me!"

"We are just not suited. We are at each other's throats

the moment we are alone, but I don't want to spoil it for Isabel. She has been so kind to me and she is so excited about having newlyweds here," Jasmine said quietly.

"I hope you don't think you can deny me. If I choose, you know you will have to let me do it," Falcon whispered savagely.

"If you lay one finger on me, I'll scream the place down," she whispered fiercely.

He always took up a challenge. He pushed her down onto the bed and she gave a piercing scream and shouted at the top of her voice, "I sat on Prick!"

"By the legs of God, Jasmine, they will think I am killing you." Then he began to laugh at the humor of the situation. "I thought he was called Quill?"

"He was," she hissed, "but you call him Prick so often, I've changed his name." She covered her face and groaned. "Oh, my lord, what will they all be thinking?"

"They will think you most passionate to cry out so that the whole castle can hear," he replied, chuckling.

"They have misconceptions about you too. They think you performed some great heroic feat by swimming a raging river to get to me. They think we have this great psychic bond that told you I needed you. I'm cast in the role of damsel in distress and you are the noble, heroic knight." She stopped and looked at him. "You really did swim that river, didn't you?" she said, amazed. "My God, you must be dead on your feet. I'm sorry," she murmured.

He sighed with the pleasure he always felt when her words to him were sweet as honey. She was apologizing to him and suddenly he remembered how roughly, though deliciously, he had forced himself upon her two nights before. She was so fragile. Perhaps he was being selfish not to let her rest tonight. He knew that he could control himself with her only up to a point. After that the demands of his powerful body ruled supreme and took what it wanted. Jasmine took him to a place where nothing else mattered but burying his body deep inside hers. "I'll sleep on the floor," he offered hoarsely. "You need your rest, we still have far to go."

"You need your rest as much as I. You will sleep in the bed on your wedding night or I am ashamed. Do not touch me but rest more at ease than on the floor."

He looked down at her. Only a child would believe that a man, any normal whole man, would rest more at ease in a bed with a near-naked woman than on the floor alone. "Very well," he agreed shortly.

He put out the candles, undressed quickly, and climbed into the bed beside her, naked. He lay silent, stiff, desperately aware of the silken body. He could feel her warmth and smell her tempting fragrance. He had never felt less like sleep. Every breath she took, every least stir she made, he was aware of.

The longer he lay the harder he became. His masculinity was an aching urgency. He willed her to touch him, to reach out to him so that he could leave her in no doubt of his readiness. He was making an endless night of it. He would be aware of each hour, but she did not move.

Slowly the realization came to him that he was a fool. Jasmine was his and he would have the joy of her, willing or no. His broad shoulders took up most of the bed, so he did not have to reach far to lay hands on her. He simply placed his hands on her waist, easily spanning it, and lifted her over him.

Jasmine stiffened, then struggled frantically, but he held her firmly to the hard, naked length of his body. "Let me go or I'll scream," she threatened tensely.

"You can scream all you want to," he said low, "but somehow I don't think you will."

She renewed her struggles until the nightgown was in shreds, but she was still pinioned against the hard length of him. He relaxed his fierce hold upon her, and she

raised her head from his chest and gazed into the searing
green flame of his smoldering eyes.

"We are husband and wife, Jasmine. There is no shame
in this, darling." One hand moved up from her waist to
cup a heavy, round breast whose taut pink tip had been
burning his chest. "Yield to me now, love," he murmured
thickly against her throat.

"Falcon, wait!" she cried desperately. Her body well
remembered the pain his great shaft had caused her, and
she knew she would do anything to keep him from entering her body again. She could feel his rigid erection pressing into the place where her thigh joined her belly only
scant inches away from its desired goal. She knew she
must distance herself from his great weapon. "May I lie
beside you?" she pleaded prettily.

Reluctantly his hand uncupped her luscious breast and
returned to her waist, then without effort he lifted her to
his side and propped himself on his elbow to gaze down
at her. "Don't tremble, love, I'll be gentle, I won't hurt
you," he breathed raggedly.

"You hurt me before," she accused, then changed her
tone and began to beg. "Don't hurt me again, please
don't hurt me."

"Lie still, darling. I don't want to hurt you, I want to
love you," he soothed. "Before that door opens again I
intend to make you my wife in every way." She lay still,
stiff, rigid. "Jasmine . . . you are so unearthly fair." His
hand caressed her moonlit hair and his lips came down
on hers gently, tentatively, savoring the soft pink mouth
for which he'd hungered long, but the moment his lips
released hers, she turned from him so that her lips and
breasts were out of reach of his hungry mouth. His arms
slid around her waist immediately and she realized with
dismay that her breasts, indeed all her most intimate
parts were open to his exploring hands. Then a new realization dawned. Her bare buttocks rested full against his

loins. His manroot was hard and bold against her soft
flesh. He drew in a swift breath each time she squirmed
and her bottom caressed the tip of his inflamed shaft. His
thumbs caressed her nipples until they were hard as tiny
jewels, and she tried to shrink from his touch. "Honey
love, I only want to hold you, touch you," he cajoled.

"I-I'll let you hold me . . . but, Falcon please . . .
don't do the other . . . please?"

An impatient retort was on his lips when he felt the
wetness of her tears. His heart and his resolve melted like
snow in summer. He cursed himself for the mating he'd
forced on her at Gloucester. He saw clearly that from her
point of view it had been nothing short of rape. No wonder she begged him never to do it again. He had his work
cut out for him if he was to persuade her that an intimate
encounter need not be brutal.

With infinite gentleness he turned her over to face him.
"My little sweetheart, trust me not to hurt you again.
Forgive me for what I forced you to do the other night?"
He stroked her hair to gentle her and coax her into a
response. "Open your legs just a tiny bit for me. I'll just
use one finger, I promise. Just relax, darling, and I'll
make you tingle."

Jasmine refused to answer him.

"Sweetheart, I know how tiny you are, especially down
there, but I know how to stop it from hurting. I'll make
you hot and slippery and I swear I won't mount you until
you're completely ready for me."

Jasmine clenched her fists and thumped them against
his hard, bare chest. "No, no, no!" she sobbed.

"I have starved for that which is mine by right of wed-
lock and I will have it," he said low, his self-control
sorely strained.

"Ah, why did you not let me drink deeply? If I were
only half-conscious I might have been able to endure it."

Her words wounded him, ate at his pride. So beautiful

yet so cruel. He was deeply stung that a woman would need to get drunk before she could endure him.

Tears spiked her eyelashes and he patiently kissed them away with a tenderness that tore at his heart. He sighed deeply, trying to cool his raging ardor. "Sshh, hush love," he crooned, "I promise I won't do the other if you let me hold you, touch you," he said reluctantly.

Her eyes searched his. "Do you really promise not to put it into me?"

He smiled and whispered, "I promise not to put it into you if you will let me have free rein with my hands and my kisses."

After a tense moment she nodded her agreement. He cradled her against him with one strong arm, while his other hand stroked her gently. He chose a nonthreatening place to begin and moved his hand to caress her arm. He brought her fingers to his lips and kissed each one with reverence, then placed her hand against his chest. She stiffened again as her fingers came into contact with the crisp hair. He told himself her shy reserve would dissolve as they became familiar with each other's bodies. His lips began his kisses at the top of her head, which was well below his chin, then with loving hands he raised her face to his and brushed his lips across her temples, her eyelids, the tip of her nose, her top lip. Then, forcing her mouth open only slightly, he allowed the tip of his tongue to touch hers with a teasing little darting motion. He must have bestowed a hundred kisses upon her before he moved on to further intimacy.

Slowly he folded back the cover from their bodies so that he could see her in all her glory, and lifted her higher against the pillows so that his lips could explore her body. She demurred, pushing her hands against his chest. "Jassy, you agreed," he said, arching her abdomen up to his mouth to let his tongue play about her navel.

Although he was low in the bed and she was much

higher, she could just reach his shoulders with her hands, but as she pushed at them it had the effect of lowering him further so that his hot mouth now rested at the cleft between her legs. Surely he wouldn't put his wicked tongue inside her again, she thought wildly. "Falcon, no!" she cried as her worst fears were realized.

"Jasmine, you agreed," he murmured against her hot center. He parted her lips slightly and allowed just the tip of his tongue to do the same teasing little darting motion it had done when he kissed her mouth.

"I know I didn't agree to this, milord." She gasped and then she remembered that before they were wed he had offered to make love to her with his tongue so that by the time they were married she would be ready for his great manroot. She hadn't really believed he would do any such wicked thing, the mere talk of it had shocked her to her very soul. But now, again, she realized he expected her to allow him any wicked fantasy that came into his head. She withdrew from him with her mind so that her body could no longer feel the things he would do to her.

Though their physical bodies touched each other intimately, there was a great gulf that separated them mentally, emotionally, and spiritually. Falcon knew he must breach that gulf or they would have no kind of marriage. As his hands and mouth grew bolder, his fingers and tongue more intimate, Jasmine withdrew further and further.

Falcon was in a fever of longing. Deep inside, his gut ached from the loveplay that had gone on for hours without reaching its natural conclusion. He cursed himself for promising not to mount her; he should have remembered how painful his swollen shaft would be if he didn't have release. He crouched above her in his great need. His entire body now screamed with the need to release the pent-up desire that surged wildly through him. He straddled her gently and slid his shaft into the valley between her upthrusting breasts, then he took the round globes into his hands and squeezed them until his hard erection was sheathed. Jasmine could keep silent no longer. She cried out in low protest, "My lord, what are you doing to me?" Falcon was beyond words. It took only a few thrusts until he was gasping with ecstasy. He had come on her breasts. He resisted the urge to massage it over her silken skin and instead reached for the shredded black nightgown and gently wiped her breasts. She snatched the gown and turned away from him, silently outraged.

When Falcon awoke he found his cheek against her hot breast and groaned with the frustration of his situation. Jasmine opened her eyes and recoiled from him, her accusing look clearly blaming him for obscene things he should never have done.

He shot up from the bed as if she had thrown ice-cold water on him. Naked, he knelt to tend the fire, which had burned to ashes. She averted her gaze from his body and her amethyst eyes widened in horror as she surveyed the remnants of Isabel's night rail. This reminded her that all below thought it had been her wedding night, but there would be no evidence of her virginity upon the sheets.

Jasmine looked about her for something sharp and spotted Falcon's sheathed dagger lying upon his clothes. She moved across the bed and took the knife from its leather sheath. She was shocked by the speed at which Falcon had moved. Her wrist was being crushed by his strong fingers as he demanded quietly, "What the hell are you doing?"

Her lashes swept to her cheeks. Surely he hadn't thought she would stab him in the back? Actually, his thought had been for her. Surely she wouldn't harm herself rather than submit to him?

She faltered, "I-we-they will expect blood upon the sheets."

He took the dagger from her and without à word made

a small slit in his thumb and squeezed half a dozen drops of blood from it. By the legs of God, he couldn't endure another night like the last. They would have to leave today. If they had to spend more time under the indulgent noses of their avid audience, touching in bed but not enjoying intercourse he would go mad. He went to the window and sighed with relief, for it had begun to snow in the night. They would have to leave today to ensure that they got through the mountain passes before they became blocked.

"It has begun to snow so we must leave today." Suddenly he felt he was being cruel to tear her away from the comfort of Chepstow. "Dress warmly, Jasmine, it will be freezing cold out there. Have a visit with your father while you have the chance." He slipped on his shirt, pants, and boots. "I'll get William to give us one of his campaign tents. I don't want you sleeping out in the open."

Jasmine shivered and moved down in the bed to the lovely warm place Falcon's body had recently vacated. How could she face a journey through the snow? She sighed deeply. It would be easier than another night where their every whisper might be overheard.

Chapter 28

Jasmine wore a woolen gown and woolen stockings and a pair of riding boots. As she sought out Isabel to see if she had some warm gloves she could borrow, she passed an open chamber door and saw her father packing his saddlebags for a journey. He beamed at her. "Did you sleep well, sweetheart?"

Suddenly her bottom lip was quivering and she covered her face with her hands as she wept hopelessly. He put his big arm about her and sat her down before the fire. "Jasmine, I want you to be happy," he said anxiously. "I'm a good judge of men; believe me when I tell you you've one of the best in the whole realm. He has qualities that mark him off from other men."

"Then why didn't you give him your precious Isobel or Ela?" she cried.

"That was precisely my plan, but from the moment he laid eyes on you, he was blind to them. He would have no other. Child, your grandmother and I painted such a portrait of your inadequacies as a wife, no man in his right mind would have wanted to wed with you. In fact, I refused him outright until he forced me to yield to his demands. He told me you had spent the night in his bed and were hopelessly compromised. He insinuated that the damage he had done was beyond repair. I wanted him for a son-in-law, Jasmine, so I gave in to his demands."

"But they inherit your lands and castles," protested Jasmine.

"De Burgh did not covet my castles, he coveted only you. Jasmine, my dear, surely he has demonstrated the depth of his feelings for you. He braved a raging river to snatch you from the arms of Chester."

She shuddered at mention of the dreaded name.

"Do you not return Falcon's affection? Are things not right between you?" he asked concerned.

"He is so arrogant. His word is law. He expects me to obey his every order, but I shall defy him till I die!" she said passionately.

Salisbury tried not to smile. "You didn't defy Chester," he pointed out.

"Because he threatened to harm Estelle!" she cried.

"And Chester wouldn't hesitate to inflict hurt upon you if you defied him. Am I right?"

"Yes," she said, remembering Chester's cruel hands on her breasts.

"You defy Falcon de Burgh because he allows you to defy him. Think about it, Jasmine." Her father kissed her brow and wished her Godspeed on her journey. He told her he would shortly take issue with John and Chester for what they had tried to do to her.

Jasmine, wrapped in the ermine cloak with another hooded cloak over it, sat her palfrey in the snow-covered courtyard of Chepstow wishing she had the chatelaine's skills of Lady Isabel Marshal. She spoke so knowledgeably to Falcon, almost like an equal.

"In a couple of days I intend to send a few supply wagons through to you at Mountain Ash. Heaven only knows what the harvest was like at your Welsh holding. I'll send some hams and wheels of cheese. Also some fine white flour so Jasmine won't have to eat black bread all winter. I'll include wine and cider casks and some ale too. If it's been a male stronghold for a long time I know it will lack decent linen and any number of things. I'm willing to bet there isn't a single mirror in the entire castle," said Isabel, laughing at the puzzled look on Falcon's face. "Men!" she said to Jasmine.

"I'll never understand them," Jasmine said faintly.

Isabel winked. "You underestimate yourself."

"Thank you so much for your kindness, Isabel," said Jasmine, her eyes looking longingly at the warm stone strength of Chepstow.

"Go with God," Isabel shouted, as de Burgh put the spurs to his destrier and led the string of packhorses away.

Mountain Ash was approximately the same distance from Chepstow as Gloucester had been, but the terrain was treacherous. There were two ranges of mountains to climb, most of which were over twenty-five hundred feet. The first part of their journey would be far easier than the last half, and Falcon hoped to make it to the vicinity of Pontypool by dusk. It was at the foot of the first mountain range where the Castle of Usk lay beside a large lake.

Jasmine followed Falcon's lead, being sure to keep up with him so he could have no complaints. She was very proud of herself for sitting her saddle for so many hours without complaint or tears through the thickly falling snow.

Just before dusk the snow stopped to give them a breathtaking view of the lake with the Castle of Usk rising from its far side. Jasmine felt the urge to capture its beauty on canvass. She swallowed her pride and spoke to her husband. "Can we stay there tonight?"

He knew she was cold and tired and hungry, and yet something about the place made him uneasy. After a slight hesitation he shook his head. "I think we'll be better off in the tent."

She flared, "You would! 'Tis no hardship for you to sleep on the cold ground. I want to go to the castle, I don't trust you alone in a tent in the wilderness with none to come to my aid!"

"You do right to fear me, lady!" he said tightly. "Never say to me again that you don't feel safe with me."

She bit her lip, for she knew she had really angered him this time.

Suddenly a lone rider with long black hair and bared arm muscles rode out from under the trees and drew rein beside Falcon. Jasmine cried out in alarm, but Falcon and the man spoke in the Welsh tongue. He gestured to the castle and Falcon asked him a question. In answer the Welshman held up the five fingers of one hand.

Falcon turned his head to look at her. "We go to the Castle of Usk after all."

"Oh, thank you, milord. I'm truly sorry if I angered you."

He cut her short. "We don't go for your sake, my lady, we go because Chester's assasins await us."

She felt herself sway and caught hold of her saddle horn desperately to keep from fainting into the snow. Falcon chose the long way around the lake, keeping under cover of the trees and coming to the postern gate of the castle. Usk was part of the vast de Clare holdings that Isabel had brought to William Marshal when they married. It was a small holding, and the marshal kept only a handful of retainers there, some Welsh, some English. It had no garrison of men-at-arms, but from his service in Wales, Falcon de Burgh was familiar with Usk.

He did not take the horses to the stables but sheltered them in a lean-to near the kitchens that was used to keep wood for the fires. As he lifted Jasmine from the saddle he felt her shaking. How in the world would this sweet child find the courage to be a helpmate to a man like himself? For her sake he never should have married her. He opened the kitchen door and pushed her through into the hot room, redolent with the smell of delicious bread and acrid smoke. He fished into a pocket for a coin and held it out to the cook. "Where do you sleep?" he asked.

She pointed to a small room off the kitchen that contained a single pallet. As he ushered Jasmine into the little chamber, he cautioned her, "You will be safe and warm here. Put the bar down on the inside and do not open to any but me."

The Welsh scout who had met him across the lake was in the kitchen when Falcon came out of the small room. "Are they all five together?" asked Falcon, hoping they were not so that he could take on one at a time.

"They are drinking in the hall," the Welshman replied.

"Let's try to separate them. I'll go up on the battlements. Tell them you were just up there and thought you saw a rider across the lake."

The Welshman nodded his understanding. He was a

member of William Marshal's household and therefore unwilling to take a hand in killing Englishmen, but as a native Welshman he was not averse to seeing English kill English. He went into the hall and told of the rider.

The leader of the men asked, "Was there a woman with him?"

"Too far off to tell." He pointed upward. "They should be easy to spot now in the snow, although the light is fading fast."

The leader dispatched two men to the battlements, then took the other two with him to the bailey where the drawbridge was clearly visible.

Falcon crouched on the battlements with his unsheathed knife at the ready. The two men were talking as they emerged on the ramparts. "If he manages to escape, we must secure the woman at all costs. I wouldn't like to face Chester without her."

"If your arrow had found its mark in Nottingham we'd not be up to our arses futtering about in bloody snow . . ." The voice was silenced forever as Falcon's knife went straight into the man's windpipe.

"What the Hellfire?" cried his companion, drawing his knife and backing off in a crouch.

"That's exactly where I'm sending you, my friend. The one fatal mistake you made in life was missing my back when you aimed that arrow." Falcon flung himself, knife first, upon the startled man. The force of his full body weight followed. The man was thinking what an utter fool de Burgh was to jump a man holding a drawn dagger, but he never got the chance to finish the thought.

Falcon bound the two bodies together by the leather thongs of their chausses then lifted the deadly bundle onto the parapet. One push and the pair dropped straight down into the lake with a splash that sprayed the men waiting by the drawbridge.

One called up, "What the hell was that? Did one of you fall off the wall?"

Falcon stepped onto the wall with raised sword. "Both!" he taunted.

"It's him," they cried in unison, running back into the castle, racing for the stone staircase that would carry them to their quarry.

"What's he done with the woman?" one asked. They gripped the hilts of their swords but did not unsheath them until they finished climbing. By then it was too late for the first man to draw. He had run straight onto de Burgh's needle-sharp weapon. Falcon lifted his foot to the man's chest to help him withdraw his sword and immediately engaged the other two. Before the space of thirty seconds had elapsed he had drawn blood on one assailant's sword arm and the man fell back in a moment's hesitation. The secret of Falcon's success in battle was that he never, ever hesitated. He slashed the other man and met his blade with a grating metallic sound, then he pulled back and swung with all the power behind his arm.

As the man fell back trying to keep his balance, Falcon slipped his sword into the gut below the armor that covered the man's chest. He turned to face the other sword but the man had fled. With decisive determination Falcon pursued the fifth man who was still alive.

On his way down the flight of stone steps the Welshman emerged from the shadows. "He has fled the castle," the man said.

De Burgh snatched the bow from the man's hand and one arrow from his quiver, then he took the stairs, going back up three at a time. High on the ramparts he took careful aim, his eye and his hand steady. The arrow sped its way to its target like a bird of prey flying through the night. The man's scream disturbed a flock of pigeons that had settled to roost for the night. A pair of screech owls took immediate advantage and selected a plump pigeon each for their supper. Then all was eerily silent until a lone wolf took up the cry and howled at the moon.

Falcon stood on the battlements a long time, oblivious to the freezing night air. Finally he went below to the kitchen and knocked on the door of the small room. "Jasmine," he whispered hoarsely.

"Falcon, are you all right?" she asked as she fumbled with the bar.

"No, don't lift the bar, Jasmine. All is well; go to sleep." He couldn't touch her that night, not with the blood of five men on his hands. He sank down at the door and laid his head back against the door jamb. For one fleeting moment he glimpsed himself through her eyes and understood exactly her distaste for him.

What dark, perverse desires had made him choose one so fragile, fair, and innocent? Jasmine was like a flower and no fit mate for a black rogue who lived by blood and sword. Splendor of God, what had made him dip his ring in her virgin's blood to stamp his brand all over the sheets? She must think herself married to a madman to do such a bastardly trick. Well, she was his now, for better or for worse. *"Pauvre petite,"* he murmured into the darkness.

By morning they were cursing each other again. She emerged from the tiny room to find him wolfing down a great slab of cold mutton, followed by hot, freshly baked bread dripping with honey.

"How dare you shove me in there for the night? It was so small I could scarcely turn around. I was choked with flour in the air that is stored in there, *and,*" she emphasized angrily, "I suspect the pallet was lousy!"

He looked at her incredulously. "I really believe you expect me to apologize."

"I doubt that a de Burgh would apologize to anyone . . . not in this lifetime."

"Put your mouth to better use, lady, and fill it with hot food." The warning in his voice boded no good for her if she disobeyed him. He strode from the kitchen to attend their horses, and the cook brought her a steaming bowl of gruel laced with cream and honey. The cook eyed the little blond creature holding the ermine fur with wonder. She had never seen a female so fair-skinned and fine-boned in her life. She seemed unreal, like a fairy princess from a child's story. Timidly she held out a parcel of food for their journey, fearing to offend the lady by the crudeness of the offering.

Jasmine was touched by the thoughtful gesture. "Oh, how very kind of you. I was wicked to complain of the bed you gave me, but I said it just to plague de Burgh."

The cook could hardly believe the lady deigned to speak with her. Finally she decided to warn her, "Don't anger him lady. Last night he killed five men who had come to seize you."

Jasmine's first thought was, Why do people tell such outrageous tales about him, as if he were some living legend? But she held her tongue. The tales usually proved to have more than a grain of truth in them.

Falcon made her sit pillion behind him as they left the Castle of Usk, and it annoyed her beyond belief that she was again being treated like a child. As they climbed higher through the mountain pass, the wind howled fiercely as if it were trying to blow them back whence they came. Fancifully she feared the mighty spirit of the Black Mountains was putting them through an ordeal, a test of wind and ice that very few would master.

De Burgh's great, wide shoulders blocked the impact of the icy wind and sleet from her. She huddled against his warmth, clinging to him for dear life as the stallion's hooves struck splinters of frozen earth from the hard ground.

It took them the whole day, but when they were safely

over the highest peaks and descended to the sheltered valley beneath, Falcon built a fire and set up the campaign tent beside it. He then proceeded to cut fir boughs to make a lean-to for the horses.

Jasmine unpacked food, candles, and the bedroll of furs and took them into the tent, leaving him to his cold task. He brushed the snow from his shoulders and came inside. His eyes softened as he saw that she had lighted the candles and warmed their food at the fire.

"I think the great spirit of the Black Mountains has approved our passage. Perhaps it will be easier from here on," he said.

She laughed, amused that their thoughts could be so alike.

He took off his cloak and doublet and spread them to dry. "That is the first smile you have gifted me with since we were wed," he said, sitting down upon the furs to eat.

"God's feet, there has been little enough to smile about. We are escaping from enemies who will take our lives if the cruel elements don't do it first. We're out here in the middle of this wild, godforsaken wilderness with a snowstorm raging above us that almost freezes our mounts in their tracks."

He stretched lazily and smiled up at her. "There is nowhere on earth I would rather be tonight than here with you," he said, caressing her with his eyes.

She flared, "You have the most infuriating habit of looking me over."

He smiled again. "A crime every bridegroom in the world could be accused of, I'm sure." He stretched out his hand to her. "Come and eat. The pleasure of the food is doubled when I share with you."

She sat down stiffly, wanting none of his soft looks, soft words. "I would rather be anywhere than here with you," she said cruelly.

He was amused. He raised his head from his food and

smiled lazily at her. "You cannot provoke me tonight. It is an impossibility." His eyes mocked her gently, clearly telling her that tricks to incite a fight between them would not work.

She knew she was trapped. She knew he was going to do it to her again. He pulled her to him. He had inherited his reckless, pulsing de Burgh blood. It made him alive with passion, and he was unashamed of it. His hand went up her gown to strip off the woolen stockings, then he ran his hands up and down her slim, silken legs, lingering long about her soft thighs.

She shivered uncontrollably and he quickly removed her remaining clothes and rolled her inside the warm furs. She was so filled with dread for what was to come her eyes brimmed with tears, mercifully blurring his hard, erect nakedness. Then he was against her and she felt the full monstrous length of him.

He enclosed her in a world that extended no farther than his encircling arms and the powerful strength of his hard body. He began to kiss her and nuzzle her with his warm persuasive mouth, but, knowing what was to come, she could not begin to enjoy the loveplay. The tighter his embrace became the further she withdrew into herself.

She withdrew further and further, the gulf between them widened and widened until at last she was able to separate mind and body. Her spirit flew high inside the silken tent and floated there, then it soared above the tent, the trees, the clouds, and up to the stars. Her body lay still, inert, motionless. Her lack of response filled Falcon with a sense of despair. His passionate hands and mouth failed to kindle a spark of desire in her. Instead of meeting his fire with fire, she met his fire with ice. In spite of her lack of response, he soon felt his seed start, then it soared into her tight, velvety sheath as he emptied himself inside her. Her body was delicious, yet without response it had been one of the most disappointing experiences of his life.

When it was safe to do so, her mind and body came together with a little jerk, and she turned from him and slept. His need for her was so intense, it was more pain than pleasure. Once again sleep obliged him to beg before it permitted him to lose consciousness.

Chapter 29

A lifetime of training awakened him at dawn. How he longed to awaken her with a kiss, to cuddle together in the warm furs, to meet the day's challenge with the taste of her on his mouth, but he did not want to see her flinch from him.

She stirred beside him and, as she reached for her clothes, he turned away quickly to hide the bleakness in his eyes. The wind had died down considerably and great flakes of soft snow drifted down, blanketing the whole world in white.

She scorned to ride with him again, but followed his lead, climbing steeply, descending cautiously, splashing through mountain streams, and picking their way through dense forest. Whenever the snow blanketed him from her vision she panicked. By midday she could no longer feel her feet. Her teeth began to chatter and would not stop, no matter her proud determination. Finally she swallowed her pride.

"Falcon," she called.

He stopped in his tracks and allowed her to come abreast of him. "What would you like?" he asked politely.

"I-I'm cold," she said in a small voice.

Again he repeated, "What would you like?"

She bit her lip. He wasn't going to make it easy for her. "I-I would like to come up with you."

He stared at her as if he were undecided.

"Please," she added as an afterthought, afraid he might refuse.

He fastened the reins of her palfrey to the string of packhorses and lifted her before him in the saddle. She tucked her cold hands between her legs to warm them and in a very short time felt her back deliciously warm from the heat of his body. He had decided to be cool and detached. If she preferred to deal with him at a distance, then so be it. Trouble was, she wasn't at a distance. She was sitting in his lap. To make matters worse, each time his horse shifted weight from forelegs to rear legs she moved slightly back against him. Her buttocks touched the tip of his shaft, causing an erection. A strand of her silver-gilt hair blew back across his cheek and he quivered at the exquisite sensations she aroused in him.

His mind conjured an erotic fantasy and he groaned. He had heard somewhere that Arab men in the desert trained their horses for what they called *coït à cheval*. A man sat his woman astride his horse facing him and made love to her as the horse galloped over the hot sands. *Coït à cheval* horses were rockers, and legend was that it was an experience a woman remembered always.

He groaned aloud this time and Jasmine turned around and looked up into his face. "Are you cold?" she asked with concern.

"Cold?" he repeated with disbelief. Bones of God, his blood was so overheated at this moment he felt he might erupt like a volcano. "Are you cold, Jasmine?" he queried.

"Only my feet, but I can't really feel them anymore."

"Why didn't you tell me?" he demanded. "We'll make camp now. I'll get a fire going right away."

"No . . . no . . . perhaps if we rode all night, we would be there in the morning," she urged him. He heard the panic in her voice at the thought of making camp for the night and vowed to keep his lust under control. Where was the pleasure in making love to an unwilling wench?

As soon as the fire was lighted, he pulled off her boots and massaged her small feet. His strong hands soon warmed them up and the numbness vanished. Jasmine yawned. She quite liked having her feet played with. In fact, if she admitted it, she quite liked this man who was her husband. She had learned to have a great deal of respect for his strength and courage and his practical common sense. He was also far more attractive than any man had the right to be. If only he didn't do *that* to her, she could almost be happy, she told herself.

Again he fashioned a lean-to for the horses and she watched him effortlessly cut huge fir branches with his knife. When he was done there was still light in the sky. "I think we would benefit from some hot food. I'll see if there's any game about. Stay close by the fire until I return. Call out if you are afraid, I won't go far."

"Afraid?" she scoffed as he disappeared into the trees. "What could there possibly be out here to fear!" She put her boots back on and walked toward the sound of a nearby stream she could hear. There beside the water she saw a young, furry cub. "Oh, how sweet, you're just a baby," she murmured. She picked the animal up in her arms trying to discern if it was a mountain lion, lynx, or snow leopard.

"Falcon, Falcon, come quickly," she called.

He came quickly through the trees, dagger already to hand. He was alarmed at what he saw. "Jasmine, put it down and get the hell out of there." His temper flared at the danger she had put herself into. "I told you to stay by the fire. I don't give orders to have them disobeyed."

The mother of the young wildcat crouched along a tree limb readying herself to spring. As Falcon came beneath the tree, the three-hundred-pound killer sprang, her forelegs splayed, and ten black claws shot out of her pads. She bared three-inch upper canines, white as bone, and stabbed them into his shoulder. He rolled with the animal, desperate to keep her fangs from his jugular. In the same split second the cat was on her back, Falcon plunged in his knife to the hilt and ripped upward. He had no choice but to kill the wildcat.

Jasmine stood white-lipped, staring in horror at the carnage. "Must you kill everything that moves?" she cried.

"Damn it, woman, you were the cause of this wildcat's death."

She knew his words were true. He plucked the kit from her arms and ordered, "Get back to the fire."

"What are you going to do?" her voice rose on a note of panic.

"What I have to do. The kit was born too late in the season. It will starve without its mother. It is more humane to kill it."

"No!" she cried. "Let me have it for a pet. Please, Falcon?" she implored.

He spoke to her as if she were being an unreasonable child. "It will grow the size of its mother. It will be a mankiller."

"I'll set it free the moment the hard winter is past. Falcon, let me have it." She was so unreasonable in the things she asked him for. It increased his temper that he must refuse her when she pleaded with him. "I'll call her Shanna," she said softly.

His patience, stretched beyond its endurance, snapped. "We are escaping with our lives and you drag along a bloody menagerie. You have a sparrow over there who's cage is wrapped in an oilskin and a hedgehog at the bottom of my saddlebags. I'm going to feed Feather to Prick, and then feed Prick to Shanna," he vowed.

Jasmine knew she could have her way with him. She knew as surely as Eve had known in her dealings with Adam. She came close to him. He was so tall she had to tilt her head to look up at him. She put her small hands upon his chest and said softly, "You gave me no wedding present, Falcon . . . I would have Shanna for my bride's gift."

He could not resist her. He commanded hundreds of men with ease but found it almost impossible to handle one small female. She looked toward the dead wildcat and the tears streamed down her sweet face.

"Don't weep. It's over and done and no tears will change it. Take the kit back to the campfire." When she had gone he stripped to the waist and washed his wound in the icy river. His chain-mail vest had prevented the fangs from disabling him and he knew his blood would soon coagulate in the freezing mountain air.

Jasmine surreptitiously fed the kit her supper while Falcon wasn't looking then took off one of her petticoats to bundle it, and put it in a basket on one of the packhorses.

The next day Falcon became concerned when he discovered Jasmine asleep in the saddle. He took her before him again but could not seem to warm her or keep her from falling into exhausted slumber. He stepped up the pace, knowing he must reach Mountain Ash this day. Her endurance was at an end, her face alarmingly pale as the snow, and he touched it repeatedly to see if she was fevered.

When at last the wearied pair rode into the courtyard at Mountain Ash, the whole castle came out to greet them. He was amazed to see every last one of his knights

there before him, including some Welsh knights he hadn't
seen since he had last been at the castle. Two of them
stepped forward now, eager to relieve him of his burden.
Gower and Tam were brothers, strapping great louts, always ready for mischief.

"My lady is nearly done. I'll need a woman to look to
her needs until she is recovered," Falcon explained.

The brothers looked at each other and said in unison,
"Big Meg."

Falcon handed Jasmine down to Gower, but only until
he dismounted, then he took her back into his own arms.
"Get her. I'll take Jasmine to the tower room above
mine." There was no need for him to point out that
would be the safest place in the castle of Mountain Ash,
for an enemy would have to first defeat Falcon to get to
her.

The men vied with each other for the honor of carrying
Jasmine's luggage to the tower room. She smiled sleepily
at Tam and he lost his heart forever. Gower bent to set
the fire to blazing while his eyes were alight with mischief. He winked suggestively to Falcon and said, "A
week in bed should put her right."

Tam gave his brother a hard punch in the ribs.
"There's no need to be lewd. Don't you know a lady
when you see one?"

"Christ, are you trying to teach me manners?" Gower
asked, doubling with laughter, for Tam was surely the
lewdest youth in all Wales.

"Ye can't teach manners to pigs," asserted Tam, giving
his brother a hard shove from the room. They jostled Big
Meg as she was about to enter the chamber and she
threatened to bang their heads together. She looked as if
she could fell a horse. "Uncouth, uncivilized half-
breeds," she cursed, referring to their parentage—English father, Welsh mother. She took one look at the
small, pale girl in Falcon's arms and the maternal urge

almost overpowered her. "Out, pigs!" she ordered. "That goes for you too, milord, beggin' your pardon. She'll not be sharin' your bed for a night or two until she can hold her own against an overdemanding bridegroom." Her eyes shone with the light of battle, daring him to countermand her orders. The three men showed mock fear, but Falcon couldn't conceal a grin.

"It's a package deal, Meg. She comes with a bird, a hedgehog, and a wildcat, and I give you fair warning that once she's had a decent night's rest and some warm food, she'll be a match for you, me, and this pair of muscle-bound swine you mistook for pigs."

Gervase had set Falcon's chamber to rights. His war chest and full armor gleamed from a fresh polishing, and Falcon didn't ask how the men had managed to get back to Wales with a full complement of weapons and armor.

Gervase said, "I've only been here a couple of days. I got through the passes before the snow started, but from what I've seen the new castellan didn't do too shabby a job here. There's enough fodder stored to last the winter and the men had a successful hunt two days back."

Falcon tossed his doublet and cloak to Gervase. "Some clean clothes will feel good." He removed his chain mail and Gervase saw the blood on his shirt. He knew better than to question him. De Burgh would tell all in his own good time. Falcon told him briefly what had happened in Gloucester and ordered a twenty-four-hour patrol on the walls.

Falcon stretched cramped shoulder muscles. "Christ, I could eat an oxen, harness and all."

Gervase grinned. "The kitchen spits are turning at double speed. Here, have some ale to tide you over."

Falcon drank the horn of ale and wiped his hand across his mouth. "Is there any of that mead they brew in these parts?"

"I'll raid the cellars," Gervase promised.

Falcon thought Gervase was back in short order, but
when he turned he saw that it was Morganna who had
entered his chamber without knocking. She had hot water and clothes.

"I don't recall sending for you," he said curtly, his eyes
unreadable.

"Nevertheless," she said with double meaning, "you
have need of me."

He held her with his eyes for long minutes, then lowered his challenging glare. The moment he did so, she
advanced and began to remove his shirt.

The master's return had a profound effect on the entire
castle. Spits and turning irons were brought out and
cooks, maids, and scullions raced about like an army of
ants. Fires were started in all the great smoking chimneys
and underneath the brick ovens. The castle itself was
small, consisting of tower, hall, kitchens, armory,
knights' quarters, and servants' rooms, but the outbuildings sprawled out behind consisting of stables, barns,
dairy, stillroom, smithy, and storage sheds.

A holiday atmosphere prevailed. They were safe and
snug for the winter with no harder tasks to accomplish
than cleaning their armor, sharpening their weapons, and
grooming their horses. When the men suffered from being cooped up they could count on Falcon taking them
on a raid or two, but for the next months the battle-weary
knights could eat, drink, dice, and lift their eyes from
their swords long enough to select a pretty face or plump
shoulder among the women servants of Mountain Ash.

Only a handful of Falcon's knights were married because most were very young men. All the men, women,
and children alike had a burning curiosity regarding the
new bride, Lady Jasmine de Burgh. Some had never seen
her and most of the knights who had, had only done so
from a distance. It was the custom that there would be a

feast the second night back at Mountain Ash and they would be able to see their new lady up close for the first time.

Jasmine awoke midmorning. She had been able to sprawl across the great bed whose curtains had been drawn back to let in the heat from the cozy fire. She yawned and stretched and threw back the luxurious fur covers.

Big Meg bullied her back into bed. "Yer feet don't touch the floor until evening," she said firmly.

"But I feel fine, Meg. There are a hundred things I must learn how to do." Jasmine's domestic shortcomings appalled her. "I'm afraid I've been brought up too frivolously. I'm in ignorance of the simplest chore."

"You'll get your beauty sleep. Tonight at the feast every eye in the hall will be fixed on you. Their curiosity about you is beyond all bounds. I've had to forbid them entrance to the tower today. You'd never believe the silly excuses they use to get up here. The men are as bad as the women. Well, not quite. Women can be right catty little bitches when confronted with a woman far more beautiful than themselves." Meg set a great tray of food before her. "You'll do nothing but eat and sleep all day and get your strength up to hold your own against that lot down there. They'll examine you so closely, they won't be satisfied until they know the color of yer drawers!"

Jasmine laughed happily. She was all woman and would love being the center of attention. She stretched her dainty feet into the depths of the feather mattress, took a large bite of the deliciously salty gamon ham, and contemplated which of her gowns would show off her unusual coloring to best advantage.

She hadn't felt this happy in a long, long time. She drifted off in a warm haze of drowsiness only to be rudely annoyed by raised voices.

"Christ, Meg, I didn't give her to you body and soul, I do still have rights of ownership!" Falcon insisted.

"A poor choice of words, de Burgh," Jasmine shouted from the bed. "Let him in, Meg, I need to sharpen my claws on some hapless fool."

As he looked at her lying in the bed, the anger in his eyes vanished immediately and was replaced by one of hunger. Big Meg moved off to respect the lovers' privacy, but still hovered in the background to prevent him from exercising his rights.

"Are you feeling stronger, Jasmine? I brought you some mead." Falcon held it out to her and watched hungrily as her pink lips touched the honey wine. His physical response to her was immediate and marked. It was ever so. He sat on the edge of the bed so that it would be less obvious. "You look luscious," he murmured. "I can't believe you've come through the ordeal so well."

She blushed and looked away from him, but it did not free her mind of his overpowering presence. He cupped her face and drew her mouth up to his, then his hands slipped beneath the covers to caress her silken breasts. He said huskily, "Leave us, Meg."

"No, sir. You put her in my hands to restore her strength. I'll not have you draining away her vitality with your lovemaking," she said bluntly.

He bit off an obscenity and stood to leave. He could see he would get absolutely nowhere with these two. Meg held the door for him and winked. "Take her twice tonight to make up for it," she whispered. The grin was restored to his face.

"Wear white for me tonight as befits a bride," he called.

Chapter 30

Big Meg was appalled when she lifted the lid on Jasmine's trunk. As the velvets and silks covered with beaded embroidery spilled to the carpet she jumped back in alarm. "I can't touch any of this finery, my big, rough hands would tear it to bits. I'll get Glynis, the little maid from the laundry to see to your clothes. She's never seen the likes of this, but she has a gentle touch and her hands are always clean," Meg said decisively. "I'll fetch her now, so she can get everything unpacked."

When she was alone, Jasmine let Feather out of his cage so he could fly about freely and explore his new home. Then she coaxed Quill to unroll by tempting him with the leftover rind from her ham. Big Meg ushered in the little maid who stood shyly by the bed, her eyes like saucers. Small and dark like most of the Welsh, she had never seen anyone like Jasmine, let alone her clothes. The sparrow on Lady de Burgh's shoulder cocked his wise little head at her to see if she posed a threat. When he was satisfied that she did not, he flew onto the rim of Jasmine's mead and helped himself.

"Oh, the dear little mite," Glynis said, clapping her hands.

Meg said darkly, "Let's hope you take to the rest of the menagerie," then pointed to Jasmine's great trunk. "It's all yours, Glynis."

The girl's ohs and ahs increased with each garment she lifted reverently from the trunk and hung in the wardrobe.

"Glynis, find me a hairbrush please. It will take me a lifetime to get the tangles from my hair. Then we must choose something for me to wear tonight. It must be spe-

cial . . . something that will catch the eye of everyone
in the hall," said Jasmine. "Something scarlet, I think."
No white for her tonight. She needed to conquer these
people, and red was the most powerful color in magic. It
had all sorts of mystic properties, sexual, physical, and
spiritual. Besides, scarlet would set off her silvery-gilt
tresses to perfection, to say nothing of irritating de
Burgh. What more could she ask? Scarlet it would be!

Glynis screamed as she opened a basket and a young
mountain lion spat in her face.

"Oh don't be afraid, Glynis, that's Shanna. Meg, I suppose we'll have to get her a litter box filled with rushes or
she'll pee all over Falcon's lovely carpets."

Meg rolled her eyes and Glynis's mouth was agape.
She closed it slowly and said with wonder, "You are a
witch lady."

Jasmine laughed. "Yes, I suppose I am, and tonight I
feel all the Power of the Universe will flow into my
body." Her eyes glowed. "I feel more alive than I have
ever felt before!"

She soaked an hour in the tub Big Meg effortlessly
hauled in for her. "Mmm, it feels heavenly not to have to
spend the day in the saddle," she said, gingerly caressing
her bottom to see if any callouses had developed. "Meg,
let me have just a little more mead, I like it excessively."

Meg obliged and wondered if she drank it to give her
courage to defy de Burgh. She knew half the castle would
walk the length of Wales to see him bested by a woman,
but she doubted it would ever happen.

Little Glynis sat amazed as she gazed at the dazzling
vision before her. Jasmine was dressed in flame color with
her moonlight tresses tumbling about her shoulders. A
bright silken poppy pinned behind one ear added another
splash of contrast.

As de Burgh's step was heard outside the chamber,
Jasmine's back straightened and her chin went up in

readiness for a confrontation. He opened without knocking as she knew he would and stopped dead on the threshold. Falcon had never seen a more ravishing vision in all his experience. She would have an immediate impact upon any man who glimpsed her. Desire flared in him as he fancied he could warm his hands at her blaze. However, his brows drew together in a warning frown. "Jasmine, I asked you to wear white."

"No, milord, you *told* me to wear white, there is a world of difference. I don't take orders kindly."

He held onto his temper. "Then I ask you now, Jasmine. Will you please wear white this first night as befits a bride?"

She tossed her head and stood her ground, unwilling to have his will imposed upon her. "Since I am to be the center of attention, I have decided I will stand out better in red. Those in the far corners of the hall will be able to get a better look at me."

"I will wait while you change," he said quietly, determined to be in control of his temper as well as the situation.

Jasmine, however, did not hold her temper. "You are ridiculous, sir! Surely I am to be allowed to choose my own clothes?"

Glynis shrank visibly in anticipation of the verbal battle while Big Meg did her best to conceal a grin.

Falcon looked at his wife with disbelief. She was well aware that she could choose her own clothes, that was not the point. He had asked her to wear white and she was deliberately thwarting him, and doing so with relish. Incredibly she was playing some sort of power game with him.

"I should take my hand to you," he said quietly, blocking the door. "If you'd had a good warming years ago you'd know your place."

"I demand that you remove yourself from the door and

let me proceed to the hall," she said, the light of fire in her eyes.

"Demand, Jasmine?" he asked lazily. By the way his brow slanted sardonically she suspected he was up to something, but he bowed formally to her. "So be it," he said, and offered his arm.

After a brief hesitation she took it and allowed him to escort her to the hall below. Big Meg shook her head. "I know this sounds ridiculous to look at them, but she is very like him, you know."

The hall was packed. The aroma of roasting meat tantalized every nose. The festive air was warm and welcoming and the great babble of voices stilled for a minute as Falcon entered with Jasmine on his arm, then it doubled in volume.

Pot boys scurried about, while female servants set the trestle tables and young pages filled their knights' drinking horns. He took Jasmine to the raised dais, which was an innovation, built so all could get a better view of their new lady.

Falcon held up his arms to silence his household and waited patiently for them to quiet. "Before the serving begins I must introduce you to my new bride. Jasmine of Salisbury is now Lady de Burgh." A cheer went up, but he raised a hand to silence it. "There is more you should know. I am afraid my lady has been spoiled and much indulged all her life." He glanced down at her shocked face and she saw the amusement in his eyes as he laughed down at her. She knew in that moment he would have his revenge in his own time, his own way. "I must warn you that she has no maidenly reserve, while I, as you already know, am no gentleman. Neither one of us will hesitate to provoke each other before all assembled. Decorum is not a word you will associate with the de Burghs."

Jasmine seethed as his insufferable laughter rang out over her head. "And so," he said, pushing back his chair and swinging her up into his arms, "I am taking her back upstairs to change into a gown of *my* choosing. She is a willful wench who needs to learn who is master at Mountain Ash. If we don't return right away, you will all know that I have seen another dish that tempts me more."

As he strode from the hall he held her so firmly she could not move because he knew she would fly at him with her fists in a fit of hot temper. "I'll give them something to talk about," he murmured against her ear.

Upstairs she threw her hairbrushes and her shoes at him. "How could you humiliate me so?" she demanded. "I cannot go back and face them all."

"Jasmine, I warned you before you went down, but you chose not to heed me. 'Tis becoming a habit with you." Then his voice lowered with quiet determination. "Now, change the gown."

Her stubbornness had truly been provoked. She said silkily through set teeth, "There is no need for me to change since I shall not be returning to the hall."

He ignored her words and opened her wardrobe. It took him only a moment to select the lovely white gown he had in mind.

She protested, "De Burgh, if I change the gown, it means I have to change everything—undergarments, stocking, shoes—you don't know a thing about women's clothes!"

"Don't I?" he asked silkily. "Do you delude yourself you're the first woman I've undressed?"

"Oh!" She gasped and turned her stubborn back to him. Immediately she felt his hands at the fastenings of her gown and she had visions of him tearing it from her. She whirled to face him, her mouth all sulky. He was so much taller, she had to tip her head back to look up at him. " 'Fore God, if you ruin this gown I'll—"

"You'll what?" he asked, his hands already inside the neckline to take up her challenge.

She was so angry she was panting, but she had guile
enough to lower her lashes to her cheeks so he wouldn't
see her hatred in that moment. In a small voice she said,
" 'Tis a particular favorite, that's all . . . I thought it
would please you."

"It does please me, Jasmine. Its color makes you so
vividly beautiful it has aroused me." As his mouth closed
over hers in a deep kiss she thought he was ready to let
her have her own way, but without her realizing it he had
the scarlet gown undone and off her as they kissed. He
took his mouth from hers and ordered, "Now the shift."

"No!" she said, her eyes stormy.

He rummaged among her things until he held a white
silken shift and a pair of white satin shoes. She made it as
difficult as possible for him to remove her undergarments, but he seemed to enjoy it as if it were a love game.
When she stood before him clad only in the red stockings, he picked her up and set her down before the mirror
so she could watch as he caressed her breasts until they
hardened and thrust up impudently. Suddenly she was
very ready to cover herself with the white gown. "De
Burgh, I concede," she cried.

He flashed his wolf's grin. "There is no hurry to return, darling. They will naturally assume I am going to
make love to you."

She looked at him in horror and saw clearly that their
assumption would be correct if she did not make haste.
She cast about for words that would cool his advances.
"Falcon, I want them to love me here at Mountain Ash. I
promise to try to be a dutiful wife. Let's go back to the
hall. I'll let you dress me," she offered temptingly.

De Burgh was well aware that she was manipulating
him, but her words and her attitude had softened considerably. Perhaps he was halfway to taming her. As he
dressed her in white he managed to touch every intimate

part of her body at least half a dozen times, so that by the time they reentered the hall she was rosy with blushes.

With de Burgh's firm hand at the small of her back, a much-chastened Jasmine took reluctant steps toward the festivities. The moment everyone saw her, a great cheer went up around the hall, and one by one they got to their feet and began to applaud her courage and her beauty. It was the beginning of a love affair as the people of Mountain Ash and Jasmine lost their hearts to each other.

After dinner and the toasts, everyone wanted to speak with her, look at her, touch her. Falcon's knights fell over each other playing gallant, which greatly amused him and pleased her. She was introduced to every female, from the youngest child to the old woman who made the brooms to sweep out the castle chambers.

Jasmine's eyes widened as a young woman came up to the dais dressed as a young warrior in a sleeveless leather tunic with golden bracelets clasped about her upper arms. De Burgh said casually, "This is Morganna. She is hostage for the Welsh king's good behavior."

Morganna's eyes slid over Jasmine's ethereal beauty with contempt and she spoke instead to Falcon. She touched his shoulder with a light, familiar hand. "How is your wound?"

"It is nothing; the scratch is healed."

"Wound?" asked Jasmine, looking at the girl, who was not beautiful in the accepted sense of the word, but clearly had a sensual quality a man would find attractive.

Morganna's eyes touched Jasmine's face again. "He was bitten by a wildcat." She made the statement as if it had two different meanings.

She is someone to reckon with, Jasmine thought warily, but she would not question de Burgh about the girl. She had more pride than that. After dinner they sat at table for two hours, watching the dancing, the gaming, the dicing. She watched Morganna easily lure Gervase from a game of chance he had been winning. "I believe Gervase is out of his depth with that one," she said wisely.

De Burgh shrugged. "By morning he will have lost his purse and gained a better understanding of women."

She flared, "Do you treat all women with contempt?"

"No. An honorable woman I treat with honor." He took her hand and she drew in her breath sharply. For a brief instant her fingers were against his mouth and the familiar panic rose up in her as the time for bed drew nigh. "Let's go up," he murmured huskily, rising and taking her with him with one strong possessive arm.

Her heart beat thickly as they began to climb the tower steps. She glanced up at his strong profile outlined against the eight-foot-thick stone walls and felt very small and vulnerable. When she would have gone on from his door up to her own chamber, he stayed her with his hand and drew her into the doorway, then leaned his arms on either side of the jamb, effectively trapping her. His head dipped to steal a kiss. As soon as he lifted his mouth from hers she begged, "Please, Falcon."

"Do you deny me?" he demanded.

"No," she said quickly, "for I do not want another battle on my hands, not tonight."

"Battle?" he questioned. "I want to make love, not war." He pushed open his chamber door and all she could see was the massive bed.

"Please no, Falcon," she breathed.

His mouth was on her throat, kissing its wildly beating pulse, while his fingers sought and made erect a taut little nipple. "Jassy, I'm starving for you," he said against her throat.

On a half-sob of fear she cried, "Oh, Falcon, I was so happy tonight. Please don't spoil it for me."

Though he was loathe to do it, his instincts told him that if he gave her time and room enough so she didn't feel compelled, perhaps she would begin to respond to his advances. He cupped her face and looked down at her with softened eyes. "I was happy tonight too. My bed will be cold to me, but I will try to understand that you need more time, my darling." His lips brushed hers and he stood aside to watch her climb the tower steps to her solitary chamber.

There were no servants waiting up for her because they assumed she would spend the night with her husband. Jasmine lighted her candles and undressed dreamily. She had told the truth when she said she had been happy that night. She swore she would become more capable and domestic. She would learn every nuance of running a castle that sometimes housed two hundred. She liked the idea that she was its center, its core, its heart.

She hung her clothes in the wardrobe, ran her hand over the flame-colored gown he had forced her to change, and laughed softly. Because she had obeyed their lord, she had won their hearts. She put on a warm velvet robe and poked up the fire. She could hear voices, low. She could not make out what they were saying, nor where they were coming from, but she could hear someone talking. She listened at the door and then the window of the tower chamber, but the voices were not coming from these. It was only at a certain place in the room she could hear the talking. The man raised his voice and she was sure it was de Burgh.

His chamber was beneath hers so the sound must be coming up through the floor. She crouched down upon her hands and knees and put her ear to the floor. The muffled voices were definitely coming from below. She was almost certain one of the voices belonged to a woman. Jasmine thought it was probably Big Meg answering de Burgh's questions about her, and she wished she could hear what was being said. She moved a chair over against the wall and turned back the carpet. That was better, already the voices were less muffled and she heard de Burgh clearly say "No!" Again on her hands and knees, she was both surprised and excited to discover a crack in the thick floorboards where two beams came together. It was a small chink to which she could put either an ear or an eye. She peeped through the crack and saw nothing, then suddenly de Burgh, stripped to the waist, was standing directly beneath her. "Leave it," she heard him say. He had a small bandage on his shoulder. He spoke again, but only two words floated up to her. She heard him say "bed" and "now."

She was intrigued to learn who was in his chamber with him. Then suddenly she saw and was deeply shocked at her own naïveté, stupidity. She saw Morganna's arms twined about his neck, her body pressed up to his in a kiss. Jasmine sat back on her heels, stunned at de Burgh's deceit. He was forever crying his needs to her when quite obviously those needs were being taken care of elsewhere. She felt anger, betrayal, and, yes, she admitted, jealousy!

How dare he? She was Lady de Burgh. Her grandfather had been the great King Henry; her bloodlines were royal. She was mistress here, she wanted to be the center, the heartroot of Mountain Ash, but her position was being undermined by a slut!

A blinding fury gripped her as she rose from the floor and ran down the cold tower steps that led to de Burgh's chamber. She threw open his door and rushed inside. He was alone. Surprise showed in every line of his face.

"How dare you keep your whore at Mountain Ash?" she demanded.

His eyes swept her from head to foot and saw that she was outraged. Even in a simple bedgown her bearing was regal. Her hair flew about her shoulders, making her wildly beautiful. He wondered briefly where she had heard the gossip, and if it would be best to deny it. He faced her blazing eyes and knew there was no point in trying to placate her. His own eyes narrowed. He was in the right mood for a good fight followed by a good bedding. "I'd have no need for a whore if you fulfilled your wifely duties," he accused.

She gasped. "You admit it, you blackhearted rogue! Your idea of wifely duties would have me chained to a bed night and day."

"Let me educate you, Jasmine. Men saddle themselves with a wife only so that they will have their sexual needs taken care of on a regular basis," he said flatly.

"That is not true. You had other reasons for marrying me, de Burgh," she accused.

"What for instance?" he taunted. "Your efficiency as a chatelaine? Your ability to bear me strong sons?"

She flew at him. "You are a devil!" she cried, tearing off his bandage so savagely that the wound began to bleed again. "Why didn't you tell me you were wounded by the wildcat? Why did you let her tend you?"

Suddenly he knew she was jealous of Morganna and he felt exultant. She would not experience jealousy unless she cared for him. She felt the need to inflict pain on him only because she had been hurt. He towered above her. His eyes were clear green crystal, his skin stretched smooth and brown over high cheekbones. He took hold of her shoulders and she watched as the dark pupils slowly obliterated the clear green. He looked down at her with his eyes stained almost black by desire.

"Princess Jasmine, the untouchable. My lovemaking turns you to ice. Take off that robe . . . get into bed," he ordered.

"De Burgh, you took knightly vows to be gentle and honorable with all womanhood."

"Damn it, Jasmine, I'm not some courtly knight from a legend . . . I'm a flesh-and-blood man, with flesh-and-blood needs. You haven't the faintest idea what I'm talking about, have you? But you're going to learn. All I have to do is think of you and I am hard and ready. When I am actually in the same room with you, where I can see you and hear your laughter, my blood races like flames until I am so hot for you I am dangerous to be near. On the rare occasions I am permitted to touch you, I almost go mad with the need to taste you, the need to bury myself in you, to hold you impaled on me all through the night, to fall asleep with my body joined to yours."

His impatient hands seized her and stripped off the bedgown, then he lifted her high against his heart and let her slide slowly down his hard body.

"You lecherous beast," she cried in anguish, "don't touch me minutes after you've held her in your arms!"

"I will decide when to touch you. You will learn that I am master in my own castle. I will take you wherever and whenever I desire you."

"Have me then!" she panted her challenge.

He tossed her onto the bed, stripped off the rest of his clothes, then came after her. He towered above her in a white heat of passion. His hot, demanding mouth came down on her breasts. He kissed and sucked and licked every inch of her satiny skin from her neck to her knees.

Suddenly she was more afraid than she had ever been for she felt a tiny spark deep within ignite and an answering response she had no control over began to pulsate inside her belly and breasts. Her mind began withdrawing the moment she felt the strange sensations. She would not let herself become a slave to this man, her body craving his the way he described how his body craved hers.

She remembered things she had heard at court, things she had closed her ears to. Whenever Falcon de Burgh's name had been mentioned one woman always said, "The man is a god. I get wet just looking at him." Jasmine hadn't known then what she meant, but she knew now.

As his fingers probed her intimately, she knew that for the first time in her life she was wet and slippery.

He was in no hurry now. His foreplay was leisurely, drawn out. He stroked her body with firm but gentle hands, savoring the feel of every delicious satiny curve and swell. Touching her was never enough for Falcon. He always had a driving need to see every inch of her. He pushed off the covers, knelt beside her on the bed, and gazed at her until his eyes were stained black with passion. Then, starting at her feet, he traced kisses all the way up her legs, not stopping until he reached the delicious golden triangle. He raised his head to again fill his eyes with her delicate loveliness, then dipped it with a ragged groan to tongue and lick the two tiny moles that sat on either side of her mons.

For seven months she had fought him, and every step of the way it had been fruitless battling against his strength. Now, locked in his embrace, it was as if she lost separate identity. She would not let it happen. She refused to become just another possession. She centered her mind on his wound just inches from her mouth and imagined the searing pain he must have experienced. At that precise moment he plunged into her, but her mind and body were separated from him. She went limp as she felt the mountain lion attack her, then plunge its fangs into her soft body. Then her mind closed off the pain as she willed herself to feel nothing. He felt his seed start and cried out in his passion, and at that precise moment she bit her sharp little teeth into his raw wound.

"You bitch!" he hissed through clenched teeth. She drew back her hand and slapped him full in the face. He would not retaliate by striking her but would have his revenge in his own time, his own way. She snatched up her bedgown to cover her nakedness. "How does it feel to have your blood on the sheets for a change?" she mocked.

They looked at each other with hatred, each vowing silently to be finished with the other. The feast at Mountain Ash had definitely ended in climax!

Chapter 31

Morganna had been shattered when Falcon de Burgh returned to Mountain Ash with an exquisite bride on his saddlebow. Though she was a hostage, she had had the freedom to escape every day she had been there, but had chosen to stay and await de Burgh's return. The months had been long because of his absence, and it had gotten to the point where she lived only for his return. She was obsessed with him. He was easily the most satisfying sexual partner she had ever known, and she had known several, including Llewellyn, self-styled King of Wales.

She had a plan to become mistress of Falcon and Mountain Ash, and all she needed was something to bind him to her forever. She knew what she must do. She knew she must bear him a child. Jasmine's appearance had thrown her plans into jeopardy.

So far she had been unsuccessful in luring him to bed, but she knew he and Jasmine had separate chambers and that all was not milk and honey between the newlyweds. There was already some bone of contention between them, so it should be simple for her to drive in her wedge and widen the distance between bride and groom.

She knew, however, she would need all her wiles as a woman to seduce him back to her bed. Even when she was in his arms she did not fool herself into thinking he received as much pleasure as he gave to her. Part of him was ever withdrawn. It was a deliberate reserve that kept his innermost being secret. It tormented her to the point of insanity. To bear his child would let her own and possess that vulnerable bit of his emotions. She knew him to be a man of honor. He would never discard a child that was his, nor the woman who bore it.

It was almost a month before the supply wagons Isabel Marshal had promised got through to Mountain Ash. At the same time, the lull in the bad weather permitted scores of de Burgh men-at-arms to get through the snow-girt passes.

Accompanying both wagons and men was the indomitable Estelle. De Burgh welcomed her briefly and politely, but he was by no means sure if her appearance would augur well for him.

Jasmine, however, was happier to see her grandmother than she had been in a very long time. Dame Winwood managed to bring with her everything Jasmine had left behind as well as a profusion of herbs, simples, ointments, decoctions, electuaries, and the precious crystal ball. In addition to all this, the things Isabel Marshal sent along with the food and fodder were invaluable. She had sent linens, spices, wines, fine materials, cushions, carpets, and, unbelievably, a great oval mirror.

Tam volunteered to carry all Estelle's luggage to her small chamber on the almost certain chance that he would get to see Jasmine. When she smiled at him and asked if he could carry the mirror up to her tower room, he lingered there a long time, looking at her feminine belongings, her brushes, perfume, bedrobe, and the soft white ermine wrap.

Estelle and Jasmine were finally alone, laughing at each other with tears of relief in their eyes. So many questions between them needed asking and answering that Jasmine insisted "You first."

"When I discovered Chester had put a guard on your

door I knew I would be of no use to you. I realized he could use me to force you to his will, so I disappeared. I went home to Salisbury, then went to Chepstow to speak with your father. I put my faith in de Burgh. If you had a psychic bond with him, he would be your salvation. Your father told me that he had indeed rescued you and carried you off to Mountain Ash. I worried over your having such an ordeal through the icy mountains, but I see that de Burgh took every care of you."

"I'll tell you all the gory details of my two weddings, they'll make your hair stand on end," Jasmine said. "But if you think de Burgh takes every care of me, you are mistaken. The moment we are together it is like setting a match to kindling. I am sure no man and woman ever fought more than we do. Estelle, whatever am I to do? I think I'm already carrying his child."

Estelle's heart stopped. All the anguish she had suffered years before when her beloved only daughter had quickened with Salisbury's seed and died in childbed came rushing back to her. Damn men to hell, why did they need to destroy the women they loved best? She saw Jasmine's delicate body and feared she would never be able to carry and safely deliver a child. She was as ethereal and fragile as a rare orchid. Why had she ever agreed to let her marry de Burgh?

Well, there was no alternative but to confront him. She'd have this out with him now. She carefully questioned Jasmine about her menstrual flow, asking about all the classical signs from morning sickness to tender breasts. When she was convinced the pregnancy was real she sought out de Burgh.

She found him in the shed that stored fodder for the animals. With Gervase at his elbow he tallied what stores they had against how many animals must be wintered, taking into account that more horses were arriving nearly every day.

"Men!" she exploded when she saw him.

De Burgh touched Gervase on the shoulder. "Leave us," he said quietly.

"Well, are you satisfied?" she demanded as the man left them.

De Burgh kept a wise silence, knowing there was a lot more she was going to get off her chest.

"Was this some sort of race to see how quickly you could make it happen?" she asked, warming to her subject. "Did you have the need to prove your virility to your hundreds of men?" She took a deep breath. "Blood of God, you must have had her abed day and night to get her with child this quickly." Estelle suddenly broke down. She covered her face and cried, "It will kill her!"

De Burgh was dismayed. "I had no idea," he said lamely.

Estelle dashed the tears from her eyes. "I warned you repeatedly . . . we all warned you she was too delicate for wife and mother, but you would not be denied, you would have her at all costs. I thought you understood that you could not play stallion and brood mare with Jasmine."

Suddenly he was afraid. It was a feeling alien to him, but he experienced it now. If he lost Jasmine his life would be empty. In spite of the enmity between them, she was his woman, and he could not bear the thought that he could bring harm to her. Above all other feelings she aroused in him was the need to protect and cherish her.

Estelle calmed a little when she saw the sobering effect her words were having on de Burgh. She would drive home her point while she had him at a disadvantage. "I watched my only child hemorrhage to death because she was too small to give birth. When I look at the size of you and imagine how big the child will be you have planted in her, I nearly run mad!"

"Estelle, what I have done can be undone," he said firmly, "with your skills."

She sighed with relief that he would be willing to let her get rid of the child. "Then we are in agreement that I will administer an abortificant to safeguard Jasmine's life. But if she conceives by you so easily it will happen again and again. You must find others who will drain your lust. I'm sure every woman at Mountain Ash between the age of fifteen and fifty would be eager for your attentions."

Inwardly Falcon recoiled, yet through the day the seeds that Estelle planted began to take root. His spirits were lower than they had been in years as it was brought home to him that he could never have legitimate children. He had coveted Jasmine from the moment he saw her riding the unicorn. He had suffered through an endless seven-month wait to get her. He had been triumphant when he snatched her from Chester and married her, feeling invincible, almost godlike. But now his emotions had sobered and his thoughts were dark and depressing. He would do whatever was necessary to keep Jasmine from harm, but he could not let himself even think of his child, which would never draw breath.

His men found him difficult and moody and gave him a wide berth. Falcon withdrew early to the privacy of his own chamber, preferring solitude over the company of others.

Jasmine had kept to her room all day, contemplating the changes in her life the baby would make. Now that Estelle was at Mountain Ash the small knot of apprehension had been replaced by joy. She couldn't really believe her own good fortune. All her life she had been told that she could never be a wife and mother, and now she was about to be both. She thought she would probably have a little girl, like herself, to love and cherish forever, but suppose, just suppose by some miracle she could have a boy. A son who would grow up to be a mirror image of

Falcon de Burgh . . . handsome, strong, a valiant knight.

Whatever she had, she decided she would be the best mother there had ever been. She had not been a successful wife, not yet, but by the love of St. Jude she would be a successful mother. De Burgh didn't know yet. What would his reaction be when she informed him? She wanted to see the light in his eyes turn to green fire as his pulses pounded hotly with the fierce wondrous knowledge that there, below her heart, she carried his child.

She quietly turned back the thick carpet and crouched down to look through the crack in the floor to his room below. She could see his dark head engrossed in books that lay on the table before him. Immediately she surmised they were secret doctrine he studied, which gave him his incredible powers. Her hand caressed her belly. Wed only a month and already he had planted the first of the de Burgh dynasty. The corners of her mouth went up at her secret thoughts. Should she go down now and tell him?

She heard him utter a foul oath as a knock came upon the door. He carefully locked away his books before he answered. She heard him say angrily, "What do you want?"

Then her joy was wiped away as she heard the unmistakable female voice say, "Estelle sent me."

She sat back upon her heels and flung the carpet back into place. Estelle? My God, didn't her grandmother know this woman was his whore? She closed her eyes as the wave of jealousy washed over her. She should be the one down there with him. She should be the one who would lie beside him in his great bed with the knowledge of his child held warmly between them. She hated the physical act of sex, but she liked to be kissed and embraced. She loved to feel the heat that came from his body, the scent of him in her nostrils gave her pleasure.

His strength lent her a feeling of absolute security, and she enjoyed their quick, barbed exchanges of parry and thrust when they pitted their wits against each other.

Yet she knew these things were not enough for a man. Not a virile stallion like Falcon de Burgh at any rate. Perhaps Estelle thought she was helping Jasmine by encouraging Morganna to seek his bed, but it hurt . . . oh, God, how it hurt!

Falcon was angered to have his solitude disturbed. His mood had been foul all day and it hadn't improved with nightfall. Morganna stood upon the threshold with a tempting flagon of amber liquid in her hands, and this was the only reason he let her pass into the room. "Did Estelle provide the potion?" he said with contempt.

Morganna was unsure of his meaning but ran her tongue around her lips seductively and replied, "I need no potion to make a man receptive to my charms." Nevertheless, she poured him a goblet of the strong Welsh liquor and brought it to him cupped in her long brown fingers.

He took it from her, drained it, and held out the goblet to be refilled, then he took it to the fireplace and leaned on the mantel to drink with his back to her. His black mood did not daunt her, in fact she welcomed it. If he needed to drown his sorrows, she could manipulate him, seduce him with the lure of her flesh. This was the only way she could get him to center his attention on her for a short time. If she was shrewd enough she could manipulate a careless moment into a permanent hold on him.

When Falcon remembered her presence he turned and saw her lying on the bed. Her feet and legs were bare, her skirt hiked up to give him an unimpeded view of her thighs. He walked to the bed and sat on its edge.

"You are troubled," she said. "I'm a good listener."

His mocking laugh rang out. "I have no desire to talk. Talk is the last thing I need."

Morganna went up on her knees and rested her hands upon the wide shoulders so that her face was close to his. Her tongue shot out to lick him and she said huskily, "Whatever it is you need . . . take! All you ever have to do is ask. I will be anything, do anything you ask."

His hands reached out roughly to her breasts. She moaned and fell back onto the bed, drawing him with her. Her long brown fingers reached out to play about his groin, now swollen with need. His mouth took hers savagely, then when he lifted his mouth from her she urged, "Fill me, Falcon, fill me with your seed. I want to give you a child."

He tore his mouth from her and flung himself from the bed. He threw back his head and laughed a hollow, mocking laugh. Fate was such a cruel bitch. The one thing you wanted above all other things you could never have, but everything else was laid out like a feast. All he need do was take it.

Estelle brought Jasmine's breakfast and stayed to feed and play with the young mountain lion, who by now was growing quite sleek. "I see you've had the good sense to cage Feather and Quill."

Jasmine ignored her words. "Surely you realize that Morganna woman is de Burgh's whore? Why did you send her to him last night?" she demanded.

"So she would drain his lust, of course. Would you rather he used you?" Estelle asked bluntly.

"Of course not, but I don't want him bedding her in the chamber beneath mine. 'Tis a disgusting situation and one I shall not tolerate."

"You had best tread softly, Jasmine. I think it would be a mistake to insist that he choose between you. The girl serves a valuable purpose, which enables him to leave you in peace. Eat your breakfast, child, you have far more important things to worry about than a Welsh slut."

Jasmine threw back the covers and reached for her white velvet bedgown after Estelle left. Habits of a lifetime were hard to break, and she always bathed and brushed her hair before she could eat. Then she sat down to nibble on the delicious bread and honey and freshly churned butter from the dairy. She hugged her knees to her and decided it was time to become domesticated. She would start with this delicious butter and learn the whole process, but first she would find out about the secret books and papers de Burgh kept locked away so safely.

She absently picked up her goblet of mead and pulled back the carpet with her other hand. If the room below was empty she would go down now. She lifted the goblet to her lips to drink, but her nose detected a peculiar scent. The mead contained the pungent odor of the juice of pennyroyal. Pennyroyal was drunk to induce abortion! As the thought struck her, she clearly heard Estelle in the chamber below say "It is done. I have given her the decoction as we agreed."

Jasmine was stunned. She had learned of so many things through this hole in the floor of which she had been totally in ignorance. Her husband and her grandmother had actually entered into a conspiracy to rid her of her child! She felt a wave of anger build in her heart and sweep up to her brain. She picked up her white velvet skirts and ran down the stone stairs that led to de Burgh's chamber. There she flung open the door to confront them. Both looked guilty.

"God damn you both to Hell!" she cried. "How dare you both take it upon yourselves to decide the course of my life for me?" she panted. She flung at Estelle, "How could you tell him? Did it not occur to you that this was something private, almost sacred, between husband and wife?"

"Your mother died in childbirth . . . you will do the same," Estelle said firmly.

"No! I am not my mother, and anyway do you not realize my child means more to me than life?"

Falcon could not take his eyes from her. She was magnificent. "Without even consulting me you give me an abortificant to drink!" Jasmine continued. "It is a damned good thing I am familiar with plants and their properties."

"I only did what was best for you," Estelle protested.

"I am Lady de Burgh, mistress of Mountain Ash. Must I remind you that you are merely a guest here?"

"Jasmine, are you really willing to risk your life to give me a child?" asked Falcon, hope mixed with admiration in his eyes.

"This child is mine, and may God strike any dead who try to harm it." Her eyes flashed their anger. "Thank God for one of the bonuses of carrying a child. Custom demands that you keep from my bed for the next few months."

His jaw tightened slightly, but it was a small price for him to pay if she was willing to go on with the pregnancy. "You have my word I will not bother you, my lady," Falcon said sincerely.

"It may interest you to know that there is a great hole in my floor through which I heard you both conspiring against me." She turned her accusing eyes on Falcon. "Before you again commit adultery with that slut who writhes and pants after you, I suggest you mend the hole in your ceiling!"

"I have not committed adultery, Jasmine," he said with narrowed eyes. "At least, not yet."

She was almost certain he was lying. The girl was like a bitch in heat with him, how could he have refused the use of her body? "Suppose I ask her?" she suggested.

He shrugged. "Perhaps by that time it will be a done thing," he drawled.

She shrugged her beautiful shoulders as if she did not

care. He wanted to take hold of those shoulders and crush her to his will. He wanted to shake from her a confession that she was mad with jealousy over Morganna . . . that she was falling in love with him . . . that she was filled with joy to be carrying his child. Instead he bowed formally. "Is that all, madame?"

"No, it is not," she said with a serene little smile. "I am going to become absolute mistress of Mountain Ash. My word will be law from now on. I am taking full charge of the household and the servants. The rest I leave to you, sir." She waved an imperious hand. "Estelle, Big Meg, and my husband won't like the idea that their delicate little Jasmine has grown up, but Estelle, Big Meg, and my husband can go to Hell." Her voice and her smile were as sweet as wild honey.

Chapter 32

William Marshal and Salisbury, John's brother, were closeted with the king at Gloucester. Hugh de Burgh, the king's newly appointed justiciar, chose not to join them. He had always played the role of Devil's advocate and he did it well. Among them the three men intended to manipulate, coerce, or shame John into more acceptable behavior.

The encounter was not going well. King John was in a seething, almost uncontrollable rage. He was the king and could do anything he pleased. He had waited years for the crown, coveting it when his father wore it and jealously obsessed by it when his brother Richard held it and sat on the throne for ten long years.

Being king was supposed to mean absolute power, yet

first his barons, then the church, and now his own chosen ministers and his brother were turning against him.

"I think I deserve an explanation of why you gave my daughter Jasmine to Chester when I had contracted her to de Burgh," said Salisbury, coming straight to the point.

"William, that wasn't my doing. It was some scheme of the queen's to amuse the court. I was told it was to be a mock wedding, a jest, an entertainment. I saw no harm in the little playlet."

William clearly saw through him and briefly wondered how much Chester had paid him. At least they had succeeded in getting John on the defensive.

"No harm has been done," John insisted. "She is safely wed to de Burgh, so I don't know why you are badgering me about it!"

"I'll tell you the harm, John: Other than a personal affront to me, you have succeeded in driving away the strongest flank of our army. A call to arms of your northern barons failed dismally. De Burgh was the best captain you ever had or could hope to have in the future. He's the best! His knights are trained better . . . his men-at-arms are loyal, fierce fighters, with more guts than a slaughterhouse. His Welsh bowmen, his English broadswordsmen, even his mercenaries are better trained than all others. What good is he to us holed up in Wales?"

John waved an arm indicating he could fix things in a trice. "When spring comes I will lure him back into the fold. The de Burghs are loyal Plantagenet men. His anger will have a chance to cool over the long winter months. There is no discord between de Burgh and me."

Salisbury sighed. There was no point in reminding John of the bad blood that existed between de Burgh and Chester, one of the few other barons still loyal to the crown. Bad blood that would never have been stirred up but for John and his insatiable appetite for money and women.

William Marshal's round with John succeeded in roiling his rage until it was almost out of control. "John, you must put an end to this trouble with the church. Splendor of God, man, don't you realize the seriousness of being excommunicated by the Pope?"

"I'll not be dictated to by that asshole! I am the King of England! I am the head of the church in England, not the bloody Pope! Do you realize the church has more wealth than the crown?" John's face was a dangerous hue of purple.

"Do you not realize that wealth can be used against you?" thundered William Marshal. "Louis of France must be laughing with glee at this rift between England and the Pope. He has taken most of Normandy, Anjou, Maine, and Poitou. Now he will be eyeing England, and he'll have the Pope on his side."

"You don't need to tell me they are thick as thieves. Mayhap you're in it with them. I note your dominions in France to the far south are still in your possession!" screamed John.

William Marshal's mouth tightened. "I will forget you said that, John. You know I paid dearly to hold my French possessions with the blood of my men. You must end this quarrel with the church by accepting Stephen Langton as Archbishop of Canterbury or the Pope will lay England under an interdict!"

"If the asshole does that I will seize possession of the bishops who obey the interdict and banish them from the kingdom!"

"Oppressing the churchmen is not the answer, John. Be guided in this by me. The Pope has the power to declare you deposed from the throne, to absolve the English people from their allegiance to you and entrust the

King of France with the carrying out of these decrees,"
William Marshal pointed out.

Salisbury joined in the fray. "Such a threat would
mean little if you were strong and popular in your own
country, but you are rapidly losing the respect and love
of all classes of your people."

John was raving now as he threatened, "I will bring
foreign mercenaries into England to overpower any resistance to my actions. I will compel the barons to put their
sons into my hands as pledges for their own good behavior. I will use the courts and the exchequer to plunder the
clergy legally."

Salisbury said bluntly, "That won't be enough to pay
for mercenaries. You'll have to make taxes and scutages
heavier and collect them more frequently, and how popular do you think that will make you?"

"Christ Almighty, was a king ever so beset? You are all
against me! Where's Hubert, he'll support me, if nobody
else will."

"Hubert is too much of a yes man. He tells you what
you want to hear to keep you pacified. William Marshal
and I know it is time you faced the truth and took a good
hard look at yourself," Salisbury said, totally ignoring the
flecks of foam that were on his brother's lips.

William Marshal's face grew ever more stern. "We are
not finished, John. There is still the matter of your morals
to be dealt with. It has come to my ears that you abducted yet another young female, but this time with fatal
results."

" 'Tis nothing but vicious gossip!" cried John, smash-
ing his fist into the table. "Women literally throw themselves at kings. You cannot deny they are lined up out
there to warm my bed. I am a normal, healthy man, I like
women! Christ Almighty, you'd have something to complain about if I was buggering my pages like my brother
Richard did for years. He had a warm relationship with

the church too . . . he screwed the Bishop of Fecamp for years. That proud prelate and others I could name were his special favorites!"

William Marshal had such strict morals, he turned white about the mouth to hear of Richard's pederasty.

"Now the bishops are calling me down from their pulpits, railing against my morals, and all because they believe some filthy gossip. Believe me when I tell you I will put a stop to it!" By now John was foaming at the mouth; his color had begun to alarm the two men.

William Marshal said in a placating tone, "If it is vicious gossip there is a simple way to put a stop to it. Cease taking other women to your bed. It is time to get an heir upon your wife, the queen."

John's answer to this quite shocked the men. "It is not my fault Isabella hasn't conceived. She has only just begun her menstrual courses this month."

The marshal opened his mouth and closed it again. Once more he tried to find words. "Do you mean to tell us that you consummated a union with a little girl not even old enough to conceive?"

At this John's eyes rolled back in his head, he fell to the rushes, and his feet began the staccato hammering that always accompanied a fit.

William Marshal hurried out to get Hubert de Burgh. Let him handle the king's temper tantrum; the marshal needed fresh air in his nostrils.

John was wily enough not to use any of Salisbury's or Hubert's men to carry out his vengeance. Instead he relied on Faulkes de Bréauté to select a handful of mercenaries who could be trusted to carry out his orders without question. He would put a stop to the rumors and gossip by making an example of one of the noble families. That bitch who had been a friend of Avisa's must have her tongue stilled forever. Mathilda de Braose refused to give her two grandsons as hostages. She had said she wouldn't entrust them to a man who killed his own nephew, Arthur.

John ordered the arrest of William and Mathilda de Braose, Lord and Lady of Hay on the Welsh border. He liked the idea of setting an example so well that he turned his attention to the church. He would do the same with one victim and watch the rest fall into line. He selected the poor Archdeacon of Norwich, who had been foolish enough to take Pope Innocent's excommunication seriously and had preached from his pulpit that any priest who served King John was contaminated. John ordered a fine new archdeacon's cope be made for Geoffrey of Norwich; however, it was made from lead, and when the mercenaries forced it over his head, it suffocated him.

Jasmine kept herself busy from dawn to dusk. She rushed about learning how to competently run a household. She consulted with the castellan and learned the duties of every person housed under her roof. The next time she came face to face with Morganna she said, "And what pray tell are your duties at Mountain Ash? Everyone must earn his keep here."

Morganna said slyly, "I perform certain services for Lord de Burgh."

"Indeed?" questioned Jasmine. "Do you perform these services well?"

Morganna's mouth thinned. "He always leaves me with a smile on his face."

Jasmine looked her straight in the eye and asked, "How is my husband in bed?"

Morganna again gave a sly reply. "I don't know . . . he prefers the floor."

Jasmine's mouth twitched with amusement. Falcon had not bothered to mend the hole, so she was certain he spent his nights alone. "You look strong to me. I think you would be suited to kitchen work. I shall inform the cook she has a new helper to fetch wood for the cooking and carry water for her."

Morganna seethed with hatred. "I am strong and carrying wood and water will only make me stronger. You are obviously too delicate for such work," she said with scorn.

Jasmine smiled sweetly. "It is my condition that is delicate. I am with child, didn't you know?"

Morganna was ice cold inside; she knew exactly what she would have to do.

Jasmine still hadn't had a look at the occult books or secret doctrine that de Burgh pored over in his solitude, but as she looked down from the tower and saw his dark head out by the stables she decided that her opportunity was at hand.

Inside his chamber, she was almost overwhelmed by the essence of the man. Everything in the room bore the strong stamp of his powerful personality, with the bed dominating. It was massive with black velvet curtains embroidered with his emblem of a golden falcon. Above the bed on the stone wall were great crossed broadswords so heavy she doubted she could even lift them. No wonder his wrists were so thick, his shoulders so heavily muscled, she mused. No rushes for de Burgh; his floor was covered by a thick red carpet no doubt brought back from a crusade to the Holy Land, and the large fireplace had half a dozen wolf skins stretched out before it, all silvery and inviting. No tapestries covered his walls, rather they were bare stone adorned with many flambeaux to give good light and a dazzling display of weapons. He was expert in the use of every single one, from longbow to knives and daggers.

Against one wall his huge war chest held his armor, which was always kept polished and in good repair. She ran her finger over the dark wooden chest that traveled everywhere with him. Even its worn hinges were lovingly polished. The very air was palpable with the maleness of the man. Everything was oversized to match him. The chairs were big with deep cushions, the desk containing his pens, maps, and books was massive and securely locked. When she opened his wardrobe to see if the keys were in one of his pockets, the scent of him almost undid her. It was a mixture of fine leather, sandalwood, and dangerous male animal. She blushed. It was the same scent that lingered on her skin after he had made love to her. She touched the fine lawn shirts, which seemed far too delicate a fabric to touch that hardened, powerful body. Her hand passed over leather jacks and steel mesh vests; yes, these were more suited to his brute strength. She felt all the doublets for keys, noting as she did that they were not padded as she had thought. Those wide shoulders were all de Burgh.

When she found no keys, she returned to the desk, picked up a wickedly sharp-looking dagger, and tried to force the lock. She heard the door and whirled about, truly caught in a compromising position. Dagger in hand, she was ready for Falcon's anger, but his eyes were alight as he said her name. "Jasmine." He made it sound like a caress. His eyes licked over her like a candle flame, taking in the pale-pink gown and silver ribbons. He came close enough to lift a tress of pale hair and rub it between thumb and forefinger. "You are so beautiful," he breathed.

"I am full of you," she said, tossing her hair back away from his possessive fingers.

His green eyes slipped down her body. "Are you sure, love? You look far too slender to be with child."

Her lashes dropped to her cheeks. He was too close. His effect on her was devastating. She began to tremble. "I'm sure," she managed to whisper.

He took her hand into his own large, warm hand and

said softly, "You've given me no chance to tell you how happy you've made me." He put his finger underneath her chin. "Look at me, Jasmine." When she did, he smiled down into her eyes. "Why are you trembling? You're the one holding the dagger," he teased.

"You're playing with me," she said, her eyes liquid with apprehension. He hardened immediately at her choice of words and groaned. "I'd like to play with you, Jassy, if only you'd let me."

"Beast!" she accused. "I'd rather you beat me than punish me by forcing me to bed."

He winced. "Why would I punish you?" he puzzled.

"Because I came to uncover your secret books of magic. Your powers are stronger than mine. I would learn that power," she flung at him defiantly.

He was amused and laughed softly to himself as he took out a key to unlock the desk. He lifted out his books and spread them upon the desktop for her to see. With a rueful grin he said, "I read Virgil and the great deeds of the Homeric heroes. Now you know my secret; I am a romantic fool. Tales of fair maids ever set my pulses beating wildly. Is it any wonder you stole my heart?"

She was in panic as she saw the telltale signs. He took her by the shoulders. His eyes were stained black with desire, his lips parted ready to cover her mouth, his manhood moved against her belly with a will of its own.

"You must not . . . I am with child," she protested.

"I will be gentle," he promised softly, dipping his head to taste her pink mouth.

"Gentle!" she cried, flaming with anger as a last defense. "You brute, you don't know the meaning of the word. Look at this chamber. Everything about you is too big, too hard, too brutal, too uncouth. Once aroused your lust knows no bounds . . . you are like a rampant stallion. You are too strong, too powerful. I cannot stop you from forcing yourself upon me."

His eyes narrowed. "I'd say you do a damned good job most of the time. Are you really afraid of me Jasmine, or are you afraid of yourself?"

"What do you mean?" she demanded.

"Afraid if you let me love you properly you might like it and want more? Afraid to touch me in all my wicked, forbidden places lest it set up a craving in you that will never be satisfied? Afraid to open wide to me, because I might enter your soul along with your body? Afraid because you might not measure up to the other women with whom I have shared passion?"

This last was too much for her. Blinded by tears, she raised the dagger.

"I wouldn't advise it," he said quietly. With one swift hand he disarmed her, then he put one foot behind her legs and tripped her. They went down together before the fire. He was sprawled dark and powerfully lithe. His dark brows slanted above his emerald eyes. His broad-shouldered frame revealed unmistakable raw strength. The silence was thick with challenge. Her tumbled gilt hair spread out across the rug, reminding him that when she was naked her beautiful hair was long enough to cover her delicious breasts.

His hands immediately loosened the silver ribbons, and one impatient hand slid down inside the neckline and went round down her back until it rested warmly at the base of her spine. Then he forced her body against his. As his demanding mouth covered hers she could feel him rising hard against her. His lips brushed twice across hers before he used the tip of his tongue to trace the outline of her mouth, sending a shocking trail of fire deep down inside her. Her hatred for him was hot. Then suddenly, clearly she realized she didn't have to be in love to feel the fire.

He held her captive against him while his strong, insistent arousal throbbed against the curve of her stomach.

Then he sat back on his heels and quickly took the pink gown off over her head. She protested repeatedly, but he was deaf to her pleas. Somehow she felt if she could keep her shift on it would protect her from his onslaught, but he seemed to have a dozen hands intent on plucking her naked. When she was nude, he clasped her hands above her head to prevent her clawing him and looked down at her hungrily. She lay like silken enchantment upon the furs, the fire highlighting her breasts and belly. He dipped his head to place a kiss deep within each armpit. He had done it before yet still she blushed deeply at the intimacy of such an act. He freed his shaft from the constriction of the tight cloth that covered him, and his magnificent erection sprang up with a will of its own. He poised over her, breathing harshly. Whenever he lay with her it was like slow torture. His mind and his body were at war with themselves. His flesh was fiercely demanding, his blood sang with delirious excitement, but always just beyond the ragged edges of his lust, his mind told him he wanted more.

The ultimate, of course, would be if Jasmine loved him, but he was a practical man and he would settle for much less than love. All he asked was that she desire him . . . no, even less than that. He would be over the moon if he could pleasure her—make her orgasmic. He lowered his body over hers and reached down to guide his shaft with trembling hands. His fingers forced her open further to accommodate his size. Because he took her so seldom, he could not control his peaking passion, then he surged upward pouring a throbbing, white-hot orgasm into her.

Jasmine felt panic rise within her, for before God what he was doing to her made her feel like nothing else mattered but his body inside hers. And she didn't even love him! Yes, you do, a voice said inside her head. "No, I don't!" she screamed the denial aloud and looked straight into the eyes of Morganna, who had entered his chamber without knocking.

The scene spread out before Morganna was like a knife twisting in her guts. Hatred exploded inside her brain as she saw that Falcon's need for his wife had been so great, so urgent he hadn't taken the time to disrobe.

When de Burgh realized the appalling intrusion he commanded harshly, "Get out!"

Blinded by hatred, Morganna fled.

"I'm sorry, Jasmine darling," he soothed softly.

"Don't apologize," she said breathlessly, "I'm glad she saw you making love to me." There was a note of triumph in her voice that Falcon found disconcerting. He looked down at her in amazement. He could see the pearl drops of his sperm on the inside of her thighs and he was hard again instantly, orgasmic but nowhere near sated.

She saw his intent and tried to rise. She got only to her knees before he pressed her to him with powerful arms.

"Not again!" she cried.

"Yes again," he insisted urgently.

"It's too soon," she protested.

"It's never too soon, I know strokes to soothe you, Jassy."

She pulled from him with blazing eyes. "Your sensual excesses are inexcusable! Have you forgotten I'm with child?"

"If that bitch hadn't interrupted me when she did . . . I had you one stroke from climax!"

"That bitch walking in was the only part I enjoyed," she spat cruelly. It was suddenly too much for Jasmine. She began to sob and shake. In truth he had brought her to climax, and her first release was so great the tears came flooding. She would never let him know what he had done to her . . . and she would make sure she controlled her betraying, treacherous body in future.

Chapter 33

That night Mountain Ash was raided. The invaders took sheep, cattle, fodder, and valuable horses. The thatched huts of the villagers that had sprung up outside the castle walls were set ablaze as a diversionary tactic to effect a clean getaway. Fire in the night was a terrifying experience, as the raiders well knew. In the blackness the flames crackled and roared, enjoying their wicked orgy of destruction.

The villagers were brought into the castle, and the next day was spent rebuilding their huts for them. Estelle and Jasmine were busy tending burns and comforting the children. Falcon de Burgh bided his time. He would be very sure of his target before he struck back. Once he did, he would make certain Mountain Ash was never raided again, for when the Welsh got inside a castle they killed, looted, and raped like wild beasts.

In the hall at supper his eyes sought out Morganna. She felt his eyes on her immediately and smiled with satisfaction. The moment he finished eating he excused himself to Jasmine and left the hall. Morganna followed him to his chamber, as he knew she would. He was stripped to the waist when he opened the door and drew her inside.

She could not keep her hands from him as she hoped to arouse him to untold heights. He undressed her quickly and lifted her to the bed, but then his caresses slowed in a tortuous, maddening, drawn-out session of foreplay that she neither wanted nor needed. In an amazingly short time she was mindless, begging him for the fulfillment she knew only he could give her.

Falcon, his hot mouth against her breast, said, "Where does Llewellyn store his treasure?"

"Mmmm . . . treasure?" she murmured thickly.

"Which castle houses what he has stolen from English castles?" He suspected she had been in communication with Llewellyn, as she rode out often through the mountains.

She didn't care if she betrayed Llewellyn to this man. She would do anything for him. All he had ever had to do was ask.

Her fingers closed about his swollen member. "Please, please." She rubbed and writhed against his marblelike thigh. Through the red haze of passion she sought a name. "Penderyn." She gasped.

He blew his warm breath over a distended nipple. "No, Morganna, that is where he stays in winter, where he launched the raid from. Where has he hidden his treasure . . . gold . . . jewels?"

"Ohhh . . . Brecon . . . now, please!"

Brecon! He might have guessed. It was a mountain fortress where at least three rivers joined to prevent attacks.

"Falcon . . ." she beseeched. He gave her thirty seconds of his attention. He manipulated her briskly with his hand to give her release, then quit the bed. Already he was miles away from her, his quick mind totally absorbed with a plan of revenge against Llewellyn. Though the hour was late, he did not hesitate to go down and rouse Gervase and Montgomery from their beds. He wanted to set his plan before them to see if they could pick any holes in it.

Morganna fell asleep in his bed, and it was there that Jasmine discovered her the next morning. She had wanted to tell Falcon that she would have her household servants move the villagers back into their rebuilt huts and supply them with food and blankets. When she saw the lithe brown form of Morganna curled up in his bed, her heart stopped. Tears immediately filled her eyes and she ran blindly down the tower steps and out into the cold morning, fighting a great wave of nausea. She leaned against the bailey wall and vomited, but somehow instead of making her feel better, it made her feel worse. She knew she was going to faint and realized how dangerous it would be to lie long in the freezing cold without a cloak. Blindly she reached out her hand then crumpled beside the wall.

Tam strode swiftly toward her and scooped the small, limp form into his arms. He swept into the hall and came face to face with de Burgh. "My lady is ill."

Falcon was startled to hear the protective tone the young knight used as he called her *his* lady, but he was so concerned over Jasmine that he let it pass. "Bring her upstairs," Falcon directed, and the two men swiftly climbed the tower steps. Tam naturally carried her into de Burgh's chamber. By this time Jasmine had opened her eyes and begun to protest weakly, "No, please."

Tam stopped only two long strides into the room and Falcon almost crashed into him. Tam took in the shameful scene of the naked girl in the bed and turned accusing eyes on de Burgh.

Jasmine turned her face into Tam's broad chest and whispered, "Please take me upstairs."

Falcon was racked with worry, anger, and guilt. He said shortly, "I'll get Estelle."

Morganna slipped on her tunic and sneaked away with excitement bubbling inside her. If Jasmine miscarried it would save her the trouble of destroying the child.

Estelle accompanied Falcon to the tower room, both deeply concerned. However, they were vastly relieved to see Jasmine sitting up in bed looking ethereal because of her slight pallor but unbelievably beautiful. Tam's doublet sported a pink and silver ribbon, and Falcon experienced a stab of jealousy as he realized Jasmine had given it to the young knight to wear as a favor. Then his common sense told him a knight who wore the ridiculously feminine colors of pink and silver would be a laughingstock. Tam averted his eyes from de Burgh and excused himself.

Estelle went to the bed and asked anxiously, "Are you bleeding?"

"No, of course not. Don't worry so, Estelle, I'll be perfectly all right. And please don't alert Big Meg or she'll keep me here for a week."

"I'll get you some chamomile and mint for the nausea," said Estelle, hurrying off to her stillroom.

Falcon sat down carefully on the edge of the bed. "Jasmine, if I am the cause of this I must ask your forgiveness."

Her best weapon she decided was indifference. "You? How could anything you do affect me?" she said lightly. "This is simply one of the small joys of pregnancy."

"I'm going to be away from Mountain Ash for a few days, but naturally I won't leave until I see you are recovered."

She knew immediately he was riding out in retaliation for the raid and icy fingers of fear crept around her heart. She might have clung to him and begged him to stay if she hadn't found Morganna in his bed. Instead she said indifferently. "Don't alter your plans on my account. I shall be up and about in an hour."

"I'm not taking all the men, I'll leave you well guarded," he reassured her.

She turned amethyst eyes upon him. "So long as you leave Tam, I'll feel perfectly safe," she said with the innocence of an asp.

He bit back a very nasty word, yet he was relieved. If she felt well enough to taunt him she couldn't be too ill. Nevertheless, he postponed leaving for one more day.

That night in the hall he was amused to see at least fifty of his knights sporting pink and silver ribbons. He also found himself on the receiving end of quite a few disapproving glances.

Later he dreamed he had to comfort and reassure a tearful Jasmine who was terrified for his safety. He held her against his heart and stroked her to sleep as the terror of losing him slowly melted away with his kisses. When he awoke a glum feeling descended upon him that Jasmine was indifferent as to whether he would make her a widow. However, his spirits lifted when he saw that she seemed perfectly recovered. Soon the hour drew near when he and forty of his best would ride through the night to plunder Brecon.

He would have been very gratified to know that Jasmine watched him leave through the narrow tower window. His men were laughing boisterously, jousting at one another with rough hands. The cold wind whipped their cloaks about them as they clattered over the stones of the bailey and through the gates. She saw Falcon lift his dark head toward her tower, his great destrier reared up, its forelegs pawing the wind, before he wheeled away from the castle. She thought man and beast were perfectly matched with the same strength and violence that was beautiful to watch. She shuddered, already lonely for him. How many times down the years to come would she stand so and watch him go directly into danger?

It took de Burgh two full weeks, for the mountain passes were treacherous and once they reached Brecon they had to build siege engines on the spot with their great axes. He knew that in the middle of winter the fortress would be manned by only a few good fighting men. Most of Llewellyn's army was kept close to the border of England where they could profit from quick raids on wealthy English castles. Before de Burgh quit Brecon he had two full chests of gold and a cache of precious jewels. But of more importance to him, he left not one man alive nor one wall of Brecon intact. His mangonels and trenchbuts had battered down the palisade and the curtain wall, and left gaping holes in the tower. Every outbuilding was burned to the ground. He took a grim satisfaction in the methodical destruction, which would never have happened if the Welsh hadn't struck first.

Jasmine and Estelle had consulted the crystal ball after carefully performing the magic ritual, and they had seen clearly that de Burgh would overcome all danger and come away with treasure enough to build half a dozen castles if he so desired.

Morganna was devastated to see Jasmine up so quickly from her sickbed because it meant she must still be carrying the child. She was actually singing and the bloom in her cheeks made her look stronger, healthier, and happier than she had ever been. Morganna decided to put an end to all that. She asked Estelle for an abortificant for herself. Naturally Estelle was only too willing to rid the Welsh girl of de Burgh's bastard.

Morganna waited until she saw Jasmine go to the kitchens as she did every day now, then took out the vial of rue, which she intended to pour into the mead Jasmine always drank. She stole up to Jasmine's tower room, terrified lest she be discovered. Once she thought she heard the padding of soft footsteps so she quickly took the stopper from the vial and reached for the mead. Suddenly she screamed as she was pounced on from behind and rolled to the floor. For a moment terror gripped her as she stared up into the amber eyes of a great mountain lion. She reached for her knife, but found her leather sheath empty. Quickly she rolled away from the cat toward the door, the spilled vial forgotten in her panic to get away. Later as she examined the two deep horizontal claw

marks across her bare breast, she knew they would probably leave a scar. With great cunning, she found her knife
and scratched a vertical cut to join the others, forming a
perfect letter F for Falcon.

Estelle found the empty vial she had given to Morganna. As she bent to retrieve it, a vision came to her of
what the girl had tried to do. She picked up the mead but
could discern no telltale smell of rue; however, to be on
the safe side she threw away the flagon's contents. Estelle
did not wish to estrange Jasmine and Falcon further by
explaining that Morganna had asked for the rue to get rid
of Falcon's child. She would simply have to watch the
girl closely, for she had almost succeeded in carrying out
her destructive plan.

When de Burgh and his men returned triumphant, it
was cause for a great celebration. Since it was well into
December, they decided to hold the Christmas festivities
early. The hall was decorated with holly and mistletoe,
an enormous Yule log was felled and made ready, and the
oxen sent from Chepstow were put on the spits to roast.

Jasmine was dressing for the celebration with the help
of Glynis when Falcon pushed open her chamber door
and strolled in. She was sitting in her brief shift pulling
on her stockings. "I'm not dressed," she protested with a
gasp.

He grinned. "So I see," he said.

She glanced guiltily at the scarlet gown laid out on the
bed. "I'm wearing red," she said defiantly.

His grin widened. "So I see," he said again.

Little Glynis made a hasty departure before the sparks
began to fly. Falcon drew close, drinking in the heady
sight of her, which he had thirsted for while they had
been separated. His eyes swept down over her tiny waist
and flat belly. "You're even slimmer than when I left."

"My breasts are fuller," she said, then blushed hotly.

His grin showed his even, white teeth. "So I see," he repeated, this time running an appreciative finger over the swell of her breast. He was glad she had chosen to wear red; he had known she would. The diamonds he intended giving her tonight would be set off magnificently.

His eyes grew smoky with desire, and she warned, "De Burgh, don't you dare!"

He teased, "Can't you find it in your heart to be kind to me after a two-week absence?"

"No," she said firmly.

"Let me take you to bed, just for an hour?" he teased.

"No!" she said sharply.

"Then take off your shift and let me see your lovely body for a little while."

"De Burgh!" she protested.

"Selfish little wench!" He gave a mock sigh. "Ah well, I'll just have to settle for the taste of you then," he said, picking her up and setting her down in his lap. His lips brushed hers. "Did I ever tell you," he said, brushing her lips again and again, "that your little bottom is heart-shaped?"

She was unused to this gentle loveplay and was quite willing to be teased and touched. His hand ran down her silken stocking. "Did I ever tell you," he said, brushing her lips, "that you have the prettiest slim legs?" He put his fingers beneath her chin and raised it so he could look into her eyes. "And what's this you have between your pretty legs? Did you ever tell me?"

She jumped off his lap quickly and grabbed up her gown. "De Burgh, we will miss all the fun."

He sighed. "We will if you don't let me take you to bed."

"There's going to be dancing," she said with excitement.

He mocked, "Why didn't you tell me? Why are we

wasting time in the bedroom when we could be having fun downstairs?"

She giggled. "Will you dance with me?"

"I thought all your dances would be reserved for Tam. Don't tell me you'd favor an old man like me with a dance?" He turned her around and hooked up her gown. Then he lifted her pale tresses and pressed a kiss to the nape of her neck. "Lord God, how you make me quiver," he murmured, all teasing gone from his voice. He knew if he didn't remove himself from her presence, her clothes would be strewn across the chamber and she'd be beneath him in the bed. Alone together in a room, the torment and temptation were too great for him. His eyes grew serious. He dropped a chaste kiss on the top of her head and hastily left her to finish dressing.

Chapter 34

The tables in the hall groaned beneath their succulent burden of food. The roasted oxen were supplemented by venison; it took a score of red deer to feed two hundred. In the dead of winter there were no fresh vegetables available, but the icy rivers teemed with fish, game was always plentiful, and the cooks had baked dozens of loaves, pastries, and egg dishes. Apple and mincemeat pies and gooseberry and quince tarts smothered in thick, rich cream were washed down by old ale, hot spiced cider, and the wine sent from Chepstow.

Laughter and music were the order of the night. Tam was the first knight to gather enough courage to ask Jasmine to dance, but he was followed in quick succession by his brother Gower, Montgomery, and Gervase. Jasmine tried without success to keep her eyes from the dark head that leaned against the wall watching her from across the hall. He was so easy with everyone, even the scullions called him Falcon, she noticed. Trust Gervase to deliver her to her husband after they had danced, she thought ruefully.

Falcon laughed down at her. "You haven't asked me to dance."

She tossed her hair back. "An ugly lout like you deserves to stand against the wall!"

His hands shot out to seize her about the waist and draw her close. "I've a present for you tucked inside my doublet," he said temptingly. Her eyes met his and she took up his challenge. Her hand slipped inside against the hard, bare flesh of his chest and she gasped as her fingers closed over what she knew must be jewels. As she drew them out, the diamonds caught the light and the reflection of her flame-colored gown. Womanlike, she took delight in the luxurious gift as she slipped the twin bracelets over her wrists.

She was breathless as Falcon fastened the matching necklace about her slender throat and whirled her off to dance before she could think of anything to say. "Let's give them something to talk about," he invited, then lifted her high to show off her pretty legs. The hall went wild. When they danced there was something between them that carried them away to another world where none of the others could follow.

After the dance Falcon went with the other men to drag in the Yule log for luck. There was much good-hearted pushing and shoving, and many of them were unsteady on their feet from what they had imbibed. Jasmine was flushed and happy. It was almost as if Falcon were courting her, and what woman could resist? What woman indeed? she asked herself as Morganna, in a low-cut, short leather tunic, fastened her eyes on Jasmine's diamonds and sneered, "I'm happy to see the two of you do something together, at least."

Jasmine refused to be baited. "Yes, I have discovered a passion for dancing," she said lightly.

"Passion?" Morganna scorned. "You don't even know the meaning of the word." She pulled aside her tunic to reveal her breast with the *F* carved into it. "There's passion! He puts his mark on everything he owns that really matters to him."

Jasmine closed her eyes. The evening had been thoroughly spoiled for her. If Falcon really cared anything at all for her, he would rid the castle of Morganna's hateful presence.

When he returned to Jasmine's side, he brought her a cup of hot, fragrant cider, but she set it aside. "What's wrong?" he asked, his brows drawing together in concern. The sparkle had gone out of her and she had withdrawn from him.

"Nothing," she said stiffly. "I'm suddenly very tired."

He searched her face, but she would not meet his eyes. Finally he said, "I'm sorry, I should have realized. I'll carry you up to bed."

She recoiled. "No! Please stay or your men will be disappointed."

Estelle came up and put her hand on de Burgh's arm. "I'll see to her," she said quietly. Inside Jasmine's tower room, Estelle warned her granddaughter, "I've never taken my eyes from her tonight because I know she is a danger to you."

"If he wants her he can have her," Jasmine cried angrily.

"He doesn't want her, that's why she's obsessed with him," said Estelle firmly.

"He's carved his initial on her breast!" cried Jasmine.

"What do you mean?" asked Estelle.

"She showed me a big *F* scratched across her breast!"

"She must have done it herself. She's capable of anything. I didn't tell you, but two days ago I know she came to your chamber to put rue in your wine to rid you of the child. I found the empty vial spilled upon the floor. She wanted me to think she carried his child, but the only child really is yours. Tonight I saw the raw hatred she bears you, darling. She'll try again tonight. I feel it. I know it."

Jasmine was still for a moment as she absorbed the truth of Estelle's words. "I will be ready for her. I will put the fear of the Devil into her."

"I'll ready the candles, you put on your gossamer robe," urged Estelle. They prepared for the ritual and silently waited. The green candles had burned themselves in half before they heard a footfall on the stone steps.

In the dim tower staircase Morganna stretched a cord low across the top step and secured the ends by wedging them tightly into deep crevices in the stone walls. She tested its tautness, smiled with satisfaction, and was about to step over the cord and descend when Estelle opened the chamber door and commanded, "Come . . . we've been expecting you." There were times when it was quite impossible to disobey Estelle, and this was one of them. As if under a spell, Morganna entered the chamber. With fascinated horror she saw Jasmine in a nimbus of light inside a circle of green candles. Her nakedness glowed through a robe transparent as a spider's web and she held a chalice of some potion on high as she sang a mystic chant. An unusual smoky miasma was filling the room until the heavy, burning fragrance almost choked Morganna.

Jasmine drank from the chalice then caressed a crystal orb before her, which began to swirl inside like a whirlwind. "I, Jasmine de Burgh, call upon the Powers of the Universe to curse Morganna of Wales. If you ever lift a

hand against a child of mine, God wither it!" Jasmine
raised a dagger and pointed it directly at Morganna.

With a strangled cry the girl fled the room. She forgot
the cord across the stairs and went down headfirst with a
scream of terror. Falcon's door flew open as he rushed
out.

"They tried to murder me," she screamed. "They are
witches!" She pointed up the stairs and de Burgh stood
horrified at the sight of Jasmine in her ritualistic robe.
Falcon tried to help Morganna to her feet. Her face and
arms were torn and bleeding from the rough stones. Her
hand was frozen into a claw. "I cannot move my hand
. . . they have crippled me!"

Big Meg had also heard the screams and came running. De Burgh spoke to her quickly. "Take the girl and
tend her wounds." He took the stairs two at a time. Both
women backed away from his terrible black anger.

"There will be no more witch's rituals in my castle.
This night puts an end to all your dabbling in black
magic! Do you understand me?" he thundered, his eyes
blazing with cold fury. He turned on his heel as if he
could no longer stand the sight of his wife.

Why did he have such an unreasoning attitude toward
the occult? Jasmine wondered angrily. Why did he take
that slut's part against her? She wanted to run to him
with the tale of the Welsh girl's wickedness against her
and their unborn child. She wanted to show him the cord
stretched across the steps, which could have killed her or
at the very least made her miscarry, but her pride forbade
her from defending herself. She would not beg him, in
fact she would not even speak to him from now on. She
would totally ignore him as if he didn't exist.

Over the next couple of days it became apparent that
Morganna was no longer at Mountain Ash, and no one

seemed to know of her whereabouts. It was assumed that de Burgh knew, but that the subject was closed.

Jasmine succeeded in ignoring Falcon, but though she looked away from him when they occupied the same room or when they dined in the hall, it did not free her mind of his strong image. When he and his men went hunting she thought she would go mad with the quiet loneliness, but when they returned their uproar shook the rafters.

She found him time and time again watching her, his eyes shadowed and moody, and she knew with the age-old knowledge of Eve that his need grew stronger and her time grew shorter. She knew he was stalking her like his prey. She knew his control would snap and he would take her, but she did not know how or when.

Falcon de Burgh fought the gnawing need in his gut and the ache in his loins with an iron determination, yet her siren song called to him day and night. The days were Hell when he could see her, hear her, smell her fragrance as she left a room, but the nights were worse. They were endless, lonely, sleepless endurance tests. When he drank himself to sleep his dreams were so erotic they shamed him. If she was in the same room he could not tear his eyes from her. She grew more beautiful each day. She was not quite so slim as she had been and yet he could probably still span her waist with his hands. She was innocent and earthy at the same time, and her breasts were ripe and luscious.

A new year was dawning and he knew he would not, could not go on this way. If he did not take her he would go mad; if he did not have her he would die. He shook his head and laughed at himself. If he didn't have her he deserved to die! He was a fool if he didn't turn their isolation to intimacy.

He stocked his chamber with plenty of food and wine and water, and stacked logs high against the hearth. He searched his mind for the things she would need and finally sent Big Meg up to Jasmine's chamber to fetch her hairbrushes, her diamonds, and the big oval mirror in its stand.

"Why does he want my diamonds and my mirror?" demanded Jasmine.

"I don't know my lady, I only know I'd better not return without them," Meg said.

"I'll see about this," Jasmine retorted, always ready to meet him more than halfway in a fight. She brushed aside Gervase and stepped into de Burgh's chamber. She swaggered over and planted herself squarely in front of him. She dug both fists into her glittering silver girdle and looked up. This battle she knew she was going to win.

He succeeded in looking very innocent.

"Why do you need my diamonds and my mirror?" she demanded.

"I don't need them, Jasmine. I just thought you might like to have them over the next three days."

"Three days?" she questioned, glancing about to see the room had been stocked with food and logs enough for three days. The hair on the nape of her neck bristled and she was suddenly aware that she was in danger. Big Meg carried in the mirror and handed the diamonds and hairbrushes to de Burgh. He set them on a nightstand beside the great bed. "That will be all, Meg," he dismissed. The servant cast a worried glance toward Jasmine and reluctantly went out.

De Burgh asked Gervase, "Do you have the key?"

Jasmine's eyes opened wide in disbelief. "You are going to imprison me!" she gasped.

"I am," he said smoothly.

She struggled to make sense of it. "At the end of three days you think I will give in to your demands? You don't know me very well, de Burgh!"

"You have put your finger on the trouble exactly,

chérie. I don't know you very well." He nodded to Gervase, whom she did not notice leave the chamber and quietly close the door.

"But all that is going to change, my love. At the end of three days we are going to be sharing a bed and we are going to be very, very intimate. At the end of three days I am going to know everything there is to know about you, and you will come to know me in every sense of the word."

Suddenly his plan became crystal clear. "You are not locking me in alone . . . you are locking us in here together!"

He smiled at her outrage.

"You are ridiculous, sir, I'll not stay!" she cried, rushing to the door. It would not open.

"It's too late, Jasmine, but it's not too late for us."

"Gervase!" she called urgently.

"He has his orders not to unlock it until three days have passed . . . and three nights," Falcon added huskily.

"You are mad," she accused, more than a little afraid now.

"I must have been mad to let you elude me for so long," he said softly. "At the end of three days I want to hear you say you love me."

"I'll not say it," she defied.

"You shall," he said, "you shall."

He closed the distance between them. She would have fled, but he reached out a strong hand to imprison her wrist. With the other hand he undid the silver girdle and untied the silver ribbons at her breast. He stepped back to wait. Her hands flew to the untied ribbons. "If you fasten them you shall regret it," he said quietly. "Undress. Take off everything." She knew he meant it. She knew if she begged and pleaded it would make no odds. She would have to obey him. Slowly she took off her pink velvet

tunic and embroidered underdress. She stood in her shift
with downcast eyes, overcome with shyness. His eyes devoured her, hungrily staring at her creamy shoulders and
luscious breasts.

"I'll be cold," she said quietly.

"I'll warm you, Jassy," he promised thickly. Jasmine
feared if she hesitated longer, his hands would tear her
shift from her. She might as well get it over, there was no
way out. She took refuge in a deeply cushioned chair and
sat to remove her shoes and peel off her stockings. Then
keeping her eyes lowered she reluctantly removed her
shift. Stealing a quick glance at him, she saw that he was
removing his own garments. Her lashes quickly swept to
her cheeks again. She sat rigid with apprehension waiting
for him to pounce. When he did not, she glanced up
again. Naked, he walked about quickly, picking up their
discarded clothing. Then to her utter disbelief she
watched him bundle it together and shove it out of the
tower window. She jumped up, forgetting her nudity for a
moment. "I have no other clothes!" she cried.

"Exactly," he said, looking most pleased. He had at
last succeeded in arousing her fiery temper.

"Do you expect me to spend three days with you,
while we are both completely naked?" she shouted.

"I can't think of a better way for us to become intimately acquainted with each other, my love."

Her cheeks flamed with anger and embarrassment. It
was not easy at any time to stand her ground with her
powerful husband, but when he towered before her dis-
playing his full naked strength she found it impossible.
She covered her face with her hands and curled into the
chair unable to stay her flow of tears.

Falcon's face softened. He would let her have her little
cry; she would feel better for it. He made no move toward
her. He had resolved that she would have to make the
first move. He knew he couldn't expect anything overt, of

course, but he would watch her closely for that first subtle sign that she might welcome his advances.

He walked over to the fire to poke it into a cozy blaze, then carefully banked it at the back with a fresh log. While he was crouched to tend the fire, she dashed the tears from her eyes and sprinted toward his wardrobe. She threw open the doors and was dismayed to find it empty. She could not even cover herself with an article of his, and worse, she realized, neither could he!

"De Burgh, whatever will we do for three days?"

He poured them wine and approached her slowly. "We could talk to each other . . . listen to each other. No lies . . . no witch's tricks. Here, have a little wine, it will warm you, give you courage, stop you from taking yourself so seriously. And if I'm lucky it will bring a bubble of laughter to your lips."

Her hand shook a little as she took it from him. My God, she could not even breathe when he was so close. "Please, your nearness disturbs me."

He laughed softly and stretched out prone on the wolf pelts before the fire. "You are so innocent. As I've warned you before, telling a man his nearness disturbs you is just the spur to make him come much closer."

Now that his manhood was covered she found it easier to look at him. He raised his head and smiled lazily at her. He began to make love to her with his eyes, lingering on every lovely secret part of her. She had never been more aware of her femininity in her life. Naked and totally vulnerable, with his eyes eating her, she felt new sensations she had never experienced. Her pulses raced and she could feel her heartbeats all fluttery as she contemplated the first hesitant step along the road to her awakening.

He loved the sense of spicy anticipation as he felt excitement stir in him . . . the tightening in his balls and shaft, the heat stealing across his loins, and the exquisitely pleasurable sensation as his shaft filled. Magic danced in the air.

She stole a look at his well-muscled back and the long shanks of his legs stretched to the fire. He was darkly attractive enough to make any woman fall in love with him. Jealousy flared up in her. She wondered if he had ever told another woman that he loved her. She doubted it, but perhaps that was just wishful thinking. Suddenly she wanted to be more beautiful to him than other woman had been.

With his intent gaze upon her it was as if he read her thoughts. "You are so very beautiful," he told her huskily.

She shook her head, "Not anymore. I'm too fat. My baby has made me—"

"*Our* baby, darling. You are more beautiful today than you've ever been before. Your body is luscious, perfect." His words worshipped her and she knew he meant every word he said. Was it the wine that made her feel so bold? Suddenly she wanted to walk before him, to stretch and pose prettily and display herself.

Again, reading her thoughts, he said, "Will you fetch us more wine?"

She stood up shyly, but as his eyes caressed every curve, her pride took over to straighten her back, thrust out her breasts, and toss her hair about her shoulders. Almost there were two Jasmines. She watched herself in fascination to see what she would do next. She cast him small, tempting glances from the corner of her eye and reached for his empty goblet. Then she glided away from him, prideful as a cat. She knew exactly what he would say as she felt his eyes on her back.

"Did I ever tell you that your little bottom is heart-shaped?"

Her mouth curved into a delicious smile and she giggled. When she turned to face him, holding the two filled wine goblets, she saw that he had gotten up from the rug and was sitting in the big chair. She loved the feel of his eyes upon her as she walked a direct path to him. It was as if he had intoxicated her. She stopped just out of arm's reach to tease him, then lifted her wine and drained it. She licked her lips with the tip of her provocative, pink tongue. She bent toward him temptingly, and as she offered him his wine, her hand brushed his in an unmistakable caress.

"You touched me," he said, laughing triumphantly.

"Falcon!" she protested.

"Ah, it's Falcon now, not de Burgh," he teased. His laugh went right inside her and made itself at home. Gently, so he wouldn't scare her off, he reached out and pulled her into his lap. The wine splashed over onto his hand and she bent to lick it off.

"You twist me round your little finger, I'm so easy for you to manage. I think it's your hair that makes all men weak."

She giggled, basking in the loveplay.

He set the wine aside and ran his hand up and down her leg. His eyes were stained black with passion. He dipped his head to taste her lips and she sighed deeply when he took his mouth away. "Did I ever tell you," he said, brushing her lips, "that you have the prettiest slim legs?"

"This all happened before," she said breathlessly.

"In another life?" he teased unmercifully.

"No, remember, when I wore the scarlet gown?"

"You were in your shift as I remember, and refused to play the game out."

"Mayhap I have more courage now," she teased.

He put his fingers beneath her chin so he could look deeply into her eyes. "And what's this you have between your pretty legs? Did you ever tell me?"

She shook her head breathlessly. He put his lips to her

ear and murmured, "I think it's a honey pot." Gently he
reached between her legs and dipped in one finger then he
brought it to his lips and tasted it. "Mmmm . . . delicious!"

"Falcon!" she protested, suffused with blushes.

He reached again for her secret place and she did not
protest overmuch. Gently he inserted his finger again and
began to move it very slowly in a circular motion as if he
were stirring her honey pot. His knowing fingertip encircled her tiny bud over and over again until she was
squirming with pleasurable sensations. The pleasure
seemed to go higher and higher in ever-widening circles
of intensity.

She slipped her arms about his neck and let her head
fall back as she gave herself up to the pleasure, then suddenly with widened eyes she cried, "Oh oh oh oh
ohhhh!"

Falcon grinned with delight. "Did you enjoy that a
little, sweetheart?"

She licked lips gone suddenly dry. "Well, perhaps just
the tiniest little bit," she admitted reluctantly.

He put her off his knee. "If you're going to lie, I don't
want to play with you," he teased.

She saw the tip of his great shaft quiver. With great
daring she pointed. "You're lying now. You do want to
play with me."

"Just ignore it and it will go away," he said solemnly.

Jasmine waited a moment, her eyes alight with mischief. "I don't believe it will."

"Oh, yes . . . it will soon be dead," he said.

"Dead?"

"Yes, of starvation!" He gathered her up into his arms.
"Lord God, Jassy, I love you so much. I'm going to take
you now, I cannot wait longer." He carried her to his
great bed and pressed her back against the pillows. He

kicked off the furs, unwilling to have this act of love covered or impeded in any way.

Jasmine soon learned that Falcon's mouth was a formidable weapon against her defenses. His persuasive mouth was hot, fierce, and demanding as it explored her from neck to navel, and between kisses it whispered and bathed her in adoration. His hands roamed over her body, caressing, exploring, teasing until he had set up a fever of need. She lifted her arms to encircle his neck and arched her soft body against his hardness. With her eyes closed she gave herself up to him to assert his mastery over her in any way he wished. For the first time ever, she longed for the act of domination and submission.

Then he fused his mouth to.hers and she opened her lips to receive his tongue. It ravished her mouth until she moaned from its thrusts. She felt an emptiness inside her that needed filling in exactly the same way he filled her mouth. She reached for him with fevered fingers then gasped and withdrew them as she felt the size of him. Realizing her hesitation, he took her hand and guided it back. She could feel him throbbing, rearing, then slowly, together, the hands of the lovers guided the invader to its destination.

They both knew that whatever he did to her now, she had agreed to it. With deft fingers he parted her to receive him. He thrust slowly, smoothly inside her, then held himself still to let her get used to the swollen fullness of him. Her sheath was so burning hot and unbelievably tight that he lengthened another inch once he was inside her.

He knew this was the critical moment where she usually withdrew from him, separating her mind from the physical act of sex. It was up to him to make her offer herself as a sacrifice to the divine gods of passion. He began to stroke deeply in and out, matching his rhythm to the throb of their pulsing blood. His tongue ran like wildfire along her neck and up to her ear where he whispered fiercely, "Stay with me, Jassy . . . feel me . . . feel everything . . . oh, God, you're so hot, so tight . . . soar away with me, love, to another world."

He was the Falcon. She let him take her higher and higher as he plunged deeper and deeper. He totally engulfed her until they were locked in love. Together they soared to the heights until triumphantly they shattered into a million fragments, fusing into each other, bathing each other, then floating, sailing together on a sea of bliss.

She clung to him as if she could never bear to be parted again. This was what he had wanted, needed from her! She had submitted to him body and soul, letting him take what he needed, and now she was limp from the loving she had received, languid, drowsy, and deliciously warm.

Falcon held her to him tightly and rolled until she lay atop of him. Her cheek was pressed against his heart, her beautiful hair spread across his chest. His strong brown hands slipped down her body until they cupped her buttocks and they drifted off to sleep, their unborn child enfolded safely between their melded bodies.

Chapter 35

In his slumber a few hours later he missed the heat of her body and came up through the layers of sleep. For a moment he was bereft that she had left their bed until his searching eyes fell upon her exquisite beauty. Jasmine had gotten up to bathe, memories of the things she had said and the things he had done covering her with pink blushes.

Falcon came to her immediately to begin the acknowledgment. He enfolded her in strong, loving arms but he knew a woman needed more than that. She wanted a kiss that remembered last night's passion and promised delightful possibilities for the hours to come. His lips told her that she filled his heart and lingered in his consciousness. He knew that without the epilogue, the cycle of lovemaking was incomplete.

She hid her face against his chest until his whispered love words aroused her out of herself, eroding away her shy inhibitions. Later he would transport her from the reality of caution and codes to a sublime paradise. He would love her until he enslaved her, encouraging her to toss and writhe and pant her way to total satiety.

"What would you like to eat?" he asked.

She sighed deeply. "I would like whatever you want," she replied. He slipped his arm about her and they selected some tempting items from their store of food. They shared the same platter and the same goblet because they wanted to be one, and he scooped her into his lap so they could share the deeply cushioned chair.

He fed her with his fingers and she sucked his fingertips erotically, sending shivers through him to that other tip at the end of his shaft. When they were replete with food they drank from the goblet, placing their lips in turn at the exact same spot. Then because their mouths had been too long apart they kissed and he fed her wine from his lips. They intoxicated each other, until their blood sang in their veins and desire built until they were dizzy from their need.

He lifted her high in powerful arms and did not set her feet to the carpet until she was before the tall mirror. "I want you to watch me make love to you. I want you to see how it makes you more beautiful," he murmured.

"Falcon . . . Falcon," she cried, and he dipped his head to taste his name on her wine-red lips. Her eyes stared at their image in the mirror and she saw him go down on his knees before her. His lips teased the tiny golden curls as his hands caressed the backs of her thighs, forcing her forward into his kisses. She felt his tongue search out her tiny bud until it swelled with passion, then he deeply probed all her soft, intimate depths. She bit her lips to keep herself from screaming with excitement. Her fingers entwined his thick, black curls and she pressed his head farther into her warm fragrance. She watched her hands dig into the wide, muscled shoulders, leaving scratches as the intensity of his mouth invaded her senses. His tongue, long and lean, lapped at her, then it stroked her hard and strong. It invaded and plundered her shamelessly until it took her.

In the mirror she saw her breasts harden, her eyelids droop, her pink mouth slacken. With a cry she fell to her knees before him and kissed him deeply. She tasted herself on his lips and it made her wild.

"Did you like that, Jassy?" he asked huskily.

"Oh, Falcon, I loved it! I love you!" she cried wildly. A whole new world was opening up for her. Her blood was so high there was no limitation to the things she wanted to do. "Oh, Falcon, what have you done to me? Have you any idea how you have made me feel?"

"Of course, darling. You want to be wild and wicked and never say no again."

"Oh, yes! I'm wildly curious about your body. Come and lie down on the furs before the fire and let me explore you." He stretched out in a supine position and she knelt above him with worshipful eyes. She brushed her palms over the slabs of muscle in his chest and bent to put the tip of her tongue to each nipple. She wanted more and more and she felt that she would never get enough of him, ever. Her hands slid over his flat belly then she bent over him with great daring to tongue his navel. He groaned with the unbearable heavy ache she had created in his loins.

"Did I hurt you?" she asked. She almost felt wild enough to hurt him and be hurt in return.

"Let me teach you," he said. "The most sensitive part is here just below the head where the skin is pulled back. You can encircle my shaft with your fingers like so, and move them up and down over the head, or you can use both hands if you want to stimulate the whole length. I feel a different sensation entirely if you put your palms on either side and roll it back and forth."

The wildness inside her erupted and she was consumed with an overwhelming desire to kiss him there. She remembered that Estelle had told her it was probably the most erotic thing a woman could do for a man. She bent and kissed the tip of his shaft then looked into his eyes to enjoy his reaction. As she had hoped, his eyes were stained black with passion, which enticed her to something more daring. She ran the tip of her tongue around the groove at the base of the head. It gave her deep satisfaction to see him rear and buck and gasp, "Jassy . . . Jassy!" Then she encircled the length of his shaft with both hands and took the head into her mouth, alternately sucking and tonguing him. He knew if he did not stop her it would be over in seconds. Quickly he reversed their positions. After flipping her down onto the silvery wolf skins, he impaled her savagely. She was so highly aroused from their foreplay that she was soon crying out with her orgasm. The moment he heard her, his hot seed flowed as he emptied himself inside her.

This time they slept while their bodies were still joined; his shaft stayed half-hard with the erotic content of his dreams. The more they made love, the more they began to talk. They shared their fears, hopes, and dreams for the future. They shared everything . . . laughter, secrets, tears. He read his favorite tales to her from Homer, and to give him pleasure she wore her diamonds to bed while he made love to her.

They shared their childhood memories, their knowledge, their likes and dislikes, and discovered more similarities than they had ever dreamed. Outside there was another great snowstorm; inside they cuddled in the big bed with the curtains drawn back to let in the heat of the fire.

She sighed to the tip of her toes, then took one foot and ran it along his bare leg. "Falcon, why are you so opposed to my magic?" she asked, not afraid anymore to bring up the forbidden.

He was silent for a moment while he gathered his thoughts. "Let me see if I can explain it so you will understand how I feel. The price for life is involvement, responsibility, effort. I don't want my men, my people to live in an imaginary world where everything or anything they fancy can be achieved effortlessly through magic."

She stretched luxuriously. "Ah, you are only opposed to fakery and hocus-pocus. I shall still practice my real magic."

"I can see I shall have to use my belt on you," he threatened, taking her roughly in his arms.

"Even you must admit some of it is real or at least unexplained," she protested between kisses.

"Well, let's see," he mused. "Take that mystical crystal ball you use to see visions. It might hold others spellbound, but I know that its swirling, smoky illusions are nothing more than colored sand particles that float in water that has a drop of glycerine in it."

She playfully took handfuls of his hair into her fists and pulled it. "You are no fun at all!" she accused.

"Fun?" he demanded fiercely. "Let me teach you what fun is all about."

His erection brushed against her thigh and she teased, "Are you always in that wretched condition?"

"Always," he admitted, lifting her above him to set her astride him. She did no more than keep him hard while he played with her silvery-gold hair and rosy breasts. She provoked every sense of his body with tantalizing guile. Lord God, he was hard. "Jassy, you make love to me this time . . . you set the pace . . . do the things you like."

She blushed and said shyly, "You will think me wanton, overbold."

He shook his head. "Modesty is misplaced in the bedchamber."

She sat like silken enchantment on his lean, muscled body. She covered his face with kisses, then flushed at her own boldness as her tongue traced the arched curve of his top lip. His mouth opened and she thrust in her tongue to duel and play with his. His mouth was like Heaven, she decided. She could feel his erection bucking and jumping between her legs, searching frantically for her entrance, and she teased him by sliding her silky thigh up its entire length. His voice dropped an octave as he said huskily, "Mayhap *next time* I'll let you set the pace." With firm hands he took hold of her bottom and lifted her onto his magnificent erection. His hardness impaled her with pleasure. "Hold on tight, darling," he murmured as his hands cupped her bottom and lifted her up and down on him effortlessly.

For long moments at a time the focus of his mind was raptly absorbed watching her take her pleasure. Her sensations were so delicious, he noted with satisfaction, it caused her breath to stop. All the way up inside her, he suddenly wished he'd imprisoned her for three weeks, rather than three days, for he knew he was going to wear himself out, and her, in the time they had left, experiencing every degree of lovemaking possible between male and female.

Finally with head thrown back in abandon, she cried out his name and her nails left bloody half-moons on his shoulders. She knew something vastly important had happened to her locked in this chamber. It would divide her life forever into before and after. She felt newborn as if she'd only just come fully alive. She was experiencing a divine, immense new power, a secret side to herself that had been unknown, unexplored. Forevermore she had the knowledge that blissful, exquisite pleasure was only an arm's length away.

It was early in the morning after their third night together that she heard someone at the door. She flew across the room and pressed herself against the huge door to try to muffle the sound of the low knocking with her naked body. Outside Gervase stood hesitating with key in hand. He was flanked by Big Meg and Estelle. Their anxious faces reflected their worry about what had gone on behind the locked door for the last three days. Falcon awoke and slipped from the bed. He came up behind Jasmine, lifted her hair to press kisses to the nape of her neck, then enfolded her in strong arms beneath her breasts. Every vulnerable part of her was open to his hands, while his insistent shaft rose up against her buttocks.

"Go away," she called through the door. "We need another day together."

As the three exchanged surprised glances, they heard the unmistakable ring of triumph in de Burgh's laugh.

Finally winter decided to give way to spring and the mountains of Wales were filled with wildflowers and birdsong. The people at Mountain Ash had had to get used to a lord and lady who were very deeply in love, but they were still a little shocked at their intimate behavior in the hall each night. They acted like newlyweds when in reality Lady Jasmine was almost ready to give birth. Falcon fed her from his own plate. She wrinkled her nose at the sweet sugarplum he offered her. "I only fancy sour things these days."

He looked at her with love in his eyes. She bent toward him and whispered, "I love the way you look at me."

"How do I look at you?" he asked.

"As if I were naked!" she said, blushing.

He took her hand and brushed her fingers with his lips. The tenderness and concern he felt for her brought a great lump into his throat, and he prayed silently for the thousandth time that she would come through her childbirth without complications. They had talked it out and he was amazed that she faced it unafraid. She was prepared for the suffering; he wished to God he could say the same.

Whenever he saw the worry mar Estelle's brow he felt guilty about impregnating his delicate wife, yet at the same time he tried to keep his fear at bay. He masked his anxiety for Jasmine's sake, knowing she would need all his strength as well as her own.

Early in the morning on the last day of May he searched everywhere for Jasmine until he became almost frantic. He found her in the laundry shed bending over a tub like a washerwoman, while half a dozen female servants stood about her wringing their hands.

"What the hell do you think you're doing?" he demanded. "Have you all gone mad?" he blasted the women.

"Don't scold, Falcon. I wanted to bring on my labor, and every woman I asked said her's began while she was doing the wash."

He wasn't amused, in fact he couldn't remember a time when he'd been angrier. "It's too soon," he said with a worried frown. "You're not supposed to have the baby for two or three weeks yet."

"Falcon, I do believe it worked . . . I think it's begun," she said faintly, experiencing a tearing pain in her back.

He swept her up in his arms and carried her to their

chamber, calling impatiently for Big Meg and Estelle. "For Christ's sake, Meg, you shouldn't have taken your eyes off her, you know she can't be trusted! Hurry and pull back these covers."

"If her labor's just started, it won't be born until next month," said Meg, laughing.

"What the hell are you talking about, woman?" Falcon asked blankly.

Jasmine put out her hand to calm him. "It's an attempt at humor, darling. This is the last day of May . . . it won't be born until June."

"It's a damned silly time for humor," he said irritably. "Estelle, thank God. I found her doing the wash!" They exchanged worried glances and he walked toward the window and beckoned her.

"Have you got that stuff for pain you told me about?"

"Yes, yes, I have colewort and poppy for if it gets very bad. Falcon, it's not going to happen in five minutes, you know. We're in for a long day and night of it. The best thing you can do is go and have a stiff drink with your men; this is women's work."

"To hell with that rubbish." He appealed to Jasmine. "You do want me to stay with you, darling, don't you?"

"Of course I do. Help me to undress, then you can rub my back."

He settled her in bed, then threw off his boots and climbed up on the bed behind her. "Here, lean against me, while I rub the pain away." He propped her between his legs and she used his long, hard thighs to rest her arms. She leaned back against him feeling warm and safe and cherished. She drowsed a little until another pain came, but it was still bearable.

"Do you remember teasing me because you thought I was too slim to be with child?" she asked, touching her enlarged stomach.

He teased her now. "No, I don't remember you ever

being slim. Haven't you always been fat as a little piglet?" She giggled happily for love really was blind. He told her over and over how lusciously beautiful she looked when in reality she felt grossly swollen and ungainly.

"We have to settle the names. If it's a boy I can't decide between Rickard and Michael. Let's see . . . Rickard de Burgh . . . Michael de Burgh."

"I like Rickard," he said definitely.

"I like Michael," she announced.

"Naturally, and if I'd said Michael, you would have said Rickard!" he pointed out.

"I think it will be a girl. What was that name you said you liked?"

He kissed her ear. "If it's a girl it will serve you right. I hope you have a willful little witch just like yourself."

It was over twelve long hours before Jasmine went into hard labor. Falcon was all but forgotten as she went down to the gates of pain in woman's usual way.

Estelle pointed imperiously to the door and he was glad to leave. He couldn't bear to watch Jasmine suffer any longer. Like many a man before him, he swore he would never do this to her again. He played hazard with his men who stayed up all night with him, but he lost at every throw of the dice. He paced the hall, alternately booting stools across the room or kicking the logs in the fireplace impatiently.

Upstairs on the big bed Jasmine bit down on a rolled linen towel to muffle her screams as the dark head of her son forced its way into the world. She was wringing wet with perspiration and was at the limit of her strength. Estelle was visibly relieved that it was almost over. So long as there was no trouble getting the afterbirth and providing no hemorrhaging began, all should be well. She carefully passed the male child to a waiting Meg and his lusty cry echoed to the rafters.

"Holy Mother of Heaven," exclaimed Estelle, "there's another child!"

"I know," Jasmine whispered faintly.

"How long have you known?" Estelle demanded, her nerves stretching to their limit.

"Weeks," Jasmine replied, closing her eyes, then opening them wide as a scream was torn from her pale lips.

De Burgh took the stairs three at a time the moment he heard the child cry out. He threw open the door and filled the chamber with his presence.

"Out!" commanded Estelle.

"To hell with that," he shouted, "I won't be ordered about in my own castle. Is she all right?"

"Get out. I haven't time for male tantrums. If you don't get out I'll have Big Meg throw you out!"

He backed off quickly. Something must be wrong. The child was born, but Jasmine was still screaming. He went out into the tower staircase feeling useless and impotent, and guilt was almost crushing his heart. He ran up to her tower room, tenderly touching items of clothing that belonged to her, each evoking memories so poignant he couldn't breathe. He clenched his fists and shook them at the heavens. "If she dies . . . if you play me such a bastardly trick . . . I'll . . ." He listened intently, but her screaming had stopped. He could hear the baby crying lustily, but he could not hear Jasmine.

He ran down the stairs and went into the chamber again. None dared to stop him this time as he fell on his knees beside the bed. "She's unconscious!" he accused.

Estelle said, "She's asleep, Falcon."

"How do you know?" he demanded.

"Because she is exhausted. It took every last ounce of her strength and mine to bring those into the world."

Big Meg held a naked male child in each arm. Falcon was stunned. "Twins? I have two sons? Jasmine gave me two sons at one time?" He felt dizzy.

"Don't go fainting on me, I have enough de Burgh men to look after," said Estelle, laughing.

"My god, it's a wonder I didn't kill her. Is she really all right?"

"You go and do the bragging and let her do the sleeping. I'm just as amazed as you. She came through this magnificently."

Mountain Ash had never been subjected to such unrestrained rejoicing and celebrating in its history. At the end of twenty-four hours the castle could have been overtaken by its weakest enemy, for there was only one man in residence who was still sober. Falcon was stretched out on the floor beside their bed waiting for Jasmine to waken. When she did finally open her eyes for a few minutes, their hands and eyes met and held. Neither of them needed words to convey their feelings to the other. Finally Jasmine whispered, "Michael and Rickard de Burgh."

He tried unsuccessfully to hide a grin. "You do realize they will inevitably be known as Mick and Rick?"

She smiled contentedly and closed her eyes.

Chapter 36

The arrival of June brought more than twin sons, it also brought messengers to Mountain Ash. Estelle had known visitors would come and one stranger would change all their lives. Strangely, each and every one was associated with Ireland. She told de Burgh and was gratified that he neither lost his temper with her extrasensory perception nor ridiculed it. She mentioned it to Jasmine, but her granddaughter's days were filled with her babies, searching out a wet nurse to help supplement their feedings, and her nights were filled with a husband who was madly in love with her. Their time alone together was all too brief to suit either of them.

If he encountered her in a hallway he would sweep her into his arms for an impassioned embrace until they were interrupted by the intrusion of a servant. Even in the company of others he found he could not keep his hands from her. They touched and burned and exchanged tender, promising looks. Occasionally he had been lucky enough to encounter her in an outbuilding such as the stillroom, and he had barely allowed her time to bar the door before he had undressed her and lifted her onto his demanding manroot. They always made love as if it were for the first time—and the last. The dark splendor of his body contrasted so sharply against her pale silken beauty.

The first people to arrive were William and Mathilda de Braose. They were fleeing from Hay, their magnificent castle on the Welsh border. King John had ordered his mercenaries to arrest them, and they had gotten away only by the skin of their teeth. They had heard rumors that de Burgh had broken with King John and hoped his strong forces would help them against the king.

William was a practical man who did not really expect de Burgh to wage war against his King, but he felt reasonably sure that Mountain Ash would harbor them.

Jasmine made Mathilda rest and provided her with all the things she had been forced to leave behind. They appealed to Estelle to see what she could predict for Mathilda's future, but for some reason Estelle reminded them that de Burgh had forbidden her to practice her witchcraft or dabble in the occult, and under no circumstances would she flaunt the lord's wishes. Mathilda quite understood her position, but Jasmine rolled her eyes ceilingward wondering what maggot had gotten into her grandmother's brain.

Falcon was frank with William de Braose. Mountain Ash would give them sanctuary, but now that the good weather was upon them, he fully expected Chester's men or the king's men—which were virtually the same thing —to ride in any day. Falcon recalled Estelle's mention of Ireland. The de Braoses had a daughter who was married to Walter de Lacey, who held the lordship of Meath in Ireland. Falcon urged William to seek refuge with them.

The next visitor to arrive brought an urgent message from William de Burgh in Ireland. Murphy would have stood out in any crowd. He was de Burgh's top captain, probably well past his prime in years, although no one would have dared suggest such a thing. He stood six-foot-four with flaming red hair, now streaked with silver. He had a craggy face and a thick accent. Falcon and Jasmine could make out what he said if they listened closely, but the Welsh were totally baffled each time he opened his mouth. He had sailed from Wexford in one of many de Burgh vessels that were now anchored in Swansea Bay about twenty miles away.

Jasmine was totally bemused by Murphy. She had never seen anyone who fit the description of an ogre quite so well, bringing to life for her the mythical figure of tales told her in childhood, yet he was so gentle it was comical. Her heart was in her throat when he picked up her babies and cooed and sang to them, for he held them both in one gigantic arm.

Falcon closeted himself with Murphy to read the messages his uncle had sent him, but also to pick his brains. He plied him with Welsh liquor, the strongest brew Falcon had ever tasted, yet it went down Murphy's throat as if it were water.

Falcon broke the seal on the thick, white parchment and read:

My trusted Captain Murphy brings greetings to
Falcon de Burgh, son of my beloved brother, God
rest his soul. I have recourse to ask your aid, but
first I must make plain my position. As you know I
was Steward to Henry II and as favor for good service he made me the Lord of Connaught. Ostensibly
everything west of the River Shannon belongs to the
de Burghs. However, what you may not know is that
I have never been able to conquer the people and live
there. I have always resided in Limerick, and since I
was the chief lord of the region, King John made me
governor.

Two Irish kings have fought each other to be
King of Connaught, and I freely admit to you that
over the years I have joined forces with each to gain
Connaught, changing sides like I would change my
coat. I deeply regret that last year with a large force
gathered from Dublin, Leinster, Limerick, and
Munster I joined forces with Cathal Carragh against
Cathal Crovderg until he fled north. Then Carragh
turned against me, assumed nominal kingship, and
harried Connaught ruthlessly into submission. I lost
King John's favor when he decided to be on
Crovderg's side. At this point I changed sides and
marched with Crovderg into Connaught. I killed
Carragh but I sustained a wound. My soldiers were
billeted over three counties of Connaught, namely
Sligo, Mayo, and Roscommon. Rumor swept
through the clans, or tribes as we call them in Ireland, that my wound had killed me, and the tribes
turned on my billeted soldiers as they slept and mas-
sacred nine hundred. What are left of Crovderg's
and my own men are holed up at the fortified
monastery of Boyle. De Burghs by royal decree own

over a fifth of Ireland, but only with your aid will
my sons and your sons rule this vast palatinate.

William de Burgh
Lord of Connaught

Falcon measured Murphy another drink and joined
him. "Tell me of William. What manner of man is he?"

Murphy scratched his head. "What is there to tell?
He's a fierce warrior who has fought all his life. In years
past all that mattered to him was loyalty to the crown.
You were his heir when he had no sons of his own, but
many years after the first Lady de Burgh died, he married
Moira and she gave him his two sons. She's no more than
a young girl still. Now I believe the most important thing
to William is his sons' inheritance. Richard, the eldest, is
barely seven years old. William knows if anything happens the boys will never be able to hold what is rightfully
theirs."

Falcon fixed Murphy with his green crystal eyes. "If
anything happens?" he repeated.

The red-haired giant looked uncomfortable as if he had
been trapped. He got to his feet and did a turn about the
room. Then he came back and faced de Burgh. "Look,
I'm tellin' secrets, an' William would flay the skin offa me
if he knew, but the wound he took was a bad one. He
coughs blood an' I think he sees the writin' on the wall."

Falcon contemplated the great baronies of Ireland.
They covered much more land than those in England and
were indeed palatinates. William Marshal held the lordship of Leinster, Walter de Lacey held Meath, and his
brother Hugh de Lacey held Ulster. Connaught was
greater than any. Never let it be said that Falcon de
Burgh was not an ambitious man. He now had sons of his
own to think of. "My wife's grandmother, Dame Estelle
Winwood, is more clever in treating ailments than any

physician. It is possible she could do something for William."

"You'll come then?" asked Murphy.

"I will consider it," Falcon said bluntly.

Jasmine had a chamber plenished for Murphy and introduced him to Estelle. "I hear your mother is a genius in treatin' a man's aches an' pains. Perhaps she could do somethin' with the misery in me shoulder," he said, rubbing his upper arm.

Estelle's eyes narrowed. "I am her grandmother, not her mother," but she was not displeased with the compliment. "I will bring you a liniment after dinner that dispels rheumatism in the joints."

As Estelle walked away he said with appreciation to Jasmine, "She's a foin figure of a woman!"

Jasmine tried to hide a smile; Murphy must have more guts than a slaughterhouse to tackle Estelle.

After dinner Falcon was amazed that Murphy was still on his feet after all he had imbibed that day. When Estelle took him a pot of her special liniment made from the ground-up root of cuckoopint boiled in oil of roses and mixed into bean flour, Murphy took off his doublet so she could apply it. "That smells too fancy for the loikes of me," he said, winking.

"Well, if you insist, I could mix in some hot ox dung," she threatened. "Sit down, man, I can't reach you."

He did as he was bidden, but he slipped his arm about her waist and pulled her down into his lap.

"Well, I'll be damned," said Estelle. "You don't have a rheumatic complaint at all, do you?" she asked, looking him straight in the eye.

He grinned at her and lowered his voice. "I have an ache elsewhere I bet you could ease."

"Oh, you're a betting man, are you? Well, I wager

you've had so much liquor you can't even get it up!" Estelle said bluntly.

Murphy's grin widened, " 'Tis a bet, my little dearling. If I put it up, will you put it in?"

"You're a cheeky old bugger, Murphy," she said, laughing. "It's so long since it was used, I'm not sure it's really there."

He kissed her ear. "Shall we find out?" he invited.

The next day brought yet another visitor bringing a message. With only a handful of men Salisbury came riding in before sunset. He had news and a request from King John. It could have easily been brought by messenger, but Salisbury himself came because he was anxious to know how his little Jasmine fared. When they last parted she had seemed so unhappy over her marriage to de Burgh.

She was overjoyed to see her father and took him by the hand up to the tower room now used as a nursery. He was a proud grandfather and couldn't get over the fact that Jasmine had borne them. He kept shaking his head and laughing. "Your relationship certainly must have undergone a metamorphosis. Things were strained between you to say the least."

Jasmine smiled her secret smile as Falcon came into the chamber to receive hearty congratulations.

"What happened between you two?" asked Salisbury, shaking his head in disbelief.

"De Burgh in heat was too hard to resist," she said lightly, causing both men to flush.

Closeted with Salisbury, Falcon learned that, in a bold attempt to avert civil war, John's advisers had suggested he take his army to conquer Ireland once and for all. Amazingly most of the barons had agreed to send their men. He had appointed a new justiciar in Ireland to look to the crown's interests in the land—an Irish baron by the name of Meiler fitz Henry.

"John knows your worth as a fighting man, he knows the loyalty your men bear you—envies it, in fact. He is calling on you as one of the Lords of the Welsh Marches to fulfill your military obligations to the crown."

Since Falcon had already decided to go to Ireland to aid William de Burgh, he reasoned that he might as well let John bear the financial burden of transporting his men and their horses. He said, "I'm ready now. All I need is ships. With Hubert de Burgh in charge of the Cinque Ports I don't think that should pose a problem, do you?"

Salisbury sighed with satisfaction. Falcon de Burgh was always so decisive, which is exactly what made him such a great general in battle.

"The navy has ships in Bristol. Don't you want to wait for the departure of the other barons? There's talk of John sailing with the army."

"Wait for John?" Falcon asked, laughing incredulously. "Unlike John I can't waste my life cowering under the bedsheets. It's now or never, providing I'm in charge of when we sail and where we make land. I'll send the ships back for the rest of your army, William."

"I don't think you need worry about Chester any longer. Rumor has it he is to wed soon."

Falcon grinned. "Me? Worry about Chester?"

The two men enjoyed a hearty laugh. "John has finally produced an heir. I left him strutting about like he was the first man to ever sire a son. I'd better not tell him you've even bettered him in that."

Falcon ran his hand down Jasmine's ever-tempting hair as she sat brushing it, then disrobed quickly and stretched himself in the bed. He had something to tell her and wasn't at all sure that she would understand. Never one for evasive words, he came right out with it. "I am going to Ireland."

Her hand stopped in midair holding the brush. She looked at him stretched with his hands behind his dark head. He had not discussed it with her. He had taken the decision himself. She sighed. She couldn't expect a man like de Burgh to seek her council, it would be like asking for her permission. The idea would not occur to him. She approached him clad only in her shift. She was about to ask softly, "When do we leave?" when he imprisoned her wrist and said thickly, "I already miss you!"

"What?" she asked incredulously, her eyes going wide.

"Come to bed, love," he urged.

"Not now! *You* are not going to Ireland; *we* are going to Ireland."

"Don't be silly, Jasmine, think of the danger."

"There is danger if you leave us here. What of Chester?"

"He is to be wed," he said quietly.

"Then John. You know he would like to get his hands on me!" she hissed.

"John needs my aid. You need fear nothing from that quarter," he assured her. "Come to bed. I had in mind a more pleasant pursuit than fighting with you."

She was angry. She flared, "Not now! There's still danger here. What if that whore of yours comes creeping back to murder me and my babes in our beds?"

"Jasmine, that's enough!" he silenced.

She ignored the warning. "You think I'm useless. I made it over those damned Black Mountains through the freezing snow. I learned how to run a castle. I gave you two sons."

"Jasmine, come here to me," he commanded.

She turned her back on him. "You can forget about that, de Burgh. Try sleeping alone!" She slammed the chamber door and ran up to the nursery. Big Meg eyed her silk shift and flushed cheeks.

Jasmine said, "I've decided to sleep up here tonight." No sooner was the declaration out of her mouth than an angry de Burgh strode in, naked as the day he was born.

"Don't ever turn your back and walk out on me again," he ground out.

"Hush, you'll wake the babes," she said.

Meg rolled her eyes as the master picked up the mistress and strode out with her in his powerful arms. He slammed their bedchamber door shut with a kick and set her feet down in front of the fire. Then he pulled her down to the furs and pushed her back into their deep pile. Fierce crystal-green eyes reflecting the flames of the fire challenged her to deny him. "I will send for you when all is secured and safe."

"No!" she spat.

"I will not allow you to pull away from me, to withdraw from me again . . . keeping yourself from me while you grow ever colder and I grow ever hotter!" His eyes burned her with his intent, unblinking, his meaning deliberate. He tore off her shift, possessively feasting on the sight of her rosy breasts in the flickering firelight. He knew she was watching his face, his eyes, his mouth as they worshipped her nudity, and he knew the effect it was having on her as her eyelids half closed. He trapped a nipple between finger and thumb and manipulated it gently, then cupped her breasts with his great scarred hands and brought them to his mouth.

Her arms slid about his neck and she clasped him to her, opening her thighs. He slid into her hot sheath, filling her completely. Wildly she wrapped her legs about him, tossing her head from side to side on the silvery furs, riding with him to that secret place only the two of them were allowed to go. "I love you," he said hoarsely.

"Take me!" It had a double meaning in that precise moment and he knew he could deny her nothing.

Afterward she lay in his arms in the big bed, whispering between kisses. "All you need do is sail straight to Connaught, secure a castle for us, then fight your way through to William at Boyle. If you can't do that in short order, I'll know you for a weak-livered, ass-eared lout." She was almost childlike in her trust and confidence in his abilities.

He kissed her again and murmured, "You have an uncommon knowledge of my business, madame."

"You forget I am a witch," she teased him with her tongue.

"Did you say bitch?" he asked, his mouth sliding down to taste her luscious breasts. His lips traced down her stomach and drifted between her legs. As his cheek rested against her soft thigh, he asked her to show him the place she liked to be touched. He captured her hand, kissed each finger, then ran his tongue across her palm. He guided her first finger to the insistent hot pulsing between her legs.

"Here?" he whispered, allowing her fingertip to touch the swollen pink flesh. "Here?" he asked huskily, moving her finger to touch the erect bud of her womanhood.

When she gasped "Please, Falcon," he smiled knowingly and raised her hand back to his mouth. He sucked the sweetness from her fingertips then took her fiercely a second time. Then he enfolded her in his arms with her back against him so he could fall asleep holding her breast as he always did.

Falcon sealed his message to William de Burgh, and Murphy was on his way. William and Mathilda de Braose decided to sail with Murphy to Meath where their son-in-law Walter de Lacey ruled, and which would bring Murphy closer to Boyle.

While the ships were being brought from Bristol, Falcon pored over his maps of Ireland. He was a direct man who chose a goal and made an unswerving path toward it, and he saw no reason to change his methods in this campaign. Most of the English in Ireland went to Dublin and never ventured beyond The Pale. He would go to the opposite coast. He would sail directly into Galway and secure it. Galway looked to have a magnificent bay. He knew it had a great Norman castle built by the Conqueror in the last century when Galway had been a thriving seaport.

It was also the heart of the de Burgh lands of Connaught. In the week before they sailed he almost despaired that he had promised to take Jasmine, for he realized that wherever she went, the menagerie followed. The twins, their wet nurse, Big Meg, and Estelle he grudgingly agreed to. She had to seduce him, however, into agreeing to take Feather and Prick. When the subject of Shanna arose, he flatly refused, and Jasmine was forced to smuggle the great cat aboard a supply ship under cover of dark. Jasmine would leave nothing behind she valued, for she knew with a deep certainty that their future lay in Ireland, for good or for ill.

Falcon was mildly surprised that his knights and men-at-arms totaled four hundred. No wonder John wanted his service again. Well, he was going to Ireland, but it sure as hell wasn't in the king's cause. It was in de Burgh's cause and would remain so for the rest of his life, he vowed.

The voyage across the Celtic Sea was unremarkable, mainly because by chance they had picked the best month of the summer to sail. Jasmine saw nothing of Falcon during the voyage for his every minute was taken up with his men, their horses, weapons, and supplies, but the last night as they stood at anchor by the Aran Isles awaiting the other ships, he came to her.

Later, she awoke with a start in the narrow bunk to find his hot mouth pressed against her breast. "Is it very late?" she asked guiltily. "I know you wanted an early start."

"You needed the sleep, I fear I kept you awake most of the night." She blushed and watched him leave the berth to dress and don his armor. Suddenly tears choked her throat. She wanted to hold him so tightly that he would never leave her, but she knew he would hate her tears. She would never cling to him to weaken his resolve. He came to the bed now and sat on the edge, his face hard. She sat up, unmindful of her nakedness in the intensity of the parting.

"You'll stay aboard until all is safe, even if it takes a month!" he commanded. "The captain has his orders to take you back out into safe waters as soon as we're landed."

She searched his face. The only fear she saw there was for her. Suddenly he grinned. "Give me a kiss to spur me on."

"Haven't you had enough?" she asked tremulously.

"Never," he whispered against her mouth.

He stood and she pulled up the furs to cover herself. "No," he protested, "let me carry a picture of you in all your loveliness."

Chapter 37

The de Burgh army swept up from the shores of Galway taking all before them in few battles and with fewer injuries. Falcon couldn't have done it with undisciplined men. De Burgh wanted no burned castles, ruined crops, raped women, or looted towns. These people were going to be his people. It was a matter of leadership.

By the second day he was in possession of Galway Castle; those of Carragh's men who had been left to hold it were dispatched without hesitation, and the Irish kerns, servants, and cooks were given a choice of serving or dying.

Falcon de Burgh stood alone on the ramparts marveling at the heartstopping beauty of the land—the pink dawns and lavender dusks, the lushest green meadows he'd ever seen, which couldn't just be a trick of the light. He looked down at the rugged coast behind him and the sound of the waves almost emptied his head. He had a sense of oneness with the land, a feeling of coming home. Connaught was a place to have and to hold forever, like the right woman, like Jasmine.

He looked off across the rolling hills and meadows. They should be dotted with sheep and filled with rich, milky herds. He'd see to it. He could travel for a week and still be on de Burgh land. Connaught . . . he'd make it a world apart or die in the attempt!

Falcon safely ensconced Jasmine and the twins in the castle and put a twenty-four-hour guard around its walls. He gave the Irish their freedom in exchange for their parole. He wanted them to think they were trusted because it gave a man self-esteem to be on an honor system. Of course he didn't trust them, not yet. Not when tribes were capable of rising in the night to murder those who slept beneath their roof.

Galway was a sizable port, though very poor at the moment. Tiny fishing vessels eked out a living, but the trading ships of the O'Malleys of adjacent Connemara had stopped sailing into Galway because its people were now too poor to buy or barter goods. The town's former prosperity could be seen by the cobblestone streets lined by neat stone cottages and taverns, which, for the most part, had closed long ago.

De Burgh men now swaggered through the streets, their authority undisputed, their spirits high with the adventure of conquering a new land. The people of Galway were surprised when the castle did not take what it needed, but offered to buy with good coin their catches of fish and fresh hay cut from the fields.

An enterprising couple with a millwheel began to grind wheat and barley to provide the castle with flour. Flax that hadn't been picked in years was gathered and spun into linen for the refined ladies who lived at Castle Galway. Daily, Falcon sent out hunting parties into the woods and forests where deer and game were abundant.

The Irish peasants had taken only rabbits and hares that could be caught with crude snares; larger game had been ignored for lack of weapons to hunt them. His horses were growing sleek on the sweet green clover, and de Burgh knew he could delay no longer the campaign that would take them up through Roscommon to Boyle where William and his decimated army had taken refuge. He hand-picked a score of his best men to leave behind in Galway; he wanted no surprises on his return.

Falcon took Tam aside and spoke to him privately.

"I want you to guard Jasmine while I'm gone. If I don't return or get a message through to you within a month, get her back under Salisbury's protection."

Tam grinned. "I wager you'll be back in half that time."

Falcon's face was grim and serious. "I hope I haven't picked the wrong man to guard Jasmine. She can be a little bitch and won't hesitate to wrap you around her little finger to get her own way. I want you to become her shadow. Don't let her get farther away from you than a tall man's pissing distance," he warned.

He also warned Jasmine severely before he departed.

"Play Tam no tricks. My men will give their lives to keep you safe for me." He had pledged his sword to William de Burgh, so to be certain they would get through to Boyle he would take half his men overland. The rest, under Montgomery, would sail up the River Shannon. This necessitated sailing south from Galway to the mouth of the river and following it all the way to Boyle. Though the overland route was shorter, it was by far the more dangerous.

If Falcon was not at Boyle Monastery first, something must have gone wrong, and Montgomery had orders to get William and his men aboard and sail back to Galway, which was comparatively safe.

In full armor astride their great war-horses, de Burgh's fighting men met only token resistance, which they overcame with a minimum of bloodshed. The only fierce battle they fought was in a narrow pass in the woods when they were within a half-day's ride of their destination. When their attackers saw the mettle of the men they were attempting to kill, they fled in boats across the Lough Gara.

Montgomery encountered clear sailing until the River Shannon narrowed at Athlone before opening up into the waters of Lough Ree. There John de Courcy's knights challenged them, but when he learned they were de Burgh men sailing on King John's ships, he grudgingly let them pass without incident.

When Falcon de Burgh's two hundred clattered into the courtyard of the fortress of Boyle Monastery, he was greeted by a man in his own exact image but who was twice his age. William de Burgh, powerfully built with the majestic pride of a lion glittering from his crystal-green eyes, welcomed his nephew with frank relief. His pallor was the only indication that he was not enjoying the best of health. Murphy stood at his right hand. He was enough to frighten anyone to death who didn't know him, Falcon thought wryly.

William introduced him to Crovderg, self-styled king, and Falcon could not help an instant dislike for the man. Though Crovderg's face was impassive, it was obvious the dislike was mutual. De Burgh and Crovderg had a hundred soldiers left between them, and Falcon estimated they could have fought their way out if they had been resolute enough and had a strong enough leader.

"How did you come? Were your losses great? Did you meet with much resistance?" asked William.

"So many questions." Falcon laughed softly. "We sailed into Galway and took the castle. I brought half my force overland, the other half is sailing up the Shannon. There was no resistance to speak of."

At this, Crovderg's dislike turned to hatred. Young de Burgh's disregard for danger seemed nothing short of contempt. The young fool had no sense of caution. He was nonchalant to the point of insolence.

Crovderg said, "You would do well to fear your enemies. In a new land you don't even know who they are."

De Burgh knew that fear in front of your men was a disastrous, fatal emotion. No wonder they had been holed up here like rats. He shrugged and answered Crovderg, "Caution comes in the planning. Once you are committed you succeed or fail by the strength of your determination and your sword arm."

William de Burgh longed to be as young again as the man who faced him with all the untamed strength and incaution. The young man had offered his sword without reservation, and in that moment William loved him.

Perhaps it was because the Irish soldiers had been caged so long at Boyle, or perhaps it was a natural antipathy that existed between the Anglo-Normans and Crovderg's men, but they constantly rubbed each other's nerves raw, and fistfights were common. William de

Burgh and Captain Murphy acknowledged Falcon now commanded all, but this did not suit Crovderg and his men, who were undisciplined and almost impossible to control.

The monks at the monastery of Boyle brewed an Irish liquor called poteen that was one of the strongest drinks Falcon had ever tasted. He warned Gervase to see that the men used it in moderation. He chafed at having to wait for Montgomery's ships to arrive. Falcon arose early, as he had done all his life, and for the second morning in a row he was offended by what he saw. The Irish and even some of his own men were sleeping off a heavy drinking bout. The place stank from an occasional pool of vomit and the odd places men had urinated.

De Burgh approached the offending men and put his boots into a soldier's ribs. When he had the attention of all, including Crovderg and his captain, he hooked his thumbs into his belt and said with deliberate contempt, "I see we have a drinking problem."

Crovderg's captain sneered. "We drink, we get drunk, we fall down. No problem."

The contempt in Falcon's eyes changed to amusement. He looked from Crovderg to the captain and asked pleasantly, "Which one of you will be their champion?" Both men were built like bulls with thick necks and massive chests, yet de Burgh knew Crovderg would let his man do his dirty work for him. He was relying on the man's natural Irish belligerence as he grinned and invited, "Would you like to get your hands on me?" He stripped off his shirt and his big, scarred hands knotted into fists. He feinted with his right hand and as his opponent tried to parry the blow de Burgh's left fist smashed into his ribs.

"Yer soft from drink," de Burgh taunted as his opponent lashed out at the dark, handsome face. Falcon ducked and drove in a succession of hammering blows to the gut and ribs.

The raging bull flung himself on de Burgh and hit him in the face, splitting his cheek below the high bone in the same place he wore Jasmine's scar. The captain was no mean opponent, and the two men rolled over the stones, marking them with blood as they struggled for mastery, exchanging terrible punishing blows. Then de Burgh was astride him and smashed his driving fist into the captain's jaw. The captain's great bulk helped heave de Burgh off and he managed to find his feet. Falcon knew the man was finished—he swayed with eyes swollen closed while de Burgh mercilessly hammered his face until he crashed over backward and lay still.

Falcon breathed hard and wiped the dripping blood from his face with swollen fists. He looked at the faces gathered about. "If there is any man who does not wish to obey me, let him speak now. We are de Burghs and you'll have to try to live up to the name."

William's men were impressed and gave him their instant loyalty. Crovderg's men were filled with sullen hatred.

"Now, lads, let's clean up this dung heap," Falcon exclaimed.

When Montgomery arrived and reported clear sailing, Falcon decided to send William and his men back down the River Shannon by ship. William eagerly agreed and decided the time was ripe to stop and get Moira and his young sons from Limerick. Falcon decided to accompany him and put Gervase in charge of the men returning overland. He scribbled a quick note to Jasmine telling her to prepare for William, the Lord of Connaught, who would be arriving with his young wife and sons to establish their residence at Galway Castle.

Falcon was glad he had chosen to sail down the beauti-

ful River Shannon, for halfway down, at a spot called
Portumna, he found a place that captured his heart and
his imagination. For him magic danced in the air. Just
there upon that cliff with a wide view he would build his
castle and upon these lush fields he would graze his own
horseflesh. From its gray stone tower he would be able to
see the whole of magnificent Lough Derg, which must
stretch for twenty or thirty miles.

Leaning on the ship's rail with William, Falcon spoke
of his future vision for Portumna. William waved his
hand magnanimously. "Do it, lad . . . do it before it's
too late, like it is for me. Build your castle; build fifty
castles!"

Falcon looked down the centuries in that moment. "I
will," he said with conviction. "The de Burgh dynasty
will encompass Connaught with strongholds along the
whole border to keep the rest of the world out. What we
don't finish, our sons will. What they don't finish, our
grandsons will."

William knew his sons' legacy would be safe with this
man, and he felt a great peace of mind descend upon him.
With eyes twinkling, he said, "If you spend all your
money on Connaught, you'll have no gold for your sons."

Falcon laughed softly. "My sons will have a stronger
heritage than gold. They'll get their own gold and be
better men for it."

Crovderg and his men decided to part forces with the
de Burghs. At that, Falcon heaved a hearty sigh of relief.
The seeds he had sown had apparently fallen on fertile
soil and sprouted, as he intended they should. He had
told Crovderg that King John himself would be arriving
in Leinster soon, most likely at its capital, Dublin, with a
sizable army from all his barons. Since Crovderg had no
chance in Hades of defeating John, he must join forces
with him.

* * *

Falcon was surprised by the soft-spoken Moira with her freckles and sandy hair. God's breath, she'd never attract him in a million years, but he conceded she had done well by William in breeding him a pair of proud, dark-headed de Burghs worthy of their birthright. Though only eight and nine, they were a sore trial to their mother as they ran from one escapade to another, fearlessly climbing the ship's rigging, then disappearing belowdecks to scramble about between the murderous hooves of the great war-horses.

They immediately adopted Falcon as their model hero and imitated his speech, his walk, and his mannerisms.

No trouble was encountered until late at night when they were sailing past Castle Bunratty in the Shannon estuary. Suddenly the first ship was assailed by flaming arrows dipped in pitch. Falcon ordered his ship to weigh anchor. Fifty of his knights disembarked with their horses and he ordered the ships to proceed. He would join them at Galway only after he had taken the castle. He was furious. Bunratty was a Connaught stronghold, and he already thought of Connaught as his.

Falcon took the offensive—he knew no other way to fight—and within half an hour his fifty knights were inside the castle's curtain wall. Falcon's horse scattered the coals of the fire used to set their arrows aflame and he felt the soft thud of a body as it fell away from the stallion's hoofs. All was in confusion as men ran about in the darkness. The surprise was complete—the enemy neatly penned in the courtyard or trapped high on the ramparts. With unsheathed broadswords and knives, his men rounded up the enemy in the center of the yard and lighted bright torches so they could get a good look at each other.

"I am de Burgh of Connaught. By whose authority do you occupy my castle?" Falcon asked incredulously.

Their leader cursed aloud and spoke up. "Meiler fitz Henry, the justiciar of Ireland."

Falcon's eyes narrowed and his voice became dangerously quiet. "You are damned fortunate we didn't slit your throats and send you back to fitz Henry slung across your saddles."

"We were only passing through—"

"To where?" de Burgh cut off coldly. There was no answer. "If fitz Henry is giving his cronies carte blanche to occupy other men's castles he won't be justiciar long, and you can tell him so." There was an uncomfortable silence then Falcon said, "Well, you'd better get started. You'll have a long walk to Dublin."

His men were grinning from ear to ear. Falcon was going to keep their horses! Fitz Henry's men marched stiffly through the gates to the accompaniment of whistles and jeers.

Falcon left half his men to hold Bunratty and waved the other twenty-five through the gate. They would ride directly north to Galway. As the last torch was doused, he felt his horse plunge sideways as if to avoid a collision, then Falcon felt a sharp stab of pain in his shoulder as he took one of the renegade's steel. Numbness began to spread through his body and he heard the clatter of hooves fade away. He put out his arms to grasp his horse's mane, but felt himself fall into blackness. He opened his eyes to see the anxious face of Gower bending close to pad his wound with moss. Another knight held a flask of poteen to his lips. It tasted raw and burned his throat, but it gave him the strength to mount.

" 'Tis good we're still at Bunratty," said Gower, his face gone pale.

De Burgh shook his head. He couldn't waste his breath on words. "Galway," he said grimly. Gower was appalled. Galway was sixty or seventy miles off.

Before they even reached Crusheen Falcon's shoulder

and arm had begun to throb incessantly. Now he felt light-headed from loss of blood. He gave the stallion his head and they rode another fifteen miles. At Gort he reined in his horse and slid from the saddle. Again the flask was pressed upon him.

"Take it all, sir." He downed the poteen without stopping; it blunted the edge of the pain.

"Send the men ahead to warn my lady." He had difficulty keeping the words from slurring together.

Gower helped him mount slowly, but it took a concentrated effort for him to stay erect in the saddle. Each jolt of his destrier made the pain seem like burning flames. He was too weary to give any more orders. All he asked was enough strength to walk into Galway Castle. He did not want to scare Jasmine by being carried into the fortress feet first.

At Oranmore he had to fight the urge to roll from the saddle to the comfort of the grass. He had begun to feel sick and dizzy with the constant sway of the stallion's stride. Dawn was lighting the sky by the time he dismounted at Galway Castle. Gower supported his sagging body. He was half-unconscious when he felt another steadying hand at his side. His eyes licked over Jasmine wearing a red velvet bedrobe, her beautiful hair tumbling wildly about her shoulders. They had him inside now.

He grinned at Jasmine. "Red is good . . . won't show blood." He sagged against the stone wall and Gervase rushed forward to lift him up to bed. Falcon closed his eyes. He was safe. His love would tend his wound.

Chapter 38

The lump in Jasmine's throat almost choked her. Falcon looked so young and vulnerable lying in the wide bed. By this time her own knowledge of herbal medicine equaled Estelle's, and she insisted upon nursing him alone, night and day, sleeping only when her weary head fell to his pillow as she knelt at his bedside. However, once the danger and the fever were passed, she gave him a wide berth, allowing William, Gervase, and even Murphy to entertain him through the days of convalescence.

Finally he would be denied no longer and dispatched Gervase with a curt message. He found her in the nursery playing with the twins. "My lady, Falcon is most unhappy; he demands that you attend him."

She bit her lips, picked up her skirts, and followed the faithful squire.

"Well, sir, I hear you are doing what you do best."

He raised a questioning brow.

"Issuing orders," she supplied coolly.

Falcon nodded toward the door and Gervase left them alone. "Jasmine, why are you avoiding me? What have I done to offend you?"

"The children need my attention. I am a busy woman. I haven't time to indulge you, so I leave the entertaining up to others," she said lightly.

He looked hurt. "Come here to me," he said quietly.

Almost reluctantly she went to stand beside the bed. An amazingly strong hand pulled her down to sit on its edge. "Look at me, Jasmine."

Slowly she lifted her eyes to his, but her throat ached too much to even speak.

"There has been too much between us—love, hate, call

it what you will—this violent feeling that has been between us since we laid eyes on each other, so please don't ask me to believe this pretended indifference."

She broke down then, all her tears and fears came pouring out. Withdrawal was her coping device. If she remained a cool distance from him, perhaps she would be able to bear the fear of separation, the threat of injury, the punishment of his death.

He held her against his tightly bandaged chest and tenderly stroked her hair as she sobbed out her fears. His voice could be very beautiful without the hard edge he used to bark out orders. He said softly, "You let Feather fly in the garden regardless of the ravens and hawks that could pick him off at any time." His thumbs brushed the tears from her cheeks. "And I see you have freed Shanna into the forest."

For a moment she thought he was changing the subject and defended her actions. "It would be cruel to cage them. They are wild and their lives would be unbearable if they were not free. I never want them to be fully tamed. They will come and go as they please, and if their lives are shortened by a natural enemy, then so be it."

"Exactly," he said.

She stared at him through tear-drenched eyes.

"We must live life to the full, Jasmine. Every minute of it."

Laughter bubbled up through her tears. "You mean you are too wild to cage and tame, Falcon de Burgh!"

"Exactly!" he said, pulling her on top of him.

"See? This is one of the reasons I kept my distance. Your lust knows no bounds. You'll open up your wound again."

"You know there are other ways, other things we can do," he tempted.

"And you know you won't be satisfied with those things." She added, blushing, "and neither will I."

He had her breasts freed now. "If I can't satisfy you, then I deserve to die," he said between kisses. "Come to bed. How many women can boast they killed their husbands with the act of love?"

"Falcon!" she protested, on the brink of surrender. He threw back the covers to prove his readiness for her. "Come and ride me," he invited.

"You're not strong enough."

"I'm stronger than you," he challenged, and she felt weak all over.

"You'll hurt yourself," she half-protested.

"I hurt already!" His shaft was erect and pulsing wildly and when he whispered, "Heal me!" she was lost.

Estelle confided to Falcon and Jasmine that William de Burgh would not recover. Occasionally he hemorrhaged from the mouth, and no matter what she did for the complaint, the plain fact was that he had perhaps a year to live.

Over the summer months more and more of William's men who had escaped the massacre arrived at Galway. As the Irish began to accept the de Burghs, Falcon offered to train them as part of his standing army. At a gathering that consisted of all the castle people and most of the town's inhabitants, he stood before all and told them, "You have fought England and poverty and each other until you've almost bled yourselves to death. All that is in the past. I intend to make us strong. Totally impregnable. In England we have walled cities. We are going to build a wall around the town of Galway."

There was a loud cheer. He held up his hands for silence. "After that, I'm going to build a defense system of castles around the whole of Connaught. I will fight to our last drop of blood to keep Connaught safe, but we will have to live together in peace."

His voice was again drowned out by cheering. "I intend to make us rich in sheep, cattle, and horseflesh." He grinned. "We de Burghs are raiders from way back." He knew they were instinctively clannish, so he'd make a clan of them. "You are every last one a de Burgh."

He marveled that it had taken so short a time to win them over, and he really had Jasmine to thank for it. He chuckled to himself. They really believed her to be a faerie woman, a faerie princess. The Irish children had seen her riding her "unicorn" and the whispers had started. Sparrows flew from the trees to sit on her golden head and mountain lions came out of the forest to feed from her hand. Some swore that she could fly, that they had seen it with their own eyes. How in Hellfire that rumor began he didn't know, but he suspected it was a new filmy robe she'd had fashioned with what looked like butterfly wings for sleeves. She and Estelle had been willing to tend any ailing children, and soon the women began asking for potions and spells and had been fascinated by her crystal ball and magic rituals. They were a people who believed in wood nymphs, water sprites, faeries, and banshees, and they took Jasmine to their hearts.

He gave himself no credit, but in reality he, too, had earned their respect. He paid attention to their children. If he saw a little girl, he picked her a flower. If he saw a lad, he reached into his doublet for a coin. He was interested in everything and everyone, and talked with them at their work. Shepherds, farmers, fisherman, weavers . . . he was curious and asked them all questions and was quick to understand their answers.

Falcon was always accessible. He listened and acted fairly when asked for justice. When he looked at a cow or a horse, he touched it and examined it intently. He touched the children's heads, tousling their hair, giving them sweets. He cared deeply about his own family. More and more often he was seen laughing in the gardens with a son on each shoulder. He was deeply in love with his lady and not ashamed to sweep her into his arms at the least provocation.

In England King John had finally seen the wisdom of capitulating to the church and accepted Stephen Langton as the Archbishop of Canterbury.

John came to Ireland with his barons, but the action was far removed from Connaught, and after long months he soon tired of Ireland and returned to England. Sometimes it seemed that his only spur for coming at all was to take his revenge upon Mathilda de Braose. No matter where she fled, he had followed ruthlessly. He had ordered her son-in-law to turn her over to the crown. When Walter de Lacey refused, he took the lordship of Meath away from him and gave it to John de Grey, a crony of Meiler fitz Henry.

Mathilda and her son tried to flee to Scotland but they were finally captured. Then King John committed the act that was the straw that broke the camel's back. He starved Mathilda de Braose and her son to death in the dungeons of Windsor Castle.

The barons had stood for enough. They met secretly at Bury St. Edmunds and took an oath before the altar to insist John renew the Charter of Henry I and return to the old laws of the land, or they would consider declaring war.

In Ireland the barons had problems of their own. On the strength of his office as justiciar, Meiler fitz Henry was aggrieving the magnates of Ireland and despoiling them of their rightful castles and lands. He took the whole of Cork and made grants to his favorites, ignoring the seignory of heirs of original grantees. Hugh de Lacey's lands were swallowed up, then John de Courcy's. The de Burghs decided Meiler fitz Henry's men were coming too close to Connaught for comfort—they were taking everything east of the Shannon. From the castle in

Galway, de Burgh mounted raids, devastating the castles acquired by fitz Henry and his allies. They also sent a formal protest to King John.

Fitz Henry's men cared nothing for the Irish people. They even plundered their churches because they had learned the Irish stored everything there, from their wealth to their crops and livestock. When fitz Henry seized Offaly in Leinster and Fircal in Meath, it was too much for William, the Marshal of England, because Leinster was his. He got permission from John to go to Ireland to see to his lands, but only after giving John his younger son Richard as hostage.

De Burgh and William Marshal joined their forces. Their army of about two thousand English and Irish fought pitched battles all that winter. Finally King John ordered de Burgh, William Marshal, and Meiler fitz Henry to cease all hostilities and to come to England where he would appoint a special commission to determine the cross complaints.

William de Burgh and Falcon stood in the vast armory at Galway Castle where the weapons had been brought. They would be cleaned, sharpened, and polished ready for future battles. Falcon said, "If you wish me to go to England in your stead, William, I am ready to do so."

"It was me the king summoned. I'll not give him the satisfaction of pleading ill health."

Falcon frowned, knowing the rigors of facing the king and his commission would take their toll. William laughed shortly. "I've felt so useless all winter with you fighting my battles for me. I intend to fight this one myself, aye, and I intend to win. I pledge you I'll return with seisin to more land and castles than we have now. I have nothing to lose, Falcon, and everything to gain for my sons. God grant me time."

Falcon advised, "I think you should take Estelle with

you. Since she has been treating your complaint you have seemed stronger."

William's eyes twinkled. "I'll bribe her by taking along Murphy." Then he became serious. "Get your castle built at Portumna. I'll leave you my ships so you can build up trade with the O'Malleys. I'll send the ship I take to England back filled to the gunwales with things we're short of here."

That night Falcon had the rare pleasure of helping Jasmine put the twins to bed. He laughed as they managed to drench both their mother and father with their bath water. "By the Rood, these little demons are all de Burgh. How did so fair a damsel produce two sons with hair as blue-black as a raven's wing?"

"They may look like you, but they have my intelligence," she teased. "Do you realize that walking and talking at one year is something of a phenomenon?"

"I thought they'd be riding by now! I have a pair of ponies picked out in the stables." He thought she'd protest with a protective shriek, but she said, "They will be riding before their next birthday."

He whispered into her ear, "May I watch you feed them?"

She gave him a hard push. "Dolt! They drink from a cup now. Would you keep them babies forever?"

Rickard reached up his arms and gave his mother a sweet kiss. Mick punched her. They left them with Big Meg, the only person who could handle them both at once.

"Double trouble," murmured Falcon, slipping his arm about Jasmine as they walked to their own chamber. "Tomorrow we start to build the castle at Portumna. It's for them really."

Jasmine raised her eyes to his face. "They have so

much more here than they would have had in Wales. Falcon, tell me how you go about building a castle."

He warmed to his subject as he insisted on undressing her, kissing each silken part of her body as he bared it. "First you build the stone tower, a simple strong donjon, then add a strong curtain wall. You build it on natural defenses—a cliff with a wide view. From our tower we'll be able to see the whole lake or lough, as they say here. The ground floor will be for storage, then the first floor will be upstairs. We'll have the hall and kitchens and a room where the guards will sleep at night, as well as chambers for the servants and retainers.

"Our chambers will be up on the second floor, and of course we will have murder holes to throw down rocks or scalding water on our enemies. Would you like a chapel up there too?"

She wrinkled her nose. "I'd much rather have a bathing room and one for the children. I've already begun painting tiles with flowers and animals and elves and rhymes. All the children of Portumna for generations will learn to read from my tiles."

He pulled her against him. "This land does that to you . . . makes you think of your children's children, and their children."

"Did you know that those vine scrolls over the window arches were done by an old stonemason who's still alive? He lives in a cottage down by the river. Can I have vine scrolls around all my embrasures?"

"You can have anything you want, my darling. All I ask in return is that you . . ." He bent and whispered his request into her ear. She slapped him and pulled his hair and he tumbled her to the bed, rolling over and over like two children playing. Finally he lay back and held her high above him with his strong hands at her waist. Deliberately she reached down to close her fingers about his long, hard shaft. He gasped at the deep pleasure she always brought him. She traced the tip of his lance up her belly, then encircled her navel. She drew him up further so she could rub him around each breast, then finally she dipped one of her nipples in the tiny opening at the end of his shaft.

He groaned and rolled with her until she was beneath him. He straddled her, pinning her to the bed with his thighs, and held her wrists captive over her head. Then he captured her nipple in his mouth and tongued it unmercifully until she writhed beneath him. She could feel the prod of his manhood against her soft thigh. She needed it to fill her, so she arched up, opening her legs wide to speed his entrance. When he thrust himself to the hilt, she locked her legs across his back and closed her sugared walls upon him tightly so that he could not begin moving in and out yet. She knew that would draw his mouth from her nipple to fuse with her mouth.

His tongue began to ravish her slowly and only then did she stop squeezing down on his marble-hard shaft, allowing him to plunge and withdraw in the exact same rhythm he had set with his tongue.

"Faster," she begged, but he knew that the slow hard strokes would sustain their bliss for a long time, drawing out their passion as it built up and up, ever higher, ever stronger. He knew when their climax came it would be an explosive hard bang, followed by perhaps twenty delicious orgasmic spasms each smaller than the last until they faded away, leaving only the feel of their pulses inside each other. The feeling of total satiety and satisfaction was overwhelming.

When they were building the outbuildings at Portumna inside the castle court or "bawn," Falcon got a wonderful idea for Bunratty. Inside the bawn here were to be a dairy, granary, larder, stables, byres, and blacksmiths. Bunratty was built on the Shannon estuary. Why not build a boat dock to allow their ships to sail right inside the bawn? He divided his time between the castles, and Jasmine was content to let him go, thankful he was not going out on raids from which he might return feet first.

Falcon was at Bunratty when the ship William had sent back to Ireland arrived. It was a hot summer day, and he and Gervase had been lifting hefty stones into place along the seawall they had built inside the bawn. They were both grimy, their bared chests sweat-streaked and tanned a dark brown. Now they would have a chance to see if it was practical to dock the great vessel right inside the bawn, close against the castle wall. He knew his men would welcome a break from hauling heavy stones. Even though unloading a ship was no lightweight chore, curiosity to see what goods had been brought and to hear the latest news from England drew the men to the ship like a lodestone.

After much jostling and shouting and free advice offered from every man at Bunratty, the vessel was docked successfully and her sails furled. Falcon grinned as he inspected the varied selection of goods the ship had brought. No doubt Murphy had been responsible for sending new armor, weapons, and saddles for the horses, and Estelle had sent back velvets, furs, and woolens, which were available in England in much greater supply.

The grin was wiped from his face as he saw a small figure standing hesitantly in the stern. Though she held her head proudly, she did not approach him until he beckoned her. Morganna held a girl child to her protectively, knowing the picture of adversity she created. Gervase's mouth tightened with anger as he strode away to give de Burgh privacy.

"Was it necessary to follow me to Ireland?" Falcon demanded.

"If there had been no need, I would never have swallowed my pride and come begging."

"I gave you gold," he reminded her.

She saw clearly that she did not tempt him. She would bide her time. She must gain his permission to stay; that would be sufficient for the present. "My gold was stolen from me," she lied. She held up her rigid hand and said bitterly, "I cannot defend myself the way I once did." The babe began to whimper. "I ask only a roof over our heads," she said proudly.

Finally he nodded his consent. "Cause no trouble," he warned her flatly as she slipped past him and went into the Castle of Bunratty. He turned to find Gervase at his shoulder.

"The brat could be mine or any other man's at Mountain Ash," he told de Burgh, thinking the girl was blackmailing him.

Falcon said, "She had more good sense than to claim the child was mine, Gervase."

"Then why let her stay?" he asked, thinking of Jasmine who was so very dear to him.

De Burgh shook his head and murmured, "It is hard for a woman with a child and no man. It is of little consequence. We have so much."

Chapter 39

They heard no news of how William de Burgh fared before the commissioners, but rumblings of the king and his English barons were rife. If rumor was to be believed, an army of over two thousand had been assembled at Stamford in Lincolnshire by John's northern barons and was prepared to move against him in war if he would not meet their demands. Finally in mid-June they trapped him on an island in the River Thames called Runnymeade and forced him to sign a document they called the Great Charter.

The Archbishop of Canterbury, the barons, and their learned clerics spent twelve days adding on clauses. John signed only because it was expedient to do so. He had no real intention of keeping it, and felt he could easily repudiate it by saying it was signed under compulsion.

King John now saw the need to gather all those who were loyal to him. He needed as many friends and allies as he could muster. He was always sure of Hubert de Burgh, the Earl of Chester, and his brother Salisbury. He now needed William Marshal as he had never needed him before. Thinking to please the king, the commissioners deciding the court case between William Marshal and Meiler fitz Henry decided in Meiler's favor. John flew into a rage, overturned their decision, and confirmed the marshal's claims for his hereditary lands in Ireland. He did likewise with William de Burgh, Lord of Connaught. John had the marshal's younger son Richard as hostage for his good behavior, and of course he asked for William de Burgh's sons also. It was an old and common custom and William agreed since his sons would be in the charge of their uncle, Hubert de Burgh, England's justiciar.

William asked for a private audience with John, who granted it on condition he bring Estelle to the castle. Her immediate reaction was to refuse, but after deep meditation she realized that her fate and John's were linked. Their paths ran together and they were not yet done with each other. It was as inevitable as a Greek tragedy.

As she and William waited for their audience, she observed her companion at close quarters. The dankness of their lodgings in London had done William de Burgh's health no good at all. He now had a permanent pallor and in spite of her dosing, lung disease was ravaging him.

She saw death in his face. The sea voyage home would likely do him some good, but it would be temporary.

Her thoughts skipped ahead as she tried to guess John's attitude and his opening gambit. Would he use force or blackmail or persuasion? She was mildly surprised that the king spoke in conciliatory tones.

"Dame Winwood, Estelle, you deserted me in my hour of need. Have you no remorse?" he bantered.

From his life of indulgent hedonism he had become fat, the girth of his belly had expanded alarmingly, and his face was bloated and mottled.

"Allow me to offer congratulations on your son and heir, your majesty," she said.

He beamed with pride at the small sop she threw his way. He is a slimey bastard, Estelle thought. He can see as plainly as I that William is ill, yet he will not offer him a seat. She looked the king directly in the eye and said, "May we sit down, sire?"

"How remiss of me. By all means be seated. We have much to discuss. It seems I too must offer congratulations. My dearest niece Jasmine has produced two sons to carry on the great bloodline of de Burgh." He turned to William. "Would you be kind enough to carry a letter for me to the lady?"

"Of course, sire," William agreed.

John's shrewd eyes saw that de Burgh was dying. "Your nephew, Falcon de Burgh, is a strong, ambitious leader who generates great loyalty in his soldiers. Are you not afraid to place your sons' lands and titles in his keeping?" William had already negotiated with John to have Falcon act as regent Lord of Connaught until his sons were of age.

"I have complete faith in Falcon de Burgh's integrity. He is building his own castle at Portumna, which will go to his sons. We are de Burghs. We do not devour ourselves."

Estelle winced inwardly. William was implying that the Plantagenets had devoured themselves. John smiled thinly and chose not to take offense, which told Estelle that the king wanted something of them.

"I have found from bitter experience that the best way to curb ambition and stop a man from taking land and titles unto himself is to give him his own to worry about," the king said.

Estelle knew John would keep her. Now she saw that he also wanted Jasmine and that he would use her children to get her. Conveniently the king had a map and a scroll on his desk. "Let's see." He pretended to ponder. "Suppose I give Falcon de Burgh the towns of Meelichard, Kilfeakle as well as Portumna . . . and, er . . . the Castle and lands of Askeaton in Limerick near Bunratty, which you told me he had turned into a dock for your ships."

"I am certain your generosity will overwhelm him, sire," replied William.

"Deeded to him and his outright, of course," John said magnanimously. "Same terms as I have with you, William—his sons hostage for proof of loyalty to the crown."

Estelle knew Jasmine, knew that she would never agree. She thought of poor Mathilda de Braose and shuddered.

John's eyes sought out Estelle's. "You are cold, Dame Winwood. How would you like to return to your cozy apartment here at the Palace? It is being held for you exactly as you left it."

She sat before him with hooded eyes. For all the years her daughter had been dead she had harbored a grudge against Salisbury and all other men. Now she let the hard lump of resentment melt away. All men were not created evil. Salisbury, de Burgh, even Murphy were saints when compared to this man before her.

"Estelle, you force me to beg," the king continued.

"The private condition for which you treated me so successfully grows ever worse. I am reduced to the ministrations of Orion," he said as a final inducement. "Will you stay and attend your king?"

She sighed. Whatever happened would be on his head. "So be it," Estelle decided.

Jasmine knelt before a great trunk filled with the most exquisite material. She had haggled with an O'Malley captain who had sailed into Galway just this morning from Morocco. She picked up a length of black silk so fine it was transparent. Half-consciously she became aware of a shadow, a sudden droop of the spirit. Something must be wrong. She stood up and looked out to sea. The clouds cast long fingers on the water. On impulse she ran up to the nursery to check on the boys and heaved a sigh of relief as she saw Rick deliberately push a bowl from the table. It broke into three pieces of crockery awash in bread and milk. Mick's hair was daubed with an unidentifiable substance that had been edible at the start of the meal.

Big Meg said, "He does it a-purpose so I'll bathe him. 'Tis unnatural the way the young imp takes to water."

Jasmine laughed. "I often look between his toes to see if he's growing webs."

Big Meg scowled at Rick who had a tentative finger on another bowl. "An' you, Rickard de Burgh! I'll give your clod of a head a thump against the stone wall if you break any more pots."

He pushed the bowl from the table and gave his mother a beatific smile. Her heart started a wild war dance at the child's resemblance to his father. Falcon was at Portumna trying to get the castle finished. Was this premonition she felt connected with him?

Faintly, from somewhere, something threatened. She was restless as a tigress. She looked down at the black material she still held in her hands. Was its color significant? She closed her eyes and meditated for a moment. She conjured a picture of Falcon so detailed she saw the blue-black shadow of the beard he always had until he shaved. He was well. The danger was not to him.

It was more a threat to the power she had over him. A slight smile curved her lips. She had powers she had not yet even tried on him. She would go to him. She would test her powers. Tam would argue against the thirty-five-mile ride, which wouldn't get her to Portumna until dark had fallen, but Tam was like putty in her fingers.

The Castle of Portumna was impressive even in the dark. It had massive walls with fretted battlements and two high towers guarding the gates. In the daylight she would be able to see its delicately carved arches, but now the things that stood out were black window slits and a great pile of stone that would gradually disappear as the castle was completed.

The only reason they were able to enter the castle at all was that the iron portcullis was not yet in place. Knowing she wished to surprise Falcon, Tam took himself and the horses off to the stables so their late arrival wouldn't rouse the sleeping castle.

Jasmine made her way silently to the battlements. She had brought only one thing with her to Portumna—the length of filmy, black silk that had evoked such disturbing vibrations the moment she touched it. She disrobed quickly and draped the fine-spun silk around her body.

Jasmine looked up to the heavens. The sky was like black velvet strewn with diamonds, and the crescent moon cast a silvery light that bathed everything in mysterious shadows. She raised her arms to the heavens and chanted softly: "Earth and Water, Air and Fire, Wand and Pentacle and Sword. Work ye unto my desire, harken ye unto my word!"

Then Jasmine held out her hands and beckoned.

Falcon came awake with a start. What had disturbed him? He listened but heard nothing, yet he could not roll over and go back to sleep. Something compelled him. The night was still and warm, and its heartstopping beauty beckoned to him. He reached for his chausses and slipped them on, then he stretched his great muscles to rid his body of its lethargy and like a nightstalking beast stole up to the battlements. He blinked, not believing his eyes. Surely that was Jasmine silhouetted against the far battlement? He took long strides toward the vision, sure in the knowledge that no other woman but his had hair the color of moonlight.

When he was close enough to see her naked form through the black wisp of silk he stopped and questioned, "Jassy . . . how did you come to me?"

"I flew on the wings of night," she whispered, adding to the magic of the improbable encounter.

His voice was a caress. "I won't ask how or why, it is enough that you are here." He thought to close the distance between them, but she stepped back into shadow and disappeared, leaving only a trace of silvery laughter upon the still night air. She knew he would follow her. He would even be drawn through fire or water by the magnet of her body.

He had all the advantages, of course. He had designed the castle himself and in his black chausses with his deeply tanned chest, she could not see him. Conversely, Jasmine could not conceal her hair, so it was inevitable that the game was soon over. He came up behind her as she ran across the lawn and scooped her into his arms.

"You chased me until I caught you," she teased.

"That's true. You are a wanton little baggage, Jasmine de Burgh, running about in the night unclothed. I flatter myself that I rid you of your inhibitions, but I don't believe you ever had any. You are a Pagan at heart." He kissed her throat, his lips traveling a fiery path up behind her ear, then his teeth found her earlobe and he gave her a love bite.

"I am a witch," she said simply.

"Nay, witch is an ugly word. You are an enchantress; *my* enchantress. Last night there were herons and swans upon the lake. I longed to share them with you. I wished so hard for you that you have come." He set her feet down in the grass, which was thick as velvet, and drew her hands to his lips.

"You've neglected me shamefully of late. I came because I needed you to tell me you love me."

His mouth found hers. It was deliciously hard and demanding. Between deep kisses he pledged, "I love you, I adore you, I cherish you, I worship you."

She sighed from the very tip of her toes.

"Lie with me beneath the stars," he urged.

She stretched upon the emerald-dark grass and watched him remove his chausses, then he came down to her. The film of black silk separated their bodies, but it acted as an aphrodisiac. It was erotically tantalizing to caress her soft breasts through the silken material until he felt them grow firm in his hands. He drew in a great breath as his lengthening shaft brushed against the seductively slippery silk and their bodies slid together deliciously as he moved upon her. "Jassy, my love is indissoluble."

"Not your love . . . *our* love, our love, my dearest darling." She clung to him as if he were the source of her life's breath, as if this act renewed her. She gave him so much passion and love and life that she needed him to replenish her. She needed his long, hard manroot to fill her emptiness with his own passion and love and life. Their joy in each other was so sharp and intense it was like pain.

After a long time she lay quiet, encircled in his arms as

they gazed at the dark sky. They watched shooting stars and wished upon them.

"At sea the crescent moon can be used to navigate," he told her. "If you fantasize that it is a bow, you will shoot your arrow directly at the sun."

"My fantasies run along different lines," she teased.

He took hold of her fiercely and pinned her beneath him. "Such as?" he demanded.

She traced her finger along the hard line of his jaw. "I always dreamed of a moonlight swim. There are so many things we can dare in the night that we couldn't do in the day with the eyes of the castle looking down on us."

"By God, you are a temptress. I think we were together in Eden." His hand, which had been absently stroking her delicious bottom through the black silk, now plucked away the material and his fingers sought the tight golden curls between her legs. He dipped his head to kiss her there, then sighed, reluctant to leave so pleasurable a diversion. "Come, we'll swim in the moonlight. I only hope I can fulfill all your wishes this easily."

They played in the water like a pair of otters. They teased and taunted and touched. When she kicked him, he kissed her. When he splashed her, she bit him. When he caught her, she pulled his hair.

Howling, he carried her from the water.

"I believe you are ready for more demanding sport, Lady Insatiable," he teased.

He expected her to bolt the moment he put her down, but she stood looking at him with an awed look on her face. "You are magnificent," she whispered. She reached out to feel the great slabs of muscle that stretched the length of his torso from shoulder to hip. His thighs were like marble. She knelt down before him to worship him with her lips, then her hot mouth covered him and he cried out in ecstasy.

By morning they were both respectably dressed and

took breakfast with the men. Falcon smiled down at her as he announced, "You can all take a holiday from the building today. I want to show off to my wife everything we've done here."

Jasmine admired every stone of Portumna that day, never tiring of hearing the enthusiasm in his voice as he explained each and every detail of their future home. It was one of the last glorious days of summer, and they packed a picnic lunch and rowed out upon the lough. They found a secluded grassy bank. After the meal Falcon stretched out with his dark head in her lap, murmuring drowsy love words, revealing secret thoughts and exchanging love promises for the future as the bees droned about them in the hot afternoon sun.

Falcon felt the warmth of her thighs against his face, and the desire flared up in him as strongly as the first time he had seen her. He wanted her and knew she was well aware of it. "By God, madame, did you put an aphrodisiac in the wine? I feel as if I have sipped the philter of a sorceress. Did you use mandrake or wolfsbane?" he teased, showing off his knowledge of herbs.

She smiled her secret smile. "Ah, let me think, did I feed you monkshood or the deadly nightshade with its poisonous black berries?"

"What does that do? Swell the size of my manhood?"

"Well, you don't need anything to swell the size of your head!"

As always their mood of teasing turned deadly serious when they made love, and afterward he couldn't understand her mood as one tear slipped down her lovely cheek. " 'Tis just that this has been one of the happiest days of my life," she tried to explain, which only baffled him further.

That night she clung to him desperately as a violent storm erupted over them when the cold air of autumn clashed with the last of summer's heat. In the morning he kissed her good-bye and promised to return to Galway in another week.

Jasmine had not covered two miles when the shadow returned to her. While she had been with him, Falcon had dispelled completely the vague unease that had taken hold of her. Suddenly she had a burning desire to see Bunratty. Tam groaned aloud his protest when she broached the subject, knowing as he listed the reasons why he should not take her, that in the end Jasmine would ride to Bunratty with him beside her.

Perhaps the threat of danger came from something unsafe about the great dock Falcon had built that brought ships right inside the castle walls. When she saw it, Jasmine could scarce believe her eyes. He had transformed the place as if by magic.

She was very weary from the long ride and frozen to the bone from the chill wind that blew in from the sea. She promised herself to come out later to view it all longer after she had warmed herself inside Bunratty. With Tam close on her heels, she made her way to the kitchen in search of hot food and came face to face with Morganna and her child. In that instant Jasmine's world crumbled. Feeling faint, she willed herself to keep her composure. A voice inside her head screamed. Here is the trouble which threatens. But she was more than a threat; she was a reality. The two women challenged each other with their eyes.

Finally Morganna held up her stiff, crooked hand and spat, "You did this to me. I will bear your curse forever!"

Jasmine said quietly, "You did it to yourself, but if your mind is bent on blaming me, I will remove the curse from you. Bathe it in the waters of the River Shannon at midnight and the stiffness will leave it forever." She knew the affliction was in the girl's mind; any ritual would unfreeze it.

Jasmine moved away from her with regal dignity, although in reality she went blindly, searching out a place where she could be alone. Tam followed her up to a bed-chamber and watched helplessly as she crumpled down in one of the window embrasures, leaning her head against the stones, so cold and weary that she could not think. Her teeth chattered and beneath her drooped eye-lids the shadows of the room swayed like water.

"My lady, I swear to you I did not know she was here," Tam said desperately. "Why did you heal her hand?" he asked in disbelief.

She stared at him for a moment as if she had not heard him, but then she answered. "Because it is not Morganna who I hate!" Suddenly her composure shattered into a million pieces as her heart broke. Tam held her closely for an hour until her sobbing ceased and she had cried herself dry. Then he helped her to bed, covered her with the warm furs, and crept from the chamber.

Chapter 40

When Jasmine rode into Galway Castle the next day, William's ship rode in the harbor. She learned that as soon as he arrived yesterday a messenger had been dis-patched to Falcon, and he was expected any hour now. Jasmine cringed at the thought of seeing him so soon. She hadn't the vaguest idea what she would say—she knew only that she hated him with an intensity that threatened to consume her. Thank God Estelle was back, she would be able to advise her.

In the kitchens she saw Murphy deeply quaffing a large horn of ale. "Ah, it's like an angel crying on my tongue," he said with satisfaction.

"I'm glad you are back safely. Was William successful? How is his health? Where is Estelle?"

"So many questions, my little darlin'. Estelle had to stay behind with the king. She gave me this letter for you."

An icy finger seemed to touch Jasmine. "But she was treating William's health. Did the king force her?" she demanded.

Murphy set down the horn. "Darlin', there's little she can do for William an' he's the first to accept it. John didn't force her outright; she insists her destiny lies with his, an' there's no arguin' with the woman." He shrugged. Then he smiled. "There now, ye've had the bad news, the rest is all wonderful. William was most successful in securing the de Burgh holdings, but I'm sure he'll be wantin' to tell you an' Falcon himself."

She tucked the letter into her belt and went up to the children. They both had the same response. After a quick kiss they both wanted Daddy and couldn't seem to understand why she had dared to come back without him.

She sat down in a large wooden chair and opened Estelle's letter.

My dearest Jasmine,
I have only a moment to pen you a brief warning. The king has granted the de Burghs all they ask and more. In return William has pledged his sons and Falcon must do the same. I know you too well. I fear that, like Mathilda de Braose, you will refuse him. If you refuse, you endanger yourself and Falcon. Not all his pride, nor courage, nor skill with a sword would protect you from the wrath of the King. The children will be perfectly safe with Hugh de Burgh and I shall remain here to guarantee their welfare.

Think long and hard before you do something foolish.

> Your loving grandmother,
> Estelle.

Jasmine rested her head on the back of the chair and
Mick crawled up into her lap. She stroked the black curls
so infinitely precious to her. She thought of the child
Falcon had made with Morganna while she thought his
heart had beat only for her. The ache in her heart was so
heavy she could scarcely endure it. No wonder she had
had a premonition of impending doom. First the woman,
now her children.

She glanced down at Rickard. He had pulled off her
shoe and was wiggling her toes, saying "This little piggy
went to market."

A woman's lot in this world was pain and tears, aching
fear and sacrifice. She hugged Mick fiercely and kissed
his temple. It would not be her sons who were sacrificed,
she vowed. Mick squirmed in her tight embrace until she
put him down. She watched him go, taking his brother
with him. They ignored the toy animals and drums,
much preferring the small wooden swords their father
had made them. They were so like Falcon it took her
breath away. She whispered, "I'll not hand over my sons
as if the king deserves anything he sets his dirty mind to
have!"

Jasmine bathed and changed her clothes. She knew de
Burgh would be arriving at any moment. She must look
her best, for it always gave her confidence. In her wardrobe she pushed aside the whites and pinks, because de
Burgh liked her best when she was soft and feminine. To
face him now she'd choose a bolder color. Her hand hesitated over the black. Perhaps she should wear mourning
for the love that he had killed. In the end she chose defi-

ant red velvet and painted her mouth as boldly scarlet as her gown.

She waited until the men arrived from Portumna and Falcon had been closeted with William for an hour before she interrupted them. By now she knew he would have poured William more than one strong Irish whisky. She could not bear to look at Falcon, but greeted William warmly with a welcoming kiss. "Congratulations, my lord, on your overwhelming success. By all accounts Meiler fitz Henry has been vanquished." She saw his ravaged state of health. "Oh, William, London has taken its toll of you."

He nodded. "It rained every day. The dampness of England is insidious, I'm afraid."

Falcon watched his wife in silence. She had neither spoken to him nor looked at him. Her attitude screamed aloud that something was very wrong between them.

William held out a sealed parchment. "The king entrusted me with a letter for you, Jasmine."

Falcon went black as iron. He snatched up the letter. "How dare he!" he exclaimed with loathing.

She turned glittering, cold eyes upon her husband. "You must be drunk, sir." She held out her hand. "My letter."

The space between them stretched incredibly wide. His mouth was ruthless and hard as he noted she was back to being the ice queen. He tore open the letter to reveal its contents and read aloud with disbelief: "My dearest Jasmine, You need not send your sons if you will come to me in their stead."

High on Falcon's cheekbones spots of red spread like blood. He threw the letter aside and grabbed her, his hands bruising her shoulders. "Holy God, I'd sooner kill you. I'd see you dead first!"

She raised her arms and threw aside his hands. "Surely the decision is mine," she said icily.

Falcon was in a black temper. "Leave us. Seek your room, madame."

She left, but she certainly did not seek her room. Instead she sought out Moira, who was happy that at last her sons would be put into service that would train them for knighthood. They were long past the age of five, when most boys became pages. She could ask for no greater household than that of the boys' uncle, Hubert de Burgh. Perhaps William would send Murphy with them to see to their daily welfare.

Moira asked nothing more than to stay by William's side to the end, no matter how long or how short that time turned out to be.

Jasmine sighed and squeezed Moira's hand. She could not burden the other woman with her own dilemma; she had quite enough with which she must cope. Jasmine climbed the stairs to her chamber and began to remove her clothes from the great wardrobe. She would sleep in the nursery with the children from now on, until it was time to leave, she thought to herself. With that last thought she realized that she had already made her decision.

She would never place her sons in John's hands. She would never separate them from their father. John had made her decision so much easier for her. Instead of disobeying his commands and bringing the wrath of the king down upon the de Burghs, she would simply go to join her grandmother. She shuddered at the thought of the journey back to England for she knew not what she had to face at the end of it. But perhaps with guile and cunning and the blessed help of St. Jude, she would not be forced to submit to him. And if she did have to submit after all, then that was the price she was willing to pay to keep her sons free.

She heard Falcon's booted step on the threshold but kept her back to the door. After he had observed her for a moment, he asked in a deadly quiet tone, "What the hell do you think you are doing?"

"I'm removing my things to the nursery," she said stiffly.

"Jasmine, I'm sorry I acted like a jealous fool over John's letter." Then after a slight pause, he said, "This isn't about that, is it?"

The bedgown she was holding slipped through her fingers as she faced him. "I went to Bunratty . . . I saw your other child."

"I have no other child!" he shouted, his temper stormy.

"I hate you!" she cried vehemently. "Have you any notion how wildly I loved you? I held nothing back, I gave you everything. You have degraded me by forcing me to live a lie."

He saw her mind was made up, no matter how he protested. She had no faith in him whatsoever. Falcon stood silent and proud, his face closed against her. He dismissed the idea of dragging Morganna before her to swear that the child was not his. His honor was at stake! His word was his bond. His whole life was based upon his integrity. When Jasmine came to realize he had kept his marriage vows sacred, he would accept her apology.

Before the week was out William de Burgh took to his bed. He relied on Falcon's judgment regarding his sons' placement. His brother Hubert was in charge of so many castles the decision was a difficult one. As justiciar of England he held all the Cinque Ports plus every castle at every other port on England's southern coast, from Sandwich to Corfe. Falcon thought it best to send William's sons to a castle that was de Burgh personal property rather than one of which Hubert was only warden. So in the end it was decided the boys would go to Castle Rising in Norfolk. It was far enough removed from the political intrigue of London and it was a safe northern haven should France ever carry out her continual threat of an invasion. Indeed, Castle Rising was the place where Falcon would send his own sons, once his delaying tactics were exhausted.

The ship that was to take the boys was being readied, as they must sail before the gales of September made the seas treacherous. Jasmine contemplated telling Gervase her intentions but reluctantly decided against it. His first loyalty would always be to Falcon, and he would feel duty-bound to reveal her intent. Her only difficulty would lie in evading Tam, for he took his duty of guarding her most seriously. She had a twinge of conscience when she thought of the punishment Falcon would mete out to him.

In the end she told only Big Meg and Glynis, the little servant from Wales. Glynis was terrified and begged her to change her mind. "My lady, when he learns what you are planning he will beat you to jelly."

"Most likely," agreed Jasmine, "so be sure to keep my confidence."

Big Meg held her tongue. She knew how much this woman loved her sons and to what degree her heart would ache for them.

"Meg, promise me you will stay with the children until they are past their second birthday. Somehow I will try to return by then." The thought came to her that likely de Burgh would not have her back. "At least I promise to come for a visit."

Getting her things aboard ship was easier than she thought. Since William's condition was rapidly deteriorating, Jasmine offered to take over the task of readying the boys for their journey to England so that Moira would be free to stay at her husband's bedside. Murphy was going with William's sons, and he saw to the horses and dogs they were taking with them, as well as an ever-growing collection of belongings that active young boys decided they could not bear to leave behind.

Falcon's temperament was dark and stormy as the gulf between himself and Jasmine widened. The moment he saw William's sons safely aboard and the ship had weighed anchor, he intended to leave for Portumna and stay there until the castle was finished. And thus three weeks elapsed before he could stand the separation no longer and returned to have it out with his wife. When he discovered that she had left him to return to England, he nearly ran mad.

He questioned all the women over and over. Each put into words her own feelings of why Jasmine had gone— so that her sons could remain free—but their words did not penetrate his brain to make any sense of it. She should have trusted him. Didn't she think him capable of protecting his own sons? The twins were the most precious part of their lives. He would have agreed to the king's demands but never actually complied with sending them as hostages, at least not while they were still babes.

Tam knew enough to keep his distance from de Burgh, and even Gower received his share of de Burgh's black temper.

William died. Because Falcon was kept busy seeing to the details of the burial and comforting Moira as best he could, he couldn't get drunk and stay drunk. Falcon found it difficult to share his feelings with another man, but finally he turned to Gervase and exposed the deep hurt he was feeling. "Why did she go?" he demanded wretchedly.

"The honor Jasmine carries in her heart cannot be explained," said Gervase. "She is a great lady. Can you imagine the courage of a woman who will not betray her sons, even though she faces disaster herself? Falcon, she had a terrible dilemma and acquitted herself with her faultless integrity."

Falcon smashed a fist into his hand. "God's breath, I'm going to go and get her. I'll not let that evil swine besmirch her."

When the de Burgh ship delivered Jasmine to Castle Rising in Norfolk, she was surprised and delighted to find Avisa with Hubert de Burgh.

"Darling, don't look so shocked. We were quietly married a few weeks ago, after Beatrice died. Poor lady had been ill a long time."

Jasmine, wondering wildly if Hubert had killed Geoffrey de Mandeville, was relieved when he read her thoughts and chuckled. "Fellow conveniently died of a fever last year; saved me the trouble of disposing of him!"

As Avisa enfolded her in a welcoming embrace, Jasmine said, "Oh, Avisa, I am so happy for you. It is what you have both wanted for years."

Avisa laughed. "Isn't there an old saying that when the Gods wish to punish us they grant us our wishes? Have a rest from what must have been a wretched voyage and after dinner we'll sit up half the night and gossip."

Jasmine put her hand out to Hubert. "Your brother William's condition is critical. He may even be gone by now, but he wouldn't want you to grieve, he only wants what is best for his sons." Jasmine's young nephews had already galloped off to explore the countryside the moment their mounts and dogs were brought ashore.

At dinner the conversation focused on the Magna Carta that the barons had forced John to sign.

Avisa said, "I don't for one moment think that John intended to honor the document, but the barons are holding him to it."

Hubert, ever the king's advocate, said, "Avisa, you are being ungenerous I think. You do not know John's intent."

She laughed. "I know John. That says it all!"

Jasmine turned to Hubert. "Can you explain the Magna Carta to me in simple terms, my lord? I am woefully ignorant."

"Well, it's more or less a contract. If the king gives his vassals good government, they will give him good service. It's basically an acknowledgment on John's part that the tenants in chief, or barons, have the right as well as the power to call the king to account."

"There! So you know automatically that John hates every word of it!" Avisa put in.

Hubert continued. "Of course whatever the king grants to his barons, they in turn must observe toward the men below them. The Great Charter has some magnificent clauses, which I have had to learn by heart, being justiciar. 'No free man shall be seized or imprisoned or dispossessed or outlawed or banished or in any way injured, nor will we attack him or send against him, except by the legal judgment of his peers or by the law of the land.' "

Avisa teased, "Hugh, stop showing off. You know what these de Burgh men are like! The main points are no taxation unless agreed by council. The church is to be free to have its rights and liberties unhurt as are the ancient customs of the cities to be preserved. No man can be kept in prison without trial, and goods and property can no longer be seized for debts if they can be discharged. Best of all, darling, women finally have some rights. Widows can no longer be forced to marry against their will!"

Hugh winked at Avisa, which prompted her to point out, "If that had always been the law, think of all the time and heartache we could have saved."

"Our love is sweeter for the waiting," Hugh said gallantly.

"Waiting?" Avisa hooted. "I haven't denied you in years. De Burgh men don't take no for an answer." Avisa saw a shadow cross Jasmine's face, and knew there was trouble with Falcon. "Come, darling, let's go upstairs where we can be private and I'll shock you with tales of the court's latest indiscretions."

Upstairs in her chamber, Avisa poured Jasmine a goblet of sweet wine and made her comfortable on a chaise longue. "Life is strange. Once upon a time you thought to serve me as your queen; now we are both Lady de Burgh."

Jasmine's heart was so heavy, she was close to tears.

"Whatever is amiss between you and Falcon?" asked Avisa.

Jasmine shook her head. "He-he was unfaithful," she whispered.

"Is that all?" asked Avisa, laughing at her innocence. "Forgive me, darling. It's simply unimportant to a woman who has had three husbands, married to a man who has had three wives."

Jasmine considered her words. "But, Avisa, being first isn't so important so long as you are his last love."

Avisa was amused. "I don't for one moment delude myself that I will be his last love. I am older than Hugh, so I don't even imagine I'll be his last wife!"

"Oh, Avisa, you make my troubles seem inconsequential."

"Darling, you are in danger of taking yourself seriously, and that can be deadly. What you need is a little flirtation, an amusing little affair, after which you'll be so much more understanding of your poor husband's peccadillos."

Jasmine shuddered slightly as a clear picture of John sprang up in her mind. What must it be like to submit to a man you despised? Pray God, she never had to find out.

"In a couple of days Hugh is taking me back to Gloucester. Why don't you come too? I'll give an entertainment for you and you'll be able to pick and choose a lover from the dozens of men I'll invite.

Jasmine laughed and shook her head. "I must see Estelle and also I wish to petition the king about something."

It was Avisa's turn to shudder. "Well, you'll soon get your chance if you stay here. Actually, that's why I'm leaving. John has been pressing Hugh to accompany him on some secret mission to the Bishop of Lincoln's Castle at Newark and naturally they'll break their journey here."

"Newark Castle is a great stronghold isn't it?" Jasmine asked curiously.

"Aye, and the Bishop of Lincoln is just about the only churchman who has remained loyal to the king through all the trouble. He's the most unlikely bishop who ever was. God must have been appalled the day John appointed him bishop. But come to think of it, God must have been appalled every day at the things John has done," Avisa said wickedly.

"I wonder what he's up to?" mused Jasmine.

"It will be something to do with money for 'tis an obsession with John, along with sex of course." Avisa laughed.

Chapter 41

When they left for Gloucester, Hugh and Avisa took their hundred knights, leaving only the small garrison of men-at-arms who always resided at Castle Rising. They had only been gone twenty-four hours when an urgent demand arrived by king's messenger for Hubert de Burgh.

The castellan exchanged furious words with the king's

messenger, and Lady Jasmine de Burgh was consulted. The young knight had cold eyes and a hard mouth; moreover, he was furious that the justiciar was not in residence. "Madame, the king has traveled from London to Cambridge with only the king's own guard because he could wait no longer for the justiciar. What is the man about?" he demanded angrily.

"The man?" asked Jasmine, taken aback by the young knight's lack of respect. "Sir, you are speaking of England's justiciar. Are you not afraid of incurring his wrath?"

"I am more afraid of the king's," he said bluntly. "In fact, I dare not return and tell him I could not find the justiciar. It is not safe for King John to travel farther north without protection of his army."

"Not safe?" asked Jasmine.

"Madame, it was only last Christmas that an army of two thousand gathered at Stamford ready to move against the king. Have you been hiding under a stone?"

Jasmine laughed prettily. "Since John signed the Great Charter I am sure the army has disbanded. This is October and ten long months have passed since Christmas," she chided.

He flushed and his eyes narrowed. She was insinuating that he was a coward, when he was only following the king's orders.

"The justiciar has been gone less than twenty-four hours. They cannot be much farther than Peterborough. I will send after him. Return to the king and tell him that Lady Jasmine de Burgh awaits him at Castle Rising." She gave him a contemptuous little smile. "I warrant he'll chance the forty miles from Cambridge without his army." She called in the castellan. "See that this man gets some ale and a fresh horse."

Jasmine was restless as a tigress. She took up a warm cloak and went up on the battlements. Castle Rising had an unimpeded view of the wash. She watched in fascination as miles and miles of pale coral sand were swallowed by the tide sweeping in from the North Sea. She nervously licked her lips and tasted the salt air upon them. The gulls and terns swooping overhead screamed with cries that pierced her heart. Why had she come? she asked herself in a panic. She must have been mad! Then she turned to face the wind and it brought a small measure of calm.

She had come to ask King John a boon. She would face a dragon in its cave to allow her sons to remain in Ireland with their father. Aye, and if she was being truthful, she had also come to punish Falcon. She loved him totally and was devastated by his faithlessness. She had run blindly away from him in hope that the separation would make him suffer so much he would value her more. But she realized bleakly that if she was unfaithful to him with the king, he would value her less—in fact, she would be worthless in his eyes.

She sighed. John would be here soon. She would have to face him alone, unprotected. Her only salvation was a small vial of hemlock with which she would render him impotent. She had brought it all the way from Ireland. It was hidden between her breasts and she would keep it on her person at all times.

She went down in search of the castellan to see which apartments he would assign to the king. He showed her into the west wing of Castle Rising where over the years the king had often stayed. It was the only wing that had enough bedrooms to accommodate his gentlemen and servants. She asked the castellan to give Estelle a chamber close to hers in the east wing, then sought out Murphy, who was housed in the tower with his two young de Burgh charges and their servants. The boys had just returned from sword practice in the yard. They were both eager to learn and thought themselves quite fierce now that they finally owned real weapons.

"The king is coming. It's possible he will be arriving as early as tomorrow. You must kneel to him and always address him as 'your majesty' or 'sire,' " she told them.

Murphy said, "Whist, lass, they've been properly trained for all that, even though they're fresh from the bogs of Ireland."

"Oh, Murphy, I didn't mean to imply that they are ignorant. They are boys and may not place the same importance on things as we do. I'm about to offer more advice and hope you won't take offense at me. Please study the tides before you go riding on the sands of the wash. The water seems to sweep around treacherously in circles. You could be marooned and drown out there if you were not wary."

Young Richard laughed and flushed. "I was already caught out there, my lady. My fear was so great it won't happen again."

She said to Murphy, "I've arranged for Estelle to have a chamber in the east wing, far from the king's apartments, so you may be private with her."

He nodded his thanks, and Jasmine warned, "It may be necessary for me to flee the king, Murphy, if he tries to hold me captive. Don't be alarmed and above all do nothing foolish to antagonize John and jeopardize the boys' safety. Together with Estelle I will be able to outwit him. I would appreciate it, however, if you would keep a couple of horses saddled and ready in case we have to steal away at a moment's notice."

Jasmine went down to the great kitchens where huge piles of game were already being dressed and sides of beef and venison were being fitted to the spits. The king's men were used to a sumptuous table, and she wanted to make sure there would be some extra-special dishes for John. She decided the first course would be a tureen of prawns and oysters broiled in herb sauce, followed by crisply browned roast duckling with orange and lemon sauce, a rack of lamb cooked crisp on the outside, but rare and pink on the inside, marrows stuffed with smoky minced ham and cheese, an artichoke salad, followed by apple, pear, and peach pie and spicy tarts decorated with marchpane.

The next day she chose her gown carefully. After much deliberation she donned a midnight-blue velvet with a demure lace collar. The dark color contrasted vividly with her pale golden tresses, but the gown was so plain and severe that it pointed out she was a woman of virtue.

At last she heard the rumble of wagons and looked out to see the king and his gentlemen riding beside the baggage carts. This was most unusual; the men customarily rode well ahead of these dust-raising carts. She heard the king order that the wagons not be unloaded and that they be guarded by a dozen men round the clock. She puzzled over the significance of this as she craned her neck to get a glimpse of Estelle. She knew her grandmother was a bad traveler and hoped she had not been forced to ride all the way. Jasmine picked up her skirts and ran, leaving the castellan and his assistants to receive the large party. She would wait to welcome the king at the door to his apartments, and at the first opportunity she would play the supplicant on her sons' behalf.

Jasmine's heart beat wildly as she heard John ascending the stairs and her thoughts scattered in a thousand directions, then a measure of calm descended as he came into view and she gathered her confidence. She was a woman; he didn't stand a chance.

King John smiled at her, deeply satisfied. "Jasmine, you came to me."

She went down on her knee before him, and he raised

her up and took her into his arms. His mouth captured hers in a possessive kiss and she almost panicked and fled.

"Majesty, I came as a supplicant to beg a favor from you," she said primly. He took her hand firmly in his and swept into the chamber with her. Half a dozen of his gentlemen crowded in after them.

"The hall has been specially decorated in your honor, sire, and they will be serving some of your favorite dishes at dinner."

His eyes traveled down to her breasts and his mouth curved with appreciation. "Lady Jasmine and I will dine here. You gentlemen may be excused now, I think we can manage with the services of a page. Send young Jamie to me." The men bowed and left them alone.

A warning bell was ringing in Jasmine's ears. She must not risk offending the king because he was so unpredictable. He was capable of turning cruel and vicious in an instant, yet she must find a plausible excuse that would allow her to leave the room. "Majesty, I am honored that you wish to dine with me. May Estelle join us? I have missed her so very much."

"No, you little minx, she may not. I want you to myself tonight, Jasmine, and I believe that's perfectly obvious."

She blushed a deep pink and he laughed. "Ah, you do understand that I am going to make love to you; I am pleased."

"Majesty," she protested, "I came to petition you to let my sons stay in Ireland. They are only babes, and I—"

His arm went about her waist and he pulled her to him. He looked down at her lovely pale face. "You may have anything you desire."

"Thank you, sire," she said with a sinking heart, for she knew that in return he would take what he desired.

She stammered. "Majesty, I-I must bathe and dress for dinner."

He shook his head and laughed. "I haven't bathed yet. We will bathe together." His eyes glittered knowingly. "Jasmine, I have waited too many years for you. I won't permit you to leave this room tonight."

"Sire, please. I have never been unfaithful to my husband. You know I am a virtuous woman."

"I should have asked de Burgh for you long ago. He would have had to give you to me, I am the king, he would have had no choice."

She thought wildly, My god, you do not know Falcon de Burgh! "Sire, I do not believe you would deliberately ruin my marriage. De Burgh would never share my favors."

"He would have no choice, littlest one. He would have more good sense than to see me ruin all the de Burghs by stripping them of their land and titles," he warned. "Jasmine, you have royal blood. Surely I don't have to explain to you the divine right of kings?"

She lowered her lashes to her cheeks as his fingers sought her soft breast. "No, your majesty," she murmured. Jasmine cursed her luck. John had outwitted her. She should never have underestimated him.

The young page knocked discreetly and entered. "Jamie, order a bath and see that the fire is banked."

"Will you remove your cloak, sire?" he asked as he saw the king still wore his sable-lined mantle.

"The lady will tend me, Jamie."

"Yes, your majesty. Which gown shall I bring for the lady?"

John licked his lips and said with relish, "The champagne satin, I think. There is nothing to compare with the feel of satin on female flesh."

Jasmine realized they were not speaking of a gown but a nightgown. She was shocked to realize the page tended

John and his women every night and that the king traveled with a selection of negligees with which to adorn the women his gentlemen procured for him.

When the page left the chamber, Jasmine reached up to remove the magnificent cloak from John's shoulders. She was glad that he wanted her to attend to his needs. She thought of the vial between her breasts and knew the degree of deviousness it would require to doctor the king's wine.

John sat down before the fire. "My boots, Jasmine."

She stiffened. All her senses were heightened and she was sensitively aware of every nuance. Was this night to be a lesson in humiliation? She came to him and knelt before him, her lashes lowered over eyes liquid with apprehension.

"By God, you look at me." His fingers forced her chin up. He laughed. "Lord, how angry you are with me at this moment." Her eyes were bright with unshed tears. She was the most ethereal creature he had ever seen, and her anger excited him. There was something else about this young woman that had always excited him. She looked as innocent and untouched as a virgin. In fact, with her silvery-gilt hair she looked angelic. A thrilling surge ran through his loins at the thought of defiling an angel.

"My doublet," he murmured. With trembling fingers she unfastened the brilliant emerald and gold doublet and wondered if she dared first remove the golden circlet from his head before she pulled off the doublet, or if he would wear it to bed. Her fear was momentarily replaced by amusement as she saw that beneath the doublet he wore a corset. John was showing signs of corpulence from his life of indulgence, but his vanity demanded he try to hide it from the world.

She choked back a laugh and coughed. "My throat is so dry, Majesty. May I have some wine?" she whispered.

He waved a negligent hand toward the sideboard, but his avid eyes never left her. She slowly poured two goblets of deep, rich wine, knowing he would see immediately if she reached for the vial. Mercifully at that moment the servants arrived with a large wooden tub and a dozen buckets of hot water.

Jasmine's hands were trembling so violently she almost dropped the small vial. Clutching it tightly, she emptied half its contents into the goblet on the right and quickly slipped the vial back between her breasts. Young Jamie arrived with bath oils, scented soap, a pile of crested towels, and a champagne satin night rail. When the page made no move to leave the chamber, she took the wine goblets over to John, handed him the one in her right hand, and murmured, "Dismiss the page."

"He's going to bathe us," explained John.

"Oh, no!" Jasmine exclaimed, appalled. She'd have no witnesses to what went on between her and the king. "I'll bathe us, sire."

John waved out the page. "Remove your gown," he said with hungry eyes. It was as if she was paralyzed. Though her shyness excited him, he was growing impatient. "Do you think your tits and pussy so special you won't even show your king?" His eyes glittered. "Will I have my gentlemen back in to undress you?"

"Oh, you wouldn't!" She was horrified at the suggestion but knew him capable of anything.

He laughed. "They'll even hold you for me while I fuck you, sweetheart."

She realized with a growing alarm that he had not even tasted his wine. She took a deep gulp from her own goblet and was vastly relieved to see him follow suit and sip his own. The vial between her breasts burned her skin. She knew that at all costs she must conceal it. Slowly she removed her gown, knowing that he watched her hungrily. Then, pretending shyness, she presented him with her back so that she could remove the vial and tuck it beneath her discarded gown on the stool. She slowly removed her undergarment and John's eyes were drawn immediately to her heart-shaped bottom. His mouth suddenly went dry and he quaffed the wine deeply.

"Leave the stockings," he said thickly. "Come to me." She had beautiful breasts, lovely ivory globes with dark-pink nipples. He grinned in appreciation. "Your tits really are something special."

She made no move toward him, so he came to her. She was relieved that he brought his wine with him. She took up her own goblet again and drank deeply. Before he set the golden cup down, he too quaffed deeply. He took her breasts into his hands, weighing them, squeezing them. "Your skin is so pale, so fair, you will be covered with finger bruises by morning."

He knelt and pulled off her garters and stockings, then turned her so that he could intimately examine her round buttocks.

She bit her lips to keep from screaming as his hands explored her. Then he reached down to remove the rest of his own clothing. She moved away, ostensibly to finish her wine, but as John stood before her naked she almost choked. He was so overendowed, like all the male Plantagenets, he was hung like a bull. She closed her eyes to blot out the horror of it all and he laughed at her.

"Silly child. You've been running away from me for years when all the time I had exactly what you wanted. Come, the water looks inviting," he ordered.

She drained her wine and John did the same. He took her hand to help her into the tub and as he climbed in his enormous erection brushed her thigh. He sat down in the scented water and pulled her into his lap.

"Damn, the hot water has made me grow limp," he cursed. Jasmine had never heard such welcome words in her life. Her legs grew weak with relief and she sank down into the water with him. The hemlock was working; pray God it kept him in this flaccid condition.

He played with her in the water and did all manner of things to titillate himself, but his member would not harden. Jasmine felt an uncontrollable revulsion as John's small hands caressed her obscenely, yet she dared not show it. The water warmed her skin until it glowed rosily, but inside she was cold as ice, frozen with horror. He decided they should quit the water, blaming the bath for his condition. He took up another bottle of wine and filled his goblet. "Put on the satin and get into bed," he commanded.

He lifted her on top of his great body and rubbed her shamelessly against him. The slippery material moving over their naked flesh would have aroused a dead man.

She closed her eyes and willed her mind to separate from her body. A great nausea was rising within her, and she wondered wildly what he would do if she threw up all over him.

He still had the desire, but the ability to perform was nonexistent. His frustration increased by the minute. He got up for another bottle of wine, then doubled his efforts, demanding that Jasmine kiss him, arouse him.

She had the temerity to suggest that his inability stemmed from the fact that he knew what he did was wrong. He silenced her with a particularly brutal squeezing of her breasts, leaving her gasping with pain. But her words started the wheels turning in his brain. The reason he was having trouble was because she looked so pure and innocent—angelic, that was it. He reached for another bottle, this time not bothering with a goblet. He said thickly, "I must get past this ridiculous barrier of your saintliness. Your pose as the Holy Virgin is all a pretense. Beneath the masquerade you are hotter than other bitches. I'll have you avid for me tomorrow night. I'll tie you to the bed and take your virginity."

"I am not a virgin," Jasmine said, greatly alarmed.

John's hand swept up to her buttocks and his finger traced the cleft of her bottom. "There is one place where you are still virgin. None has been before me in here," he said, pressing home the finger.

Finally his exertions, greatly aided by the wine he had imbibed, took their toll and he fell asleep. Jasmine was also exhausted, yet sleep was the farthest thing from her mind. For a moment she couldn't stop shaking from revulsion, then she forced herself to slip quietly from the bed. Her skin crawled as if there had been maggots on her and she wondered if she would ever feel clean again, but she forced herself to shake off the horror of the previous hours and like a ghost melted into the shadows and materialized in the east wing at Estelle's door.

Chapter 42

"My God, child, what has he done to you?"

Jasmine shook her head wearily. "No intercourse. I fed him some hemlock. We must get away from him. It's so much more abhorrent than I ever imagined, and the night to come will be even worse. I asked Murphy to keep two horses saddled for me. We can't go now, for soon as he awoke he would follow. The tide comes in just at the hour of noon today. We will ride across the sands at the last possible minute. Then the tide will sweep in and make it impossible for them to follow us. Find out exactly where Murphy will have the horses. I must go back now. I don't want him to know I ever left the chamber."

John slept late and awoke with a bad head and a worse

temper. Jasmine was most grateful that he almost ignored her. He was incensed, however, that his justiciar had not yet arrived. Jasmine listened to his conversation with his gentlemen intently, and was amazed to learn that the guarded wagons that accompanied him contained the royal coffers and the crown jewels of England. King John was so suspicious of being robbed that he was taking his chests of gold and all the crown's wealth from London to the Bishop of Lincoln's massive stronghold of Newark Castle. No wonder he was livid that Hubert de Burgh was not on hand to safeguard the transfer!

As the morning wore on John became ever more agitated. He used every filthy obscenity he could curl his tongue around to describe the miserable, disloyal men who served him. Jasmine poured all the remaining hemlock into a goblet of wine and urged John to drink it to soothe his nerves. She watched him drain the cup and closed her eyes in relief.

The time was getting closer to noon by the minute and she knew she must get out of the room soon if she hoped to escape the castle. In fact, the very tide she awaited was keeping her husband's ship standing out to sea. Falcon impatiently paced the deck watching for the tide to turn. Once it did so, it would carry his ship into the wash and he would be able to anchor close to Castle Rising where he knew she had taken his two nephews. He experienced fear such as he had not known since her ordeal with childbirth. When he imagined her at the mercy of John's sexual excesses he nearly went mad. He prayed that he could rescue her while she was still untouched. The only means he had of dispelling his fear was to give his temper full rein. He became angry with Jasmine in the extreme. When he got his hands on her he intended to beat some sense into her.

He anticipated a confrontation such as they had never had before, but when it was over and the dust had settled,

there would be no doubt whatsoever who would rule
their household from this time forward. His jaw was set,
his mouth was grim, and his determination was inflexible.
He was outraged that he must risk leaving his Irish holdings vulnerable while he had to come chasing after her.
He intended to give her a lesson she would never forget.

King John began to foam at the mouth and to roll his
eyes alarmingly. Jasmine immediately took advantage of
the moment. "I will get Estelle, your majesty. You need
some of her medicine." He was in a terrible state. She
knew that hemlock could be a deadly poison. Perhaps she
had given him too much. She had no cloak, but wore the
midnight-blue gown from the previous day. She moved as
if her feet had wings. She flung open Estelle's chamber
door and grabbed her by the hand. Breathlessly she
urged, "Come quickly before 'tis too late!"

Estelle, ever practical, took up her cloak, but did not
bother with her bottles and herbs. "Murphy is waiting
with the horses," she said as the two of them ran down
the stone staircase of Castle Rising. The faithful Murphy
stood quieting two saddled horses. Jasmine mounted immediately and he helped Estelle into the saddle. "Keep
away from the king, he is in a terrible state," Jasmine
warned.

He clung to the harness of the two animals, most apprehensive about letting the women ride off on their own.
Estelle grabbed his big hand to reassure him. "Years back
I had a prophetic vision that is now unfolding. The final
page will soon be turned. All things come at their appointed time. You must let us go to meet our destiny,
Murphy."

The first fingers of the incoming tide were stretching
across the sands of the wash as Murphy reluctantly let go
the reins. Jasmine and Estelle dug their heels into the
sides of their mounts to urge them out onto the vast
stretch of sand.

As he looked down from above, King John saw Jasmine and Estelle immediately. The bitches were fleeing! He was enraged. He screamed at his gentlemen to follow them and fetch them back immediately. How dare anyone disobey direct orders from the king? Flecks of foam flew from his mouth as he rushed from the chamber to the castle's bailey. His face was bright red with anger and humiliation. He looked truly demented as he ran raving and screaming and issuing orders. "My horse, my horse! After them, damn you lily-livered, useless, ass-licking parasites."

His men ran to saddle his horse as well as their own. He waved frantically toward the stables. "Move out, move out." He grabbed his horse, vaulted into the saddle, and wheeled it toward the sands of the wash. The men who were guarding the treasure wagons became alarmed. The king was waving to them frantically to move out. Were they being attacked? Quickly they harnessed the horses to the wagons to follow the king out of Castle Rising onto the flat sands.

The king led the chase, oblivious of the creeping, swirling water beneath his horse's hooves. His gentlemen followed and then, lagging behind somewhat, came the treasure wagons.

The de Burgh ship came in on the tide and the men on deck stood aghast at what they saw. A large party of king's men and wagons were racing across the treacherous sands of the wash. From their vantage point it was obvious that not all of them were going to make it across the salty flats. The tide was devious. It formed large circles that marooned and trapped whatever was unwise enough to be out there on the sand.

The king's gentlemen became aware of their predicament long before the king. They raced to catch up with their monarch and warn him of the tide that was ready at their heels to swallow them. As they came up behind him, the king turned and to his horror saw his treasure wagons floating. He heard the harnessed horses screaming as they were sucked under and the cries of the drowning wagon drivers.

The king ordered his gentlemen to go back to save his treasure, but they totally ignored him and sped past in an effort to save themselves from a like fate.

Jasmine and Estelle thundered from the sands of the wash onto dry land, but they were aware that the king and some of his men were in pursuit just behind them. "We are taken, we are taken." Jasmine sobbed in despair.

"Do not fear, child, it was meant to be," soothed Estelle, gentling her horse as the king's men surrounded them.

There was so much shouting and confusion that it took Estelle a few moments to realize that half of the king's party had not made it to safety across the sands. The king did not seem to care that his men and their horses had drowned in his service, only that the crown jewels were lost to the insatiable sea. It was clear that madness had descended upon him, and his gentlemen tried every tactic in their power to calm him. They lied to him blatantly, assuring him that when the tide went out they would be able to ride back out over the wash and retrieve his fortune in gold.

Jasmine was blue with the cold. She whispered to Estelle, "I knew I gave him too much hemlock. The moment he drank it he began to foam at the mouth."

"Too bad it didn't kill him," whispered Estelle. "It still might," she added hopefully.

King John had unfurled a long whip from his saddlebow and was lashing any man foolish enough to draw close. His gentlemen, in a panic, did not know what to do. Estelle managed to make herself heard over the pandemonium. "We are at Swineshead. There is an abbey nearby where we may take refuge for the night."

Three of the men broke away to search out the abbey and prepare its holy residents for the king's party. The light was fading from the afternoon sky when they dismounted at Swineshead Abbey and wearily ushered the still-raving king inside. The monks made themselves scarce. The man in robes at the entrance who admitted travelers was the only monk in evidence. After lifting his arms to indicate that the available chambers were on the second floor, he melted away into the shadowed cloisters.

Jasmine was not so naive as to think she would go unscathed, and it came as no surprise when John looked about for someone on whom he could vent his spleen and his red eyes alighted upon her.

"Bitch! Whore! You are the cause of all my trouble." He still held the whip and none of his gentlemen had the guts to take it from him. He cracked the whip and it snaked across the floor, catching Jasmine on the ankle. She screamed and ran. "Upstairs, bitch!" he commanded.

She fled. Upstairs was the only avenue of escape from the madman. His gentlemen tried to appease him, but it was halfhearted since they had learned long ago that a tyrant cannot be appeased.

John ran halfway up the staircase after Jasmine, then turned, remembering Estelle. He pointed a terrible finger. "Hag! Witch! The only reason I let you live is to prepare the decoction I need. Get me some now! The longer you take, the more time I will have to punish the little bitch upstairs." King John laughed wildly as he moved on up the stairs, brandishing his long whip.

Estelle could not reason with the deranged king that she had nothing at all from which to make a herbal drink. She ran down the cloistered hall looking for the kitchens. At last she found them, but only one monk was in evidence and from what she could see the room was quite bare. Almost no food was being prepared for the evening meal, and there appeared to be no stores of food or herbs from which she could draw.

"My good man, what do you intend to feed the king and his men for dinner?" she commanded.

The monk uttered one word in a low, well-modulated tone. "Peaches."

"Peaches?" cried Estelle, feeling her heart sink.

Upstairs, Jasmine thought her heart would burst. She had tried her best, but she could not escape the wrath of John. She had struggled and scratched and clawed and bitten him, but in the end he had managed to tear off her clothes and was in the process of tying her wrists and ankles to the four bed posts. Horror of horror, he had tied her facedown. She knew that not only would he use the whip on her naked flesh, but when he tired of the whip, he would rape her in the deviant manner he had promised.

She lay exhausted yet rigid with fear and apprehension, sobbing for every breath. She wished herself dead, then real fear gripped her that before John was finished with her, she could very easily be dead. She had long since blocked out the stream of filth and invective that poured from his mouth as he described in horrific detail what he was about to do to her. He cracked the whip over the bed and its tail end caught her across her pale back and curled under her breast, leaving a thin red stripe of blood.

She heard a woman's scream followed by a loud pounding on a door. She dully realized the voice was her own, but who knocked? Would someone come to her rescue? John had begun to divest himself of his clothes when the pounding came through to him. He ignored it at first, then realized it could only be Estelle come with his needed decoction. He left the inner chamber door ajar and went into the small anteroom. At the door he shouted, "Dame Winwood?"

"Aye" came the reply.

He opened the door cautiously and saw that she held out a goblet. Beneath her gown, Estelle's knees literally knocked together. Some half-forgotten knowledge of peaches had surfaced from her subconscious while she had been in the kitchens. She had taken a rolling pin and broken open the peach pits. Then she had pulverized the contents and mixed it with syrup from the peaches, hoping against hope it would disguise the bitter taste until King John had ingested some of the powerful poison. Her ears were cocked for more sounds of anguish from Jasmine, but an ominous silence was all that now met them.

She offered up the goblet and held him in an hypnotic stare. She began to talk; it was almost a chant. "Long ago I had a prophetic vision that has all come to pass. I saw your brother Richard die and knew you would be crowned king. In the vision you were a wild boar. I saw you murder your nephew Arthur and take the crown across the water to England. I saw Philip of France and his cub Louis swallow whole your Angevin possessions, Brittany, and finally Normandy. Then they set their eyes on England because its monarch was weak. I believe your ancestors, all those men you betrayed, reached up from the water and took everything you possessed. You were too vain, caring only for the jewels in the crown, rather than the power it represented."

John snatched up the cup and drained it. Immediately he went into a seizure. The whip slipped from his fingers and he fell to the floor, drumming his heels and banging his head. Estelle turned and fled. She called loudly for his gentlemen, and one by one they crept cautiously from their rooms.

"He is dying," she said in a decisive voice. "So that none of you will be blamed for this I suggest you get him to the stronghold of Newark Castle and the Bishop of Lincoln. He is too weak to ride, in fact I expect him to lapse into a coma any minute. Prepare a bed in a wagon, hurry." She retraced her steps back to the king. He lay still now. He had vomited and his face was turning black. Alarmed, she knelt to see if he was breathing. He was not. Frantically she felt for a pulse . . . there was none. The king was dead!

She pulled off her cloak and wrapped it about him in a way that covered his face. Immediately she heard his men approaching. She stood up and faced them. "Quickly now, he is in a coma, as I feared. Handle him with care, lest he cease to breathe. At all costs you must see that he gets to Newark where both he and yourselves will be safe."

They carried him down the stairs and out of the abbey to a mule and wagon. "Let me just check him," Estelle said with great concern. The men mounted their horses and Estelle drew back the cloak from King John's face. He was dead; very, very dead. She heaved an enormous sigh of relief and urged the men to hurry. She stood in a trance staring after them long after they were gone from sight.

When a frustrated Falcon finally navigated his ship to anchor at Castle Rising, Murphy told him what had taken place. Falcon had seen for himself the horse-drawn wagons being dragged unmercifully beneath the flood-tide, but when he learned that Jasmine had ridden out across the wash he was filled with apprehension.

He paced about like a caged animal, waiting for the tide to sweep back out so that he could ride across the sands of the wash and discover Jasmine's fate. His face had gone white when Murphy told him that after only one night under the same roof as King John, Jasmine had fled.

Before Falcon could continue his journey, Hubert de Burgh and his men arrived back at Castle Rising. He listened with disbelief as Murphy repeated the tale of the king's men riding across the sands and being trapped by the tides of the wash. All were mounted and ready when the tide retreated sufficiently to allow horses to gallop the damp sands.

Falcon de Burgh spurred his destrier and its strong legs dug deeply into the wet sand, sending clods flying behind into the faces of those who followed. Soon, however, Falcon had outdistanced the others in the race to Swineshead. From the distance he could see a slow party of travelers leave the abbey and decided to pursue it. However, as he drew close to Swineshead Abbey he saw Estelle frantically waving to him, and swerved his destrier in her direction.

"Where is she?" He shouted the words as he dismounted and ran as she waved her arm.

"Upstairs!"

Sword in hand, he flew down the corridor like an avenging angel. As he drew closer to her, he felt her presence and rushed through the small anteroom into her chamber. Falcon de Burgh, who had never flinched from anything in his life, recoiled physically as he saw his naked wife trussed spread-eagle to the bedposts. His legs were unsteady as he crossed the room to the bed. With trembling hands he cut her bonds with his sword. The whip marks on her flesh registered in his brain, blocking out everything save the need for revenge.

Jasmine turned her head, knowing who it was before she ever saw him. She whispered, "Falcon . . . I—"

"No!" he cried. "I ask no questions . . . leave it, Jasmine." He took off his cloak to cover her nakedness, and she huddled miserably upon the bed as her husband left her without even the comfort of his embrace.

Falcon emerged from the abbey to see Hubert in deep conversation with Estelle. He had not sheathed his sword, nor did he intend to until it had found its royal target. "She needs you," he told Estelle grimly. He began to remount when Hubert's voice cut through the red mist that fogged his brain.

"Where are you going?"

"To slay John," he said evenly.

"You are too late it seems. The king is dead."

"I won't believe it until I see it for myself," swore Falcon.

"It's true, my lord. He is very, very dead. I sent his body on to Newark, to the Bishop of Lincoln," Estelle confirmed.

Falcon looked at his uncle the justiciar with alienation in his eyes. "He despoiled everything he ever touched. You will be the only man in England who is not happy at the news."

Hubert grasped his shoulder hard. "Nay, lad, I'm happier than anyone for I've the most to gain. John's heir Henry is yet a child. Once he is crowned, I'll undoubtedly be named regent. I'll be the uncrowned King of England for many years to come. Don't stand there gaping. Get your women out of here. Get on that ship and go back to Ireland as fast as the wind will carry you. I have the business of the realm to see to," said Hubert.

Chapter 43

Although Jasmine occupied the captain's cabin aboard the de Burgh vessel, Falcon had so far not shared it with her. When she had come aboard yesterday with her grandmother, the wind was blowing strong. The ship had strained against its anchors, making the timbers groan. Jasmine's amethyst eyes were half-closed against the wind as she searched the forcastle deck for the dark, powerful figure of her husband. She saw that he was busy, but refused to go below with Estelle.

Not too many minutes had passed after he weighed anchor before a gigantic wave poised just above the ship long enough for him to shout "Hard astarboard." The wave struck and Jasmine frantically clung to the binnacle head as the ship turned on her side as if she would roll completely, then incredibly she righted, water streaming from her, washing across the decks. Then she lifted. Jasmine heard Falcon order "Hands to braces" in the maintops. She felt the ship shudder and buck and heard the storm canvas rattle in the wind as the squall heeled her over again. Jasmine was soaked to the skin and waited no longer to seek safety belowdecks.

She warmed herself at the cabin stove and found a velvet bedrobe of Falcon's to wear while her clothes dried. She expected de Burgh to come for dry clothes after he had weathered the storm, but her wait was in vain. Jasmine knew the storm they had just experienced was nothing compared to the one that was brewing between her and Falcon. She was of a mind to get it all out in the open. She wanted to have at him about his whore, Morganna, and she wanted to explain everything to him about the king. She clenched her fists and ground her teeth in frustration when he did not come. The welts from the whip on her leg and back had crusted over in a thin red line, and she knew she would be able to prevent scars if she rubbed her flesh with a paste of honey and calamint. It became apparent to her that Falcon was avoiding her. Each day when she went up on deck he was in exactly the same spot as the day before. He stood on the ship's prow as it fell and rose in the waves, staring stonily out to sea.

The situation became unbearable for her. She had a great need to confess all to him and receive his forgiveness, as she would forgive him Morganna, after they had

had a go at each other. Finally she knew he would not come to her aboard ship, so she pushed him from her mind and thought only of the joy of seeing her children again.

When the ship arrived at Galway, she and Estelle disembarked together without any aid from de Burgh. The anticipation of being reunited with her twins almost overwhelmed Jasmine. The moment she saw them she froze for a full minute, wondering how she could touch them when such a short time ago she had committed murder, then in a rush all was forgotten as they ran into her arms, embracing her as hard as she did them.

Jasmine was undone. The tears flowed unbidden as relief washed over her that the only man who could separate them was gone forever. She chose to sleep in their room this first night home. She told herself she was happy. So long as they loved her, that was all that mattered. She had a long, relaxing bath, after which Estelle dabbed on the honeyed calamint, then in a warm bedgown, she cuddled her babies and rocked them until they fell asleep. She too needed rest, needed to heal. She was asleep before ten o'clock, but after the witching hour, along about one in the morning, she awoke restless as a tigress. She put on her slippers and the velvet bedgown and went silently up to the castle ramparts. Her eyes crinkled against the wind as she looked out over the battlements, her silvery hair streaming out behind her.

She did not know how long she had been there before she realized she was not alone. She was startled and then unnerved to see Falcon staring at her in the shadowed moonlight. He did not speak. He did not move. She knew he was angrier with her than he had ever been before. She knew she would have to be the one to force a confrontation.

"Well, haven't you the guts to face me?" she accused, taking the offensive while it was still open to her.

"If I come any closer I will knock you down, madame," he said with suppressed violence.

She swaggered over to him, planting herself squarely in front of him, and dug both fists into the red velvet bedgown. Falcon was all in black. "You are a Devil!" she threw at him. "An unfaithful, lecherous Devil to boot!"

"You dare speak to me of faithlessness?" he roared.

"Dare? I'd dare anything! What will you do, take a whip to me?" She tore open her bedgown to expose her breasts. "Will you put more scars upon me?" she taunted. "Perhaps you'd carve your initials into my breast as you did to your whore!"

"That is a damned lie," he bellowed, "and she is not my whore! After you left I confronted her and she admitted she picked the child up on the docks. You owned me heart and soul, yet you had not one grain of faith in me," he accused. "You couldn't wait to run off to whore for the king."

The hate, love, all-consuming passion between them boiled over. She swung back her arm and slapped him full across the face.

He retaliated immediately and slapped her back. He had no idea of his own strength. The blow felled her, and he looked down at the crumpled figure of his beloved in horror. "My little love, my sweeting, what have I done?" he crooned as he bent to pick her up and cradle her against him. She clung to him sobbing and he rocked her until she cried out.

"Falcon, let me confess to you what I did," she whispered.

"Nay, nay, there is no need for confessions between us. I will always adore you and cherish you no matter what you have done," he promised, almost alarmed at what she would tell him.

"Falcon, please, I must," she insisted.

He braced himself for the blow to come.

In a contrite low voice she said, "Falcon, I murdered King John."

"You . . . murder?" he questioned.

"Yes, yes, I did. I gave him hemlock to make him impotent. It worked too well."

Falcon began to shake. It came to her that he was laughing. "Jassy, Jassy, do you mean to tell me that he didn't abuse you?"

"No," she said, shaking her head, "so I had no real justification in killing him."

"Darling, Estelle claims she poisoned him with peach pits," he assured her.

"Oh my God, it feels wonderful to share the guilt," she said, a bubble of laughter rising through the tears.

"I think we have done enough shouting and brawling on the ramparts for one night. I think we should finish our conversation in bed, don't you?" he invited.

"Yes, please," she murmured, snuggling against him for warmth.

He carried her to their chamber where he laid her in their bed and removed her bedrobe. "You are the loveliest woman on earth," he vowed.

"When you look at me, I feel that is true."

"My God, I've near starved to death for you," he said, climbing into bed and pulling her softness against the hard length of him. He kissed her a thousand times before he moved on to more intimate play. "Do you forgive me, darling?"

"I've never seen you so angry with me."

"You stir my pirate's blood," he whispered, burying his face in her delicious silken hair.

"Mmm, I do it apurpose to provoke you," she teased.

He knew he was the luckiest man alive. She was lovely and hot-tempered, but had a beguiling way of turning sweet as honeyed mead.

"I was dreadful jealous," she said quietly, and he felt exultant at her admission.

Her fingers closed around his shaft and he groaned. "Oh, that feels wonderful, Hyacinth, don't stop."

"Hyacinth?" she cried, pretending to pull out handfuls of his dark hair.

"I mean my little flower," he teased, shaking with laughter. He turned over and imprisoned her on top of him. She could feel his manhood seeking her center. Suddenly they were very serious. Face to face, he looked deeply into her eyes as he slowly impaled her inch by delicious inch onto his lance.

The feel and smell and taste of him excited her to a wildness she had not experienced in months. Though they tried to prolong their pleasure, they could not control themselves and took their release together. She collapsed onto him and he gently laid her beside him and whispered to her of the beauty of their castle at Portumna.

"The last night I was there the beauty of the place was haunting. The garden was filled with the last of the large summer roses. They seemed to float in the moonlight. Then a big white owl flew silently through the trees and I knew it was the perfect place for my enchantress." He smiled into the darkness as he realized Jasmine was asleep in his arms.

Reckless abandon. Intrigue. And spirited love. A magnificent array of tempestuous, passionate historical romances to capture your heart.

- ☐ **THE RAVEN AND THE ROSE**
  by Virginia Henley   17161-X $3.95

- ☐ **TO LOVE AN EAGLE**
  by Joanne Redd   18982-9 $3.95

- ☐ **DESIRE'S MASQUERADE**
  by Kathryn Kramer   11876-X $3.95

- ☐ **SWEET TALKIN' STRANGER**
  by Lori Copeland   20325-2 $3.95

- ☐ **IF MY LOVE COULD HOLD YOU**
  by Elaine Coffman   20262-0 $3.95

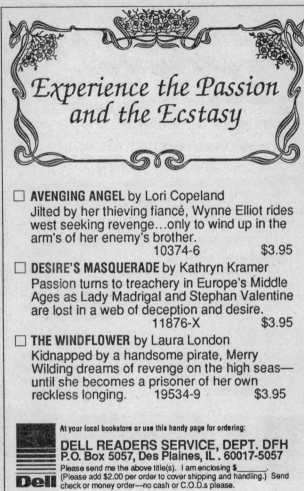